PRAISE FOR

CROOKED KINGDOM

AND SIX OF CROWS

'A delicious blend of masterfully executed elements . . .
Bardugo outdoes herself in this exhilarating follow-up'
—BOOKLIST, STARRED REVIEW

'Unputdownable excitement from beginning to end'
—KIRKUS, STARRED REVIEW

'*Ocean's Eleven* set in a *Game of Thrones*-esque world . . . a pacey
read with electric prose'
—INDEPENDENT

'Crackling dialogue and sumptuous description. Bardugo
dives deep into this world . . . If you're not careful, it'll steal
all your time'
—NEW YORK TIMES

'Cracking page-turner with a multi-ethnic, band of misfits
with differing sexual orientations who satisfyingly, believably
jell into a family'
—KIRKUS, STARRED REVIEW

CROOKED
KINGDOM

LEIGH BARDUGO

Orion

ORION CHILDREN'S BOOKS

First published in Great Britain in 2016 by Hodder and Stoughton
This edition first published in 2017 by Hodder and Stoughton

11

ISBN: 978 1 78062 231 6

Typeset by Input Data Services Ltd, Somerset

Printed and bound by Clays Ltd, Elcograf S.p.A.

The paper and board used in this book are
made from wood from responsible sources.

Orion Children's Books
An imprint of Hachette Children's Group
Part of Hodder and Stoughton
Carmelite House
50 Victoria Embankment
London EC4Y 0DZ

An Hachette UK Company

www.hachette.co.uk

To Holly and Sarah, who helped me build;
Noa, who made sure the walls stayed standing;
Jo, who kept me standing too.

THE WANDERING ISLE

LEFLIN

JELKA

VILKI

THE BONE ROAD

NOVYI ZEM

WEDDLE

THE TRUE SEA

REB HARBOR

EAMES HARBOR

SHRIFTPORT

EAMES CHIN

COFTON

KETTERDAM

BELENDT

KERCH

LAND BRIDGE

SOUTHERN COLONIES

6th Harbor

Imperjum

Sweet Reef

Eil Komedie

5th Harbor

Warehouse
District

The Lid

East
Stave

West
Stave

The Barrel

Council of Tides
Watchtower

Hellgate

Anvil

The Emerald
Palace

White Rose

Menagerie

Goedmedbridge

The Crow Club

Kaelish Prince

Black Veil Island

The Slat

Van Eck Mansion

Smeet Residence

The Exchange

Zentsbridge

Geldrenner Hotel

The Boeksplein

Morgue

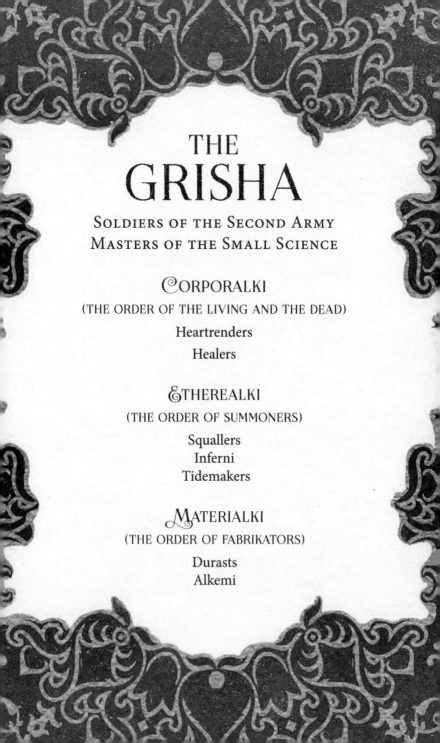

THE
GRISHA

SOLDIERS OF THE SECOND ARMY
MASTERS OF THE SMALL SCIENCE

CORPORALKI
(THE ORDER OF THE LIVING AND THE DEAD)
Heartrenders

Healers

ETHEREALKI
(THE ORDER OF SUMMONERS)
Squallers

Inferni

Tidemakers

MATERIALKI
(THE ORDER OF FABRIKATORS)
Durasts

Alkemi

PART ONE

FORSAKEN

1

RETVENKO

Retvenko leaned against the bar and tucked his nose into his dirty shot glass. The whiskey had failed to warm him. Nothing could get you warm in this Saintsforsaken city. And there was no escaping the smell, the throat-choking stew of bilge, clams, and wet stone that seemed to have soaked into his pores as if he'd been steeping in the city's essence like the world's worst cup of tea.

It was most noticeable in the Barrel, even more so in a miserable dump like this one—a squat tavern wedged into the lower floor of one of the slum's grimmest apartment buildings, its ceiling bowed by weather and shoddy construction, its beams blackened by soot from a fireplace that had long since ceased to function, the flue clogged by debris. The floor was covered in sawdust to soak up spilled lager, vomit, and whatever else the bar's patrons lost control of. Retvenko wondered how long it had been since the boards had been swept clean. He buried his nose more deeply in the glass, inhaling the sweet perfume of bad whiskey. It made his eyes water.

"You're supposed to drink it, not snort it," said the barkeep with a laugh.

Retvenko put his glass down and gazed at the man blearily. He was thick necked and barrel chested, a real bruiser. Retvenko had seen him toss more than one rowdy patron into the street, but it was hard to take him seriously dressed in the absurd fashion favored by the young men of the Barrel—a pink shirt with sleeves that looked fit to split over huge biceps, a garish red-and-orange plaid waistcoat. He looked like a dandified soft-shell crab.

"Tell me," said Retvenko. His Kerch wasn't good to begin with, and it was worse after a few drinks. "Why does city smell so bad? Like old soup? Like sink full of dishes?"

The barman laughed. "That's just Ketterdam. You get used to it."

Retvenko shook his head. He didn't want to get used to this city or its stink. His job with Councilman Hoede had been dull, but at least his rooms had been dry and warm. As a treasured Grisha indenture, Retvenko had been kept in comfort, his belly full. He'd cursed Hoede at the time, bored with his work shepherding the merchant's expensive cargo shipments across the sea, resenting the terms of his contract, the foolish bargain he'd made to get himself out of Ravka after the civil war. But now? Now he couldn't help thinking of the Grisha workshop at Hoede's house, the fire burning merrily in the grate, brown bread served with slabs of butter and thick cuts of ham. After Hoede had died, the Kerch Merchant Council had let Retvenko take on sea voyages to pay his way out of the indenture. The money was terrible, but what other options did he have? He was a Grisha Squaller in a hostile city with no skills but the gifts with which he'd been born.

"Another?" the barman asked, gesturing at Retvenko's empty glass.

Retvenko hesitated. He shouldn't waste his money. If he was smart with his pennies, he would only need to rent himself out for one more voyage, maybe two, and he'd have enough money to pay off his indenture and buy himself a ticket to Ravka in a third-class berth. That was all he needed.

He was due on the docks in less than an hour. Storms had been predicted, so the crew would rely on Retvenko to master the air currents and guide the ship calmly to whatever port they needed to reach. He didn't know where and he didn't care. The captain would call coordinates; Retvenko would fill the sails or calm the skies. And then he would collect his pay. But the winds hadn't picked up yet. Maybe he could sleep through the first part of the voyage. Retvenko tapped the bar and nodded. What was a man to do? He deserved some comfort in this world.

"I am not errand boy," he muttered.

"What's that?" the barman asked as he poured out another drink.

Retvenko gave a dismissive wave. This person, this common lout, could never understand. He toiled away in obscurity. Hoping for what? An extra coin in his pocket? A warm glance from a pretty girl? He knew nothing of glory in battle, what it was to be revered.

"You Ravkan?"

Through the muzzy blur the whiskey had created, Retvenko came alert. "Why?"

"No reason. You just sound Ravkan."

Retvenko told himself to relax. Plenty of Ravkans came through Ketterdam looking for work. There was nothing on him that said Grisha. His cowardice filled him with disgust—at himself, the barman, this city.

He wanted to sit and enjoy his drink. There was no one in the bar to jump him, and despite the barman's muscles, Retvenko knew he could handle him easily. But when you were Grisha, even staying still could mean courting trouble. There had been more rumors of disappearances in Ketterdam recently—Grisha vanishing from the streets or their homes, probably snapped up by slavers and sold to the highest bidder. Retvenko would not let that happen to him, not when he was so close to buying his way back to Ravka.

He downed his whiskey, slammed a coin on the counter, and rose from the barstool. He left no tip. A man could work for a living.

Retvenko felt a little unsteady as he headed outside, and the moist stink of the air didn't help. He put his head down and set his feet toward Fourth Harbor, letting the walk clear his head. *Two more voyages*, he repeated to himself, a few more weeks at sea, a few more months in this city. He'd find a way to make it bearable. He wondered if some of his old friends might be waiting for him in Ravka. The young king was said to be handing out pardons like penny candy, eager to rebuild the Second Army, the Grisha military that had been decimated by the war.

"Just two more trips," he said to no one, stamping his boots against the spring damp. How could it be this cold and wet this late in the year? Living in this city was like being trapped in the chilly armpit of a frost giant. He passed along Grafcanal, shivering as he glimpsed Black Veil Island tucked into the water's bend. That was where the Kerch wealthy had once buried their dead, in little stone houses above water level. Some trick of the climate kept the island shrouded in shifting mists, and there were rumors that the place was haunted. Retvenko hastened his steps. He wasn't a superstitious man—when you had power like his, there was no reason to fear what might lurk in the shadows—but who liked to walk by a graveyard?

He burrowed deeper into his coat and made quick time down Havenstraat, keeping alert to the movements in every twisting alley. Soon he'd be back in Ravka, where he could stroll the streets without fear. Assuming he got his pardon.

Retvenko squirmed uncomfortably in his coat. The war had pitted Grisha against Grisha, and his side had been particularly brutal. He'd murdered former comrades, civilians, even children. But what was done could not be undone. King Nikolai needed soldiers, and Retvenko was a very good soldier.

Retvenko nodded once to the guard stashed in the little booth at the entrance to Fourth Harbor and glanced over his shoulder, confirming he hadn't been followed. He made his way past the cargo containers to the docks, found the appropriate berth, and stood in line to register with the first mate. Retvenko recognized him from past voyages, always harried and ill-humored, scrawny neck poking from the collar of his coat. He held a thick sheaf of documents, and Retvenko glimpsed the purple wax seal of one of the members of the Kerch Merchant Council. Those seals were better than gold in this city, guaranteeing the best berths in the harbor and preferred access to the docks. And why did the councilmen garner such respect, such advantage? Because of coin. Because their missions brought profit to Ketterdam. Power meant something more in Ravka, where the elements bent to the will of the Grisha and the country was ruled by a proper king instead of a cadre of upstart merchants. Admittedly, Retvenko had tried to depose that king's father, but the point remained.

"We're not ready for the rest of the crew just yet," the first mate said as Retvenko gave his name. "You can keep warm in the harbormaster's office. We're waiting on our signal from the Council of Tides."

"Good for you," Retvenko said, unimpressed. He glanced up at one of the black obelisk towers that loomed over the harbor. If there were any chance that the high and mighty Council of Tides could see him from their watchtower, he would have let them know exactly what he thought with a few choice gestures. They were supposedly Grisha, but had they ever lifted a finger to help the other Grisha in the city? To help those down on their luck who might have welcomed a bit of kindness? "No, they have not," he answered himself.

The first mate winced. "*Ghezen*, Retvenko. Have you been drinking?"

"No."

"You stink of whiskey."

Retvenko sniffed. "Little bit whiskey."

"Just dry out. Get yourself some coffee or strong *jurda*. This cotton has to be in Djerholm in two weeks' time, and we aren't paying you to nurse a hangover belowdecks. Understood?"

"Yes, yes," Retvenko said with a dismissive wave, already heading toward the harbormaster's office. But when he was a few steps away, he flicked his wrist. A tiny whirlwind caught the papers the first mate was holding, sending them flying over the docks.

"Damn it!" he shouted as he went scrambling over the wooden planks, trying to capture the pages of his manifest before they blew into the sea.

Retvenko smiled with grim pleasure, then felt a wave of sadness overtake him. He was a giant among men, a gifted Squaller, a great soldier, but here he was just an *employee*, a sad old Ravkan who spoke broken Kerch and drank too much. *Home*, he told himself. *Soon I'll be home.* He would get his pardon and prove himself once more. He would fight for his country. He would sleep under a roof that didn't leak and wear a blue wool *kefta* lined with silver fox fur. He would be Emil Retvenko again, not this pathetic shadow.

"There's coffee," said the clerk when Retvenko entered the harbormaster's office, gesturing toward a copper urn in the corner.

"Tea?"

"There's coffee."

This country. Retvenko filled a mug full of the dark sludge, more to warm his hands than anything. He couldn't bear the taste of it, certainly not without a healthy dose of sugar, which the harbormaster had neglected to supply.

"Wind blowing in," said the clerk as a bell clanged outside, shaken by the rising breeze.

"I have ears," Retvenko grumbled.

"Don't think it will amount to much here, but once you get out of the harbor—"

"Be silent," Retvenko said sharply. He was on his feet, listening.

"What?" said the clerk. "There's—"

Retvenko put a finger to his lips. "Someone cries out." The sound had come from where the ship was docked.

"It's just gulls. Sun's coming up soon and—"

Retvenko raised a hand, and a gust of air slammed the clerk back into the wall. "I said *be silent*."

The clerk's mouth dropped open as he hung pinned to the slats. "You're the Grisha they got for the crew?"

For Saints' sake, was Retvenko going to have to pull the air from this boy's lungs and suffocate him into quiet?

Through the waxy windows, Retvenko could see the sky beginning to turn blue as dawn arrived. He heard the squawking of gulls searching the waves for breakfast. Maybe the liquor was muddling his mind.

Retvenko let the clerk drop to the ground. He'd spilled his coffee, but he didn't want to bother with another cup.

"Told you it was nothing," said the clerk as he dragged himself to his feet. "Didn't have to get all heated up." The clerk dusted himself off and got resettled behind the desk. "I never met one of you before. Grisha." Retvenko snorted. The clerk probably had and simply didn't know it. "You get paid pretty good for the voyages?"

"Not good enough."

"I—" But whatever the clerk was going to say next was lost as the door to the office exploded in a hail of splinters.

Retvenko's hands went up to shield his face. He ducked and rolled behind the clerk's desk for cover. A woman entered the office—black hair, golden eyes. *Shu.*

The clerk reached for a shotgun Retvenko saw strapped beneath the desk. "They've come for the payroll!" he shouted. "Ain't no one taking the payroll."

Retvenko watched in shock as the gangly clerk stood like some kind of avenging warrior and opened fire. By all that was holy, nothing could motivate the Kerch like cash.

Retvenko peeked around the desk in time to see the shotgun blast strike the woman directly in the chest. She was thrown backward and collided with the doorjamb, crumpling to the floor. He smelled the sharp burn of gunpowder, the metallic tang of blood. Retvenko's belly gave a shaming lurch. It had been a long time since he'd seen someone shot down in front of him—and that had been in a time of war.

"Ain't no one taking the payroll," the clerk repeated with satisfaction.

But before Retvenko could reply, the Shu woman wrapped her bloody hand around the door frame, hauling herself to her feet.

Retvenko blinked. Just how much whiskey had he had?

The woman marched forward. Through the remains of her tattered blouse, Retvenko saw blood, flesh pocked with buckshot, and the glint of what looked like metal.

The clerk fumbled to reload, but the woman was too fast. She grabbed the gun from his hands and swatted him down with it, knocking him sideways with terrible force. She tossed the gun aside and turned her golden eyes on Retvenko.

"Take payroll!" Retvenko shouted, clambering backward. He dug in his pockets and tossed his nearly empty wallet at her. "Take what you want."

The woman smiled slightly at that—with pity? Amusement? Retvenko did not know. But he understood that she had not come for the money at all. She had come for him. And it didn't matter if she was a slaver or a mercenary or something else entirely. She would face a soldier, not some cowering weakling.

He leapt to his feet, muscles responding reluctantly to his demands, and shifted into fighting stance. His arms arced forward. A howling wind swept through the room, tossing a chair, then the clerk's desk, then the steaming coffee urn at the woman. She batted each item away with little interest, as if she were brushing aside stray cobwebs.

Retvenko focused his power and shoved both his hands forward, feeling his ears pop as the pressure dropped and the wind swelled in a surging thunderhead. Maybe this woman couldn't be stopped by bullets. Let's see how she fared against the fury of a storm.

The woman growled as the gale seized her, hurtling her back through the open doorway. She seized the jamb, trying to keep hold.

Retvenko laughed. He'd forgotten how good it felt to fight. Then, from behind him, he heard a loud *crack*, the shriek of nails torn free and rending timber. He looked over his shoulder and caught the briefest glimpse of the dawn sky, the wharf. The wall was gone.

Strong arms seized him, clasping his hands to his sides, preventing him from using his power. He was rising, sailing upward, the harbor shrinking beneath him. He saw the roof of the harbormaster's office, the body of the first mate in a heap on the dock, the ship Retvenko had been meant to sail on—its deck a mess of broken boards, bodies piled near the shattered masts. His attackers had been there first.

The air was cold on his face. His heart pounded a ragged rhythm in his ears.

"Please," he begged as they soared higher, unsure of what he was pleading for. Afraid to move too suddenly or too much, he craned his neck to look at his captor. Retvenko released a terrified moan, somewhere between a sob and the panicked whine of an animal caught in a trap.

The man holding him was Shu, his black hair pulled into a tight bun, his golden eyes narrowed against the rush of the wind—and from his back emerged two vast wings that beat against the sky, hinged, gracefully wrought in looping silver filigree and taut canvas. Was he an angel? A demon? Some strange mechanical come to life? Had Retvenko simply lost his mind?

In the arms of his captor, Emil Retvenko saw the shadow they made cast upon the glittering surface of the sea far below: two heads, two wings, four legs. He had become a great beast, and yet that beast would devour him. His prayers turned to screams, but both went unanswered.

2

WYLAN

What am I doing here?

That thought had run through Wylan's head at least six times a day
since he'd met Kaz Brekker. But on a night like this, a night when they
were "working," it rose and fell in his head like a nervous tenor practic-
ing his scales: *WhatamIdoingherewhatamIdoingherewhatamIdoinghere.*

Wylan tugged at the hem of his sky-blue jacket, the uniform worn
by the waiters of Club Cumulus, and tried to look at ease. *Think of it as a
dinner party*, he told himself. He'd endured countless uncomfortable meals
at his father's house. This was no different. In fact, it was easier. No awkward conversations about his studies or when he planned to start classes
at the university. All he had to do was stay quiet, follow Kaz's instructions, and figure out what to do with his hands. Clasp them in front? Too
much like a singer at a recital. In back? Too military. He tried just dangling them at his sides, but that didn't feel right either. Why hadn't he
paid better attention to the way waiters stood? Despite Kaz's assurances
that the second-floor parlor was theirs for the night, Wylan felt certain
that at any minute a real member of the staff would enter the room, point

at him, and shout, "Impostor!" Then again, Wylan felt like an impostor most days.

It had been just under a week since they'd reached Ketterdam, almost a month since they'd left Djerholm. Wylan had been wearing Kuwei's features for most of that time, but whenever he caught a glimpse of his reflection in a mirror or a shop window, it took a long moment to realize he wasn't looking at a stranger. This was his face now—golden eyes, wide brow, black hair. His old self had been scrubbed away, and Wylan wasn't sure he knew the person who remained—the person who was standing in a private parlor in one of the Lid's most luxurious gambling dens, caught up in another of Kaz Brekker's schemes.

A player at the table lifted his champagne glass for a refill, and Wylan darted forward from his perch against the wall. His hands were shaking as he took the bottle from the silver ice bucket, but there were some benefits to the years he'd spent at his father's social functions. He at least knew how to pour a proper glass of champagne without it foaming over. Wylan could almost hear Jesper's mocking voice. *Marketable skills, merchling.*

He dared a glance at Jesper now. The sharpshooter was seated at the table, hunched over his cards. He wore a battered navy waistcoat embroidered with small gold stars, and his rumpled shirt shone white against his dark brown skin. Jesper rubbed a tired hand over his face. They'd been playing cards for more than two hours. Wylan couldn't tell if Jesper's fatigue was real or part of the act.

Wylan filled another glass, focusing on Kaz's instructions.

"Just take the players' orders and keep one ear on Smeet's conversation," he'd said. "It's a job, Wylan. Get it done."

Why did they all call it a job? It didn't feel like working. It felt like missing a step and suddenly finding yourself falling. It felt like panic. So Wylan took stock of the room's details—a trick he'd often used to steady himself whenever he arrived someplace new or when his father was in a particularly foul mood. He inventoried the pattern of interlocking starbursts that formed the polished wood floor, the shell-shaped nodes of the blown-glass chandelier, the cobalt silk wallpaper flocked with silver clouds. No windows to allow in natural light. Kaz said none of the gambling dens had them, because the bosses wanted players to lose track of time.

Wylan watched Kaz deal another hand to Smeet, Jesper, and the other players at the round table. He wore the same sky-blue staff jacket as Wylan and his hands were bare. Wylan had to fight not to stare at them. It wasn't just the strangeness, the wrongness of seeing Kaz without his gloves, it was that his hands seemed animated by a secret machinery Wylan didn't understand. When he had started to learn figure drawing, Wylan had studied anatomy illustrations. He had a good grasp of musculature, the way bones and joints and ligaments fit together. But Kaz's hands moved as if they'd been made for no other purpose than to manipulate cards, long white fingers flexing in easy rhythm, the shuffle precise, each turn economical. Kaz had claimed he could control any deck. So why was Jesper losing so badly?

When Kaz had outlined this part of the plan at the hideout on Black Veil, Wylan had been incredulous, and for once, he hadn't been the only one with questions.

"Let me get this straight," Nina had said. "Your grand scheme is to give Jesper a line of credit and make him play cards with Cornelis Smeet?"

"Smeet likes high-stakes Three Man Bramble and blondes," said Kaz. "So we're going to give him both. I'll deal the first half of the night, then Specht will take over."

Wylan didn't know Specht well. He was a former navy seaman, a member of the Dregs who had piloted their ship to and from the Ice Court. If Wylan was honest, between the grizzled jaw and the tattoos that ran halfway up Specht's neck, he found the sailor slightly frightening. But even Specht had looked concerned when he said, "I can deal cards, Kaz, but I can't control a deck."

"You don't have to. From the time you sit down, it will be an honest game. The important thing is to keep Smeet at the tables until midnight. The shift change is when we risk losing him. As soon as I stand up, he's going to start thinking about moving on to another game or calling it a night, so you all need to do everything you can to keep his ass firmly planted at that table."

"I can handle it," Jesper said.

Nina had just scowled. "Sure, and maybe for phase two of this plan I can masquerade as a *jurda parem* dealer. What could possibly go wrong?"

Wylan wouldn't have put it that way exactly, but he agreed. Strongly. They should be keeping Jesper away from gambling dens, not encouraging his love of risk. But Kaz hadn't been moved.

"Just do your job and keep Smeet thoroughly enthralled until midnight," he'd said. "You know what's on the line." They all did. Inej's life. And how could Wylan argue with that? He felt a pang of guilt every time he thought about it. Van Eck had said he would give them seven days to give up Kuwei Yul-Bo—then he would begin torturing Inej. They were almost out of time. Wylan knew he couldn't have prevented his father from double-crossing the crew and kidnapping her. He *knew* that, but he still felt responsible.

"What am I supposed to do with Cornelis Smeet after midnight?" Nina asked.

"Try to talk him into spending the night with you."

"What?" Matthias had sputtered, red flooding his face all the way up to his ears.

"He won't say yes."

Nina sniffed. "Like hell he won't."

"Nina—" Matthias growled.

"Smeet never cheats at cards or on his wife," Kaz said. "He's like half the amateurs strutting around the Barrel. Most of the time he's respectable, scrupulous—strict economies and half a glass of wine at dinner. But once a week he enjoys feeling like he's an outlaw matching wits with the high rollers on East Stave, and he likes a pretty blonde on his arm when he does it."

Nina pursed her lips. "If he's so moral, then why do you want me to try to—"

"Because Smeet's rolling in coin, and any self-respecting girl from West Stave would at least make the effort."

"I don't like this," said Matthias.

Jesper had smiled his reckless gunslinger's grin. "To be fair, Matthias, you don't like much."

"Keep Smeet at Club Cumulus from eight bells until midnight," Kaz said. "That's four hours of play, so stay smart about it."

Nina was certainly doing her best, and Wylan didn't know whether to be impressed or concerned. She was dressed in a sheer lavender gown rigged with some kind of corset that pushed her cleavage to alarming heights, and though she'd lost weight since her battle with *parem*, there was still plenty of her for Smeet to grab onto. She'd settled her rump firmly on his knee, arm around his shoulder, and was cooing prettily in his ear, her hands caressing his chest and occasionally slipping beneath his jacket like a beagle searching for treats. She stopped only to order oysters or another bottle of champagne. Wylan knew Nina could handle just about any man and any situation, but he didn't think she should have to sit half-dressed in a drafty gambling parlor, perched on some leering lawyer's lap. At the very least, she was probably going to catch cold.

Jesper folded yet again and blew out a long, exasperated breath. He'd been losing slowly for the last two hours. He'd kept his bids cautious, but neither luck nor Kaz seemed to be on his side tonight. How were they supposed to keep Smeet at the table if Jesper ran out of funds? Would the other high-stakes players be enough of a lure? There were a few of them in the room, lingering by the walls, watching the game, each hoping to nab a seat if someone cashed out. None of them knew the real game Kaz was running.

As Wylan leaned down to refill Nina's glass, he heard Smeet murmur,

"A card game is like a duel. It's the little cuts and slashes that set the stage for the final killing stroke." He glanced across the table to Jesper. "That lad is bleeding all over the table."

"I don't know *how* you keep the rules straight in your head," Nina said with a giggle.

Smeet grinned, clearly pleased. "This is nothing compared to managing a business."

"I can't imagine how you do that either."

"Sometimes I don't know myself," Smeet said on a sigh. "It's been a hard week. One of my clerks never came back from his holiday, and that meant I was stuck shorthanded."

Wylan nearly dropped the bottle he was holding; champagne splashed onto the floor.

"I'm paying to drink it, not wear it, boy," snapped Smeet. He wiped at his trousers and muttered, "That's what comes of hiring foreigners."

He means me, Wylan realized as he backed away hurriedly. He didn't know how to make the reality of his new Shu features sink in. He couldn't even speak Shu, a fact that hadn't worried him until two Shu tourists with a map in hand had waylaid him on East Stave. Wylan had panicked, made an elaborate shrugging gesture, and bolted for the servants' entrance to Club Cumulus.

"Poor baby," Nina said to Smeet, running her fingers through his thinning hair and adjusting one of the flowers tucked into her silky blonde tresses. Wylan wasn't sure if she'd actually told Smeet she was from the House of the Blue Iris, but he certainly would have assumed so.

Jesper leaned back in his seat, fingers tapping the handles of his revolvers. The movement seemed to draw Smeet's eye.

"Those guns are remarkable. Real mother-of-pearl in the handles, if I'm not mistaken," Smeet said in the tones of a man who was rarely mistaken. "I have a fine collection of firearms myself, though nothing in the line of Zemeni repeating revolvers."

"Oh, I'd love to see your guns," Nina cooed, and Wylan looked at the ceiling in an attempt to avoid rolling his eyes. "Are we going to sit here all night?"

Wylan tried to hide his confusion. Wasn't the whole point to get him to stay? But apparently Nina knew better, because Smeet's face took on a slightly mulish cast. "Hush now. If I win big, I may buy you something pretty."

"I'll settle for some more oysters."

"You haven't finished those."

Wylan caught the quiver of Nina's nostrils and thought she might be drawing a fortifying breath. She'd had no appetite since she'd recovered from her bout with *parem*, and he didn't know how she'd managed to slurp down nearly a dozen oysters.

Now he watched her swallow the last of them with a shudder. "Delicious," she managed with a glance at Wylan. "Let's have some more."

That was the signal. Wylan swooped in and picked up the big dish laden with ice and discarded shells.

"The lady has a craving," Smeet said.

"Oysters, miss?" Wylan asked. His voice sounded too high. "Buttered prawns?" Too low.

"She'll have both," said Smeet indulgently. "And another flute of champagne."

"Marvelous," Nina said, looking slightly green.

Wylan rushed through the swinging door to the servants' pantry. It was stocked with plates, glassware, napkins, and a tin tub full of ice. A dumbwaiter took up a large section of the far wall, and there was a trumpet-shaped speaking tube next to it to allow the staff to communicate with the kitchen. Wylan set the dish of ice and shells on the table, then called down to the kitchen for oysters and buttered prawns.

"Oh, and another bottle of champagne."

"What vintage?"

"Uh . . . more of the same?" Wylan had heard his father's friends talk about which wines made for good investments, but he didn't quite trust himself to choose a year.

By the time he returned to the parlor with Nina's order, Kaz was standing up from the table. He made a gesture as if he was dusting off his hands—the sign that a dealer had finished his shift. Specht sat down, a blue silk cravat tied at his throat to hide his tattoos. He shook out his cuffs and called for players to ante up or cash out.

Kaz's eyes met Wylan's as he vanished into the pantry.

This was the moment. According to Kaz and Jesper, a player often thought his luck was bound to the dealer and would stop play at the shift change.

Wylan watched in distress as Smeet stretched and gave Nina's bottom a firm pat. "We've had a good run," he said, glancing at Jesper, who was staring dejectedly at his meager pile of remaining chips. "We may find fatter game elsewhere."

"But my food just came," pouted Nina.

Wylan stepped forward, unsure of what to say, only knowing that they had to delay Smeet. "Is everything to your liking, sir? Can I offer you and the lady something more?"

Smeet ignored him, hand still hovering over Nina's backside. "There's finer vittles and better service to be had all over the Lid, my dear."

A big man in a striped suit approached Smeet, eager to snag his seat. "Cashing out?"

Smeet gave Jesper a friendly nod. "Looks like we both are, eh, lad? Better luck next time."

Jesper didn't return the smile. "I'm not done here."

Smeet gestured to Jesper's sad stack of chips. "Certainly looks like you are."

Jesper rose and reached for his guns. Wylan clutched the bottle of champagne in his hands as the other players pushed back from the table, ready to grab their own weapons or dive for cover. But all Jesper did was unsling his gun belt. Gently, he laid the revolvers on the table, fingers brushing over their high-gloss ridges with care.

"How much for these?" he asked.

Wylan tried to catch Jesper's eye. Was this part of the plan? And even if it was, what was Jesper thinking? He loved those guns. He might as well cut off his own hand and throw it into the pot.

Specht cleared his throat and said, "The Cumulus isn't a pawnshop. We accept cash and credit from the Gemensbank only."

"I'll stake you," Smeet said with studied disinterest, "if it will get the game moving again. One thousand *kruge* for the guns?"

"They're worth ten times that."

"Five thousand *kruge*."

"Seven."

"Six, and that's only because I'm feeling generous."

"Don't!" Wylan blurted. The room went silent.

Jesper's voice was cold. "I don't remember asking for your advice."

"The insolence!" said Smeet. "Since when do waiters involve themselves in game play?"

Nina glared at Wylan, and Specht's tone was furious with disbelief when he said, "Gentlemen, shall we get this game rolling again? Ante up!"

Jesper shoved his revolvers across the table to Smeet, and Smeet slid a tall stack of chips over to Jesper in return.

"All right," said Jesper, his gray eyes bleak. "Deal me in."

Wylan stepped back from the table and disappeared into the pantry as quickly as he could. The dish of ice and shells was gone, and Kaz was waiting. He'd thrown a long orange cape over his blue jacket. His gloves were already back in place.

"Kaz," Wylan said desperately. "Jesper just put his guns up."

"How much did he get for them?"

"Why does that matter? He—"

"Five thousand *kruge*?"

"Six."

"Good. Not even Jesper should be able to run through that in less than two hours." He tossed Wylan a cape and mask, the trappings of the Gray Imp, one of the characters of the Komedie Brute. "Let's go."

"Me?"

"No, the idiot behind you." Kaz picked up the speaking trumpet and said, "Send up another waiter. This one managed to spill champagne on some high roller's shoes."

Someone in the kitchen laughed and said, "You got it."

They were down the stairs and out the servants' entrance bare moments later, their costumes allowing them to move anonymously through the crowds of East Stave.

"You knew Jesper would lose. You made sure of it," Wylan accused. Kaz rarely used his cane when they were roaming parts of the city where he might be recognized. But despite his lopsided gait, Wylan had to jog to keep up with him.

"Of course I did. I control the game, Wylan, or I don't play. I could have made sure Jesper won every hand."

"Then why—"

"We weren't there to win at cards. We needed Smeet to stay at the tables. He was ogling those guns almost as much as Nina's cleavage. Now he's feeling confident, like he's in for a good night—if he loses, he'll still keep playing. Who knows? Jesper may even win his revolvers back."

"I hope so," said Wylan as they hopped onto a browboat crowded with tourists and headed south down the Stave.

"You would."

"What's that supposed to mean?"

"Someone like Jesper wins two hands and starts to call it a streak. Eventually he loses, and that just leaves him hungrier for the next run of good luck. The house relies on it."

Then why make him walk into a gambling den? Wylan thought but didn't say. And why make Jesper give up something that meant so much to him?

21

There had to be another way to keep Smeet playing. But those weren't even the right questions. The real question was why Jesper did it all without hesitating. Maybe he was still looking for Kaz's approval, hoping to earn back his favor after Jesper's slip had led them into the ambush at the docks that had nearly cost Inej her life. Or maybe Jesper wanted something more than forgiveness from Kaz.

What am I doing here? Wylan wondered again. He found himself gnawing on his thumb and forced himself to stop. He was here for Inej. She'd saved their lives more than once, and he wasn't going to forget that. He was here because he desperately needed the money. And if there was another reason, a tall, lanky reason with a too-strong taste for games of chance, he wasn't going to think about that right now.

As soon as they made it to the outskirts of the Barrel, Wylan and Kaz ditched their capes and sky-blue jackets and wended their way east into the Zelver district.

Matthias was waiting for them beneath a darkened doorway on Handelcanal. "All clear?" Kaz asked.

"All clear," said the big Fjerdan. "The lights went out on the top floor of Smeet's house more than an hour ago, but I don't know if the servants are awake."

"He only has a daily maid and cook," Kaz said. "He's too cheap for full-time servants."

"How is—"

"Nina is fine. Jesper is fine. Everyone is fine except for me because I'm stuck with a gang of hand-wringing nursemaids. Keep a watch."

Wylan shrugged apologetically at Matthias, who looked like he was considering dashing Kaz's skull against a wall, then hurried along the cobblestones after Kaz. Smeet's home also served as his office, and it was located on a dark street with sparse foot traffic. The lamps were lit along the canal and candles burned in some of the windows, but after ten bells, most of the neighborhood's respectable citizens had already retired.

"Are we just going in through the front door?"

"Use your eyes instead of running your mouth," said Kaz, lockpicks already flashing in his gloved hands.

I am, Wylan thought. But that wasn't strictly true. He'd taken in the house's proportions, the pitch of its gabled roof, the roses beginning to bloom in its window boxes. But he hadn't looked at the house as a puzzle. With some frustration, Wylan could admit this was an easy solve. The Zelver district was prosperous, but not truly wealthy—a place for successful artisans, bookkeepers, and barristers. Though the houses were well built and tidy, with views of a wide canal, they were tightly packed together, and there were no grand gardens or private docks. To access the windows of the upper floors, he and Kaz would have had to break into a neighboring home and go through two sets of locks instead of one. Better to risk the front door, to simply act as if they had every right to be there—even if Kaz was carrying picks instead of keys.

Use your eyes. But Wylan didn't like looking at the world the way Kaz did. And once they'd gotten their money, he'd never have to again.

A bare second later, Kaz pressed down on the handle and the door swung open. Immediately, Wylan heard the patter of paws, claws on hard wood, low snarls, as Smeet's pack of hounds rushed the door, white teeth flashing, growls rumbling deep in their chests. Before they could realize someone other than their master had come to call, Kaz pushed Smeet's whistle between his lips and blew. Nina had managed to slip it from the chain the lawyer always wore around his neck, then tucked it beneath an empty oyster shell for Wylan to whisk into the kitchen.

There was no sound from the whistle—at least not one that Wylan could hear. *It's not going to work*, he thought, imagining those huge jaws tearing into his throat. But the dogs skittered to a halt, bumping into one another in a confused tangle.

Kaz blew again, lips pursing in time with the pattern of a new command. The dogs quieted and flopped to the floor with a disgruntled whine. One even rolled over on its back.

"Now why can't people be this easily trained?" Kaz murmured as he crouched to oblige the dog with a belly rub, black-gloved fingers smoothing the short fur. "Close the door behind you."

Wylan did and stood with his back pressed to it, keeping a wary eye on the pile of slavering hounds. The whole house smelled of dog—damp fur, oily hides, warm breath moist with the stink of raw meat.

"Not fond of animals?" Kaz asked.

"I like dogs," Wylan said. "Just not when they're the size of bears."

Wylan knew the real puzzle of Smeet's house had been a thorny one for Kaz to solve. Kaz could pick just about any lock and outthink any system of alarms, but he hadn't been able to come up with a simple way around Smeet's bloodthirsty hounds that wouldn't leave their plan exposed. During the day, the dogs were kept in a kennel, but at night they were given free run of the house while Smeet's family slept peacefully in the richly appointed rooms of the third floor, the staircase closed off by an iron gate. Smeet walked the dogs himself, up and down the Handelcanal, trailing after them like a tubby sled in an expensive hat.

Nina had suggested drugging the dogs' food. Smeet went to the butcher every morning to select cuts of meat for the pack, and it would have been easy enough to switch the parcels. But Smeet wanted his dogs hungry at night, so he fed them in the mornings. He would have noticed if his prized pets had been sluggish all day, and they couldn't risk Smeet staying home to care for his hounds. He had to spend the evening on East Stave, and when he returned home, it was essential that he find nothing amiss. Inej's life depended upon it.

Kaz had arranged for the private parlor in the Cumulus, Nina had caressed the whistle from beneath Smeet's shirt, and, piece by piece, the plan had come together. Wylan did not want to think about what they'd done to obtain the whistle commands. He shivered when he remembered what Smeet had said: *One of my clerks never came back from his holiday.* He never would. Wylan could still hear the clerk screaming as Kaz dangled him by the ankles from the top of the Hanraat Point Lighthouse. *I'm a good man*, he'd shouted. *I'm a good man.* They were the last words he'd spoken. If he'd talked less, he might have lived.

Now Wylan watched Kaz give the drooling dog a scratch behind the ears and rise. "Let's go. Watch your feet."

They sidestepped the pile of dog bodies in the hall and made their way quietly up the stairs. The layout of Smeet's house was familiar to Wylan. Most businesses in the city followed the same plan: a kitchen and public rooms for meeting with clients on the ground floor, offices and storage on the second floor, sleeping rooms for the family on the third floor. Very wealthy homes had a fourth floor for servants' quarters. As a boy, Wylan had spent more than a few hours hiding from his father in his own home's upper rooms.

"Not even locked," Kaz murmured as they entered Smeet's office. "Those hounds have made him lazy."

Kaz closed the door and lit a lamp, turning the flame down low.

The office had three small desks arranged by the windows to take advantage of the natural light, one for Smeet and two for his clerks. *I'm a good man.*

Wylan shook off the memory and focused on the shelves that ran from floor to ceiling. They were lined with ledgers and boxes full of documents, each carefully labeled with what Wylan assumed were the names of clients and companies.

"So many pigeons," Kaz murmured, eyes scanning the boxes. "Naten Boreg, that sad little skiv Karl Dryden. Smeet represents half the Merchant Council."

Including Wylan's father. Smeet had served as Jan Van Eck's attorney and property manager for as long as Wylan could remember.

"Where do we start?" Wylan whispered.

Kaz pulled a fat ledger from the shelves. "First we make sure your father has no new acquisitions under his name. Then we search under your stepmother's name, and yours."

"Don't call her that. Alys is barely older than I am. And my father won't have kept property in my name."

"You'd be surprised at what a man will do to avoid paying taxes."

They spent the better part of the next hour digging through Smeet's files. They knew all about Van Eck's public properties—the factories, hotels, and manufacturing plants, the shipyard, the country house and farmland in southern Kerch. But Kaz believed Wylan's father had to have private holdings, places he'd kept off the public registers, places he'd stash something—or someone—he didn't want found.

Kaz read names and ledger entries aloud, asking Wylan questions and trying to find connections to properties or companies they hadn't yet discovered. Wylan knew he owed his father nothing, but it still felt like a betrayal.

"Geldspin?" asked Kaz.

"A cotton mill. I think it's in Zierfoort."

"Too far. He won't be keeping her there. What about Firma Allerbest?"

Wylan searched his memory. "I think that one's a cannery."

"They're both practically printing cash, and they're both in Alys' name. But Van Eck keeps the big earners to himself—the shipyard, the silos at Sweet Reef."

"I told you," Wylan said, fiddling with a pen on one of the blotters. "My father trusts himself first, Alys only so far. He wouldn't leave anything in my name."

Kaz just said, "Next ledger. Let's start with the commercial properties."

Wylan stopped fiddling with the pen. "*Was* there something in my name?"

Kaz leaned back. His look was almost challenging when he said, "A printing press."

The same old joke. So why did it still sting? Wylan set the pen down. "I see."

"He's not what I would call a subtle man. Eil Komedie is in your name too."

"Of course it is," Wylan replied, wishing he sounded less bitter. Another private laugh for his father to enjoy—an abandoned island with nothing on it but a broken-down amusement park, a worthless place for his worthless, illiterate son. He shouldn't have asked.

As the minutes ticked away and Kaz continued reading aloud, Wylan became increasingly agitated. If he could just read, they'd be moving twice as fast through the files. In fact, Wylan would already know his father's business inside out. "I'm slowing you down," he said.

Kaz flipped open another sheaf of documents. "I knew exactly how long this would take. What was your mother's family name?"

"There's nothing in her name."

"Humor me."

"Hendriks."

Kaz walked to the shelves and selected another ledger. "When did she die?"

"When I was eight." Wylan picked up the pen again. "My father got worse after she was gone." At least that was how Wylan remembered it. The months after his mother's death were a blur of sadness and silence. "He wouldn't let me go to her funeral. I don't even know where she's buried. Why do you guys say that, anyway? No mourners, no funerals? Why not just say good luck or be safe?"

"We like to keep our expectations low." Kaz's gloved finger trailed down a column of numbers and stopped. His eyes moved back and forth between the two ledgers, then he snapped the leather covers shut. "Let's go."

"Did you find something?"

Kaz nodded once. "I know where she is."

Wylan didn't think he imagined the tension in the rasp of Kaz's voice. Kaz never yelled the way Wylan's father did, but Wylan had learned to listen for that low note, that bit of black harmony that crept into Kaz's tone when things were about to get dangerous. He'd heard it after the fight at the docks when Inej lay bleeding from Oomen's knife, then when Kaz had learned it was Pekka Rollins who had tried to ambush them, again when they'd been double-crossed by Wylan's father. He'd heard it loud and clear atop the lighthouse as the clerk screamed for his life.

Wylan watched as Kaz set the room to rights. He moved an envelope a little more to the left, pulled a drawer on the largest file cabinet out a bit farther, pushed the chair back just so. When he was done he scanned the room, then plucked the pen from Wylan's hands and set it carefully in its place on the desk.

"A proper thief is like a proper poison, merchling. He leaves no trace." Kaz blew the lamp out. "Your father much for charity?"

"No. He tithes to Ghezen, but he says charity robs men of the chance at honest labor."

"Well, he's been making donations to the Church of Saint Hilde for the last eight years. If you want to pay your respects to your mother, that's probably the place to start."

Wylan stared at Kaz dumbly in the shadowy room. He'd never heard of the Church of Saint Hilde. And he'd never known Dirtyhands to share any bit of information that wouldn't serve him. "What—"

"If Nina and Jesper did their jobs right, Smeet will be home soon. We can't be here when he gets back or the whole plan goes to hell. Come on."

Wylan felt like he'd been bashed over the head with a ledger and then told to just forget about it.

Kaz cracked opened the door. They both stopped short.

Over Kaz's shoulder, Wylan saw a little girl standing on the landing, leaning on the neck of one of the massive gray dogs. She had to be about five, her toes barely visible beneath the hem of her flannel nightgown.

"Oh Ghezen," Wylan whispered.

Kaz stepped out into the hall, pulling the door nearly shut behind him.

Wylan hesitated in the darkened office, unsure of what he should do, terrified of what Kaz might do.

The girl looked up at Kaz with big eyes, then removed her thumb from her mouth. "Do you work for my da?"

"No."

The memory came at Wylan again. *I'm a good man.* They'd ambushed the clerk coming out of the Menagerie and hauled him to the top of the lighthouse. Kaz had held him by his ankles and the clerk had wet himself, screaming and begging for mercy before he'd finally given up Smeet's whistle commands. Kaz had been about to reel him back up when the clerk had started offering things: money, bank account numbers for Smeet's clients, and then—*I've got information on one of the girls at the Menagerie, the Zemeni.*

Kaz had paused. *What do you have on her?*

Wylan had heard it then, that low, dangerous note of warning. But the clerk didn't know Kaz, didn't recognize the change in the rough scrape of his voice. He thought he'd found a wedge, something Kaz wanted.

One of her clients is giving her expensive gifts. She's keeping the money. You know what the Peacock did to the last girl she caught holding out on her?

I do, Kaz said, his eyes glinting like the edge of a straight razor. *Tante Heleen beat her to death.*

Kaz—Wylan had attempted, but the clerk kept talking.

Right there in the parlor. This girl knows she's cooked if I tell. She sees me for free just so I keep my mouth shut. Sneaks me in. She'll do the same for you, your friends. Whatever you like.

If Tante Heleen found out, she'd kill your Zemeni, said Kaz. *She'd make an example of her to the other girls.*

Yes, the clerk gasped eagerly. *She'll do anything you want, everything.*

Slowly, Kaz began to let the man's legs slide through his grasp. *It's terrible, isn't it? Knowing someone holds your life in his hands.*

The clerk's voice rose another octave as he realized his mistake.

She's just a working girl, he screamed. *She knows the score! I'm a good man. I'm a good man!*

There are no good men in Ketterdam, Kaz said. *The climate doesn't agree with them.* And then he'd simply let go.

Wylan shuddered. Through the crack in the door, he saw Kaz squat down so he could look the little girl in the eye. "What's this big fellow's name?" Kaz said, laying a hand on the dog's wrinkled neck.

"This is Maestro Spots."

"Is that so?"

"He has a very fine howl. Da lets me name all the puppies."

"Is Maestro Spots your favorite?" asked Kaz.

She appeared to think, then shook her head. "I like Duke Addam Von Silverhaunch best, then Fuzzmuzzle, *then* Maestro Spots."

"That's good to know, Hanna."

Her mouth opened into a little O. "How do you know my name?"

"I know all children's names."

"You do?"

"Oh, yes. Albert who lives next door and Gertrude on Ammberstraat. I live under their beds and in the backs of the closets."

"I knew it," the girl breathed, fear and triumph in her voice. "Mama said there was nothing there, but I knew it." She cocked her head to one side. "You don't look like a monster."

"I'll tell you a secret, Hanna. The really bad monsters never look like monsters."

Now the little girl's lip trembled. "Did you come to eat me? Da says monsters eat children who don't go to bed when they're told."

"They do. But I won't. Not tonight. If you do two things for me." His voice was calm, almost hypnotic. It had the coarse rasp of an over-rosined bow. "First, you must crawl into bed. And second, you must never tell *anyone* you've seen us, especially your da." He leaned forward and gave Hanna's braid a playful tug. "Because if you do, I'll slit your mother's throat and then your father's, and then I'll cut out the hearts of all these sweet slobbering hounds. I shall save Duke Silverhaunch for last so that you will know it's all your fault." The little girl's face was as white as the lace on the neck of her nightgown, her eyes wide and bright as new moons. "Do you understand?" She nodded frantically, chin wobbling. "Now, now, no tears. Monsters see tears and it only whets their appetites. Off to bed with you, and take that useless Maestro Spots along too."

She skittered backward over the landing and up the stairs. When she was halfway up, she cast a terrified glance back at Kaz. He raised one gloved finger to his lips.

When she was gone, Wylan slipped out from behind the door and followed Kaz down the steps. "How could you say something like that to her? She's just a child."

"We were all just children once."

"But—"

"It was that or snap her neck and make it look like she fell down the stairs, Wylan. I think I showed remarkable restraint. Move."

They picked their way past the rest of the dogs still flopped down in the hallway. "Incredible," Kaz said. "They'd probably stay like that all night." He blew on the whistle and they leapt up, ears pricked, ready to guard the house. When Smeet returned home, all would be as it should: hounds pacing the ground floor; office intact on the second floor; wife snoozing comfortably on the third floor, and daughter pretending to do the same.

Kaz checked the street and then waved Wylan outside, pausing only to lock the door behind them.

They hurried down the cobblestones. Wylan peered over his shoulder. He couldn't quite believe they'd gotten away with it.

"Stop looking around like you think someone's following you," Kaz said. "And stop scurrying. You couldn't look guiltier if you were performing the role of Thief Number Three in a penny play on East Stave. Next time walk normally. Try to look like you belong."

"There isn't going to be a next time."

"Of course not. Keep your collar up."

Wylan didn't argue. Until Inej was safe, until they'd gotten the money they'd been promised, he couldn't make any grand ultimatums. But there would be an end to this. There had to be, didn't there?

Matthias gave a high birdcall from the other end of the street. Kaz glanced at his watch and ran a hand through his hair, ruffling it wildly. "Right on time."

They rounded the corner and slammed directly into Cornelis Smeet.

3
MATTHIAS

Matthias kept to the shadows, watching this strange play unfold.

Cornelis Smeet tipped, losing his footing, hat sliding from his nearly bald head. The boy who had run into him stepped forward, offering assistance.

The boy was Kaz, but he was not Kaz. His dark hair was mussed, his manner flustered. He kept his eyes averted, his chin tucked into his collar as if hopelessly embarrassed—a green youth, respectful of his elders. Wylan hovered behind him, shrunken so deeply into his coat Matthias thought he might actually disappear.

"Watch where you're going!" Smeet huffed indignantly, resettling the hat on his head.

"Terribly sorry, sir," Kaz said, brushing the shoulders of Smeet's jacket. "Curse my clumsiness!" He bent to the cobblestones. "Oh dear, I think you dropped your wallet."

"So I did!" Smeet said in surprise. "Thank you. Thank you very much." Then, as Matthias watched in disbelief, Smeet opened his billfold and drew out a crisp five-*kruge* bill. "There you are, young man. Pays to be honest."

Kaz kept his head down but somehow managed to convey humble appreciation as he murmured, "Too kind, sir. Too kind. May Ghezen be as generous."

The portly lawyer went on his way, hat askew, humming a little tune, oblivious to the fact that he'd just run directly into the card dealer who had sat across from him for two hours in Club Cumulus. Smeet arrived at his door and pulled a chain from his shirt, then frantically patted his waistcoat, searching for his whistle.

"You didn't put it on the chain?" asked Matthias as Kaz and Wylan joined him in the dark doorway. He knew such tricks were well within Kaz's abilities.

"Didn't bother."

Smeet rooted around in his shirt, then fished out the whistle and unlocked the door, humming once more. Matthias could not fathom it. He'd kept his gaze trained on Kaz's gloved hands as he'd fussed over Smeet, but even knowing that Kaz intended to return the whistle, Matthias hadn't been able to detect the moment of deception. He was tempted to drag Smeet back and make Kaz perform the trick again.

Kaz neatened his hair with his fingers and handed the five *kruge* to Wylan. "Don't spend it all in one place. Let's move."

Matthias ushered them along to the narrow side canal where he'd moored the rowboat. He tossed Kaz his cane, and they clambered down. Kaz had been wise not to allow himself the use of his walking stick this night. If someone noticed a boy with a crow's head cane lurking around the offices of Cornelis Smeet at an unusual hour, if an offhand mention of that fact somehow reached Van Eck's ears, all their work would be for nothing. To get Inej back, they would need surprise on their side, and the *demjin* was not the type to leave anything to chance.

"Well?" Matthias asked as the boat slid along the dark waters of the canal.

"Hold your tongue, Helvar. Words like to ride the water. Put yourself to use and help work the oars."

Matthias fought the urge to snap his oars in half. Why was Kaz incapable of keeping a civil tongue? He gave orders as if he simply expected everyone to follow his commands, and he'd been twice as insufferable since Van Eck had taken Inej. But Matthias wanted to get back to Black Veil and Nina as fast as possible, so he did as he was bid, feeling his shoulders flex as the boat moved against the current.

He put his mind to keeping track of the landmarks they passed, trying to remember street and bridge names. Though Matthias studied a map of the city every night, he had found Ketterdam's knots of alleys and canals nearly impossible to untangle. He'd always prided himself on a good sense of direction, but this city had defeated it, and he frequently found himself cursing whatever mad hand had thought it wise to raise a city from a swamp and then arrange it without order or logic.

Once they passed beneath Havenbridge, he was relieved to find his surroundings becoming familiar again. Kaz tipped his oars, steering them into the murky waters of Beggars' Bend, where the canal widened, and guided them into the shallows of Black Veil Island. They tucked the boat behind the drooping limbs of a white willow and then picked their way up through the graves that dotted the steep bank.

Black Veil was an eerie place, a miniature city of white marble mausoleums, many carved into the shape of ships, their stone figureheads weeping as they cut across an invisible sea. Some bore the stamp of Ghezen's Coins of Favor, others the three flying fishes of Kerch that Nina said indicated a member of the family had served in the government. A few were watched over by Ravkan Saints in flowing marble robes. There was no sign of Djel or his ash tree. Fjerdans would not want to be interred above the earth, where they could not take root.

Almost all the mausoleums had fallen into disrepair, and many were little more than piles of slumped rock overgrown with vines and clusters of spring flowers. Matthias had been horrified at the idea of using a cemetery as a safe house, no matter how long it had been abandoned. But of course, nothing was sacred to Kaz Brekker.

"Why don't they use this place anymore?" Matthias had asked when they'd taken over a vast tomb at the island's center as their hideout.

"Plague," Kaz replied. "The first bad outbreak was more than a hundred years ago, and the Merchant Council prohibited burial within city limits. Now bodies have to be cremated."

"Not if you're rich," Jesper added. "Then they take you to a cemetery in the country, where your corpse can enjoy the fresh air."

Matthias hated Black Veil, but he could acknowledge it had served them well. The rumors of hauntings kept squatters at bay, and the mist that surrounded the twisting willows and stone masts of the graves obscured the occasional lantern light.

Of course, none of that would matter if people heard Nina and Jesper arguing at the top of their lungs. They must have returned to the island and left their *gondel* on the north side. Nina's irritated voice floated over the graves, and Matthias felt a surge of relief, his steps quickening, eager for the sight of her.

"I don't think you're showing proper appreciation for what I just went through," Jesper was saying as he stomped through the cemetery.

"You spent a night at the tables losing someone else's money," Nina shot back. "Isn't that essentially a holiday for you?"

Kaz knocked his cane hard against a gravestone and they both went quiet, moving swiftly into fighting stances.

Nina relaxed as soon as she caught sight of the three of them in the shadows. "Oh, it's you."

"Yes, it's us." Kaz used his cane to herd them both toward the center of the island. "And you would have heard us if you hadn't been busy shouting at each other. Stop gawking like you've never seen a girl in a dress before, Matthias."

"I wasn't gawking," Matthias said with as much dignity as he could muster. But for Djel's sake, what was he supposed to look at when Nina had irises tucked between . . . everything.

"Be quiet, Brekker," Nina said. "I like it when he gawks."

"How did the mission go?" Matthias asked, trying to keep his eyes on her face. It was easy when he realized how tired she looked beneath the cosmetics she'd applied. She even took the arm he offered, leaning on him slightly as they made their way over the uneven terrain. The night had taken a toll. She shouldn't be traipsing around the Barrel in scraps of silk; she should be resting. But the days until Van Eck's deadline were dwindling, and Matthias knew Nina would allow herself no comfort until Inej was safe.

"It's not a mission; it's a job," Nina corrected. "And it went splendidly."

"Yeah," said Jesper. "*Splendidly.* Except that my revolvers are currently collecting dust in the Club Cumulus safe. Smeet was afraid to walk home with them, the hopeless podge. Just thinking of my babies in his sweaty hands—"

"No one told you to wager them," said Kaz.

"You dealt me into a corner. How the hell else was I supposed to get Smeet to stay at the tables?"

Kuwei poked his head out of the huge stone tomb as they approached.

"What did I tell you?" Kaz growled, pointing his cane at him.

"My Kerch isn't very good," protested Kuwei.

"Don't run game on me, kid. It's good enough. Stay in the tomb."

Kuwei hung his head. "Stay in the tomb," he repeated glumly.

They followed the Shu boy inside. Matthias loathed this place. Why build such monuments to death? The tomb was constructed to look like an ancient cargo ship, its interior carved into a vast stone hull. It even had stained-glass portholes that cast rainbows on the crypt floor in the late afternoon. According to Nina, the carvings of palm trees and snakes on the walls indicated that the family had been spice traders. But they must have fallen on hard times or simply taken their dead elsewhere, because only one of the vaults had a resident, and the narrow passages on either side of the main hull were equally empty.

Nina pulled the pins from her hair, shucked off the blonde wig, and tossed it on the table they'd set in the middle of the tomb. She slumped into a chair, rubbing her fingers along her scalp. "So much better," she said with a happy sigh. But Matthias could not ignore the almost green-ish cast to her skin.

She was worse tonight. Either she'd run into trouble with Smeet or she'd simply overexerted herself. And yet, watching her, Matthias felt something in him ease. At least now she looked like Nina again, her brown hair in damp tangles, her eyes half-shut. Was it normal to be fascinated by the way someone slouched?

"Guess what we saw on our way out of the Lid?" she asked.

Jesper started digging through their food stores. "Two Shu warships sitting in the harbor."

She threw a hairpin at him. "I was going to make them guess."

"Shu?" asked Kuwei, returning to where he'd spread his notebooks over the table.

Nina nodded. "Cannons out, red flags flying."

"I talked to Specht earlier," said Kaz. "The embassies are full up with diplomats and soldiers. Zemeni, Kaelish, Ravkan."

"You think they know about Kuwei?" Jesper asked.

"I think they know about *parem*," said Kaz. "Rumors, at least. And there were plenty of interested parties at the Ice Court to pick up gossip about Kuwei's . . . liberation." He turned his gaze on Matthias. "The Fjerdans are here too. They've got a whole contingent of *drüskelle* with them."

Kuwei sighed mournfully, and Jesper plunked down next to him, giving him a nudge with his shoulder. "Isn't it nice to be wanted?"

Matthias said nothing. He did not like to think about the fact that his old friends, his old commander, might be only a few miles from them.

38

He wasn't sorry for the things he'd done at the Ice Court, but that didn't mean he had made peace with them either.

Wylan reached for one of the crackers Jesper had dumped on the table. It was still disconcerting to see him and Kuwei in the same room. Nina's tailoring had been so successful that Matthias often had trouble telling them apart until they spoke. He wished one of them would do him the courtesy of wearing a hat.

"This is good for us," said Kaz. "The Shu and the Fjerdans don't know where to start looking for Kuwei, and all those diplos making trouble at the Stadhall are going to create some nice noise to distract Van Eck."

"What happened at Smeet's office?" Nina asked. "Did you find out where Van Eck is keeping her?"

"I have a pretty good idea. We strike tomorrow at midnight."

"Is that enough time to prepare?" asked Wylan.

"It's all the time we have. We're not going to wait for an engraved invitation. What's your progress on the weevil?"

Jesper's brows shot up. "The weevil?"

Wylan removed a small vial from his coat and set it down on the table.

Matthias bent to peer at it. It looked like a bunch of pebbles. "That's a weevil?" He thought of weevils as pests that got into grain stores.

"Not a real weevil," said Wylan. "It's a chemical weevil. It doesn't really have a name yet."

"You've got to give it a name," said Jesper. "How else will you call it to dinner?"

"Forget what it's called," Kaz said. "What matters is that this little vial is going to eat Van Eck's bank accounts and his reputation."

Wylan cleared his throat. "Possibly. The chemistry is complicated. I was hoping Kuwei would help."

Nina said something to Kuwei in Shu. He shrugged and looked away, lip jutting out slightly. Whether it was the recent death of his father or the fact that he'd found himself stuck in a cemetery with a band of thieves, the boy had become increasingly sullen.

"Well?" Jesper prodded.

"I have other interests," Kuwei replied.

Kaz's black gaze pinned Kuwei like the tip of a dagger. "I suggest rethinking your priorities."

Jesper gave Kuwei another nudge. "That's Kaz's way of saying, 'Help Wylan or I'll seal you up in one of these tombs and see how that suits your interests.'"

Matthias was no longer sure what the Shu boy understood or didn't, but apparently he'd received the message. Kuwei swallowed and nodded grudgingly.

"The power of negotiation," Jesper said, and shoved a cracker in his mouth.

"Wylan—and the obliging Kuwei—will get the weevil working," Kaz continued. "Once we have Inej, we can move on Van Eck's silos."

Nina rolled her eyes. "Good thing this is all about getting our money and not about saving Inej. Definitely not about that."

"If you don't care about money, Nina dear, call it by its other names."

"*Kruge?* Scrub? Kaz's one true love?"

"Freedom, security, retribution."

"You can't put a price on those things."

"No? I bet Jesper can. It's the price of the lien on his father's farm." The sharpshooter looked at the toes of his boots. "What about you, Wylan? Can you put a price on the chance to walk away from Ketterdam and live your own life? And Nina, I suspect you and your Fjerdan may want something more to subsist on than patriotism and longing glances. Inej might have a number in mind too. It's the price of a future, and it's Van Eck's turn to pay."

Matthias was not fooled. Kaz always spoke logic, but that didn't mean he always told truth. "The Wraith's life is worth more than that," said Matthias. "To all of us."

"We get Inej. We get our money. It's as simple as that."

"Simple as that," said Nina. "Did you know I'm next in line for the Fjerdan throne? They call me Princess Ilse of Engelsberg."

"There is no princess of Engelsberg," said Matthias. "It's a fishing town."

Nina shrugged. "If we're going to lie to ourselves, we might as well be grand about it."

Kaz ignored her, spreading a map of the city over the table, and Matthias heard Wylan murmur to Jesper, "Why won't he just say he wants her back?"

"You've met Kaz, right?"

"But she's one of us."

Jesper's brows rose again. "One of us? Does that mean she knows the secret handshake? Does that mean you're ready to get a tattoo?" He ran a finger up Wylan's forearm, and Wylan flushed a vibrant pink. Matthias couldn't help but sympathize with the boy. He knew what it was to be out of your depth, and he sometimes suspected they could forgo all of Kaz's planning and simply let Jesper and Nina flirt the entirety of Ketterdam into submission.

Wylan pulled his sleeve down self-consciously. "Inej is part of the crew."

"Just don't push it."

"Why not?"

"Because the practical thing would be for Kaz to auction Kuwei to the highest bidder and forget about Inej entirely."

"He wouldn't—" Wylan broke off abruptly, doubt creeping over his features.

None of them really knew what Kaz would or wouldn't do. Sometimes Matthias wondered if even Kaz was sure.

"Okay, Kaz," said Nina, slipping off her shoes and wiggling her toes. "Since this is about the almighty plan, how about you stop meditating over that map and tell us just what we're in for."

"I want you focused on what we have to do tomorrow night. After that, you'll get all the information you want."

"Really?" asked Nina, tugging at her corset. Pollen from one of the irises had scattered over her bare shoulder. Matthias had the overwhelming urge to brush it away with his lips. *It's probably poisonous*, he told himself sternly. Maybe he should take a walk.

"Van Eck promised us thirty million *kruge*," said Kaz. "That's exactly what we're going to take. With another one million for interest, expenses, and just because we can."

Wylan broke a cracker in two. "My father doesn't have thirty million *kruge* lying around. Even if you took all his assets together."

"You should leave, then," said Jesper. "We only associate with the disgraced heirs of the very *finest* fortunes."

Kaz stretched his bad leg out, flexing his foot slightly. "If Van Eck had that kind of money on hand, we would have just robbed him instead of breaking into the Ice Court in the first place. He could only offer a reward that big because he claimed the Merchant Council was putting city funds toward it."

"What about that chest full of bills he brought to Vellgeluk?" asked Jesper.

"Bunk," said Kaz, disgust in his voice. "Probably quality counterfeits."

"So then how do we get the money? Rob the city? Rob the Council?" Jesper sat up straighter, hands drumming eagerly on the table. "Hit twelve vaults in one night?"

Wylan shifted in his chair, and Matthias saw the disquiet in his expression. At least someone else in this band of miscreants was reluctant to keep committing crimes.

"No," said Kaz. "We're going to make like merchers and let the market do the work for us." He leaned back, gloved hands resting on his crow's head cane. "We're going to take Van Eck's money, and then we're going to take his reputation. We're going to make sure he can never do business in Ketterdam or anywhere in Kerch ever again."

"And what happens to Kuwei?" asked Nina.

"Once the job is done, Kuwei—and any other convicts, Grisha, and disinherited youths who may or may not have prices on their heads—can lie low in the Southern Colonies."

Jesper frowned. "Where will you be?"

"Right here. I've still got plenty of business that requires my attention."

Though Kaz's tone was easy, Matthias heard the dark anticipation in his words. He had often wondered how people survived this city, but it was possible Ketterdam would not survive Kaz Brekker.

"Wait a minute," said Nina. "I thought Kuwei was going to Ravka."

"Why would you think that?"

"When you sold your Crow Club shares to Pekka Rollins, you asked him to send a message to the Ravkan capital. We all heard it."

"I thought it was a request for aid," said Matthias, "not an invitation to bargain." They had never discussed giving Kuwei to Ravka.

Kaz considered them with some amusement. "It was neither. Let's just hope Rollins is as gullible as you two."

"It was a decoy," Nina moaned. "You were just keeping Rollins busy."

"I wanted Pekka Rollins preoccupied. Hopefully, he has his people trying to chase down our Ravkan contacts. They should prove difficult to find, given that they don't exist."

Kuwei cleared his throat. "I would prefer to go to Ravka."

"I'd prefer a pair of sable-lined swimming trunks," said Jesper. "But we can't always get what we want."

A furrow appeared between Kuwei's brows. The limits to his understanding of Kerch had apparently been reached and surpassed.

"I would prefer to go to Ravka," he repeated more firmly. Kaz's flat black gaze fastened on Kuwei and held. Kuwei squirmed nervously. "Why is he looking at me this way?"

"Kaz is wondering if he should keep you alive," said Jesper. "Terrible for the nerves. I recommend deep breathing. Maybe a tonic."

"Jesper, stop," said Wylan.

"Both of you need to relax." Jesper patted Kuwei's hand. "We're not going to let him put you in the ground."

Kaz raised a brow. "Let's not make any promises just yet."

"Come on, Kaz. We didn't go to all that trouble to save Kuwei just to make him worm food."

"Why do you want to go to Ravka?" Nina asked, unable to hide her eagerness.

"We never agreed to that," Matthias said. He did not want to argue about this, especially not with Nina. They were supposed to set Kuwei loose to live an anonymous life in Novyi Zem, not hand him over to Fjerda's greatest enemy.

Nina shrugged. "Maybe we need to rethink our options."

Kuwei spoke slowly, choosing his words with care. "It's safer there. For Grisha. For me. I don't want to hide. I want to train." Kuwei touched the notebooks in front of him. "My father's work can help find——" He hesitated, exchanged a few words with Nina. "An antidote for *parem*."

Nina clasped her hands together, beaming.

Jesper tipped back farther in his chair. "I think Nina may be about to burst into song."

An antidote. Was that what Kuwei had been scribbling about in his notebooks? The prospect of something that might neutralize the powers of *parem* was appealing, and yet Matthias couldn't help but be wary. "To put this knowledge in the hands of one nation——" he began.

But Kuwei interrupted. "My father brought this drug into the world. Even without me, what I know, it will be made again."

"You're saying someone else is going to solve the riddle of *parem*?" Matthias asked. Was there truly no hope this abomination could be contained?

"Sometimes scientific discoveries are like that," said Wylan. "Once people know something is possible, the pace of new findings increases. After that, it's like trying to get a swarm of hornets back into their nest."

"Do you really think an antidote is possible?" Nina asked.

"I don't know," said Kuwei. "My father was a Fabrikator. I am just an Inferni."

"You're our chemist, Wylan," said Nina hopefully. "What do you think?"

Wylan shrugged. "Maybe. Not all poisons have an antidote."

Jesper snorted. "That's why we call him Wylan Van Sunshine."

"In Ravka, there are more talented Fabrikators," Kuwei said. "They could help."

Nina nodded emphatically. "It's true. Genya Safin knows poisons like no one else, and David Kostyk developed all kinds of new weapons for King Nikolai." She glanced at Matthias. "And other things too! Nice things. Very peaceable."

Matthias shook his head. "This isn't a decision to be made lightly."

Kuwei's jaw set. "I would prefer to go to Ravka."

"See?" said Nina.

"No, I do not," said Matthias. "We can't just hand such a prize over to Ravka."

"He's a person, not a prize, and he wants to go."

"Do we all get to do what we want now?" asked Jesper. "Because I have a list."

There was a long, tense pause, then Kaz ran a gloved thumb over the crease of his trousers and said, "Nina, love, translate for me? I want to make sure Kuwei and I understand each other."

"Kaz——" she said warningly.

Kaz shifted forward and rested his hands on his knees, a kind older brother offering some friendly advice. "I think it's important that you understand the changes in your circumstances. Van Eck knows the first place you'd go for sanctuary would be Ravka, so any ship bound for its shores is going to be searched top to bottom. The only Tailors powerful enough to make you look like someone else are in Ravka, unless Nina wants to take another dose of *parem*."

Matthias growled.

"Which is unlikely," Kaz conceded. "Now, I assume you don't want me to cart you back to Fjerda or the Shu Han?"

It was clear Nina had finished the translation when Kuwei yelped, "No!"

"Then your choices are Novyi Zem and the Southern Colonies, but the Kerch presence in the colonies is far lower. Also, the weather is better, if you're partial to that kind of thing. You are a stolen painting, Kuwei. Too recognizable to sell on the open market, too valuable to leave lying around. You are worthless to me."

"I'm not translating that," Nina snapped.

"Then translate this: My sole concern is keeping you away from Jan Van Eck, and if you want me to start exploring more definite options, a bullet is a lot cheaper than putting you on a ship to the Southern Colonies."

Nina did translate, though haltingly.

Kuwei responded in Shu. She hesitated. "He says you're cruel."

"I'm pragmatic. If I were cruel, I'd give him a eulogy instead of a conversation. So, Kuwei, you'll go to the Southern Colonies, and when the heat has died down, you can find your way to Ravka or Matthias' grandmother's house for all I care."

"Leave my grandmother out of this," Matthias said.

Nina translated, and at last, Kuwei gave a stiff nod. Though Matthias had gotten his way, the dejection on Nina's face left a hollow feeling in his chest.

Kaz checked his watch. "Now that we're in agreement, you all know what your responsibilities are. There are a lot of things that can go wrong between now and tomorrow night, so talk through the plan and then talk through it again. We only have one shot at this."

"Van Eck will set up a perimeter. He'll have her heavily guarded," said Matthias.

"That's right. He has more guns, more men, and more resources. All we have is surprise, and we're not going to squander it."

A soft scraping sounded from outside. Instantly, they were on their feet and ready, even Kuwei.

But a moment later Rotty and Specht slipped into the tomb.

Matthias released a breath and returned his rifle to where he kept it, always within arm's reach.

"What business?" asked Kaz.

"The Shu have set up at their embassy," said Specht. "Everyone on the Lid is talking about it."

"Numbers?"

"Forty, give or take," said Rotty, kicking the mud from his boots. "Heavily armed, but still operating under diplomatic flags. No one knows exactly what they want."

"We do," said Jesper.

"I didn't get too near the Slat," said Rotty, "but Per Haskell's antsy, and he's not being quiet about it. Without you around, work's piling up for the old man. Now there are rumors you're back in the city and had a run-in with a merch. Oh, and there was some kind of attack at one of the harbors a few days ago. Bunch of sailors killed, harbormaster's office turned into a pile of splinters, but no one knows details."

Matthias saw Kaz's expression darken. He was hungry for more information. Matthias knew the *demjin* had other reasons for going after Inej, but the fact remained that, without her, their ability to gather intelligence had been severely compromised.

"All right," said Kaz. "But no one's connected us to the raid at the Ice Court or *parem*?"

"Not that I heard," said Rotty.

"Nope," said Specht.

Wylan looked surprised. "That means Pekka Rollins hasn't talked."

"Give him time," said Kaz. "He knows we have Kuwei stashed somewhere. The letter to Ravka will only keep him chasing his tail for so long."

Jesper tapped his fingers restlessly on his thighs. "Has anyone noticed this whole city is looking for us, mad at us, or wants to kill us?"

"So?" said Kaz.

"Well, usually it's just half the city."

Jesper might joke, but Matthias wondered if any of them really understood the powers arraying against them. Fjerda, the Shu Han, Novyi Zem, the Kaelish, the Kerch. These were not rival gangs or angry business partners. They were nations, determined to protect their people and secure their futures.

"There's more," said Specht. "Matthias, you're dead."

"Pardon?" Matthias' Kerch was good, but perhaps there were still gaps.

"You were shanked in the Hellgate infirmary."

The room went quiet. Jesper sat down heavily. "Muzzen is dead?"

"Muzzen?" Matthias could not place the name.

"He took your place in Hellgate," Jesper said. "So you could join the Ice Court job."

Matthias remembered the fight with the wolves, Nina standing in his cell, the prison break. Nina had covered a member of the Dregs in false sores and given him a fever to make sure he was quarantined and kept from the larger prison population. *Muzzen.* Matthias should not have forgotten such a thing.

"I thought you said you had a contact in the infirmary," said Nina.

"To keep him sick, not to keep him safe." Kaz's face was grim. "It was a hit."

"The Fjerdans," said Nina.

Matthias folded his arms. "That's not possible."

"Why not?" Nina said. "We know there are *drüskelle* here. If they came to town looking for you and made noise at the Stadhall, they would have been told you were in Hellgate."

"No," said Matthias. "They wouldn't resort to such an underhanded tactic. Hiring a killer? Murdering someone in his sickbed?" But even as he said the words, Matthias wasn't sure he believed them. Jarl Brum and his officers had done worse without a twinge of conscience.

"Big, blond, and blind," Jesper said. "The Fjerdan way."

He died in my stead, Matthias thought. *And I didn't even recognize his name.*

"Did Muzzen have family?" Matthias asked at last.

"Just the Dregs," said Kaz.

"No mourners," Nina murmured.

"No funerals," Matthias replied quietly.

"How does it feel to be dead?" asked Jesper. The merry light had gone from his eyes.

Matthias had no answer. The knife that had killed Muzzen had been meant for Matthias, and the Fjerdans might well be responsible. The *drüskelle*. His brothers. They'd wanted him to die without honor, murdered in an infirmary bed. It was a death fit for a traitor. It was the death he had earned. Now Matthias owed Muzzen a blood debt, but how would he ever pay it? "What will they do with his body?" he asked.

"It's probably already ashes on the Reaper's Barge," said Kaz.

"There's something else," said Rotty. "Someone's kicking up dust looking for Jesper."

"His creditors will have to wait," said Kaz, and Jesper winced.

"No," Rotty said with a shake of his head. "A man showed up at the university. Jesper, he claims he's your father."

4

INEJ

Inej lay on her belly, arms extended in front of her, wriggling like a worm through the dark. Despite the fact that she'd been as good as starving herself, the vent was still a tight fit. She couldn't see where she was going; she just kept moving forward, pulling herself along by her fingertips.

She'd woken sometime after the fight on Vellgeluk, with no sense of how long she'd been unconscious and no idea where she was. She remembered plummeting from a great height as one of Van Eck's Squallers dropped her, only to be snatched up by another—arms like steel bands around her, the air buffeting her face, gray sky all around, and then pain exploding over her skull. The next thing she knew she was awake, head pounding, in the dark. Her hands and ankles were bound, and she could feel a blindfold tight across her face. For a moment, she was fourteen, being tossed into the hold of a slaver ship, frightened and alone. She forced herself to breathe. Wherever she was, she felt no ship's sway, heard no creak of sails. The ground was solid beneath her.

Where would Van Eck have brought her? She could be in a warehouse, someone's home. She might not even be in Kerch anymore. It didn't matter. She was Inej Ghafa, and she would not quiver like a rabbit in a snare. *Wherever I am, I just have to get out.*

She'd managed to nudge her blindfold down by scraping her face against the wall. The room was pitch-black, and all she could hear in the silence was her own rapid breathing as panic seized her again. She'd leashed it by controlling her breath, in through the nose, out through the mouth, letting her mind turn to prayer as her Saints gathered around her. She imagined them checking the ropes at her wrists, rubbing life into her hands. She did not tell herself she wasn't afraid. Long ago, after a bad fall, her father had explained that only fools were fearless. *We meet fear,* he'd said. *We greet the unexpected visitor and listen to what he has to tell us. When fear arrives, something is about to happen.*

Inej intended to make something happen. She'd ignored the ache in her head and forced herself to inch around the room, estimating its dimensions. Then she'd used the wall to push to her feet and felt along it, shuffling and hopping, searching for any doors or windows. When she'd heard footsteps approaching, she'd dropped to the ground, but she hadn't had time to get her blindfold back in place. From then on, the guards tied it tighter. But that didn't matter, because she'd found the vent. All she needed then was a way out of her ropes. Kaz could have managed it in the dark and probably underwater.

The only thorough look she got at the room where she was being held was during meals, when they brought in a lantern. She'd hear keys turning in a series of locks, the door swinging open, the sound of the tray being placed on the table. A moment later, the blindfold would be gently lifted from her face—Bajan was never rough or abrupt. It wasn't in his nature. In fact, she suspected it was beyond the capabilities of his manicured musician's hands.

There was never any cutlery on the tray, of course. Van Eck was wise enough not to trust her with so much as a spoon, but Inej had taken advantage of each unblindfolded moment to study every inch of the barren room, seeking clues that might help her to assess her location and plan her escape. There wasn't much to go on—a concrete floor marked by nothing but the pile of blankets she'd been given to burrow into at night, walls lined with empty shelves, the table and chair where she took her meals. There were no windows, and the only hint that they might still be near Ketterdam was the damp trace of salt in the air.

Bajan would untie her wrists, then bind them again in front of her so that she could eat—though once she'd discovered the vent, she'd only picked at her food, eating enough to keep up her strength and nothing more. Still, when Bajan and the guards had brought her tray tonight, her stomach had growled audibly at the smell of soft sausages and porridge. She'd been woozy with hunger, and when she'd tried to sit down, she'd tipped the tray from its perch on the table, smashing the white ceramic mug and bowl. Her dinner slopped to the floor in a steaming heap of savory mush and broken crockery and she'd landed ungracefully next to it, barely avoiding a face full of porridge.

Bajan had shaken his dark, silky head. "You are weak because you don't eat. Mister Van Eck says I must force-feed you if necessary."

"Try," she'd said, looking up at him from the floor and baring her teeth. "You'll have trouble teaching piano without all your fingers."

But Bajan had only laughed, white grin flashing. He and one of the guards had helped her back into the chair, and he'd sent for another tray.

Van Eck could not have chosen her jailer better. Bajan was Suli, only a few years older than Inej, with thick black hair that curled around his collar and black gem eyes framed by lashes long enough to swat flies. He told her he was a music teacher indentured to Van Eck, and Inej wondered that the merch would bring a boy like that into his household given that his new wife was less than half his own age. Van Eck was either very confident or very stupid. *He double-crossed Kaz*, she reminded herself. *He's leaning heavily into the stupid column.*

Once the mess had been cleaned up—by a guard; Bajan didn't stoop to such work—and a new meal procured, he'd leaned against the wall to watch her eat. She'd scooped up a lump of porridge with her fingers, allowing herself only a few awkward bites.

"You must eat more than that," Bajan chided. "If you make yourself a bit more obliging, if you answer his questions, you'll find Van Eck is a reasonable man."

"A reasonable liar, cheat, and kidnapper," she said, then cursed herself for replying.

Bajan couldn't hide his pleasure. They had the same routine at each meal: She picked at her food. He made small talk, peppering his chatter with pointed questions about Kaz and the Dregs. Every time she spoke, he considered it a victory. Unfortunately, the less she ate, the weaker she got, and the harder it was to keep her wits about her.

"Given the company you keep, I'd think lying and cheating would be points in Mister Van Eck's favor."

"*Shevrati,*" Inej said distinctly. *Know-nothing.* She'd called Kaz that on more than one occasion. She thought of Jesper toying with his guns, Nina squeezing the life from a man with the flick of a wrist, Kaz picking a lock in his black gloves. Thugs. Thieves. Murderers. And all worth more than a thousand Jan Van Ecks.

Then where are they? The question tore at some hastily stitched seam inside of her. *Where is Kaz?* She didn't want to look at that question too closely. Above everything else, Kaz was practical. Why would he come for her when he could walk away from Van Eck with the most valuable hostage in the world?

Bajan wrinkled his nose. "Let's not speak Suli. It makes me maudlin." He wore tapered silk trousers and an elegantly cut coat. Pinned to his lapel, a golden lyre crowned with laurel leaves and a small ruby indicated both his profession and the house of his indenture.

Inej knew she shouldn't continue to talk with him, but she was still a gatherer of secrets. "What instruments do you teach?" she said. "Harp? Pianoforte?"

"Also flute, and voice for ladies."

"And how does Alys Van Eck sing?"

Bajan gave her a lazy grin. "Most prettily under my instruction. I could teach you to make all manner of pleasing sounds."

Inej rolled her eyes. He was just like the boys she'd grown up with, a head full of nonsense and a mouth full of easy charm. "I am bound and facing the prospect of torture or worse. Are you actually flirting with me?"

Bajan tsked. "Mister Van Eck and your Mister Brekker will reach an arrangement. Van Eck is a businessman. From what I understand, he is simply protecting his interests. I cannot imagine he would resort to torture."

"Were you the one tied up and blindfolded every night, your imagination might not fail you so completely."

And if Bajan had known Kaz at all, he wouldn't be so certain of an exchange.

In the long hours she was left alone, Inej tried to rest and put her mind to escape, but inevitably her thoughts turned to Kaz and the others. Van Eck wanted to trade her for Kuwei Yul-Bo, the Shu boy they had stolen from the deadliest fortress in the world. He was the only person who had a hope of re-creating his father's work on the drug known as *jurda parem*, and the price of his ransom would give Kaz all he had ever wanted—all the money and prestige he needed to take his rightful place among the bosses of the Barrel, and the chance at revenge on Pekka Rollins for the death of his brother. The facts lined up one after another, an army of doubts assembled against the hope she tried to keep steady inside her.

Kaz's course was obvious: Ransom Kuwei, take the money, find himself a new spider to scale the walls of the Barrel and steal secrets for him. And hadn't she told him she planned on leaving Ketterdam as soon as they were paid? *Stay with me.* Had he meant it? What value did her life carry in the face of the reward Kuwei might garner? Nina would never let Kaz abandon her. She'd fight with everything she had to free Inej even if she was still in the grips of *parem*. Matthias would stand by her with that great heart full of honor. And Jesper . . . well, Jesper would never do Inej harm, but he needed money badly if he didn't want his father to lose his livelihood. He would do his best, but that might not necessarily mean what was best for her. Besides, without Kaz, were any of them a match for Van Eck's ruthlessness and resources? *I am*, Inej told herself. *I may not have Kaz's devious mind, but I am a dangerous girl.*

Van Eck had sent Bajan to her every day, and he'd been nothing but amiable and pleasant even as he'd prodded her for the locations of Kaz's safe houses. She suspected that Van Eck didn't come himself because he knew Kaz would be keeping a close eye on his movements. Or maybe he thought she'd be more vulnerable to a Suli boy than a wily merch. But tonight something had changed.

Bajan usually left when Inej had made it clear she would eat no more—a parting smile, a small bow, and away he went, duty dispatched until the following morning. Tonight he had lingered.

Instead of taking his cue to vanish when she used her bound hands to nudge away her dish, he'd said, "When did you see your family last?"

A new approach. "Has Van Eck offered you some reward if you can extract information from me?"

"It was just a question."

"And I am just a captive. Did he threaten you with punishment?"

Bajan glanced at the guards and said quietly, "Van Eck could bring you back to your family. He could pay off your contract with Per Haskell. It is well within his means."

"Was this your idea or your master's?"

"Why does it matter?" Bajan asked. There was an urgency in his voice that pricked at Inej's defenses. *When fear arrives, something is about to happen.* But was he afraid of Van Eck or afraid for her? "You can walk away from the Dregs and Per Haskell and that horrid Kaz Brekker free and clear. Van Eck could give you transport to Ravka, money to travel."

An offer or a threat? Could Van Eck have found her mother and father? The Suli were not easy to track, and they would be wary of strangers asking questions. But what if Van Eck had sent men claiming to have knowledge of a lost girl? A girl who had vanished one chilly dawn as if the tide had reached up to the shore to claim her?

"What does Van Eck know about my family?" she asked, anger rising.

"He knows you're far from home. He knows the terms of your indenture with the Menagerie."

"Then he knows I was a slave. Will he have Tante Heleen arrested?"

"I . . . don't think—"

"Of course not. Van Eck doesn't care that I was bought and sold like a bolt of cotton. He's just looking for leverage."

But what Bajan asked next took Inej by surprise. "Did your mother make skillet bread?"

She frowned. "Of course." It was a Suli staple. Inej could have made skillet bread in her sleep.

"With rosemary?"

"Dill, when we had it." She knew what Bajan was doing, trying to make her think of home. But she was so hungry and the memory was so strong that her stomach growled anyway. She could see her mother damping the fire, see her flipping the bread with quick pinches of her fingers, smell the dough cooking over the ashes.

"Your friends are not coming," said Bajan. "It is time to think of your own survival. You could be home with your family by summer's end. Van Eck can help you if you let him."

Every alarm inside Inej had sounded danger. The play was too obvious. Beneath Bajan's charm, his dark eyes, his easy promises, there was fear. And yet amid the clamor of suspicion, she could hear the soft chiming of another bell, the sound of *What if?* What if she let herself be comforted, gave up the pretense of being beyond the things she'd lost? What if she simply let Van Eck put her on a ship, send her home? She could taste the skillet bread, warm from the pan, see her mother's dark braid twined with ribbons, strands of silk the color of ripe persimmons.

But Inej knew better than that. She'd learned from the best. *Better terrible truths than kind lies.* Kaz had never offered her happiness, and she didn't trust the men promising to serve it up to her now. Her suffering had not been for nothing. Her Saints had brought her to Ketterdam for a reason—a ship to hunt slavers, a mission to give meaning to all she'd been through. She would not betray that purpose or her friends for some dream of the past.

Inej hissed at Bajan, an animal sound that made him flinch backward. "Tell your master to honor his old deals before he starts making new ones," she said. "Now leave me alone."

Bajan had scurried away like the well-dressed rat he was, but Inej knew it was time to go. Bajan's new insistence could mean nothing good for her. *I have to get out of this trap*, she'd thought, *before this creature lures me with memories and sympathy.* Maybe Kaz and the others were coming for her, but she didn't intend to wait around and see.

Once Bajan and the guards had left, she'd slipped the shard of broken bowl from where she'd hidden it beneath the ropes around her ankles and set to work. Weak and wobbly as she'd felt when Bajan had arrived with that heavenly smelling bowl of mush, she'd only pretended to swoon so that she could deliberately knock her tray off the table. If Van Eck had really done his research, he would have warned Bajan that the Wraith did not fall. Certainly not in a clumsy heap on the floor where she could easily tuck a sharp piece of crockery between her bonds.

After what seemed like a lifetime of sawing and scraping and bloodying her fingertips on the shard's edge, she'd finally severed her ropes and freed her hands, then untied her ankles and felt her way to the vent. Bajan and the guards wouldn't be back until morning. That gave her the whole night to escape this place and get as far away as she possibly could.

The passage was a miserably tight fit, the air inside musty with smells she couldn't quite identify, the dark so complete she might as well have kept her blindfold on. She had no idea where the vent might lead. It could run for a few more feet or for half a mile. She needed to be gone by morning or they'd find the grating that covered the vent loosened on its hinges and know exactly where she was.

Good luck getting me out, she thought grimly. She doubted any of Van Eck's guards could squeeze inside the air shaft. They'd have to find some kitchen boy and grease him down with lard.

She inched forward. How far had she gone? Every time she took a deep breath, it felt like the air shaft was tightening around her ribs. For all she knew, she could be atop a building. She might pop her head out the other side only to find a busy Ketterdam street far below. Inej could contend with that. But if the shaft just ended? If it was walled up on the other side? She'd have to squirm backward the entire distance and hope to refasten her ropes so that her captors wouldn't know what she'd done. Impossible. There could be no dead ends tonight.

Faster, she told herself, sweat beading on her brow. It was hard not to imagine the building compressing around her, its walls squeezing the breath from her lungs. She couldn't make a real plan until she reached the end of this tunnel, until she knew just how far she'd have to go to evade Van Eck's men.

Then she felt it, the barest gust of air brushing against her damp forehead. She whispered a quick prayer of thanks. There must be some kind of opening up ahead. She sniffed, searching for a hint of coal smoke or the wet green fields of a country town. Cautiously, she wiggled forward until her fingers made contact with the slats of the vent. There was no light trickling through, which she supposed was a good thing. The room she was about to drop into must be unoccupied. Saints, what if she was in Van Eck's mansion? What if she was about to land on a sleeping merch? She listened for some human sound—snores, deep breathing. Nothing.

She wished for her knives, for the comforting weight of them in her palms. Did Van Eck still have them in his possession? Had he sold them off? Tossed them into the sea? She named the blades anyway—*Petyr, Marya, Anastasia, Lizabeta, Sankt Vladimir, Sankta Alina*—and found courage in each whispered word. Then she jiggled the vent and gave it a hard shove. It flew open, but instead of swinging on its hinges, it came completely loose. She tried to grab it, but it slid past her fingertips and clattered to the floor.

Inej waited, heart pounding. A minute passed in silence. Another. No one came. The room was empty. Maybe the whole building was empty. Van Eck wouldn't have left her unguarded, so his men must be stationed outside. If that was the case, she knew slipping past them would present little challenge. And at least now she knew roughly how far away the floor was.

There was no graceful way to accomplish what came next. She slid down headfirst, gripping the wall. Then, when she was more than half-way out and her body began to tip, she let momentum carry her forward, curling into a ball and tucking her arms over her head to protect her skull and neck as she fell.

The impact was fairly painless. The floor was hard concrete like the floor of her cell, but she rolled as she struck and came up against what seemed to be the back of something solid. She pulled herself to her feet, hands exploring whatever she'd banged into. It was upholstered in velvet. As she moved along, she felt another identical object next to it. *Seats*, she realized. *I'm in a theater.*

There were plenty of music halls and theaters in the Barrel. Could she be so close to home? Or maybe in one of the respectable opera houses of the Lid?

She moved slowly, hands out before her until she reached a wall at what she thought was the back of the theater. She groped along it, seeking a door, a window, even another vent. Finally, her fingers hooked over a door frame and her hands wrapped around the knob. It wouldn't budge. Locked. She gave it a tentative rattle.

The room flooded with light. Inej shrank back against the door, squinting in the sudden brightness.

"If you wanted a tour, Miss Ghafa, you might simply have asked," said Jan Van Eck.

He stood on the stage of the decrepit theater, his black mercher's suit cut in severe lines. The theater's green velvet seats were moth-eaten. The curtains bracketing the stage hung in shreds. No one had bothered to take down the set from the last play. It looked like a child's terrified vision of a surgeon's operating room, oversized saws and mallets hanging from the walls. Inej recognized it as the set for *The Madman and the Doctor*, one of the short plays from the Komedie Brute.

Guards were stationed around the room, and Bajan stood beside Van Eck, wringing his elegant hands. Had the vent been left open to tempt her? Had Van Eck been toying with her all along?

"Bring her here," Van Eck told the guards.

Inej didn't hesitate. She sprang onto the narrow back of the nearest theater seat, then raced toward the stage, leaping from row to row as the guards tried to scramble over the seats. She vaulted onto the stage, past a startled Van Eck, neatly skirting two more guards, and seized one of the stage ropes, shinnying up its length, praying it would hold her weight until she made it to the top. She could hide in the rafters, find a way to the roof.

"Cut her down!" Van Eck called, his voice calm.

Inej climbed higher, faster. But seconds later she saw a face above her. One of Van Eck's guards, a knife in his hand. He slashed through the rope.

It gave way and Inej fell to the floor, softening her knees to take the impact. Before she could right herself, three guards were on her, holding her in place.

"Really, Miss Ghafa," Van Eck chided. "We're well aware of your gifts. Did you think I wouldn't take precautions?" He did not wait for an answer. "You are not going to find your way out of this without my help or Mister Brekker's. As he does not seem to be making an appearance, perhaps you should consider a change in alliance."

Inej said nothing.

Van Eck tucked his hands behind his back. It was strange to look at him and see the ghost of Wylan's face. "The city is awash in rumors of *parem*. A delegation of Fjerdan *drüskelle* has arrived in the embassy sector. Today the Shu sailed two warships into Third Harbor. I gave Brekker seven days to broker a trade for your safety, but they are all looking for Kuwei Yul-Bo, and it is imperative that I get him out of the city before they find him."

Two Shu warships. That was what had changed. Van Eck was out of time. Had Bajan known it or simply sensed the difference in his master's mood?

"I had hoped Bajan might prove good for something other than bettering my wife's talent at the pianoforte," Van Eck continued. "But it seems you and I must now come to an arrangement. Where is Kaz Brekker keeping the boy?"

"How could I possibly know that?"

"You must know the locations of the Dregs' safe houses. Brekker does nothing without preparation. He'll have warrens to hide in all over the city."

"If you know him so well, then you know he'd never keep Kuwei somewhere that I could lead you to him."

"I don't believe that."

"I can't help what you do or don't believe. Your Shu scientist is probably long gone already."

"Word would have reached me. My spies are everywhere."

"Clearly not everywhere."

Bajan's lips quirked.

Van Eck shook his head wearily. "Get her on the table."

Inej knew it was pointless to struggle, but she did anyway. It was fight or give in to the terror that rushed through her as the guards hefted her onto the table and pinned down her limbs. Now she saw one of the prop tables was set with instruments that looked nothing like the oversized mallets and saws hanging from the walls. They were real surgeon's tools. Scalpels and saws and clamps that gleamed with sinister intent.

"You are the *Wraith*, Miss Ghafa, legend of the Barrel. You've gathered the secrets of judges, councilmen, thieves, and killers alike. I doubt there is anything in this city you do not know. You will tell me the locations of Mister Brekker's safe houses now."

"I can't tell you what I don't know."

Van Eck sighed. "Remember that I have tried to treat you with civility." He turned to one of the guards, a heavyset man with a sharp blade of a nose. "I'd prefer this didn't go on too long. Do what you think is best."

The guard let his hand hover over the table of instruments as if deciding which cruelty would be most efficient. Inej felt her courage wobble, her breath coming in panicked gasps. *When fear arrives, something is about to happen.*

Bajan leaned over her, face pale, eyes full of concern. "Please tell him. Surely Brekker isn't worth being scarred or maimed? Tell him what you know."

"All I know is that men like you don't deserve the air they breathe."

Bajan looked stung. "I've been nothing but kind to you. I'm not some sort of monster."

"No, you're the man who sits idly by, congratulating yourself on your decency, while the monster eats his fill. At least a monster has teeth and a spine."

"That isn't fair!"

Inej couldn't believe the softness of this creature, that he would bid for her approval in this moment. "If you still believe in fairness, then you've led a very lucky life. Get out of the monster's way, Bajan. Let's get this over with." The blade-nosed guard stepped forward; something gleamed in his hand. Inej reached for a place of stillness inside of herself, the place that had allowed her to endure a year at the Menagerie, a year of nights marked by pain and humiliation, of days counted in beatings and worse. "Go on," she urged, and her voice was steel.

"Wait," said Van Eck. He was studying Inej as if he were reading a ledger, trying to make the figures line up. He cocked his head to one side and said, "Break her legs."

Inej felt her courage fracture. She began to thrash, trying to get free of the guards' hold.

"Ah," said Van Eck. "That's what I thought."

The blade-nosed guard selected a heavy length of pipe.

"No," said Van Eck. "I don't want it to be a clean break. Use the mallet. Shatter the bone." His face hovered above her, his eyes a bright, clear blue—Wylan's eyes, but devoid of any of Wylan's kindness. "No one will be able to put you back together again, Miss Ghafa. Maybe you can earn your way out of your contract by begging for pennies on East Stave and then crawl home to the Slat every night, assuming Brekker still gives you a room there."

"Don't." She didn't know if she was pleading with Van Eck or herself. She didn't know who she hated more in this moment.

The guard took up a steel mallet.

Inej writhed on the table, her body coated in sweat. She could smell her own fear. "Don't," she repeated. *"Don't."*

The blade-nosed guard tested the mallet's weight in his hands. Van Eck nodded. The guard lifted it in a smooth arc.

Inej watched the mallet rise and reach its apex, light glinting off its wide head, the flat face of a dead moon. She heard the crackle of the campfire, thought of her mother's hair twined with persimmon silk.

"He'll never trade if you break me!" she screamed, the words tearing loose from some deep place inside her, her voice raw and undefended. "I'll be no use to him anymore!"

Van Eck held up a hand. The mallet fell.

Inej felt it brush against her trousers as the impact shattered the surface of the table a hair's breadth from her calf, the entire corner collapsing beneath the force.

My leg, she thought, shuddering violently. *That would have been my leg.* There was a metallic taste in her mouth. She'd bitten her tongue. *Saints protect me. Saints protect me.*

"You make an interesting argument," Van Eck said meditatively. He tapped a finger against his lips, thinking. "Ponder your loyalties, Miss Ghafa. Tomorrow night I may not be so merciful."

Inej could not control her shaking. *I'm going to cut you open*, she vowed silently. *I'm going to excavate that pathetic excuse of a heart from your chest.* It was an evil thought, a vile thought. But she couldn't help it. Would her Saints sanction such a thing? Could forgiveness come if she killed not to survive but because she burned with living, luminous hatred? *I don't care*, she thought as her body spasmed and the guards lifted her trembling form from the table. *I'll do penance for the rest of my days if it means I get to kill him.*

They dragged her back to her room through the lobby of the dilapidated theater and down a hall to what she now knew must be an old equipment room. They bound her hands and feet again.

Bajan moved to place the blindfold over her eyes. "I'm sorry," he whispered. "I didn't know he intended . . . I—"

"Kadema mehim."

Bajan flinched. "Don't say that."

The Suli were a close people, loyal. They had to be, in a world where they had no land and where they were so very few. Inej's teeth were chattering, but she forced out the words. "You are forsaken. As you have turned your back on me, so will they turn their backs on you." It was the worst of Suli denunciations, one that forbade you the welcome of your ancestors in the next world, and doomed your spirit to wander without a home.

Bajan paled. "I don't believe any of that."

"You will."

He secured the blindfold around her head. She heard the door close.

Inej lay on her side, her hip and her shoulder digging into the hard floor, and waited for the tremors to pass.

In her early days at the Menagerie, she'd believed someone would come for her. Her family would find her. An officer of the law. A hero from one of the stories her mother used to tell. Men had come, but not to set her free, and eventually her hope had withered like leaves beneath a too-bright sun, replaced by a bitter bud of resignation.

Kaz had rescued her from that hopelessness, and their lives had been a series of rescues ever since, a string of debts that they never tallied as they saved each other again and again. Lying in the dark, she realized that for all her doubts, she'd believed he would rescue her once more, that he would put aside his greed and his demons and come for her. Now she wasn't so sure. Because it was not just the sense in the words she'd spoken that had stilled Van Eck's hand but the truth he'd heard in her voice. *He'll never trade if you break me.* She could not pretend those words had been conjured by strategy or even animal cunning. The magic they'd worked had been born of belief. An ugly enchantment.

Tomorrow night I may not be so merciful. Had tonight been an exercise meant to frighten her? Or would Van Eck return to carry out his threats? And if Kaz did come, how much of her would be left?

PART TWO

A
KILLING WIND

5

JESPER

Jesper felt like his clothes were crawling with fleas. Whenever the crew left Black Veil Island to skulk around the Barrel, they wore the costumes of the Komedie Brute—the capes, veils, masks, and occasionally horns that tourists and locals alike used to disguise their identities while enjoying the pleasures of the Barrel.

But here on the respectable avenues and canals of the university district, Mister Crimson and the Gray Imp would have drawn a lot of stares, so he and Wylan had ditched their costumes as soon as they were clear of the Staves. And if Jesper was honest with himself, he didn't want to meet his father for the first time in years dressed in a goggle-eyed mask or an orange silk cape or even his usual Barrel flash. He'd dressed as respectably as he could. Wylan had lent him a few *kruge* for a secondhand tweed jacket and a gloomy gray waistcoat. Jesper didn't look precisely reputable, but students weren't supposed to look too prosperous anyway.

Once again he found himself reaching for his revolvers, longing for the cool, familiar feel of their pearl handles beneath his thumbs. That skiv of a lawyer had ordered the floor boss to store them in a safe at the

Cumulus. Kaz said they'd get them back in good time, but he doubted Kaz would be so calm and collected if someone had swiped his cane. *You're the one who put them on the table like a nub,* Jesper reminded himself. He'd done it for Inej. And if he was honest, he'd done it for Kaz too, to show he was willing to do what it took to make things right. Not that it seemed to matter much.

Well, he consoled himself, *it's not like I could have worn my revolvers on this errand anyway.* Students and professors didn't go from class to class packing powder. Might make for a more interesting school day if they did. Even so, Jesper had hidden a sad lump of a pistol beneath his coat. This was Ketterdam, after all, and it was possible he and Wylan were walking into a trap. That was why Kaz and Matthias were shadowing their steps. He'd seen no sign of either of them, and Jesper supposed that was a good thing, but he was still grateful Wylan had offered to come along. Kaz had only allowed it because Wylan said he needed supplies for his work on the weevil.

They walked past student cafés and booksellers, shop windows crammed with textbooks, ink, and paper. They were less than two miles from the noise and clatter of the Barrel, but it felt like they'd crossed a bridge into another country. Instead of packs of sailors fresh off the boats looking for trouble, or tourists jostling into you from every angle, people stepped aside to let you pass, kept their conversations low. No barkers shouted from storefronts hoping to garner business. The crooked little alleys were full of bookbinders and apothecaries, and the corners were free of the girls and boys who lacked an association with one of the West Stave houses and who had been forced to ply their trade on the street.

Jesper paused below an awning and took a deep breath through his nose.

"What?" asked Wylan.

"It smells so much better here." Expensive tobacco, morning rain still damp on the cobblestones, blue clouds of hyacinths in the window boxes.

No urine, no vomit, no cheap perfume or garbage rot. Even the tang of coal smoke seemed fainter.

"Are you stalling?" Wylan asked.

"No." Jesper exhaled and sagged a bit. "Maybe a little." Rotty had taken a message to the hotel where the man claiming to be Jesper's father was staying, so they could set a time and place to meet. Jesper had wanted to go himself, but if his father really was in Ketterdam, it was possible he was being used as bait. Better to meet in broad daylight, on neutral ground. The university had seemed safest, far away from the dangers of the Barrel or any of Jesper's usual stomping grounds.

Jesper didn't know if he wanted his father to be waiting for him at the university or not. It was so much more pleasant to think of facing a fight than the shame of how horribly he'd botched everything, but talking about that felt like trying to climb a scaffold made of rotting boards. So he said, "I always liked this part of town."

"My father likes it too. He places a high value on learning."

"Higher than money?"

Wylan shrugged, eyeing a window full of hand-painted globes. "Knowledge isn't a sign of divine favor. Prosperity is."

Jesper cast him a swift glance. He still wasn't used to Wylan's voice coming out of Kuwei's mouth. It always left him feeling a little off-kilter, like he'd thought he was reaching for a cup of wine and gotten a mouthful of water instead. "Is your papa really that religious, or is that just an excuse for being a mean son of a bitch when it comes to business?"

"When it comes to anything, really."

"Particularly thugs and canal rats from the Barrel?"

Wylan shifted the strap of his satchel. "He thinks the Barrel distracts men from work and industry and leads to degeneracy."

"He may have a point," said Jesper. He sometimes wondered what might have happened if he'd never gone out with his new friends that night, if he'd never walked into that gambling parlor and taken that first spin at Makker's Wheel. It was meant to be harmless fun. And for everyone else, it had been. But Jesper's life had split like a log into two distinct and uneven pieces: the time before he'd stepped up to that wheel and every day since. "The Barrel eats people."

"Maybe," Wylan considered. "But business is business. The gambling parlors and brothels meet a demand. They offer employment. They pay taxes."

"What a good little Barrel boy you've become. That's practically a page out of the bosses' books." Every few years some reformer got it into his head to clean up the Barrel and purge Ketterdam of its unsavory reputation. That was when the pamphlets came out, a war of propaganda between the owners of the gambling dens and pleasure houses on one side and the black-suited merch reformers on the other. In the end, it all came down to money. The businesses of East and West Stave turned a serious profit, and the denizens of the Barrel dumped very righteous coin into the city's tax coffers.

Wylan tugged on the satchel strap again. It had gotten twisted at the top. "I don't think it's much different from wagering your fortune on a shipment of silk or *jurda*. Your odds are just a lot better when you're playing the market."

"You have my attention, merchling." Better odds were always of interest. "What's the most your father's ever lost on a trade?"

"I don't really know. He stopped talking about those things with me a long time ago."

Jesper hesitated. Jan Van Eck was three kinds of fool for the way he'd treated his son, but Jesper could admit he was curious about Wylan's supposed "affliction." He wanted to know what Wylan saw when he tried to read, why he seemed fine with equations or prices on a menu, but not sentences or signs. Instead he said, "I wonder if proximity to the Barrel makes merchers more uptight. All that black clothing and restraint, meat only twice a week, lager instead of brandy. Maybe they're making up for all the fun we're having."

"Keeping the scales balanced?"

"Sure. I mean, just think of the heights of debauchery we could reach if no one kept this city in check. Champagne for breakfast. Naked orgies on the floor of the Exchange."

Wylan made a flustered noise that sounded like a bird with a cough and looked anywhere but at Jesper. He was so wonderfully easy to rattle, though Jesper could admit he didn't think the university district needed a dose of the dirty. He liked it just fine as it was—clean and quiet and smelling of books and flowers.

"You don't have to come, you know," Jesper said, because he felt he should. "You have your supplies. You could wait this out safe and snug in a coffeehouse."

"Is that what you want?"

No. I can't do this alone. Jesper shrugged. He wasn't sure how he felt about what Wylan might witness at the university. Jesper had rarely seen his father angry, but how could he fail to be angry now? What explanations could Jesper offer him? He'd lied, put the livelihood his father had worked so hard for into jeopardy. And for what? A steaming pile of nothing.

But Jesper couldn't bear the thought of facing his father on his own. Inej would have understood. Not that he deserved her sympathy, but there was something steady in her that he knew would recognize and ease his own fears. He'd hoped that Kaz would offer to accompany him. But when they'd split up to approach the university, Kaz had spared him only one dark glance. The message had been clear: *You dug this grave. Go lie in it.* Kaz was still punishing him for the ambush that had nearly ended the Ice Court job before it began, and it was going to take more than Jesper sacrificing his revolvers for him to earn his way back into Kaz's good graces. Did Kaz even have good graces?

Jesper's heart beat a little harder as they walked beneath the vast stone archway into the courtyard of the Boeksplein. The university wasn't one building but a series of them, all built around parallel sections of the Boekcanal and joined by Speaker's Bridge, where people met to debate or drink a friendly pint of lager, depending on the day of the week. But the Boeksplein was the heart of the university—four libraries built around a central courtyard and the Scholar's Fountain. It had been nearly two years since Jesper had set foot on university grounds. He'd never officially withdrawn from school. He hadn't even really decided not to attend. He'd simply started spending more and more time on East Stave, until he looked up one day and realized the Barrel had become his home.

Even so, in his brief time as a student, he'd fallen in love with the Boeksplein. Jesper had never been a great reader. He loved stories, but he hated sitting still, and the books assigned to him for school seemed designed to make his mind wander. At the Boeksplein, wherever his eyes strayed, there was something to occupy them: leaded windows with stained-glass borders, iron gates worked into figures of books and ships, the central fountain with its bearded scholar, and best of all, the gargoyles—bat-winged grotesques in mortarboard caps, and stone dragons falling asleep over books. He liked to think that whoever had built this place had known not all students were suited to quiet contemplation.

But as they entered the courtyard, Jesper didn't look around to savor the stonework or listen to the splashing of the fountain. All his attention focused on the man standing near the eastern wall, gazing up at the stained-glass windows, a crumpled hat clasped in his hands. With a pang, Jesper realized his father had worn his best suit. He'd combed his Kaelish red hair tidily back from his brow. There was gray in it now that hadn't been there when Jesper left home. Colm Fahey looked like a farmer on his way to church. Totally out of place. Kaz—hell, anyone in the Barrel— would take one look at him and just see a walking, talking target.

Jesper's throat felt dry-sand parched. "Da," he croaked.

His father's head snapped up and Jesper steeled himself for what might come next—whatever insults or outrage his father hurled at him, he deserved. But he wasn't prepared for the relieved grin that split his father's craggy features. Someone might as well have put a bullet right in Jesper's heart.

"Jes!" his father cried. And then Jesper was crossing the courtyard and his father's arms were tight around him, hugging him so hard Jesper thought he actually felt his ribs bend. "All Saints, I thought you were dead. They said you weren't a student here anymore, that you'd just vanished and—I was sure you'd been stuck through by bandits or the like in this Saintsforsaken place."

"I'm alive, Da," Jesper gasped. "But if you keep squeezing me like that, I won't be for long."

His father laughed and released him, holding him at arm's length, big hands on Jesper's shoulders. "I swear you're a foot taller."

Jesper ducked his head. "Half a foot. Um, this is Wylan," he said, switching from Zemeni to Kerch. They'd spoken both at home, his mother's language and the language of trade. His father's native Kaelish had been reserved for the rare times Colm sang.

"Nice to meet you. Do you speak Kerch?" his father practically shouted, and Jesper realized it was because Wylan still looked Shu.

"*Da*," he said, cringing in embarrassment. "He speaks Kerch just fine."

"Nice to meet you, Mister Fahey," said Wylan. Bless his merch manners.

"And you too, lad. Are you a student as well?"

"I . . . have studied," said Wylan awkwardly.

Jesper had no idea how to fill the silence that followed. He wasn't sure what he'd expected from this meeting with his father, but a friendly exchange of pleasantries wasn't it.

Wylan cleared his throat. "Are you hungry, Mister Fahey?"

"Starving," Jesper's father replied gratefully.

Wylan gave Jesper a poke with his elbow. "Maybe we could take your father to lunch?"

"Lunch," Jesper said, repeating the word as if he'd just learned it. "Yes, lunch. Who doesn't like lunch?" Lunch felt like a miracle. They'd eat. They'd talk. Maybe they'd drink. Please let them drink.

"But Jesper, what has been happening? I received a notice from the

Gemensbank. The loan is coming due, and you'd given me to believe it was temporary. And your studies—"

"Da," Jesper began. "I . . . the thing is—"

A shot rang out against the walls of the courtyard. Jesper shoved his father behind him as a bullet pinged off the stones at their feet, sending up a cloud of dust. Suddenly, gunfire was echoing across the courtyard. The reverberation made it hard to tell where the shots were coming from.

"What in the name of all that is holy—"

Jesper yanked on his father's sleeve, pulling him toward the hooded stone shelter of a doorway. He looked to his left, prepared to grab hold of Wylan, but the merchling was already in motion, keeping pace beside Jesper in what passed for a reasonable crouch. *Nothing like being shot at a few times to make you a fast learner*, Jesper thought as they reached the protective curve of the overhang. He craned his neck to try to see up to the roofline, then flinched back as more shots rang out. Another smattering of gunfire rattled from somewhere above and to the left of them, and Jesper could only hope that meant Matthias and Kaz were returning fire.

"Saints!" his father gasped. "This city is worse than the guidebooks said!"

"Da, it isn't the city," Jesper said, pulling the pistol from his coat. "They're after me. Or after us. Hard to say."

"Who's after you?"

Jesper exchanged a glance with Wylan. Jan Van Eck? A rival gang looking to settle a score? Pekka Rollins or someone else Jesper had borrowed money from? "There's a long list of potential suitors. We need to get out of here before they introduce themselves more personally."

"Brigands?"

Jesper knew there was a good chance he was about to be riddled with holes, so he tried to restrain his grin. "Something like that."

He peered around the edge of the door, peeled off two shots, then ducked back when another spate of gunfire exploded.

"Wylan, tell me you're packing more than pens, ink, and weevil makings."

"I've got two flash bombs and something new I rigged up with a little more, um, wallop."

"Bombs?" Jesper's father asked, blinking as if to wake himself from a bad dream.

Jesper shrugged helplessly. "Think of them as science experiments?"

"What kind of numbers are we up against?" asked Wylan.

"Look at you, asking all the right questions. Hard to tell. They're somewhere on the roof, and the only way out is back through the archway. That's a lot of courtyard to cross with them firing from high ground. Even if we make it, I'm guessing they're going to have plenty more thunder waiting for us outside the Boeksplein unless Kaz and Matthias can somehow clear a path."

"I know another way out," said Wylan. "But the entrance is on the other side of the courtyard." He pointed to a door beneath an arch carved with some kind of horned monster gnawing on a pencil.

"The reading room?" Jesper gauged the distance. "All right. On three, you make a break. I'll cover you. Get my father inside."

"Jesper—"

"Da, I swear I'll explain everything, but right now all you need to know is that we're in a bad situation, and bad situations happen to be my area of expertise." And it was true. Jesper could feel himself coming alive, the worry that had been dogging his steps since he'd gotten news of his father's arrival in Ketterdam falling away. He felt free, dangerous, like lightning rolling over the prairie. "Trust me, Da."

"All right, boy. All right."

Jesper was pretty sure he could hear an unspoken *for now*. He saw Wylan brace himself. The merchling was still so new to all this. Hopefully Jesper wouldn't get everyone killed.

"One, two . . ." He started firing on *three*. Leaping into the courtyard, he rolled for cover behind the fountain. He'd gone in blind, but he

77

picked out the shapes on the roof quickly, aiming by instinct, sensing movement and firing before he could think his way clear of a good shot. He didn't need to kill anyone, he just needed to scare the hell out of them and buy Wylan and his father time.

A bullet struck the fountain's central statue, the book in the scholar's hand exploding into fragments of stone. Whatever ammunition they were using, they weren't messing around.

Jesper reloaded and popped up from behind the fountain, shooting.

"All *Saints*," he shouted as pain tore through his shoulder. He really hated being shot. He shrank back behind the stone lip. He flexed his hand, testing the damage to his arm. Just a scratch, but it hurt like hell, and he was bleeding all over his new tweed jacket. "This is why it doesn't pay to try to look respectable," he muttered. Above him, he could see the silhouettes on the roof moving. Any minute, they were going to circle around the other side of the fountain and he'd be done for.

"Jesper!" Wylan's voice. Damn it. He was supposed to get clear. "Jesper, at your two o'clock."

Jesper looked up and something was arcing through the sky. Without thinking, he aimed and fired. The air exploded.

"Get in the water!" Wylan shouted.

Jesper dove into the fountain, and a second later the air sizzled with light. When Jesper poked his soaked head out of the water, he saw that every exposed surface of the courtyard and its gardens was pocked with holes, tendrils of smoke rising from the tiny craters. Whoever was up on the roof was screaming. Just what kind of bomb had Wylan let loose?

He hoped Matthias and Kaz had found cover, but there was no time to stew on it. He bolted for the doorway beneath the pencil-chewing demon. Wylan and his father were waiting inside. They slammed the door shut.

"Help me," said Jesper. "We need to barricade the entrance."

The man behind the desk wore gray scholar's robes. His nostrils were flared so wide in effrontery that Jesper feared being sucked up one of them. "Young man—"

Jesper pointed his gun at the scholar's chest. "Move."

"Jesper!" his father said.

"Don't worry, Da. People point guns at each other all the time in Ketterdam. It's basically a handshake."

"Is that true?" his father asked as the scholar grudgingly moved aside and they shoved the heavy desk in front of the door.

"Absolutely," said Wylan.

"Certainly *not*," said the scholar.

Jesper waved them on. "Depends on the neighborhood. Let's go."

They pelted down the main aisle of the reading room between long tables lit by lamps with curving necks. Students huddled against the wall and under their chairs, probably thinking they were all about to die.

"Nothing to worry about, everyone!" Jesper called. "Just a little target practice in the courtyard."

"This way," said Wylan, ushering them through a door covered in elaborate scrollwork.

"Oh, you mustn't," said the scholar rushing after them, robes flapping. "Not the rare books room!"

"Do you want to shake hands again?" Jesper asked, then added, "I promise we won't shoot anything we don't have to." He gave his father a gentle shove. "Up the stairs."

"Jesper?" said a voice from beneath the nearest table.

A pretty blonde girl looked up from where she was crouched on the floor.

"Madeleine?" Jesper said. "Madeleine Michaud?"

"You said we'd have breakfast!"

"I had to go to Fjerda."

"Fjerda?"

Jesper headed up the stairs after Wylan, then poked his head back into the reading room. "If I live, I'll buy you waffles."

"You don't have enough money to buy her waffles," Wylan grumbled.

"Be quiet. We're in a library."

Jesper had never had cause to enter the rare books room while he was at school. The silence was so deep it was like being underwater. Illuminated manuscripts were displayed in glass cases lit by golden falls of lamplight, and rare maps covered the walls.

A Squaller in a blue *kefta* stood in the corner, arms raised, but shrank back as they entered.

"Shu!" the Squaller cried when he saw Wylan. "I won't go with you. I'll kill myself first!"

Jesper's father held up his hands as if gentling a horse. "Easy, lad."

"We're just passing through," said Jesper, giving his father another push.

"Follow me," said Wylan.

"What is a Squaller doing in the rare books room?" Jesper asked as they raced through the labyrinth of shelves and cases, past the occasional scholar or student crouched against the books in fear.

"Humidity. He keeps the air dry to preserve the manuscripts."

"Nice work if you can get it."

When they reached the westernmost wall, Wylan stopped in front of a map of Ravka. He looked around to make sure they weren't being observed, then pressed the symbol marking the capital—Os Alta. The country seemed to tear apart along the seam of the Unsea, revealing a dark gap barely wide enough to squeeze through.

"It leads to the second floor of a printmaker's shop," said Wylan as they edged inside. "It was built as a way for professors to get from the library to their homes without having to deal with angry students."

"Angry?" Jesper's father said. "Do all the students have guns?"

"No, but there's a long-standing tradition of rioting over grades."

The map slid closed, leaving them in the dark as they shuffled along sideways.

"Not to be a podge," Jesper murmured to Wylan, "but I wouldn't have thought you'd know your way around the rare books room."

"I used to meet with one of my tutors here, back when my father still thought . . . The tutor had a lot of interesting stories. And I always liked the maps. Tracing the letters sometimes made it easier to . . . It's how I found the passage."

"You know, Wylan, one of these days I'm going to stop underestimating you."

There was a brief pause and then, from somewhere up ahead, he heard Wylan say, "Then you're going to be a lot harder to surprise."

Jesper grinned, but it didn't quite feel right. From behind them, he could hear shouting from the rare books room. It had been a close call, he was bleeding from his shoulder, they'd made a grand escape—these were the moments he lived for. He should be buzzing from the excitement of the fight. The thrill was still there, fizzing through his blood, but beside it was a cold, unfamiliar sensation that felt like it was draining the joy from him. All he could think was, *Da could have been hurt. He could have died.* Jesper was used to people shooting at him. He would have been a little insulted if they'd *stopped* shooting at him. This was different. His father hadn't chosen this fight. His only crime had been putting his faith in his son.

That's the problem with Ketterdam, Jesper thought as they stumbled uncertainly through the dark. *Trusting the wrong person can get you killed.*

Nina couldn't stop staring at Colm Fahey. He was a bit shorter than his son, broader in the shoulders, his coloring classically Kaelish—vibrant, dark red hair and that salt-white skin, densely clouded with freckles by the Zemeni sun. And though his eyes were the same clear gray as Jesper's, they had a seriousness to them, a kind of sure warmth that differed from Jesper's crackling energy.

It wasn't only the pleasure of trying to find Jesper in his father's features that kept Nina's attention focused on the farmer. There was just something so strange about seeing a person that *wholesome* standing in the stone hull of an empty mausoleum surrounded by Ketterdam's worst—herself among them.

Nina shivered and drew the old horse blanket she'd been using as a wrap more tightly around her. She'd started tallying her life in good days and bad days, and thanks to the Cornelis Smeet job, this was turning out to be a very bad day. She couldn't afford to let it get the best of her, not when they were this close to rescuing Inej. *Be all right*, Nina willed silently, hoping her thoughts could somehow cut through the air, speed over the waters of the Ketterdam harbors, and reach her friend. *Stay safe and whole and wait for us.*

Nina hadn't been on Vellgeluk when Van Eck had taken Inej hostage. She'd still been trying to purge the *parem* from her body, caught in the haze of suffering that had begun on the voyage from Djerholm. She told herself to be grateful for the memory of that misery, every shaking, aching, vomiting minute of it. The shame of Matthias witnessing it all, holding back her hair, dabbing her brow, restraining her as gently as he could as she argued, cajoled, screamed at him for more *parem*. She made herself remember every terrible thing she'd said, every wild pleasure offered, each insult or accusation she'd hurled at him. *You enjoy watching me suffer. You want me to beg, don't you? How long have you been waiting to see me like this? Stop punishing me, Matthias. Help me. Be good to me and I'll be good to you.* He'd absorbed it all in stoic silence. She clutched tight to those memories. She needed them as vivid and bright and cringe-inducing as possible to fight her hunger for the drug. She never wanted to be like that again.

Now she looked at Matthias, his hair coming in thick and gold, long enough that it was just starting to curl over his ears. She loved the sight of him, and she hated it too. Because he wouldn't give her what she wanted. Because he knew how badly she needed it.

After Kaz had settled them on Black Veil, Nina had managed to last two days before she'd broken down and gone to Kuwei to ask him for another dose of *parem*. A small one. Just a taste of it, something to ease this relentless need. The sweats were gone, the bouts of fever. She could walk and talk, and listen to Kaz and the others hatching their plans. But even as she went about her business, drank the cups of broth and tea heaped with sugar that Matthias set before her, the need was there, a ceaseless, serrated sawing at her nerves, back and forth, minute to minute. She hadn't made a conscious decision to ask Kuwei when she'd sat down beside him. She'd spoken to him softly in Shu, listened to him complain about the dampness of the tomb. And then the words were out of her mouth: "Do you have any more?"

He didn't bother to ask what she meant. "I gave it all to Matthias."

"I see," she'd said. "That's probably for the best."

She'd smiled. He'd smiled. She'd wanted to claw his face to shreds.

Because she couldn't possibly go to Matthias. Ever. And for all she knew, he'd thrown whatever supply of the drug Kuwei had into the sea. The thought filled her with so much panic that she'd had to race outside and vomit the spare contents of her stomach in front of one of the ruined mausoleums. She'd covered the mess with dirt, then found a quiet place to sit beneath a trellis of ivy and wept in jags of unsteady tears.

"You're all a bunch of useless skivs," she'd said to the silent graves. They didn't seem to care. And yet somehow the stillness of Black Veil comforted her, quieted her. She couldn't explain why. The places of the dead had never held solace for her before. She rested for a while, dried her tears, and when she knew she wouldn't give herself away with blotchy skin and watery eyes, she'd made her way back to the others.

You survived the worst of it, she had told herself. *The* parem *is out of reach, and now you can stop thinking about it.* And she'd managed for a while.

Then last night, when she'd been preparing to cozy up to Cornelis Smeet, she'd made the mistake of using her power. Even with the wig and the flowers and the costume and the corset, she hadn't quite felt up to the role of seductress. So she'd found a looking glass inside Club Cumulus and attempted to tailor the circles beneath her eyes. It was the first time she'd tried to use her power since her recovery. She'd broken into a sweat from the effort, and as soon as the bruised color faded, the hunger for *parem* hit, a swift, hard kick to her chest. She'd bent double, clutching the sink, her mind filled with breakneck thoughts of how she could get away, who might have a supply, what she could trade. She'd forced herself to think of the shame on the boat, the future she might be able to make with Matthias, but the thought that had brought her back to sanity was Inej. She owed Inej her life, and there was no way she was leaving her stranded with Van Eck. She wasn't that person. She refused to be.

Somehow, she had pulled herself together. She splashed water on her face, pinched her cheeks to pinkness. She still looked haggard, but with resolution, she'd hitched up her corset and flashed the brightest smile she could muster. *Do this right and Smeet won't be looking at your face*, Nina had told herself, and she'd sailed out the doors to snag herself a pigeon.

But once the job was done, when the information they needed was secured, and everyone had fallen asleep, she'd dug through Matthias' few belongings, through the pockets of his clothes, her frustration growing with every passing second. She hated him. She hated Kuwei. She hated this stupid city.

Disgusted with herself, she'd slipped beneath his blankets. Matthias always slept with his back to a wall, a habit from his days in Hellgate. She'd let her hands wander, seeking his pockets, trying to feel along the linings of his trousers.

"Nina?" he'd asked sleepily.

"I'm cold," she said, her hands continuing their search. She pressed a kiss to his neck, then below his ear. She'd never let herself kiss him this way before. She'd never had the chance. They'd been too busy untangling the skein of suspicion and lust and loyalty that bound them together, and once she'd taken the *parem* . . . It was all she could think of, even now. The desire she felt was for the drug, not for the body she felt shift beneath her hands. She didn't kiss his lips, though. She wouldn't let *parem* take that from her too.

He'd groaned slightly. "The others—"

"Everyone is asleep."

Then he'd seized her hands. *"Stop."*

"Matthias—"

"I don't have it."

She yanked herself free, shame crawling over her skin like fire over a forest floor. "Then who does?" she hissed.

"Kaz." She stilled. "Are you going to creep into his bed?"

Nina released a huff of disbelief. "He'd slit my throat." She wanted to scream her helplessness. There would be no bargaining with Kaz. She couldn't bully him the way she might have bullied Wylan or plead with him the way she might have managed Jesper.

Fatigue came on suddenly, a yoke at her neck, the exhaustion at least tempering her frantic need. She rested her forehead against Matthias' chest. "I hate this," she said. "I hate you a little, *drüskelle*."

"I'm used to it. Come here." He'd wrapped his arms around her and gotten her talking about Ravka, about Inej. He'd distracted her with stories, named the winds that blew across Fjerda, told her of his first meal in the *drüskelle* hall. At some point, she must have drifted off, because the next thing she knew, she was burrowing her way out of a heavy, dreamless sleep, woken by the sound of the tomb door slamming open.

Matthias and Kaz had returned from the university, holes burned into their clothing from some kind of bomb Wylan had made, Jesper and Wylan close on their heels, wild-eyed and soaked from the spring rain that had begun to fall—with a beefy Kaelish-looking farmer in tow. Nina felt like she'd been given some kind of lovely gift from the Saints, a situation mad and baffling enough to actually distract her.

Though the hunger for *parem* had dulled since last night's frenzy, it was still there, and she had no idea how she was going to get through the mission tonight. Seducing Smeet had only been the first part of their plan. Kaz was counting on her, Inej was counting on her. They needed her to be a Corporalnik, not an addict with the shakes who wore herself out with the barest bit of tailoring. But Nina couldn't think about any of that with Colm Fahey standing there mangling his hat, and Jesper looking like he'd rather be eating a stack of waffles topped with ground glass than facing him, and Kaz . . . She had no idea what to expect from Kaz. Anger, maybe worse. Kaz didn't like surprises or potential vulnerabilities, and Jesper's father was one very stocky, wind-chafed vulnerability.

But after hearing Jesper's breathless—and, Nina suspected, abbreviated—description of how they'd escaped the university, Kaz simply leaned on his cane and said, "Were you followed?"

"No," Jesper replied with a decisive shake of his head.

"Wylan?"

Colm bristled. "You doubt my son's word?"

"It isn't personal, Da," said Jesper. "He doubts everyone's word."

Kaz's expression had been unruffled, his rough stone voice so easy and pleasant that Nina felt the hair rise on her arms. "Apologies, Mister Fahey. A habit one develops in the Barrel. Trust but verify."

"Or don't trust at all," muttered Matthias.

"Wylan?" Kaz repeated.

Wylan set his satchel down on the table. "If they'd known about the passage, they would have followed us or had people waiting in the print-maker's shop. We lost them."

"I counted about ten on the roof," said Kaz, and Matthias nodded confirmation.

"Sounds right," said Jesper. "But I can't be sure. They had the sun at their backs."

Kaz sat down, his black eyes focused on Jesper's father. "You were the bait."

"Pardon, lad?"

"The bank called in your loan?"

Colm blinked, surprised. "Well, yes, as a matter of fact, they sent me a rather sternly worded letter that I'd become an unstable credit risk. They said that if I didn't pay in full, they would be forced to take legal action." He turned to his son. "I wrote to you, Jes." His voice was confused, not accusing.

"I . . . I haven't been able to collect mail." After Jesper had stopped attending university, had he still managed to receive letters there? Nina wondered how he'd maintained this ruse for so long. It would have been made easier by the fact that Colm was an ocean away—and by his desire to believe in his son. *An easy mark*, Nina thought sadly. No matter his reasons, Jesper had been conning his own father.

"Jesper—" said Colm.

"I was trying to get the money, Da."

"They're threatening to take the farm."

Jesper's eyes were firmly fixed on the tomb floor. "I was close. I *am* close."

"To the money?" Now Nina heard Colm's frustration. "We're sitting in a tomb. We were just shot at."

"What got you on a ship to Ketterdam?" Kaz asked.

"The bank moved up the collection date!" Colm said indignantly. "Simply said I'd run out of time. I tried to reach Jesper, but when there was no reply, I thought—"

"You thought you'd see what your brilliant boy was up to here on the dark streets of Ketterdam."

"I feared the worst. The city does have a reputation."

"Well deserved, I promise you," said Kaz. "And when you arrived?"

"I made inquiries at the university. They said he wasn't enrolled, so I went to the constabulary."

Jesper winced. "Oh, Da. The *stadwatch*?"

Colm crushed his hat with fresh vigor. "And where was I supposed to go, Jes? You know how dangerous it is for . . . for someone like you."

"Da," Jesper said, looking his father in the eye at last. "You didn't tell them I'm—"

"Of course not!"

Grisha. Why won't either of them say it?

Colm threw down the lump of felt that had been his hat. "I don't understand any of this. Why would you bring me to this horrible place? Why were we shot at? What has become of your studies? What has become of you?"

Jesper opened his mouth, closed it. "Da, I . . . I—"

"It was my fault," Wylan blurted. Every eye turned to him. "He uh . . . he was concerned about the bank loan, so he put his studies on hold to work with a . . ."

"Local gunsmith," Nina offered.

"Nina," Matthias rumbled warningly.

"He needs our help," she whispered.

"To lie to his father?"

"It's a fib. Totally different." She had no idea where Wylan was going with this, but he was clearly in need of assistance.

"Yes!" said Wylan eagerly. "A gunsmith! And then I . . . I told him about a deal—"

"They were swindled," Kaz said. His voice was as cold and steady as ever, but he held himself stiffly, as if walking over uncertain ground. "They were offered a business opportunity that seemed too good to be true."

Colm slumped into a chair. "If it seems that way, then—"

"It probably is," said Kaz. Nina had the strangest sense that for once he was being sincere.

"Did you and your brother lose everything?" Colm asked Wylan.

"My brother?" Wylan asked blankly.

"Your *twin brother*," Kaz said with a glance at Kuwei, who sat quietly observing the proceedings. "Yes. They lost everything. Wylan's brother hasn't spoken a word since."

"Does seem the quiet type," Colm said. "And you are all . . . students?"

"Of a sort," said Kaz.

"Who spend your free hours in a graveyard. Can we not go to the authorities? Tell them what happened? These swindlers may have other victims."

"Well—" Wylan began, but Kaz silenced him with a look. A strange hush fell in the tomb. Kaz took a seat at the table.

"The authorities can't help you," he said. "Not in this city."

"Why not?"

"Because the law here is profit. Jesper and Wylan tried to take a short-cut. The *stadwatch* won't so much as wipe their tears. Sometimes, the only way to get justice is to take it for yourself."

"And that's where you come in."

Kaz nodded. "We're going to get your money. You won't lose your farm."

"But you're going to step outside the law to do it," Colm said. He shook his head wearily. "You barely look old enough to graduate."

"Ketterdam was my education. And I can tell you this: Jesper never would have turned to me for help if he'd had anywhere else to go."

"You can't be so bad, boy," said Colm gruffly. "You haven't been alive long enough to rack up your share of sin."

"I'm a quick study."

"Can I trust you?"

"No."

Colm took up his crumpled hat again. "Can I trust you to help Jesper through this?"

"Yes."

Colm sighed. He looked around at all of them. Nina found herself standing up straighter. "You lot make me feel very old."

"Spend a little more time in Ketterdam," said Kaz. "You'll feel ancient." Then he tilted his head to one side and Nina saw that distant, considering look cross his features. "You have an honest face, Mister Fahey."

Colm shot Jesper a puzzled glance. "Well. I should hope so, and thank you for marking it."

"It's not a compliment," said Jesper. "And I know that look, Kaz. Don't you dare start those wheels spinning."

Kaz's only response was a slow blink. Whatever scheme had been set in motion in his diabolical brain, it was too late to stop it now. "Where are you staying?"

"The Ostrich."

"It isn't safe to go back there. We're moving you to the Geldrenner Hotel. We'll register you under a different name."

"But why?" Colm sputtered.

"Because some people want Jesper dead, and they already used you to lure him out of hiding once. I have no doubt they'd be willing to take you hostage, and there's too much of that going around already." Kaz scribbled a few instructions to Rotty and handed him a very thick stack of *kruge*. "Feel free to take your meals in the dining room, Mister Fahey, but I'd ask that you forgo the sights and stay inside the hotel until we contact you. If anyone asks your business, you're here for a bit of rest and relaxation."

Colm considered Rotty and then Kaz. He expelled a decisive breath. "No. I thank you, but this is a mistake." He turned to Jesper. "We'll find another way to pay the debt. Or we'll start over somewhere else."

"You're not giving up the farm," Jesper said. He lowered his voice. "*She's* there. We can't leave her."

"Jes—"

"Please, Da. Please let me make this right. I know—" He swallowed, his bony shoulders bunching. "I know I let you down. Just give me one more chance." Nina suspected he wasn't only speaking to his father.

"We don't belong here, Jes. This place is too loud, too lawless. Nothing makes sense."

"Mister Fahey," Kaz said quietly. "You know what they say about walking in a cow pasture?"

Jesper's brows shot up, and Nina had to stifle a nervous laugh. What did the bastard of the Barrel know about cow pastures?

"Keep your head down and watch your step," Colm replied.

Kaz nodded. "Just think of Ketterdam as a really big cow pasture." The barest smile tugged at the furrow of Colm's mouth. "Give us three days to get your money and get you and your son out of Kerch safely."

"Is that really possible?"

"Anything can happen in this city."

"That thought doesn't fill me with confidence." He rose, and Jesper shot to his feet.

"Da?"

"Three days, Jesper. Then we go home. With or without the money."

He rested a hand on Jesper's shoulder. "And for Saints' sake, be careful. All of you."

Nina felt a sudden lump in her throat. Matthias had lost his family to war. Nina had been taken from her family to train when she was just a little girl. Wylan had been as good as evicted from his father's house. Kuwei had lost his father and his country. And Kaz? She didn't want to know what dark alley Kaz had crawled out of. But Jesper had somewhere to go, someone to take care of him, somebody to say, *It's going to be all right*. She had a vision of golden fields beneath a cloudless sky, a clapboard house protected from the wind by a line of red oaks. Someplace safe. Nina wished Colm Fahey could march over to Jan Van Eck's office and tell him to give Inej back or get a mouth full of knuckles. She wished someone in this city would help them, that they weren't so alone. She wished Jesper's father could take them all with him. She'd never been to Novyi Zem, but the longing for those golden fields felt just like homesickness. *Silly*, she told herself, *childish*. Kaz was right—if they wanted justice, they would have to take it for themselves. That didn't ease the starved-heart pang in her chest.

But then Colm was saying his goodbyes to Jesper and disappearing through the stone graves with Rotty and Specht. He turned to wave and was gone.

"I should go with him," Jesper said, hovering in the doorway.

"You already almost got him killed once," said Kaz.

"Do we know who set up the ambush at the university?" Wylan asked.

"Jesper's father went to the *stadwatch*," said Matthias. "I'm sure many of the officers are susceptible to bribes."

"True," said Nina. "But it can't be coincidence that the bank called in his loan when they did."

Wylan sat down at the table. "If the banks are involved, my father may be behind it."

"Pekka Rollins has influence at the banks too," Kaz said, and Nina saw his gloved hand flex over the crow's head of his cane.

"Could they be working together?" she asked.

Jesper rubbed his hands over his face. "All the Saints and your Aunt Eva, let's hope not."

"I'm not ruling anything out," said Kaz. "But none of this changes what has to happen tonight. Here." He reached inside one of the niches in the wall.

"My revolvers!" Jesper exclaimed, clutching them to his chest. "Oh, hello, you gorgeous things." His grin was dazzling. "You got them back!"

"The safe at the Cumulus is an easy crack."

"Thank you, Kaz. Thank you."

Any hint of the warmth Kaz had shown Jesper's father was gone, as fleeting as the dream of those golden fields. "What good is a shooter without his guns?" Kaz asked, seemingly oblivious to the way Jesper's smile collapsed. "You've been in the red too long. We all have. This is the night we start paying our debts."

Now night had fallen and they were on their way to do just that, a waxing moon glaring down at them like a white and watchful eye. Nina shook out her sleeves. The cold snap had broken, and they were in the middle of a proper late spring. Or what passed for that in Kerch—the moist, claustrophobic warmth of an animal's mouth relieved only by brief, unpredictable storms. Matthias and Jesper had left for the docks early to make sure the *gondel* was in place. Then they'd all headed to the launch point, leaving Kuwei on Black Veil with Rotty and Specht.

The boat cut silently through the water. Ahead, Nina could see the gleam of lights guiding them onward.

Jesper's revolvers were back at his hips, and both he and Matthias had rifles slung across their shoulders. Kaz had a pistol in his coat and that demonic cane, and Nina saw Wylan rest a hand on his satchel. It was packed with explosives, flash bombs, and who knew what else.

"We better be right about all this," Wylan said on a sigh. "My father is going to be ready."

"I'm counting on it," Kaz replied.

Nina let her fingers brush against the grip of the pistol tucked into the pocket of her light spring coat. She had never needed a gun before, never wanted to carry one. *Because I was the weapon.* But she didn't trust herself now. Her control over her power felt flimsy, like she kept reaching for something that was just a bit farther away than she'd thought. She needed to know it would be there tonight. She couldn't make a mistake, not when Inej's life depended on it. Nina knew that if she'd been on Vellgeluk, the battle would have gone differently. Inej never would have been taken if Nina had been strong enough to face Van Eck's henchmen.

And if she'd had *parem*? No one could have stood against her.

Nina gave her head a firm shake. *If you'd had* parem, *you'd be completely addicted and well on your way to the Reaper's Barge.*

No one spoke as they reached shore and disembarked as quickly and quietly as possible. Kaz gestured for them to get to their positions. He would approach from the north, Matthias and Wylan from the east. Nina and Jesper would be responsible for the guards on the western edge of the perimeter.

Nina flexed her fingers. Silence four guards. That should be easy. A few weeks ago it would have been. Slow their pulses. Send them quietly into unconsciousness without ever letting an alarm sound. But now she wondered if it was the damp or her own nervous perspiration that made her clothes cling so uncomfortably to her skin.

Too soon, she saw the shapes of the first two guards at their post. They leaned against the low stone wall, rifles propped beside them, their conversation rising and falling in a lazy hum. Easy.

"Take 'em shut-eye," said Jesper.

Nina focused on the guards, letting her own body become attuned to theirs, seeking out their heartbeats, the rushing rhythm of their blood. It was like stumbling blind through the dark. There was simply nothing there. Dimly, she was aware of the suggestion of their frames, a trace of knowing, but that was all. She saw them with her eyes, heard them with her ears, but the rest was silence. That other sense inside her, the gift that had been there for as long as she could remember, the heart of the power that had been her constant companion since she was a child, had simply ceased to beat. All she could think of was *parem*, the exhilaration, the ease, as if the universe lay at her fingertips.

"What are you waiting for?" said Jesper.

Alerted by some sound or simply their presence, one of the guards glanced in their direction, peering into the shadows. He lifted his rifle and signaled to his companion to follow.

"They're headed this way." Jesper's hands went to his guns.

Oh, Saints. If Jesper had to shoot, the other guards would be alerted. The alarm would be raised, and this whole endeavor might go straight to hell.

Nina focused with all her will. The hunger for *parem* seized her, quaking through her body, digging into her skull with determined talons. She ignored it. One of the guards faltered, went to his knees.

"Gillis!" said the other guard. "What is it?" But he was not foolish enough to lower his weapon. "Halt!" he shouted in their direction, still trying to support his friend. "Identify yourselves."

"*Nina*," Jesper whispered furiously. "Do something."

Nina clenched her fist, trying to squeeze the guard's larynx shut to prevent him from calling for help.

"Identify yourselves!"

Jesper drew his gun. *No, no, no.* She was not going to be the reason this went wrong. *Parem* was supposed to kill her or leave her alone, not stick her in this miserable, powerless purgatory. Rage swept through Nina, clean, perfect, focusing anger. Her mind reached out and suddenly, she had hold of something, not a body, but something. She caught a movement from the corner of her eye, a dim shape emerging from the shadows—a cloud of dust. It shot toward the standing guard. He swatted at it as if trying to drive away a swarm of mosquitoes, but it whirred faster, faster, a nearly invisible blur. The guard opened his mouth to scream and the cloud vanished. He let out a grunt and toppled backward.

His compatriot was still balancing woozily on his knees. Nina and Jesper strode forward, and Jesper gave the kneeling guard a whack to the back of the head with the butt of his revolver. The man slumped to the ground, unconscious. Cautiously, they examined the other guard. He lay with eyes open, staring up at the starry sky. His mouth and nostrils were choked with fine white dust.

"Did you do that?" said Jesper.

Had she? Nina felt like she could taste the dust in her own mouth. This shouldn't be possible. A Corporalnik could manipulate the human body, not inorganic matter. This was the work of a Fabrikator—a powerful one. "It wasn't you?"

"I appreciate the vote of confidence, but this was all you, gorgeous."

"I didn't mean to kill him." What had she meant to do? Just keep him quiet. Dust dribbled from the corner of his parted lips in a fine line.

"There are two more guards," said Jesper. "And we're already running late."

"How about we just knock them over the head?"

"Sophisticated. I like it."

Nina felt a strange crawling sensation all over her body, but the need for *parem* wasn't screaming through her any longer. *I didn't mean to kill him.* It didn't matter. It couldn't right now. The guards were down and the plan was in motion.

"Come on," she said. "Let's go get our girl."

7

INEJ

Inej spent a sleepless night in the dark. When her stomach started to growl, she suspected it was morning, but no one arrived to remove her blindfold or offer her a tray. It seemed Van Eck didn't feel the need to coddle her anymore. He'd seen the fear in her clearly enough. That would be his leverage now, not Bajan's Suli eyes and attempts at kindness.

When her shivering had passed, she had struggled over to the vent, only to find that it had been bolted firmly shut. It had to have been done while she was in the theater. She wasn't surprised. She suspected Van Eck had left it unsecured just to give her hope and then snatch it away.

Eventually, her mind had begun to clear, and as she'd lain in the silence, she'd made a plan. She would talk. There were plenty of safe houses and hideouts that the Dregs had ceased to use because they'd been compromised or simply stopped being convenient. She'd start there. Then there were the supposedly secure places that belonged to some of the other Barrel gangs. She knew of a converted shipping container in Third Harbor that the Liddies occasionally used. The Razorgulls liked to hole up in a dingy hotel only a few streets over from the Slat. They called it

Jam Tart House because of its faded raspberry color and the white eaves that looked like they were decorated in icing. It should take Van Eck the better part of a night to search all the rooms. She would stall. She'd lead Van Eck and his men all over Ketterdam looking for Kaz. She'd never been much of an actress, but she'd been forced to tell her share of lies at the Menagerie, and surely she'd spent enough time around Nina to learn a thing or two.

When Bajan finally appeared and removed her blindfold, he had six armed guards with him. She wasn't sure how much time had passed, but she suspected the entire day had gone. Bajan's face looked sallow and he had trouble meeting her eyes. She hoped he'd lain awake all night, the weight of her words heavy on his chest. He cut her ankles free but replaced the ropes with shackles. They clanked heavily as the guards led her down the hall.

This time they took her through the back door of the theater, past flats of scenery and discarded props covered in dust, to the stage. The moth-eaten green curtains had been lowered so that the cavernous seating area and balconies were no longer visible. Closed off from the rest of the theater, warmed by the heat radiating from the stage lights, the set had a curious feeling of intimacy. It seemed less like a stage than a real surgeon's operating room. Inej's gaze touched the wrecked corner of the table where she'd lain the previous night and then quickly darted away.

Van Eck was waiting with the blade-nosed guard. Inej made a silent promise. Even if her plan failed, even if he smashed her legs to pulp, even if she never walked again, she'd find a way to pay him back in kind. She didn't know how, but she'd manage it. She'd survived too much to let Jan Van Eck destroy her.

"Are you afraid, Miss Ghafa?" he asked.

"Yes."

"Such honesty. And are you prepared to tell me what you know?"

Inej took a deep breath and hung her head in what she hoped was a convincing display of reluctance. "Yes," she whispered.

"Go on."

"How do I know you won't take the information and hurt me anyway?" she asked carefully.

"If the information is good, you have nothing to fear from me, Miss Ghafa. I am not a brute. I've employed the methods you are most accustomed to—threats, violence. The Barrel has trained you to expect such treatment." He sounded like Tante Heleen. *Why do you make me do these things? You bring these punishments on yourself, girl.*

"I have your word, then?" she asked. It was absurd. Van Eck had made clear exactly what his word was worth when he'd broken their arrangement on Vellgeluk and tried to have them all killed.

But he nodded solemnly. "You do," he said. "The deal is the deal."

"And Kaz must never know—"

"Of course, of course," he said with some impatience.

Inej cleared her throat. "The Blue Paradise is a club not far from the Slat. Kaz has used the rooms above it to stow stolen merchandise before." It was true. And the rooms should still be empty. Kaz had stopped using the place after he'd discovered one of the barkeeps was in debt to the Dime Lions. He didn't want anyone reporting on his comings and goings.

"Very good. What else?"

Inej worried her lower lip. "An apartment on Kolstraat. I don't remember the number. It has a view of the back entrances to some of the dens on East Stave. We've used it for stakeouts before."

"Is that so? Please go on."

"There's a shipping container—"

"Do you know something, Miss Ghafa?" Van Eck stepped closer to her. There was no anger on his face. He looked almost gleeful. "I don't think any of these places are real leads."

"I wouldn't—"

"I think you intend to send me off chasing my tail while you wait for rescue or plan some other misbegotten escape attempt. But Miss Ghafa, you needn't wait. Mister Brekker is on his way to rescue you this very minute." He gestured to one of the guards. "Raise the curtain."

Inej heard the creak of ropes and, slowly, the ragged curtains rose. The theater was packed with guards lining the aisles, thirty at least, maybe more, all heavily armed with rifles and cudgels, an overwhelming display of force. *No*, she thought, as Van Eck's words sank in.

"That's right, Miss Ghafa," said Van Eck. "Your hero is coming. Mister Brekker likes to believe that he's the smartest person in Ketterdam, so I thought I'd indulge him and let him outsmart himself. I realized that instead of hiding you, I should simply let you be found."

Inej frowned. It couldn't be. *It couldn't be.* Had this merch actually outwitted Kaz? Had he used her to do it?

"I've been sending Bajan back and forth from Eil Komedie every day. I thought a Suli boy would be most conspicuous and any traffic to a supposedly deserted island was bound to be remarked upon. Until tonight, I wasn't sure Brekker would bite; I was growing most anxious. But he did. Earlier this evening, two of his team were spotted on the docks preparing a *gondel* to launch—that big Fjerdan and the Zemeni boy. I did not have them intercepted. Much like you, they are mere pawns. Kuwei is the prize, and your Mister Brekker is finally going to give me what I am owed."

"If you'd treated fairly with us, you'd have Kuwei already," she said. "We risked our lives to get him out of the Ice Court. We risked everything. You should have honored your word."

"A patriot would have offered to free Kuwei without the promise of reward."

"A patriot? Your scheme for *jurda parem* will bring chaos to Kerch."

"Markets are resilient. Kerch will endure. It may even be strengthened by the changes to come. But you and your ilk may not fare so well. How do you think the parasites of the Barrel will manage when we are at war? When honest men have no coin to squander and put their minds to toil instead of vice?"

Inej felt her lip curl. "Canal rats have a way of surviving, no matter how hard you try to stamp us out."

He smiled. "Most of your friends won't survive this night."

She thought of Jesper, Nina and Matthias, sweet Wylan who deserved so much better than this filth for a father. It wasn't just about winning for Van Eck. It was personal. "You hate us."

"Frankly, *you* are of little interest to me—an acrobat or dancer or whatever you were before you became a blight on this city. But I confess Kaz Brekker does offend me. Vile, ruthless, amoral. He feeds corruption with corruption. Such a remarkable mind might have been put to great use. He might have ruled this city, built something, created profit that would have benefited all. Instead he leeches off the work of better men."

"Better men? Like you?"

"It pains you to hear it, but it is true. When I leave this world, the greatest shipping empire ever known will remain, an engine of wealth, a tribute to Ghezen and a sign of his favor. Who will remember a girl like you, Miss Ghafa? What will you and Kaz Brekker leave behind but corpses to be burned on the Reaper's Barge?"

A shout came from outside the theater, and a sudden hush fell as the guards turned toward the entrance doors.

Van Eck consulted his watch. "Midnight on the dot. Brekker has a flair for the dramatic."

She heard another shout, then a brief rattle of gunfire. Six guards behind her, shackles at her feet. Helplessness rose up to choke her. Kaz and the others were about to walk into a trap, and she had no way to warn them.

"I thought it best not to leave the perimeter completely unguarded," said Van Eck. "We wouldn't want to make it too easy and give away the game."

"He'll never tell you where Kuwei is."

Van Eck's smile was indulgent. "I only wonder which will prove more effective—torturing Mister Brekker or having him watch as I torture you." He leaned in, his voice conspiratorial. "I can tell you the first thing I'm going to do is peel off those gloves and break every one of his thieving fingers."

Inej thought of Kaz's pale trickster hands, the shiny rope of scar tissue that ran atop his right knuckle. Van Eck could break every finger and both of Kaz's legs and he'd never say a word, but if his men stripped away Kaz's gloves? Inej still didn't understand why he needed them or why he'd fainted in the prison wagon on the way into the Ice Court, but she knew Kaz couldn't bear the touch of skin on skin. How much of this weakness could he hide? How quickly would Van Eck locate his vulnerability, exploit it? How long until Kaz came undone? She couldn't bear it. She was glad she didn't know where Kuwei was. She would break before Kaz did.

Boots were clattering down the hall, a thunder of footsteps. Inej surged forward and opened her mouth to cry out warning, but a guard's hand clamped down hard over her lips as she struggled in his arms.

The door flew open. Thirty guards raised thirty rifles and thirty triggers cocked. The boy in the doorway flinched backward, his face white, his corkscrew brown curls disarrayed. He wore the Van Eck livery of red and gold.

"I—Mister Van Eck," he panted, hands held up in defense.

"Stand down," Van Eck commanded the guards. "What is it?"

The boy swallowed. "Sir, the lake house. They approached from the water."

Van Eck stood, knocking over his chair. "Alys—"

"They took her an hour ago."

Alys. Jan Van Eck's pretty, pregnant wife. Inej felt hope spark, but she tamped it down, afraid to believe.

"They killed one of the guards and left the rest tied up in the pantry," the boy continued breathlessly. "There was a note on the table."

"Bring it here," Van Eck barked. The boy strode down the aisle, and Van Eck snatched the note from his hand.

"What does it . . . what does it say?" asked Bajan. His voice was tremulous. Maybe Inej had been right about Alys and the music teacher.

Van Eck backhanded him. "If I find out you knew anything about this—"

"I didn't!" Bajan cried. "I knew nothing. I followed your orders to the letter!"

Van Eck crumpled the note in his fist, but not before Inej made out the words in Kaz's jagged, unmistakable hand: *Noon tomorrow. Goedmedbridge. With her knives.*

"The note was weighted down with this." The boy reached into his pocket and drew out a tie pin—a fat ruby surrounded by golden laurel leaves. Kaz had stolen it from Van Eck back when they'd first been hired for the Ice Court job. Inej hadn't had the chance to fence it before they left Ketterdam. Somehow Kaz must have gotten hold of it again.

"Brekker," Van Eck snarled, his voice taut with rage.

Inej couldn't help it. She started to laugh.

Van Eck slapped her hard. He grabbed her tunic and shook her so that her bones rattled. "Brekker thinks we're still playing a game, does he? She is my wife. She carries my heir."

Inej laughed even harder, all the horrors of the past week rising from her chest in giddy peals. She wasn't sure she could have stopped if she wanted to. "And you were foolish enough to tell Kaz all of that on Vellgeluk."

"Shall I have Franke fetch the mallet and show you just how serious I am?"

"Mister Van Eck," Bajan pleaded.

But Inej was done being frightened of this man. Before Van Eck could take another breath, she slammed her forehead upward, shattering his nose. He screamed and released her as blood gushed over his fine mercher suit. Instantly, his guards were on her, pulling her back.

"You little wretch," Van Eck said, holding a monogrammed handkerchief to his face. "You little whore. I'll take a hammer to both your legs myself—"

"Go on, Van Eck, threaten me. Tell me all the *little* things I am. You lay a finger on me and Kaz Brekker will cut the baby from your pretty wife's stomach and hang its body from a balcony at the Exchange." Ugly words, speech that pricked her conscience, but Van Eck deserved the images she'd planted in his mind. Though she didn't believe Kaz would do such a thing, she felt grateful for each nasty, vicious thing Dirtyhands *had* done to earn his reputation—a reputation that would haunt Van Eck every second until his wife was returned.

"Be silent," he shouted, spittle flying from his mouth.

"You think he won't?" Inej taunted. She could feel the heat in her cheek from where his hand had struck her, could see the mallet still resting in the guard's hand. Van Eck had given her fear and she was happy to return it to him. "Vile, ruthless, amoral. Isn't that why you hired Kaz in the first place? Because he does the things that no one else dares? Go on, Van Eck. Break my legs and see what happens. *Dare him.*"

Had she really believed a merch could outthink Kaz Brekker? Kaz would get her free and then they'd show this man exactly what whores and canal rats could do.

"Console yourself," she said as Van Eck clutched the ragged corner of the table for support. "Even better men can be bested."

8

MATTHIAS

Matthias would be atoning for the mistakes he'd made in this life long into the next one, but he'd always believed that despite his crimes and failings, there was a core of decency inside him that could never be breached. And yet, he felt sure that if he had to spend another hour with Alys Van Eck, he might murder her just for the sake of a little quiet.

The siege on the lake house had gone off with a precision that Matthias couldn't help but admire. Only three days after Inej was taken, Rotty had alerted Kaz to the lights that had appeared on Eil Komedie, and the fact that boats had been seen coming and going there at odd hours, often carrying a young Suli man. He'd quickly been identified as Adem Bajan, a music teacher indentured to Van Eck for the last six months. He'd apparently joined the Van Eck household after Wylan had left home, but Wylan wasn't surprised his father had secured professional musical instruction for Alys.

"Is she any good?" asked Jesper.

Wylan had hesitated, then said, "She's very enthusiastic."

It had been easy enough to surmise that Inej was being kept on Eil Komedie, and Nina had wanted to go after her immediately.

"He didn't take her out of the city," she'd said, cheeks glowing with color for the first time since she'd emerged from her battle with *parem*. "It's obvious he's keeping her there."

But Kaz had simply gazed into the middle distance with that odd look on his face and said, "Too obvious."

"Kaz—"

"How would you like a hundred *kruge*?"

"What's the catch?"

"Exactly. Van Eck's making it too easy. He's treating us like marks. But he isn't Barrel born, and we aren't a bunch of dumb culls ready to jump at the first shiny lure he flashes. Van Eck wants us to think she's on that island. Maybe she is. But he'll have plenty of firepower waiting for us too, maybe even a few Grisha using *parem*."

"Always hit where the mark isn't looking," Wylan had murmured.

"Sweet Ghezen," said Jesper. "You've been thoroughly corrupted."

Kaz had tapped his crow's head cane on the flagstones of the tomb floor. "Do you know what Van Eck's problem is?"

"No honor?" said Matthias.

"Rotten parenting skills?" said Nina.

"Receding hairline?" offered Jesper.

"No," said Kaz. "Too much to lose. And he gave us a map to what to steal first."

He'd pushed himself to his feet and begun laying out the plans for kidnapping Alys. Instead of trying to rescue Inej as Van Eck expected, they would force Van Eck to trade her for his very pregnant wife. The first trick had been finding her. Van Eck was no fool. Kaz suspected that he'd gotten Alys out of the city as soon as he'd made his false deal with them, and their initial investigations supported that. Van Eck wouldn't keep his wife in a warehouse or factory or industrial building, and she was at neither of the hotels he owned, or at the Van Eck country house or his two farms near Elsmeer. It was possible he'd spirited her away to some farm or holding across the True Sea, but Kaz doubted he'd put the woman carrying his heir through a grueling sea voyage.

"Van Eck must be keeping property off the books," Kaz had said. "Probably income too."

Jesper frowned. "Isn't not paying your taxes . . . I don't know, sacrilegious? I thought he was all about serving Ghezen."

"Ghezen and Kerch aren't the same thing," Wylan said.

Of course, uncovering those secret properties had meant gaining access to Cornelis Smeet's office, and another series of deceptions. Matthias hated the dishonesty of it all, but he couldn't deny the value of the information they'd obtained. Thanks to Smeet's files, Kaz had located the lake house, a fine property ten miles south of the city, easy to defend, comfortably appointed, and listed under the Hendriks name.

Always hit where the mark isn't looking. It was sound thinking, Matthias could admit—military thinking, in fact. When you were outgunned and outmanned, you sought the less defended targets. Van Eck had expected a rescue attempt on Inej, so that was where he'd concentrated his forces. And Kaz had encouraged that, telling Matthias and Jesper to be as conspicuous as possible when they brought a *gondel* down to one of the private berths at Fifth Harbor. At eleven bells, Rotty and Specht had left Kuwei at Black Veil and, dressed in heavy cloaks to hide their faces, launched the boat, making a tremendous show of shouting to supposed compatriots setting out from other berths—most of them confused tourists who weren't sure why strange men were yelling at them from a *gondel*.

It had taken everything in Matthias not to argue when Kaz had paired Nina with Jesper in the assault on the lake house, despite the fact that he knew the partnership made sense. They needed to take out the guards quietly to prevent anyone from raising an alarm or panicking. Matthias' combat training made that possible, as did Nina's Grisha abilities, so they'd been split up. Jesper and Wylan had noisier talents, so they would enter the fray only as a last resort. Also, Matthias knew if he started trailing after Nina on missions like some kind of watchdog, she'd put her hands on those glorious hips and demonstrate her knowledge of profanity in several different languages. Still, he was the only one besides perhaps Kuwei who knew how she'd suffered since they'd returned from the Ice Court. It had been hard to watch her go.

They'd approached from across the lake and made quick work of the few guards on the perimeter. Most of the villas along the shore were empty, as it was too early in the season for the weather to have gotten properly warm. But lights had burned in the windows of the Van Eck house—or, rather, the Hendriks house. The property had belonged to Wylan's mother's family for generations before Van Eck had ever set foot through the door.

It almost didn't feel like a break-in; one of the guards had actually been dozing in the gazebo. Matthias didn't realize there had been a casualty until the count on the guards had come up short, but there hadn't been time to question Nina and Jesper about what had gone wrong. They'd tied up the remaining guards, herded them and the rest of the staff into the pantry, and then swept up the stairs to the second floor wearing the masks of the Komedie Brute. They'd stopped outside the music room, where Alys was perched precariously on the bench of a pianoforte. Though they had expected to find her asleep, she was laboring her way through some piece of music.

"Saints, what is that noise?" Nina had whispered.

"I think it's 'Be Still, Little Bumble Bee,'" said Wylan from behind the mask and horns of his Gray Imp ensemble. "But it's hard to tell."

When they'd entered the music room, the silky-haired terrier at her feet had the sense to growl, but poor, pretty, pregnant Alys had just looked up from her sheet music and said, "Is this a play?"

"Yes, love," said Jesper gently, "and you're the star."

They'd tucked her into a warm coat, then shepherded her out of the house and into the waiting boat. She'd been so docile that Nina had become concerned. "Maybe she's not getting enough blood to her brain?" she'd murmured to Matthias.

Matthias hadn't been sure how to account for Alys' demeanor. He remembered his mother muddling the simplest things when she was pregnant with his baby sister. She'd walked all the way down to the village from their little house before she'd realized she was wearing her boots on the wrong feet.

But halfway back to the city, when Nina had bound Alys' hands and tied a blindfold over her eyes, securing it tightly to the neat braids coiled atop her head, the reality of her situation must have started to sink in. She'd begun to sniffle, wiping her running nose on her velvet sleeve. The sniffling became a kind of wobbly deep breathing, and by the time they'd gotten Alys settled comfortably at the tomb and even found a little cushion for her feet, she'd let out a long wail.

"I want to go hooooooome," she'd cried. "I want my dog."

From then on, the crying hadn't stopped. Kaz had eventually thrown his hands up in frustration, and they'd all stepped outside the tomb to try to find some quiet.

"Are pregnant women always like this?" Nina had moaned.

Matthias glanced inside the stone hull. "Only the kidnapped ones."

"I can't hear myself think," she said.

"Maybe if we took the blindfold off?" Wylan suggested. "We could wear our Komedie Brute masks."

Kaz shook his head. "We can't risk her leading Van Eck back here."

"She's going to make herself ill," said Matthias.

"We're in the middle of a job," Kaz said. "There's a lot that has to happen before the exchange tomorrow. Someone find a way to shut her up, or I will."

"She's a frightened girl—" Wylan protested.

"I didn't ask for a description."

But Wylan kept on. "Kaz, promise me you won't—"

"Before you finish that sentence, I want you to think about what a promise from me costs and what you're willing to pay for it."

"It's not her fault her parents shoved her into a marriage with my father."

"Alys isn't here because she did something wrong. She's here because she's leverage."

"She's just a pregnant girl—"

"Getting pregnant isn't actually a special talent. Ask any luckless girl in the Barrel."

"Inej wouldn't want—"

In the space of a breath, Kaz had shoved Wylan against the tomb wall with his forearm, the crow head of his cane wedged beneath Wylan's jaw. "Tell me my business again." Wylan swallowed, parted his lips. "Do it," said Kaz. "And I'll cut the tongue from your head and feed it to the first stray cat I find."

"Kaz—" Jesper said cautiously. Kaz ignored him.

Wylan's lips flattened to a thin, stubborn line. The boy really didn't know what was good for him. Matthias wondered if he'd have to try to intercede on Wylan's behalf, but Kaz had released him. "Someone stick a cork in that girl before I get back," he said, and strode off into the graveyard.

Matthias rolled his eyes heavenward. These lunatics all needed a solid six months in boot camp and possibly a sound beating.

"Best not to mention Inej," Jesper said as Wylan dusted himself off. "You know, if you feel like continuing to live."

Wylan shook his head. "But isn't this all about Inej?"

"No, it's all about the *grand plan*, remember?" Nina said with a snort. "Getting Inej away from Van Eck is just the first phase."

They headed back into the tomb. In the lantern light, Matthias could see that Nina's color was good. Maybe the distraction of the break-in at the lake house had been a positive thing, though he couldn't ignore the fact that a guard had died during a mission that wasn't meant to have a body count.

Alys had quieted and was sitting with her hands folded on her belly, releasing small, unhappy hiccups. She made a lackluster attempt at removing her blindfold, but Nina had been clever with the knots. Matthias glanced at Kuwei, who was perched across from her at the table. The Shu boy just shrugged.

Nina sat down next to Alys. "Would you um . . . like some tea?"

"With honey?" Alys asked.

"I, uh . . . I think we have sugar?"

"I only like tea with honey and lemon."

Nina looked like she might tell Alys exactly where she could put her honey and lemon, so Matthias said hurriedly, "How would you like a chocolate biscuit?"

"Oh, I *love* chocolate!"

Nina's eyes narrowed. "I don't remember saying you could give away my biscuits."

"It's for a good cause," Matthias said, retrieving the tin. He'd purchased the biscuits in the hope of getting Nina to eat more. "Besides, you've barely touched them."

"I'm saving them for later," said Nina with a sniff. "And you should not cross me when it comes to sweets."

Jesper nodded. "She's like a dessert-hoarding dragon."

Alys' head had swiveled right and left behind her blindfold. "You all sound so young," she said. "Where are your parents?" Wylan and Jesper burst out laughing. "Why is that funny?"

"It's not," Nina said reassuringly. "They're just being idiots."

"Hey, now," said Jesper. "We're not the ones dipping into your cookie stash."

"I don't let just anyone into my cookie stash," Nina said with a wink.

"She certainly doesn't," Matthias grumped, somewhere between delighted to see Nina back to herself and jealous that Jesper was the one making her smile. He needed to dunk his head in a bucket. He was behaving like a besotted ninny.

"So," Jesper said, throwing an arm around Alys' shoulder. "Tell us about your stepson."

"Why?" Alys asked. "Are you going to kidnap him too?"

Jesper scoffed, "I doubt it. I hear he's twelve kinds of trouble to keep around."

Wylan crossed his arms. "I hear he's talented and misunderstood."

Alys frowned. "I can understand him perfectly well. He doesn't mumble or anything. In fact, he sounds a bit like you." Wylan flinched as Jesper doubled over with laughter. "And yes, he's very talented. He's studying music in Belendt."

"But what is he *like*?" Jesper asked. "Any secret fears he confided? Bad habits? Ill-conceived infatuations?"

Wylan shoved the tin of biscuits at Alys. "Have another cookie."

"She's had three!" protested Nina.

"Wylan was always nice to my birds. I miss my birds. And Rufus. I want to go hoooooome." And then she was blubbering again.

Nina had plunked her head down on the table in defeat. "Well done. I thought we might actually get a moment of silence. I've sacrificed my biscuits for nothing."

"Have none of you people ever encountered a pregnant woman before?" Matthias grumbled. He remembered his mother's discomfort and moods well, though he suspected Alys' behavior might owe nothing to the child she was carrying. He tore a strip from one of the ragged blankets in the corner. "Here," he said to Jesper. "Dip this in water so we can make a cool compress." He squatted down and said to Alys, "I'm going to take off your shoes."

"Why?" she said.

"Because your feet are swollen, and it will soothe you to have them rubbed."

"Oh, now *this* is interesting," Nina said.

"Don't get any ideas."

"Too late," she said, wiggling her toes.

Matthias slid off Alys' shoes and said, "You haven't been kidnapped. You're just being held for a brief time. By tomorrow afternoon you'll be home with your dog and your birds. You know that no one is going to hurt you, yes?"

"I'm not sure."

"Well, you can't see me, but I'm the biggest person here, and I promise that no one will hurt you." Even as he spoke the words, Matthias knew he might be lying. Alys was currently having her feet rubbed and a cool towel placed on her forehead in a pit full of some of the deadliest vipers slithering the streets of this misbegotten city. "Now," he said, "it's very important that you stay calm so that you don't make yourself ill. What helps to cheer you?"

"I . . . I like to go for walks by the lake."

"All right, maybe we can go for a walk later. What else?"

"I like doing my hair."

Matthias gave Nina a meaningful look.

She scowled. "Why do you assume I know how to arrange hair?"

"Because yours always looks so nice."

"Wait," said Jesper. "Is he being charming?" He peered at Matthias. "How do we know this isn't an impostor?"

"Perhaps *someone* could do your hair," said Nina grudgingly.

"Anything else?" asked Matthias.

"I like singing," said Alys.

Wylan shook his head frantically, mouthing, *No, no, no.*

"Shall I sing?" Alys asked hopefully. "Bajan says that I'm good enough to be on the stage."

"Maybe we save that for later—" suggested Jesper.

Alys' lower lip began to wobble like a plate about to break.

"Sing," Matthias blurted, "by all means, sing."

And then the real nightmare began.

It wasn't that Alys was so bad, she just never stopped. She sang between bites of food. She sang while she was walking through the graves. She sang from behind a bush when she needed to relieve herself. When she finally dozed off, she hummed *in her sleep*.

"Maybe this was Van Eck's plan all along," Kaz said glumly when they'd assembled outside the tomb again.

"To drive us mad?" said Nina. "It's working."

Jesper shut his eyes and groaned. "Diabolical."

Kaz consulted his pocket watch. "Nina and Matthias should get going, anyway. If you get into position early, you can catch a few hours of sleep." They had to be careful coming and going from the island, so they couldn't afford to wait until dawn to assume their posts.

"You'll find the masks and capes at the furrier," Kaz continued. "Look for the golden badger on the sign. Get as close to the Lid as possible before you start handing them out and then head south. Don't stay in any one place too long. I don't want you drawing too much attention from the bosses." Kaz met each of their gazes in turn. "Everyone needs to be in final position before noon. Wylan on the ground. Matthias on the roof of the Emporium Komedie. Jesper will be across from you on the roof of the Ammbers Hotel. Nina, you'll be on the hotel's third floor. The room has a balcony overlooking Goedmedbridge. Make sure your sight lines are clear. I want you with eyes on Van Eck from moment one. He'll be planning something, and we need to be ready."

Matthias saw Nina cast a furtive glance at Jesper, but all she said was, "No mourners."

"No funerals," they replied.

Nina headed toward where the rowboat was moored. Kaz and Wylan stepped back into the tomb, but before Jesper could vanish inside, Matthias blocked his path.

"What happened at the lake house?"

"What do you mean?"

"I saw the look she just gave you."

Jesper shifted uneasily. "Why don't you ask her?"

"Because Nina will claim she's fine until she's suffering too much to form the words."

Jesper touched his hands to his revolvers. "All I'm going to say is be careful. She's not . . . quite herself."

"What does that mean? What happened at the Hendriks house?"

"We ran into some trouble," admitted Jesper.

"A man died."

"Men die all the time in Ketterdam. Just stay alert. She may need backup."

Jesper darted through the door, and Matthias released a growl of frustration. He hurried to catch up to Nina, turning Jesper's warning over in his mind, but said nothing as she stepped into the boat and he launched them into the canal.

The smartest thing he'd done since they'd returned from the Ice Court was to give Kaz the remaining *parem*. It hadn't been an easy decision. He was never sure how deep the well inside Kaz was, where to locate the limits of what he would or would not do. But Nina had no hold on Kaz, and when she'd crept into Matthias' bed the night of the Smeet job, he'd been certain he'd made the right choice because, Djel knew, Matthias had been ready to give her anything she wanted if she would just keep kissing him.

She'd woken him from the dream that had been plaguing him since the Ice Court. One moment he had been wandering in the cold, blind from the snow, wolves howling in the distance, and in the next, he'd been awake, Nina beside him, all warmth and softness. He thought again of what she'd said to him on the ship, when she'd been in the worst grips of the *parem*. *Can you even think for yourself? I'm just another cause for you to follow. First it was Jarl Brum, and now it's me. I don't want your cursed oath.*

He didn't think she had meant it, but the words haunted him. As a *drüskelle*, he'd served a corrupt cause. He could see that now. But he'd had a path, a nation. He'd known who he was and what the world would ask of him. Now he was sure of nothing but his faith in Djel and the vow he'd made to Nina. *I have been made to protect you. Only in death will I be kept from this oath.* Had he simply substituted one cause for another? Was he taking shelter in his feelings for Nina because he was afraid of choosing a future for himself?

Matthias put his mind to rowing. Their fates would not be settled this night, and they had much to do before dawn came. Besides, he liked the rhythm of the canals at night, the streetlamps reflected off the water, the silence, the feeling of passing unseen through the sleeping world, glimpsing a light in a window, someone rising restless from his bed to close a curtain or look out at the city. They tried to come and go from Black Veil as little as possible during the day, so this was the way he'd gotten to know Ketterdam. One night he'd glimpsed a woman in a bejeweled evening gown at her dressing table, unpinning her hair. A man—her husband, Matthias assumed—had stepped behind her and taken over the task, and she'd turned her face up to him and smiled. Matthias couldn't name the ache he felt in that moment. He was a soldier. So was Nina. They weren't meant for such domestic scenes. But he'd envied those people and their ease. Their comfortable home, their comfort with each other.

He knew he asked Nina too often, but as they disembarked near East Stave, Matthias couldn't stop himself from saying, "How do you feel?"

"Quite well," she said dismissively, adjusting her veil. She was dressed in the glittering blue finery of the Lost Bride, the same costume she'd been wearing the night she and the other members of the Dregs had appeared in his cell. "Tell me, *drüskelle*, have you ever actually been to this part of the Barrel?"

"I didn't have much opportunity for sightseeing while I was in Hellgate," Matthias said. "And I wouldn't have come here anyway."

"Of course not. This many people having fun in one place might have shocked the Fjerdan right out of you."

"Nina," Matthias said quietly as they made their way to the furrier. He didn't want to push, but he needed to know. "When we went after Smeet, you used a wig and cosmetics. Why didn't you tailor yourself?"

She shrugged. "It was easier and faster."

Matthias was silent, unsure of whether to press her further.

They passed a cheese shop, and Nina sighed. "How can I walk by a window full of wheels of cheese and feel nothing? I don't even know myself anymore." She paused, then said, "I tried to tailor myself. Something feels off. Different. I only managed the circles under my eyes, and it took every bit of my focus."

"But you were never a gifted Tailor."

"Manners, Fjerdan."

"Nina."

"This was different. It wasn't just challenging, it was painful. It's hard to explain."

"What about compelling behaviors?" Matthias asked. "The way you did at the Ice Court when you used the *parem*."

"I don't think it's possible anymore."

"Have you tried?"

"Not exactly."

"Try it on me."

"Matthias, we have work to do."

"Try it."

"I'm not going to go rattling around in your head when we don't know what might happen."

"Nina—"

"Fine," she said in exasperation. "Come here."

They had nearly reached East Stave and the crowds of revelers had grown thicker. Nina pulled him into an alley between two buildings. She lifted his mask and her own veil; then slowly, she placed a hand on either side of his face. Her fingers slid into his hair and Matthias' focus shattered. It felt like she was touching him everywhere.

She looked into his eyes. "Well?"

"I don't feel anything," he said. His voice sounded embarrassingly hoarse.

She arched a brow. "Nothing?"

"What did you try to make me do?"

"I'm trying to compel you to kiss me."

"That's foolish."

"Why is that?"

"Because I always want to kiss you," he admitted.

"Then how come you never do?"

"Nina, you just went through a terrible ordeal—"

"I did. That's true. You know what would help? A lot of kissing. We haven't been alone since we were aboard the *Ferolind*."

"You mean when you almost died?" said Matthias. Someone had to remember the gravity of this situation.

"I prefer to think of the good times. Like when you held my hair as I was vomiting into a bucket."

"Stop trying to make me laugh."

"But I like your laugh."

"Nina, this is not the time to flirt."

"I need to catch you off your guard, otherwise you're too busy protecting me and asking me if I'm okay."

"Is it wrong to worry?"

"No, it's wrong to treat me like I might break apart at any moment. I'm not that fine or that fragile." She shoved his mask down none too gently, yanked her veil back in place, and strode past him out of the alley, across the street to a shop with a golden badger over the door.

He followed. He knew he'd said the wrong thing, but he had no idea what the right thing was. A little bell rang as they entered the shop.

"How can this place be open at such hours?" he murmured. "Who wants to buy a coat in the dead of night?"

"Tourists."

And in fact, a few people were browsing the stacks of furs and pelts. Matthias followed Nina to the counter.

"We're picking up an order," Nina said to the bespectacled clerk.

"The name?"

"Judit Coenen."

"Ah!" the clerk said, consulting a ledger. "Golden lynx and black bear, paid in full. Just a moment." He vanished into the back room and emerged a minute later, struggling beneath the weight of two huge parcels wrapped in brown paper and tied with twine. "Do you need help getting these to—"

"We're fine." Matthias hefted the packages with little effort. The people of this city needed more fresh air and exercise.

"But it may rain. At least let me—"

"We're fine," Matthias growled, and the clerk took a step backward.

"Ignore him," Nina said. "He needs a nap. Thank you so much for your help."

The clerk smiled weakly and they were on their way.

"You know you're terrible at this, right?" Nina asked once they were on the street and entering East Stave.

"At lies and deception?"

"At being polite."

Matthias considered. "I didn't mean to be rude."

"Just let me do the talking."

"Nina—"

"No names from here on out."

She was vexed with him. He could hear it in her voice, and he didn't think it was because he'd been short with the clerk. They paused only so that Matthias could exchange his Madman's costume for one of the many Mister Crimson ensembles folded into the packages from the furrier. Matthias wasn't sure if the clerk had known what was stuffed in the brown-paper wrapping, if the costumes had been made in the shop, or if the Golden Badger was just some kind of drop spot. Kaz had mysterious connections throughout Ketterdam, and only he knew the truth of their workings.

Once Matthias found a large enough red cloak and placed the red-and-white lacquered mask over his face, Nina handed him a bag of silver coins.

Matthias bounced the bag once in his palm, and the coins gave a cheerful jingle. "They aren't real, are they?"

"Of course not. But no one ever knows if the coins are real. That's part of the fun. Let's practice."

"Practice?"

"Mother, Father, pay the rent!" Nina said in a singsong voice.

Matthias stared at her. "Is it possible you're running a fever?"

Nina shoved her veil up onto her head so he could experience the full force of her glare. "It's from the Komedie Brute. When Mister Crimson comes onstage, the audience shouts—"

"Mother, Father, pay the rent," Matthias finished.

"Exactly. Then you say, 'I can't, my dear, the money's spent,' and you toss a handful of coins into the crowd."

"Why?"

"The same reason everyone hisses at the Madman and throws flowers at the Scarab Queen. It's tradition. Tourists don't always get it, but the Kerch do. So tonight, if someone yells, 'Mother, Father, pay the rent . . .'"

"I can't, my dear, the money's spent," Matthias intoned gloomily, casting a handful of coins into the air.

"You have to do it with more enthusiasm," Nina urged. "It's supposed to be fun."

"I feel foolish."

"It's good to feel foolish sometimes, Fjerdan."

"You only say that because you have no shame."

To his surprise, instead of offering a sharp retort, she went silent and remained that way until they took up their first position in front of a gambling parlor on the Lid, joining the musicians and buskers, only a few doors down from Club Cumulus. Then it was as if someone had flipped a switch in Nina.

"Come one, come all to the Crimson Cutlass!" she declared. "You there, sir. You're too skinny for your own good. What would you think of a little free food and a flagon of wine? And you, miss, now you look like you know how to have a bit of fun. . . ."

Nina lured tourists to them one by one as if she'd been born to it, offering free food and drink and handing out costumes and flyers. When one of the bouncers from the gambling parlor emerged to see what they were up to, they moved along, heading south and west, continuing to give away the two hundred costumes and masks Kaz had procured. When people asked what it was all about, Nina claimed it was a promotion for a new gambling hall called the Crimson Cutlass.

As Nina had predicted, occasionally someone would spot Matthias' costume and shriek, "Mother, Father, pay the rent!"

Dutifully, Matthias replied, doing his best to sound jolly. If the tourists and revelers found his performance lacking, no one said so, possibly distracted by the showers of silver coins.

By the time they reached West Stave, the stacks of costumes were gone and the sun was rising. He caught a brief flash from the roof of the Ammbers Hotel—Jesper signaling with his mirror.

Matthias escorted Nina up to the room reserved for Judit Coenen on the third floor of the hotel. Just as Kaz had said, the balcony had a perfect view of the wide expanse of Goedmedbridge and the waters of West Stave, bordered on both sides by hotels and pleasure houses.

"What does that mean?" Matthias asked. "Goedmedbridge?"

"Good maiden bridge."

"Why is it called that?"

Nina leaned against the doorway and said, "Well, the story is that when a woman found out her husband had fallen in love with a girl from West Stave and planned to leave her, she came to the bridge and, rather than live without him, hurled herself into the canal."

"Over a man with so little honor?"

"You'd never be tempted? All the fruits and flesh of West Stave before you?"

"Would you throw yourself off a bridge for a man who was?"

"I wouldn't throw myself off a bridge for the king of Ravka."

"It's a terrible story," said Matthias.

"I doubt it's true. It's just what happens when you let men name the bridges."

"You should rest," he said. "I can wake you when it's time."

"I'm not tired, and I don't need to be told how to do my job."

"You're angry."

"Or told how I feel. Get to your post, Matthias. You're looking a little ragged around those gilded edges too."

Her voice was cold, her spine straight. The memory of the dream came at him so hard he could almost feel the bite of the wind, the snow lashing his cheeks in stinging gusts. His throat burned, scraped raw as he shouted Nina's name. He wanted to tell her to be careful. He wanted to ask her what was wrong.

"No mourners," he murmured.

"No funerals," she replied, her eyes trained on the bridge.

Matthias left quietly, descended the stairs, and crossed over the canal via the wide expanse of Goedmedbridge. He looked up at the balcony of the Ammbers Hotel but saw no sign of Nina. That was good. If he couldn't see her from the bridge, then Van Eck wouldn't be able to either. A few stone steps took him down to a dock where a flower seller was poling his barge full of blossoms into place in the rosy wash of morning light. Matthias exchanged a brief word with the man as he tended to his tulips and daffodils, noting the marks Wylan had chalked above the waterline on both sides of the canal. They were ready.

He made his way up the stairs of the Emporium Komedie, surrounded on all sides by masks and veils and glittering capes. Every floor had a different theme, offering fantasies of all kinds. He was horrified to see a rack of *drüskelle* costumes. Still, it was a good place to avoid notice.

He hurried to the roof and signaled to Jesper with his mirror. They were all in position now. Just before noon, Wylan would descend to wait in the canal-side café that always drew a noisy collection of street performers—musicians, mimes, jugglers—busking for tourist money. For now, the boy lay on his side, tucked beneath the stone ledge of the roof and dozing lightly. Matthias' rifle lay bundled in oilcloth beside Wylan, and he'd set out a whole string of fireworks, their fuses curled like mice tails.

Matthias settled his back against the ledge and shut his eyes, floating in and out of consciousness. He was used to these long stretches with little sleep from his time with the *drüskelle*. He would wake when he needed to. But now, he marched across the ice, the wind howling in his ears. Even the Ravkans had a name for that wind, *Gruzeburya*, the brute, a killing wind. It came from the north, a storm that engulfed everything in its path. Soldiers died mere steps from their tents, lost in the whiteness, their cries for help eaten by the faceless cold. Nina was out there. He knew it and he had no way to reach her. He screamed her name again and again, feeling his feet going numb in his boots, the ice seeping through his clothes. He strained to hear an answer, but his ears were full of the roar of the storm and somewhere, in the distance, the howl of wolves. She would die on the ice. She would die alone and it would be his fault.

He woke, gasping. The sun was high in the sky. Wylan stood above him, shaking him gently. "It's almost time." Matthias nodded and rose, rolling his shoulders, feeling the warm spring air of Ketterdam around him. It felt alien in his lungs. "Are you all right?" Wylan asked tentatively, but apparently Matthias' glower was answer enough. "You're great," Wylan said, and hurried down the stairs.

Matthias consulted the cheap brass watch Kaz had acquired for him. Almost twelve bells. He hoped Nina had rested more easily than he had. He flashed his mirror once at her balcony and felt a surge of relief when a bright light flashed back to him. He signaled to Jesper, then leaned over the roof's ledge to wait.

Matthias knew Kaz had chosen West Stave for its anonymity and its crowds. Already its denizens had started to come awake again after the previous evening's revels. The servants who tended to the needs of their various houses were doing their shopping, accepting shipments of wine and fruit for the next night's activities. Tourists who had just arrived in the city were strolling down both sides of the canal, pointing to the elaborately decorated signs that marked each house, some famous, some notorious. He could see a many-petaled rose fashioned in white wrought iron and gilded with silver. The House of the White Rose. Nina had worked there for nearly a year. He'd never questioned her about her time there. He had no right to. She had stayed in the city to help him, and she could do as she wished. And yet he'd been unable to keep from imagining her there, the curves of her body laid bare, green eyes heavy-lidded, cream-colored petals caught in the dark waves of her hair. There were nights when he imagined her beckoning him closer, others when it was someone else she welcomed in the dark, and he'd lie awake, wondering if it would be jealousy or desire that drove him mad first. He tore his eyes from the sign and pulled a long glass from his pocket, forcing himself to scan the rest of the Stave.

Just a few minutes before noon, Matthias caught sight of Kaz advancing from the west, his dark shape a blot moving through the crowd, his cane keeping time with his uneven gait. The crowd seemed to part around him, perhaps sensing the purpose that drove him. It reminded Matthias of villagers making signs in the air to ward off evil spirits. Alys Van Eck waddled along beside him. Her blindfold had been removed, and through his long glass, Matthias could see her lips moving. *Sweet Djel, is she still singing?* Judging from the sour expression on Kaz's face, it was a distinct possibility.

Beyond the other side of the bridge, Matthias saw Van Eck approach. He held himself rigidly, his posture erect, arms kept tight to his body as if he feared that the sin-rich air of the Barrel would stain his suit.

Kaz had been clear: Taking out Van Eck was a last resort. They didn't want to kill a member of the Merchant Council, not in broad daylight in front of witnesses.

"Wouldn't it be cleaner?" Jesper asked. "A heart attack? A brain fever?" Matthias would have preferred an honest kill, an open battle. But that was not the way things were done in Ketterdam.

"He can't suffer if he's dead," Kaz had said, and that had been the end of it. The *demjin* brooked no argument.

Van Eck had come surrounded by guards dressed in the red-and-gold livery of his house. Their heads swiveled left and right, taking in their surroundings, looking for threats. From the hang of their coats, Matthias could tell they were all armed. But there, surrounded by three huge guards, was a tiny hooded figure. *Inej.*

Matthias was surprised at the gratitude that flooded him. Though he'd only known the little Suli girl for a short while, he'd admired her courage from the first. And she'd saved their lives multiple times, putting herself at risk to do so. He'd questioned many of his choices, but never his commitment to seeing her freed from Van Eck. He only wished she'd separate herself from Kaz Brekker. The girl deserved better. Then again, maybe Nina deserved better than Matthias.

Both parties reached the bridge. Kaz and Alys walked forward. Van Eck signaled the guards holding Inej.

Matthias looked up. From the other rooftop, Jesper's mirror was flashing frantically. Matthias scanned the area around the bridge, but he couldn't see what had gotten Jesper so panicked. He peered through the long glass, training it on the labyrinthine streets that flowed outward from both sides of the Stave. Kaz's retreat appeared clear. But when Matthias looked past Van Eck to the east, his heart filled with dread. The streets were dotted with clusters of purple, all of them moving toward the Stave. *Stadwatch.* Was it just a coincidence or something Van Eck had planned?

Surely he wouldn't want to risk city officials finding out what he'd been up to? Could the Fjerdans be involved? What if they were coming to arrest both Van Eck and Kaz?

Matthias flashed his mirror twice at Nina. From her lower vantage point, she wouldn't see the *stadwatch* until it was too late. Again he felt the cold lash of the wind, heard his voice calling her name, felt his terror rise as no answer came. *She'll be fine*, he told himself. *She's a warrior.* But Jesper's warning ran in his ears. *Be careful. She's not quite herself.* He hoped Kaz was ready. He hoped Nina was stronger than she seemed. He hoped the plans they'd laid were enough, that Jesper's aim was true, that Wylan's calculations were correct. Trouble was coming for them all.

Matthias reached for his rifle.

9

KAZ

Kaz's first thought when he glimpsed Van Eck moving toward Goedmedbridge was, *This man should never play cards.* His second was that someone had broken the merch's nose. It was crooked and swollen, a dark circle of bruising forming beneath one eye. Kaz suspected a university medik had treated the worst of the damage, but without a Grisha Healer, there was only so much you could do to hide a break like that.

Van Eck was trying to keep his expression neutral, but he was working so hard to look impassive that his high forehead was shiny with sweat. His shoulders were fixed stiffly and his chest jutted forward as if someone had attached a string to his sternum and yanked him upward. He walked onto Goedmedbridge at a stately pace, surrounded by liveried guards in red and gold—now *that* surprised Kaz. He'd thought Van Eck would prefer to enter the Barrel with as little pomp as possible. He turned this new information over in his mind.

It was dangerous to ignore the details. No man liked to be shown up, and for all his attempts at a dignified promenade, Van Eck's vanity had to be wounded. A merch prided himself on his business sense, his ability to strategize, to manipulate men and markets. He'd be looking to get a bit of his own back after having his hand forced by a lowly Barrel thug.

Kaz let his eyes pass over the guards once, briefly, searching for Inej. She was hooded, barely visible between the men Van Eck had brought, but he would have recognized that knife-edge posture anywhere. And if the temptation was there to crane his neck, to look closer, to make sure she was unharmed? He could acknowledge it, set it aside. He would not break his focus.

For the briefest moment, Kaz and Van Eck sized each other up from across the bridge. Kaz couldn't help but be reminded of when they'd faced each other this way seven days ago. He'd thought too much about that meeting. Late at night, when the day's work was done, he'd lain awake, taking apart every moment of it. Again and again, Kaz thought of those few crucial seconds when he'd let his attention shift to Inej instead of keeping his eyes on Van Eck. It wasn't a mistake he could afford to make again. That boy had betrayed his weakness in a single glance, had ceded the war for the sake of a single battle, and put Inej—*all of them*—in danger. He was a wounded animal who needed to be put down. And Kaz had done it gladly, choked the life from him without pause for regret. The Kaz that remained saw only the job: Free Inej. Make Van Eck pay. The rest was useless noise.

He'd thought about Van Eck's mistakes on Vellgeluk too. The mercher had been stupid enough to trumpet the fact that his precious heir was cooking in the womb of his new wife—young Alys Van Eck, with her milk-white hair and dumpling hands. He'd been goaded by pride, but also by his hatred for Wylan, his desire to clear his son from the books like a failed business venture.

Kaz and Van Eck exchanged the shortest of nods. Kaz kept a gloved hand on Alys' shoulder. He doubted she would try to run off, but who knew what ideas were pinging around in the girl's head? Then Van Eck signaled to his men to bring Inej forward, and Kaz and Alys started across the bridge. In the blink of an eye, Kaz took in Inej's odd gait, the way she held her arms behind her back. They'd bound her hands and shackled her ankles. *A reasonable precaution*, he told himself. *I'd have done the same thing.* But he felt that flint inside him, scraping against the hollow places, ready to ignite into rage. He thought again about simply killing Van Eck. *Patience*, he reminded himself. He'd practiced it early and often. Patience would bring all his enemies to their knees in time. Patience and the money he intended to take off this merch scum.

"Do you think he's handsome?" Alys asked.

"What?" Kaz said, unsure he had heard her correctly. She'd been humming and singing all the way from the market where Kaz had removed her blindfold, and he'd been doing his best to tune her out.

"Something has happened to Jan's nose," Alys said.

"I suspect he caught a bad case of the Wraith."

Alys wrinkled her own small nose, considering. "I think Jan would be handsome, if he were not quite so old."

"Lucky for you, we live in a world where men can make up for being old by being rich."

"It would be nice if he were both young and rich."

"Why stop there? How about young, rich, and royal? Why settle for a merch when you could have a prince?"

"I suppose," said Alys. "But it's the money that's important. I've never really seen the point in princes."

Well, no one would ever doubt this girl was Kerch born and raised. "Alys, I'm shocked to find you and I are in agreement."

Kaz monitored the periphery of the bridge as they drew closer to the center, keeping a careful eye on Van Eck's guards, noting the open doors of the third-floor balcony at the Ammbers Hotel, the flower barge parked below the west side of the bridge as it was every morning. He assumed Van Eck would have people positioned in the surrounding buildings just as he did. But none of them would be permitted to land a kill shot. No doubt Van Eck would love to see him floating facedown in a canal, but

Kaz could lead Van Eck to Kuwei, and that knowledge should keep him from taking a bullet to the skull.

They stopped a good ten paces apart. Alys tried to step forward, but Kaz held her firmly in place.

"You said you were bringing me to Jan," she objected.

"And here you are," Kaz said. "Now be still."

"Jan!" she yelped sharply. "It's me!"

"I know, my dear," Van Eck said calmly, his gaze locked on Kaz. He lowered his voice. "This isn't over, Brekker. I want Kuwei Yul-Bo."

"Are we here to repeat ourselves? You want the secret to *jurda parem*, and I want my money. The deal is the deal."

"I don't have thirty million *kruge* to part with."

"Isn't that a shame? I'm sure someone else does."

"And have you had any luck securing a new buyer?"

"Don't trouble yourself on my account, merch. The market will provide. Do you want your wife back or did I drag poor Alys here for nothing?"

"Just a moment," said Van Eck. "Alys, what are we naming the child?"

"Very good," Kaz said. His team had passed off Wylan as Kuwei Yul-Bo on Vellgeluk, and Van Eck had been well fooled. Now the merch wanted confirmation he was actually getting his wife and not some girl with a radically tailored face and a false belly. "Seems an old dog can learn a new trick. Besides rolling over."

Van Eck ignored him. "Alys," he repeated, "what name are we giving the child?"

"The baby?" replied Alys in confusion. "Jan if it's a boy. Plumje if it's a girl."

"We agreed Plumje is what you're naming your new parakeet."

Alys' lip jutted out. "*I* never agreed."

"Oh, I think Plumje is a lovely name for a girl," said Kaz. "Satisfied, merch?"

"Come," Van Eck said, ushering Alys forward as he signaled to the guard holding Inej to release her.

As Inej passed Van Eck, she turned her face to him and murmured something. Van Eck's lips pinched.

Inej shuffled forward, somehow graceful, even with her arms bound behind her and shackles around her ankles. Ten feet. Five feet. Van Eck embraced Alys as she let loose a stream of questions and chatter. Three feet. Inej's gaze was steady. She was thinner. Her lips were chapped. But despite long days in captivity, the sun caught the dark gleam of her hair beneath her hood. Two feet. And then she was before him. They still needed to get clear of the bridge. Van Eck would not let them go this easily.

"Your knives?" he asked.

"They're packed inside my coat."

Van Eck had released Alys, and she was being led away by his guards. Those red-and-gold uniforms still bothered Kaz. Something was off.

"Let's get out of here," he said, an oyster knife in his hands to see to her ropes.

"Mister Brekker," Van Eck said. Kaz heard the excitement in Van Eck's voice and froze. Maybe the man was better at bluffing than he'd given him credit for. "You gave me your word, Kaz Brekker!" Van Eck shouted in theatrical tones. Everyone within earshot on the Stave turned to stare. "You swore you would return my wife and son to me! Where are you keeping Wylan?"

And then Kaz saw them—a tide of purple moving toward the bridge, *stadwatch* flooding onto the Stave, rifles raised, cudgels drawn.

Kaz lifted a brow. The merch was finally making it interesting.

"Seal off the bridge!" one of them shouted. Kaz glanced over his shoulder and saw more *stadwatch* officers blocking their retreat.

Van Eck grinned. "Shall we play for real now, Mister Brekker? The might of my city against your band of thugs?"

Kaz didn't bother to answer. He shoved Inej's shoulder and she spun around, offering her wrists so he could slash through her bonds. He tossed the knife in the air, trusting her to catch it as he knelt to deal with her shackles, his picks already sliding between his fingers. Kaz heard the clomp of boots approaching, felt Inej bend backward over his kneeling form, and heard a soft *whoosh*, then the sound of a body falling. The lock gave beneath Kaz's fingers and the shackles fell free. He rose, whirled, saw one *stadwatch* officer down, the shaft of the oyster knife protruding from between his eyes, and more purple uniforms rushing toward them from all directions.

He raised his cane to signal Jesper.

"West side flower boat," he said to Inej. That was all it took—she leapt onto the railing of the bridge and vanished over the side without a second guess.

The first set of fireworks exploded overhead, pale color in the noon light. The plan was in motion.

Kaz yanked a loop of climbing line from inside his pocket and hooked it to the rail. He snagged the head of his cane on the railing beside it, hauled himself up, and vaulted over the side, his momentum carrying him out above the canal. The cord snapped taut, and he arced back toward the bridge like a pendulum, dropping onto the deck of the flower barge beside Inej.

Two *stadwatch* boats were already moving toward them quickly as more officers raced down the ramps to the canal. Kaz hadn't known what Van Eck would try—he certainly hadn't expected him to bring the *stadwatch* into it—but he'd been sure Van Eck would attempt to close off all their escape routes. Another series of booms sounded, and bursts of pink and green exploded in the sky above the Stave. The tourists cheered. They didn't seem to notice that two of the explosions had come from the canal and had blown holes in the prow of one of the *stadwatch* boats, sending men scurrying for the sides and into the canal as the craft sank. *Nicely done, Wylan.* He'd bought them time—and done it without panicking the bystanders on the Stave. Kaz wanted the crowd in a very good mood.

He heaved a flat of wild geraniums into the canal over the protests of the flower seller and grabbed the clothes Matthias had stashed there earlier that morning. He swept the red cloak around Inej's shoulders in a rain of petals and blossoms as she continued to strap on her knives. She looked almost as startled as the flower seller.

"What?" he asked as he tossed her a Mister Crimson mask that matched his own.

"Those were my mother's favorite flower."

"Good to know Van Eck didn't cure you of sentiment."

"Nice to be back, Kaz."

"Good to have you back, Wraith."

"Ready?"

"Wait," he said, listening. The fireworks had ceased, and a moment later he heard the sound he'd been waiting for, the musical tinkle of coins hitting the pavement, followed by shrieks of delight from the crowd.

"Now," he said.

They grabbed the cord and he gave a sharp tug. With a high-pitched whir, the cord retracted, yanking them upward in a burst of speed. They were back on the bridge in moments, but the scene awaiting them was decidedly different from the one they'd escaped less than two minutes before.

West Stave was in chaos. Mister Crimsons were everywhere, fifty, sixty, seventy of them in red masks and cloaks, tossing coins into the air as tourists and locals alike pushed and shoved, laughing and shouting, crawling on hands and knees, completely oblivious to the *stadwatch* officers trying to get past them.

"Mother, Father, pay the rent!" shouted a crowd of girls from the doorway of the Blue Iris.

"I can't, my dear, the money's spent!" the Mister Crimsons chorused back, and tossed another cloud of coins into the air, sending the crowd into freshly delirious shrieks of joy.

"Clear the way!" shouted the captain of the guard.

One of the officers tried to unmask a Mister Crimson standing by a lamppost, and the crowd began booing. Kaz and Inej plunged into the swirl of red capes and people scrambling for coins. To his left, he heard Inej laugh behind her mask. He'd never heard her laugh like that, giddy and wild.

Suddenly a deep, thunderous *boom* shook the Stave. People toppled, grabbed at one another, at walls, at whatever was closest. Kaz almost lost his footing, righted himself with his cane.

When he looked up, it was like trying to peer through a thick veil. Smoke hung heavy in the air. Kaz's ears were ringing. As if from a great distance, he heard frightened screams, cries of terror. A woman ran past him, face and hair coated in dust and plaster like a pantomime ghost, hands clapped over her ears. There was blood trickling from beneath her palms. A gaping hole had been blown in the facade of the House of the White Rose.

He saw Inej lift her mask, and he pulled it back down over her face. He shook his head. Something was wrong. He'd planned a friendly riot, not a mass disaster, and Wylan wasn't the type to miscalculate so gravely. Someone else had come to make trouble on West Stave, someone who didn't mind doing more than a little damage.

All Kaz knew was he'd invested a lot of time and money in getting his Wraith back. He sure as hell wasn't going to lose her again.

He touched Inej's shoulder briefly. That was all the signal they needed. He raced for the nearest alleyway. He didn't have to look to know she was beside him—silent, sure-footed. She could have outpaced him in an instant, but they ran in tandem, matching each other step for step.

10
JESPER

Now this was Jesper's kind of chaos.

Jesper had two jobs, one before the exchange of hostages, and one after. While Inej was in Van Eck's possession, Nina was the first line of defense if the guards tried to remove her from the bridge or anyone threatened her. Jesper was to keep Van Eck in his rifle sights—no kill shots, but if the guy started brandishing a gun, Jesper was allowed to leave him without the use of an arm. Or two.

"Van Eck's going to pull something," Kaz had said back on Black Veil, "and it's going to be messy, because he has less than twelve hours to plan it."

"Good," said Jesper.

"Bad," said Kaz. "The more complicated a plan is, the more people he has to involve, the more people talk, the more ways it can go wrong."

"It's a law of systems," Wylan murmured. "You build in safeguards for failures, but something in the safeguards ends up causing an unforeseen failure."

"Van Eck's move won't be elegant, but it will be unpredictable, so we need to be prepared."

"How do we prepare for the unpredictable?" Wylan asked.

"We broaden our options. We keep every possible avenue of escape open. Rooftops, streets and alleys, waterways. There's no chance Van Eck is going to let us just stroll off that bridge."

Jesper had seen trouble coming a ways off when he'd spotted the groups of *stadwatch* headed for the bridge. It could just be a rousting. That happened once or twice a year in the Staves, the Merchant Council's way of showing the gamblers, procurers, and performers that no matter how much money they poured into the city coffers, the government was still in charge.

He had signaled Matthias and waited. Kaz had been clear: "Van Eck won't act until he has Alys back and out of harm's way. That's when we need to keep sharp."

And sure enough, once Alys and Inej had traded places, some kind of ruckus had started on the bridge. Jesper's trigger finger itched, but his second job had been simple too: Watch Kaz for the sign.

Seconds later, Kaz's cane shot into the air, and he and Inej were hurtling over the bridge railing. Jesper struck a match and one, two, three, four, five of the rockets Wylan had prepared were screaming toward the sky, exploding in crackling bursts of color. The last was a shimmer of pink. *Strontium chloride*, Wylan had told him, working away on his collection of fireworks and explosives, flash bombs, weevils, and whatever else was needed. *In the dark, it burns red.*

Things are always more interesting in the dark, Jesper had replied. He hadn't been able to help it. Really, if the merchling was going to offer those kinds of opportunities, he had a duty to take them.

The first batch of fireworks was a signal to the Mister Crimsons whom Nina and Matthias had recruited last night—or very early this morning—offering free food and wine to anyone who came to Goedmedbridge when the fireworks went off just after noon. All a big promotion for the nonexistent Crimson Cutlass. Knowing only a fraction of the people would actually show up, they'd given away more than two hundred costumes and bags of fake coins. "If we get fifty, it will be enough," said Kaz.

Never underestimate the public's desire to get something for nothing. Jesper figured there had to be at least one hundred Mister Crimsons flooding the bridge and the Stave, singing the chant that accompanied his entrance in any of the Komedie Brute plays, tossing coins into the air. Sometimes the coins were real. It was why he was a crowd favorite. People were laughing, whirling each other around, grabbing for coins, chasing after the Mister Crimsons as the *stadwatch* tried in vain to keep order. It was glorious. Jesper *knew* the money was fake, but he would have loved to be down there scrambling for silver anyway.

He had to keep still a little while longer. If the bombs Wylan had planted in the canal didn't go off when they were supposed to, Kaz and Inej were going to need a lot more cover to get off the flower seller's boat.

A series of glittering booms exploded across the sky. Matthias had released the second batch of fireworks. These weren't a signal; they were camouflage.

Far below, Jesper saw two huge gouts of water spurt up from the canal as Wylan detonated his water mines. *Right on time, merchling.*

Now he stowed his rifle beneath his Mister Crimson cloak and descended the stairs, stopping only to join Nina as they raced out of the hotel. They'd marked each of their red-and-white masks with a large black tear to make sure they'd be able to tell one another apart from the other revelers, but in the midst of the melee, Jesper wondered if they should have chosen something more conspicuous.

As they sped across the bridge, Jesper thought he spotted Matthias and Wylan in their red capes, tossing coins as they steadily made their way off the Stave. If they started running, it might draw *stadwatch* attention. Jesper struggled not to laugh. That was definitely Matthias and Wylan. Matthias was hurling the money with way too much force and

Wylan with way too much enthusiasm. The kid's throwing arm needed serious work. He looked like he was actively trying to dislocate his shoulder.

From here, they'd go separate directions, each through a different alley or canal that led off the Stave, discarding their Mister Crimson costumes for other Komedie Brute characters and disguises. They were to wait for sunset before they returned to Black Veil.

Plenty of time to get into trouble.

Jesper could feel the pull of East Stave. He could wend his way there, find a card game, spend a few hours at Three Man Bramble. Kaz wouldn't like it. Jesper was too well known. It was one thing to play at the Cumulus in a private parlor as part of a job. This would be something different. Kaz had vanished with promises of a huge haul and several valued members of the Dregs. People were speculating wildly about where he'd gone and Rotty had said Per Haskell was looking for all of them. *Stadwatch* officers would probably be visiting the Slat tonight to ask a lot of uncomfortable questions, and there was Pekka Rollins to worry about too. *Just a couple of hands*, Jesper promised himself, *enough to scratch the itch. Then I'll go visit Da.*

Jesper's stomach turned at that. He wasn't ready to face his father alone just yet, to tell him the truth of all this madness. Suddenly the need to be at the tables was overwhelming. To hell with not running. Since Kaz hadn't obliged him with something to shoot at, Jesper needed a pair of dice and long odds to clear his mind.

That was when the world went white.

The sound was something between a thunderbolt and a lightning crack. It lifted Jesper off his feet, sent him sprawling as a roaring *whoosh* filled his ears. He was suddenly lost in a storm of white smoke and dust that clogged his lungs. He coughed, and whatever he'd inhaled grated against the lining of his throat as if the air had turned to finely powdered glass. His eyelids were coated in grit and he fought not to rub at them, blinking rapidly, trying to dislodge bits of debris.

He pushed himself up to his hands and knees, gasping for air, head ringing. Another Mister Crimson lay on the ground beside him, a black tear painted onto his red lacquer cheek. Jesper dislodged the mask. Nina's eyes were closed and blood ran from her temple. He shook her shoulder.

"Nina!" he shouted above the screams and wailing around him.

Her eyelids fluttered and she drew a sharp breath, then started coughing as she sat up.

"What was that? What happened?"

"I don't know," said Jesper. "But someone other than Wylan is setting off bombs. Look."

A huge black hole gaped in the front of the House of the White Rose. A bed hung precariously from the second floor, ready to collapse into the lobby. The rose vines that climbed the front of the house had caught fire, and a heavy perfume had risen in the air. From somewhere inside, they could hear shouting.

"Oh, Saints, I have to help them," Nina said, and Jesper's addled mind remembered that she'd worked at the White Rose for the better part of a year. "Where's Matthias?" she asked, eyes searching the crowd. "Where's Wylan? If this is one of Kaz's surprises—"

"I don't think—" Jesper began. Then another *boom* shook the cobblestones. They flattened themselves on the ground, arms thrown over their heads.

"What in the name of every Saint who suffered is going on?" Nina yelled in fear and exasperation. People were shrieking and running all around them, trying to find some kind of shelter. She pulled herself to her feet and peered south down the canal toward the plume of smoke rising from another of the pleasure houses.

"Is it the Willow Switch?"

"No," said Nina, an expression of horror dawning on her face as she came to some realization Jesper didn't understand. "It's the Anvil."

As she said it, a shape shot skyward from the hole in the side of what had been the Anvil. It soared toward them in a blur. "Grisha," said Jesper. "They must have *parem*." But as the shape zoomed overhead and they twisted their necks to follow its progress, Jesper saw he was very wrong. Or he'd completely lost his mind. It wasn't a Squaller flying above them. It was a man *with wings*—huge, metallic things that moved in a hummingbird whir. He had someone clutched in his arms, a boy screaming in what sounded like Ravkan.

"Did you just see that? Tell me you saw that," said Jesper.

"It's Markov," Nina said, the fear and anger clear on her face. "That's why they targeted the Anvil."

"Nina!" Matthias was striding across the bridge, Wylan at his heels. Both of them had their masks shoved atop their heads, but the *stadwatch* had to have bigger concerns right now. "We have to get out of here," Matthias said. "If Van Eck—"

But Nina grabbed his arm, "That was Danil Markov. He worked at the Anvil."

"The guy with wings?" asked Jesper.

"No," Nina said, shaking her head frantically. "The captive. Markov is an Inferni." She pointed down the canal. "They hit the Anvil, the House of the White Rose. They're hunting Grisha. They're looking for me."

At that moment, a second winged figure burst from the White Rose. Another *boom* sounded, and as the lower wall caved in, a huge man and woman strode forward. They had black hair and bronze skin, just like the men with wings.

"Shu," said Jesper. "What are they doing here? And since when do they *fly*?"

"Masks down," said Matthias. "We need to get to safety."

They slid their masks into place. Jesper felt grateful for the uproar surrounding them. But even as he had the thought, one of the Shu men sniffed the air, a deep inhale. In horror, Jesper watched him turn slowly and lock eyes on them. He barked something to his companions, and then the Shu were headed straight for them.

"Too late," said Jesper. He tore off his mask and cape and shouldered his rifle. "If they came looking for fun, let's give them some. I'll take the flyer!"

Jesper had no intention of getting swept up by some kind of Shu bird-boy. He didn't know where the second flyer had gone and could only hope he was occupied with his Inferni captive. The winged man darted left, right, swooping and zooming like a drunken honeybee. "Stay still, you big bug," Jesper grunted, then squeezed off three shots that struck the flyer's chest dead center, flinging him backward.

But the flyer righted himself in a graceful somersault and sped toward Jesper.

Matthias was blasting away at the two huge Shu. Every shot was a direct hit, but though the Shu stumbled, they just kept coming.

"Wylan? Nina?" said Jesper. "Any time you want to jump in, feel free!"

"I'm trying," Nina growled, hands raised, fists clenched. "They're not feeling it."

"Get down!" said Wylan. They dropped to the cobblestones. Jesper heard a *thunk* and then saw a black blur as something hurtled at the winged man. The flyer dodged left, but the black blur split and two crackling balls of violet flame exploded. One landed with a harmless hiss in the canal water. The other struck the flyer. He screamed, clawing at himself as violet flames spread over his body and wings, then careened off course and slammed into a wall, the flames still burning, their heat palpable even from a distance.

"Run!" Matthias yelled.

They bolted for the nearest alley, Jesper and Wylan in the lead, Nina and Matthias on their heels. Wylan tossed a flash bomb recklessly over his shoulder. It smashed through a window and released a burst of use-less brilliance.

"You probably just scared the hell out of some hapless working girl," Jesper said. "Give me that." He snatched the other flash bomb and lobbed it directly into the path of their pursuers, turning to protect his eyes from the explosion. "And that's how it's done."

"Next time, I'm not saving your life," Wylan panted.

"You'd miss me. Everyone does."

Nina cried out. Jesper turned. Nina's thrashing body was covered in silver netting, and she was being dragged backward by the Shu woman, who stood with legs planted in the center of the alley. Matthias opened fire, but she didn't budge.

"Bullets don't work!" Wylan said. "I think there's metal beneath their skin."

Now that he said it, Jesper could see metal glinting from under the bloody bullet wounds. But what did that mean? Were they mechanicals of some sort? How was it possible?

"The net!" Matthias roared.

They all grabbed hold of the metal net, trying to pull Nina to safety. But the Shu woman kept yanking her backward, hand over hand, with impossible strength.

"We need something to cut the cord!" Jesper shouted.

"To hell with the cord," Nina snarled between gritted teeth. She snatched a revolver from Jesper's holster. "Let go!" she commanded.

"Nina—" protested Matthias.

"Do it."

They let go, and Nina zipped down the alley in a sudden burst of momentum. The Shu woman took an awkward step back, then seized the edge of the net, yanking Nina up.

Nina waited until the last possible second, then said, "Let's see if you're metal all the way through."

She shoved the revolver directly into the Shu woman's eye socket and squeezed the trigger.

The blast didn't just take her eye but most of the top of her skull. For a moment, she still stood, clutching Nina, a gaping mess of bone, soft pink brain matter, and shards of metal where the rest of her face should have been. Then she crumpled.

Nina gagged and scrabbled at the net. "Get me out of this thing before her friend comes looking for us."

Matthias tore the net away from Nina and they all ran, hearts hammering, boots pounding over the cobblestones.

Jesper could hear his father's fearful words, hastening him through the streets, a wind of warning at his back. *I'm afraid for you. The world can be cruel to your kind.* What had the Shu sent after Nina? After the city's Grisha? After *him*?

Jesper's existence had been a string of close calls and near disasters, but he'd never been so sure he was running for his life.

PART THREE

BRICK BY BRICK

11

INEJ

As Inej and Kaz moved farther from West Stave, the silence between them spread like a stain. They'd abandoned their capes and masks in a rubbish heap behind a run-down little brothel called the Velvet Room, where Kaz had apparently stashed another change of clothes for them. It was as if the whole city had become their wardrobe, and Inej couldn't help but think of the conjurers who drew miles of scarves from their sleeves and vanished girls from boxes that always reminded her uncomfortably of coffins.

Dressed in the bulky coats and roughspun trousers of dockworkers, they made their way into the warehouse district, hair covered by hats, collars pulled up despite the warm weather. The eastern edge of the district was like a city within a city, populated mostly by immigrants who lived in cheap hotels and rooming houses or in shantytowns of plywood and corrugated tin, segregating themselves into ramshackle neighborhoods by language and nationality. At this time of day, most of the area's denizens were at work in the city's factories and docks, but on certain corners, Inej saw men and women gathered, hoping some foreman or boss would come along to offer a lucky few of them a day's work.

After she'd been freed from the Menagerie, Inej had wandered the streets of Ketterdam, trying to make sense of the city. She'd been overwhelmed by the noise and the crowds, certain that Tante Heleen or one of her henchmen would catch her unawares and drag her back to the House of Exotics. But she'd known that if she was going to be useful to the Dregs and earn her way out of her new contract, she couldn't let the strangeness of the clamor and cobblestones best her. *We greet the unexpected visitor.* She would have to learn the city.

She always preferred to travel along the rooftops, out of sight, free from the shuffle of bodies. There, she felt most herself again—the girl she'd once been, someone who hadn't had the sense to be afraid, who hadn't known what cruelty the world could offer. She'd gotten to know the gabled peaks and window boxes of the Zelverstraat, the gardens and wide boulevards of the embassy sector. She'd traveled far south to where the manufacturing district gave way to foul-smelling slaughterhouses and brining pits hidden at the very outskirts of the city, where their offal could be sluiced into the swamp at Ketterdam's edge, and their stink was less likely to be sent wafting over the residential parts of town. The city had revealed its secrets to her almost shyly, in flashes of grandeur and squalor.

Now she and Kaz left the rooming houses and street carts behind, plunging deeper into the busy warehouse district and the area known as the Weft. Here, the streets and canals were clean and orderly, kept wide for the transportation of goods and cargo. They passed fenced-in acres of raw lumber and quarried stone, closely guarded stockpiles of weapons and ammunition, huge storehouses brimming with cotton, silk, canvas, and furs, and warehouses packed with the carefully weighed bundles of dried *jurda* leaves from Novyi Zem that would be processed and packaged into tins with bright labels, then shipped out to other markets.

Inej still remembered the jolt she'd felt when she saw the words *Rare Spices* painted on the side of one of the warehouses. It was an advertisement, the words framed by two Suli girls rendered in paint, brown limbs bare, the embroidery of their scant silks hinted at by golden brushstrokes. Inej had stood there, gaze fastened to the sign, less than two miles from where the rights to her body had been bought and sold and haggled over, her heart jackrabbiting in her chest, panic seizing her muscles, unable to stop staring at those girls, the bangles on their wrists, the bells around their ankles. Eventually she'd willed herself to move, and as if some spell had been broken, she'd run faster than she ever had, back to the Slat, racing over the rooftops, the city passing in gray glimpses below her reckless feet. That night she'd dreamed the painted girls had come to life. They were trapped in the brick wall of the warehouse, screaming to be set free, but Inej was powerless to help them.

Rare Spices. The sign was still there, faded from the sun. It still held power for her, made her muscles clench, her breath hitch. But maybe when she had her ship, when she'd brought down the first slaver, the paint would blister from the bricks. The cries of those girls in their mint-colored silks would turn to laughter. They would dance for no one but themselves. Ahead, Inej could see a high column topped by Ghezen's Hand, casting its long shadow over the heart of Kerch's wealth. She imagined her Saints wrapping ropes around it and sending it toppling to the ground.

She and Kaz drew no stares in their shapeless coats, two boys looking for work or on their way to the next shift. Still Inej could not breathe easily. The *stadwatch* patrolled the streets of the warehouse district regularly, and just in case that wasn't enough protection, the shipping companies employed private guards to make sure the doors stayed locked and that none of the workers stocking, stacking, and transporting goods got too free with their hands. The warehouse district was one of the most secure places in Ketterdam, and because of that, it was the last spot Van Eck would look for them.

They approached an abandoned linen storehouse. The windows of its lower floors were broken, the bricks above them blackened by soot. The fire must have been recent, but the storehouse wouldn't remain unoccupied for long; it would be cleaned out and rebuilt or simply razed for a new structure. Space was precious in Ketterdam.

The padlock on the back door was little challenge to Kaz, and they entered a lower story that had been badly damaged by the fire. The stairway near the front of the building seemed largely intact. They climbed, Inej moving lightly over the boards, Kaz's tread punctuated by the rhythmic *thunk* of his cane.

When they reached the third floor, Kaz directed them to a stock room where bolts of linen were still piled high in giant pyramids. They were largely undamaged, but those on the bottom were stained with soot, and the fabric had a burnt, unpleasant smell. They were comfortable, though. Inej found a perch by a window that let her rest her feet on one bolt and her back on another. She was grateful to simply sit, to look out the window into the watery afternoon light. There wasn't much to see, just the bare brick walls of the warehouses and the grove of huge sugar silos that loomed over the harbor.

Kaz took a tin from beneath one of the old sewing machines and passed it to her. She popped it open, revealing hazelnuts, crackers wrapped in wax paper, and a stoppered flask. So this was one of the safe houses Van Eck had been so eager to learn about. Inej uncorked the flask and sniffed.

"Water," he said.

She drank deeply and ate a few of the stale crackers. She was famished, and she doubted she'd be getting a hot meal anytime soon. Kaz had warned her that they couldn't return to Black Veil until nightfall, and even then, she didn't think they'd be doing much cooking. She watched him push himself up onto the stack of bolts across from her, resting his cane beside him, but she forced her eyes back to the window, away from the precision of his movements, the taut line of his jaw. Looking at Kaz felt dangerous in a way it hadn't before. She could see the mallet rise, glinting in the stage lights on Eil Komedie. *He'll never trade if you break me.* She was grateful for the weight of her knives. She touched her hands to them as if greeting old friends, felt some of the tension inside her ease.

"What did you say to Van Eck on the bridge?" Kaz asked at last. "When we were making the trade?"

"You will see me once more, but only once."

"More Suli proverbs?"

"A promise to myself. And Van Eck."

"Careful, Wraith. You're ill-suited to the revenge game. I'm not sure your Suli Saints would approve."

"My Saints don't like bullies." She rubbed her sleeve over the dirty window. "Those explosions," she said. "Will the others be all right?"

"None of them were stationed near where the bombs went off. At least not the ones we saw. We'll know more when we're back on Black Veil."

Inej didn't like that. What if someone had been hurt? What if all of them didn't make it back to the island? After days of fear and waiting, sitting still while her friends might be in trouble was a new kind of frustration.

She realized Kaz was studying her, and turned her gaze to his. Sunlight slanted through the windows, turning his eyes the color of strong tea. *He'll never trade if you break me.* She could feel the memory of the words, as if they'd burned her throat in the speaking.

Kaz didn't look away when he said, "Did he hurt you?"

She wrapped her arms around her knees. *Why do you want to know? So that you can be sure I'm capable of taking on some new danger? So that you can add to the list of wrongs for which Van Eck must be held to account?*

Kaz had been clear about his arrangement with her from the beginning. Inej was an investment, an asset worthy of protection. She had wanted to believe they'd become more to each other. Jan Van Eck had robbed her of that illusion. Inej was whole, unharmed. She bore no scars or trauma from her ordeal on Eil Komedie that food and sleep would not ease. But Van Eck had taken something from her nonetheless. *I'll be no use to him anymore.* Words torn from some hidden place inside her, a truth she could not unknow. She should be glad of it. Better terrible truths than kind lies.

She let her fingers drift to the place where the mallet had brushed her leg, saw Kaz's eyes track the movement, stopped. She folded her hands in her lap, shook her head.

"No. He didn't hurt me."

Kaz leaned back, his gaze dismantling her slowly. He didn't believe her, but she could not bring herself to try and convince him of this lie.

He propped his cane on the floor and used it to brace himself as he slid off the fabric pile. "Rest," he said.

"Where are you going?"

"I have business near the silos, and I want to see what information I can pick up." He left his cane leaning against one of the bolts.

"You're not taking it?"

"Too conspicuous, especially if Van Eck has gotten the *stadwatch* involved. Rest," he repeated. "You'll be safe here."

Inej closed her eyes. She could trust him enough for that.

When Kaz woke her, the sun was setting, gilding the tower of Ghezen in the distance. They left the storehouse, locking it behind them, and joined the workers walking home for the night. They continued south and east, dodging the busiest parts of the Barrel, where no doubt the *stadwatch* would be prowling, and headed toward a more residential area. In a narrow canal, they boarded a smallboat that they piloted down Grafcanal, and into the mists shrouding Black Veil Island.

Inej felt her excitement increasing as they picked their way through the mausoleums toward the center of the island. *Let them be okay*, she prayed. *Let them all be okay.* Finally, she glimpsed a dim light and heard the faint murmur of voices. She broke into a run, not caring when her cap slipped from her head to the vine-covered ground. She tore open the door to the tomb.

The five people inside rose, guns and fists raised, and Inej skidded to a halt.

Nina shrieked, "Inej!"

She flew across the room and crushed Inej in a tight hug. Then they were all around her at once, hugging her, clapping her on the back. Nina would not let go of her. Jesper threw his arms around both of them and crowed, "The Wraith returns!" as Matthias stood back, formal as ever but smiling. She looked from the Shu boy seated at the table in the center of the tomb to the identical Shu boy hovering in front of her.

"Wylan?" she asked of the one closest to her.

He broke into a grin, but it slipped sideways when he said, "Sorry about my father."

Inej pulled him into the hug and whispered, "We are not our fathers."

Kaz rapped his cane on the stone floor. He was standing in the doorway to the tomb. "If everyone is done cuddling, we have a job to do."

"Hold up," said Jesper, arm still slung around Inej. "We're not talking about the job until we figure out what those things were on the Stave."

"What things?" asked Inej.

"Did you miss half the Stave blowing up?"

"We saw the bomb at the White Rose go off," said Inej, "and then we heard another explosion."

"At the Anvil," said Nina.

"After that," Inej said, "we ran."

Jesper nodded sagely. "That was your big mistake. If you'd stuck around, you could have nearly been killed by a Shu guy with wings."

"Two of them," said Wylan.

Inej frowned. "Two wings?"

"Two guys," said Jesper.

"With wings?" Inej probed. "Like a bird?"

Nina dragged her toward the cluttered table, where a map of Ketterdam had been spread. "No, more like a moth, a deadly, mechanical moth. Are you hungry? We have chocolate biscuits."

"Oh sure," said Jesper. "She gets the cookie hoard."

Nina planted Inej in a chair and plunked the tin down in front of her. "Eat," she commanded. "There were two Shu with wings, and a man and a woman who were . . . not normal."

"Nina's power had no effect on them," said Wylan.

"Hmm," Nina said noncommittally, nibbling daintily at the edge of a biscuit. Inej had never seen Nina nibble daintily on anything. Her appetite clearly hadn't returned, but Inej wondered if there was more to it.

Matthias joined them at the table. "The Shu woman we faced was stronger than me, Jesper, and Wylan put together."

"You heard right," said Jesper. "Stronger than Wylan."

"I did my part," objected Wylan.

"You most definitely did, merchling. What was that violet stuff?"

"Something new I've been working on. It's based on a Ravkan invention called *lumiya*; the flames are almost impossible to extinguish, but I changed the formulation so that it burns a lot hotter."

"We were lucky to have you there," said Matthias with a small bow that left Wylan looking pleased and entirely flustered. "The creatures were nearly impervious to bullets."

"Nearly," Nina said grimly. "They had nets. They were looking to hunt and capture Grisha."

Kaz rested his shoulders against the wall. "Were they using *parem*?"

She shook her head. "No. I don't think they were Grisha. They didn't display any powers, and they weren't healing their wounds. It looked like they had some kind of metal plating beneath their skin."

She spoke to Kuwei rapidly in Shu.

Kuwei groaned. "Kherguud." They all looked at him blankly. He sighed and said, "When my father made *parem*, the government tests it on Fabrikators."

Jesper cocked his head to one side. "Is it just me or is your Kerch getting better?"

"My Kerch is good. You all talk too fast."

"Okay," drawled Jesper. "Why did your dear Shu friends test *parem* on Fabrikators?" He was sprawled in his chair, hands resting on his revolvers, but Inej did not quite believe his relaxed pose.

"They have more Fabrikators in captivity," said Kuwei.

"They're the easiest to capture," Matthias put in, ignoring Nina's sour look. "Until recently, they received little combat training, and without *parem* their powers are poorly suited to battle."

"Our leaders want to conduct more experiments," Kuwei continued. "But they don't know how many Grisha they can find—"

"Maybe if they hadn't killed so many?" Nina suggested.

Kuwei nodded, missing or ignoring the sarcasm in Nina's voice. "Yes. They have few Grisha, and using *parem* shortens a Grisha's life. So they bring doctors to work with the Fabrikators already sick from *parem*. They plan to make a new kind of soldier, the Kherguud. I don't know if they succeeded."

"I think I can answer that question with a big fat yes," said Jesper.

"Specially tailored soldiers," Nina said thoughtfully. "Before the war, I heard they tried something similar in Ravka, reinforcing skeletons, tampering with bone density, metal implants. They experimented on First Army volunteers. Oh, stop grimacing, Matthias. Your Fjerdan masters probably would have gotten around to trying the exact same thing, given the time."

"Fabrikators deal in solids," said Jesper. "Metal, glass, textiles. This seems like Corporalki work."

Still talking as if he isn't one of them, Inej noted. They all knew Jesper was a Fabrikator; even Kuwei had discovered it in the chaos that followed their escape from the Ice Court. And yet, Jesper rarely acknowledged his power. She supposed it was his secret to tend as he wished.

"Tailors blur the line between Fabrikator and Corporalnik," said Nina. "I had a teacher in Ravka, Genya Safin. She could have been either a Heartrender or a Fabrikator if she'd wanted to—instead she became a great Tailor. The work you're describing is really just an advanced kind of tailoring."

Inej could not quite fathom it. "But you're telling us you saw a man with wings somehow grafted onto his back?"

"No, they were mechanical. Some kind of metal frame, and canvas, maybe? But it's more sophisticated than just slapping a pair of wings between someone's shoulder blades. You'd have to link the musculature, hollow out the bones to decrease body weight, then somehow compensate for the loss of bone marrow, maybe replace the skeleton entirely. The level of complexity—"

"*Parem*," said Matthias, his pale blond brows furrowed. "A Fabrikator using *parem* could manage that kind of tailoring."

Nina shoved back from the table. "Won't the Merchant Council do anything about the Shu attack?" she asked Kaz. "Are they just allowed to waltz into Kerch and start blowing things up and kidnapping people?"

"I doubt the Council will act," he said. "Unless the Shu who attacked you were wearing uniforms, the Shu Han government will probably deny any knowledge of the attack."

"So they just get away with it?"

"Maybe not," Kaz said. "I spent a little time gathering intelligence at the harbors today. Those two Shu warships? The Council of Tides dry-docked them."

Jesper's boots slid off the table and hit the floor with a thud. "What?"

"They pulled back the tide. All of it. Used the sea to carve a new island with both of those warships beached on it. You can see them lying on their sides, sails dragging in the mud, right there in the harbor."

"A show of force," said Matthias.

"On behalf of Grisha or the city?" Jesper asked.

Kaz shrugged. "Who knows? But it might make the Shu a little more careful about hunting on the Ketterdam streets."

"Could the Council of Tides help us?" asked Wylan. "If they know about *parem*, they have to be worried about what might happen if the wrong people get their hands on it."

"How would you find them?" Nina asked bitterly. "No one knows the Tides' identities, no one ever sees them coming or going from those watchtowers." Inej suddenly wondered if Nina had tried to garner help from the Tides when she'd first arrived in Ketterdam, sixteen years old, a Grisha separated from her country with no friends or knowledge of the city. "The Shu won't stay cowed forever. They created those soldiers for a reason."

"It's smart when you think about it," said Kaz. "The Shu were maximizing their resources. A Grisha addicted to *parem* can't survive for long, so the Shu found another way to exploit their powers."

Matthias shook his head. "Indestructible soldiers who outlive their creators."

Jesper rubbed a hand over his mouth. "And who can go out and hunt more Grisha. I swear to the Saints one of them found us by our smell."

"Is that even possible?" Inej asked, horrified.

"I've never heard of Grisha giving off a particular scent," said Nina, "but I guess it's possible. If the soldiers' olfactory receptors were improved . . . Maybe it's a scent ordinary people can't detect."

"I don't think this was the first attack," Jesper said. "Wylan, remember how terrified that Squaller in the rare books room was? And what about that merch ship Rotty told us about?"

Kaz nodded. "It was torn apart, a bunch of sailors were found dead. At the time, they thought the crew's Squaller might have gone rogue, busted out of his indenture. But maybe he didn't disappear. Maybe he was captured. He was one of old Councilman Hoede's Grisha."

"Emil Retvenko," said Nina.

"That's the one. You knew him?"

"I knew *of* him. Most of the Grisha in Ketterdam know about each other. We share information, try to keep an eye out for one another. The Shu must have spies here if they knew where to look for each of us. The other Grisha——" Nina stood up, then grabbed the back of her chair, as if the sudden movement had made her woozy.

Inej and Matthias were on their feet instantly.

"Are you all right?" Inej asked.

"Splendid," Nina said with an unconvincing smile. "But if the other Grisha in Ketterdam are in danger——"

"You're going to do what?" Jesper said, and Inej was surprised by the harsh edge to his voice. "You're lucky to be alive after what happened today. Those Shu soldiers can *smell* us, Nina." He turned on Kuwei. "Your father made that possible."

"Hey," said Wylan, "go easy."

"Go easy? Like things weren't bad enough for the Grisha before? What if they track us to Black Veil? There are three of us here."

Kaz rapped his knuckles against the table. "Wylan's right. Go easy. The city wasn't safe before and it isn't safe now. So let's all get rich enough to relocate."

Nina placed her hands on her hips. "Are we really talking about money?"

"We're talking about the job and making Van Eck pay up."

Inej looped her arm through Nina's. "I want to know what we can do to help the Grisha who are still in Ketterdam." She saw the mallet glint as it reached the top of its arc. "And I'd also like to know how we're going to make Van Eck suffer."

"There are bigger issues here," said Matthias.

"Not for me," Jesper said. "I have two days left to get right with my father."

Inej wasn't sure she'd heard correctly. "Your father?"

"Yup. Family reunion in Ketterdam," said Jesper. "Everyone's invited."

Inej wasn't fooled by Jesper's airy tone. "The loan?"

His hands returned to his revolvers. "Yeah. So I'd really like to know just how we intend to settle this score."

Kaz shifted his weight on his cane. "Have any of you wondered what I did with all the cash Pekka Rollins gave us?"

Inej's gut clenched. "You went to Pekka Rollins for a loan?"

"I would never go into debt with Rollins. I sold him my shares in Fifth Harbor and the Crow Club."

No. Kaz had built those places from nothing. They were testaments to what he'd done for the Dregs. "Kaz—"

"Where do you think the money went?" he repeated.

"Guns?" asked Jesper.

"Ships?" queried Inej.

"Bombs?" suggested Wylan.

"Political bribes?" offered Nina. They all looked at Matthias. "This is where you tell us how awful we are," she whispered.

He shrugged. "They all seem like practical choices."

"Sugar," said Kaz.

Jesper nudged the sugar bowl down the table to him.

Kaz rolled his eyes. "Not for my coffee, you podge. I used the money to buy up sugar shares and placed them in private accounts for all of us—under aliases, of course."

"I don't like speculation," said Matthias.

"Of course you don't. You like things you can see. Like piles of snow and benevolent tree gods."

"Oh, there it is!" said Inej, resting her head on Nina's shoulder and beaming at Matthias. "I missed his glower."

"Besides," Kaz said, "it's hardly speculation if you know the outcome."

"You know something about the sugar crop?" Jesper asked.

"I know something about the supply."

Wylan sat up straighter. "The silos," he said. "The silos at Sweet Reef."

"Very good, merchling."

Matthias shook his head. "What's Sweet Reef?"

"It's an area just south of Sixth Harbor," said Inej. She remembered the view of the vast silos towering over the warehouse district. They were the size of small mountains. "It's where they keep molasses, raw cane, and the processing plants to refine sugar. We were right near there today. That wasn't a coincidence, was it?"

"No," said Kaz. "I wanted you to get a look at the terrain. Most sugar cane comes from the Southern Colonies and Novyi Zem, but there won't be another crop until three months from now. This season's crop has already been harvested, processed, refined, and stored in the Sweet Reef silos."

"There are thirty silos," said Wylan. "My father owns ten of them."

Jesper whistled. "Van Eck controls one-third of the world's sugar supply?"

"He owns the *silos*," said Kaz, "but only a fraction of the sugar inside them. He maintains the silos at his own expense, supplies guards for them, and pays the Squallers who monitor the humidity inside the silos to make sure the sugar stays dry and separated. The merchants who own the sugar pay him a small percentage of every one of their sales. It adds up quickly."

"Such enormous wealth under one man's protection," Matthias considered. "If anything were to happen to those silos, the price of sugar—"

"Would go off like a cheap pair of six-shooters," Jesper said, popping to his feet and starting to pace.

"The price would climb and keep climbing," said Kaz. "And as of a few days ago, we own shares in the companies that *don't* store sugar with Van Eck. Right now, they're worth about what we paid for them. But once we destroy the sugar in Van Eck's silos—"

Jesper was bouncing on the balls of his feet. "Our shares will be worth five—maybe ten—times what they are now."

"Try twenty."

Jesper hooted. "Don't mind if I do."

"We could sell at a huge profit," said Wylan. "We'd be rich overnight."

Inej thought of a sleek schooner, weighted with heavy cannon. It could be hers. "Thirty million *kruge* rich?" she asked. The reward Van Eck owed them for the Ice Court job. One he'd never intended to pay.

The barest smile ghosted over Kaz's lips. "Give or take a million."

Wylan was gnawing on his thumbnail. "My father can weather a loss. The other merchants, the ones who own the sugar in his silos, will be hit worse."

"True," said Matthias. "And if we destroy the silos, it will be clear Van Eck was targeted."

"We could try to make it look like an accident," suggested Nina.

"It will," said Kaz. "Initially. Thanks to the weevil. Tell them, Wylan."

Wylan sat forward like a schoolboy eager to prove he had the answers. He drew a vial from his pocket. "This version works."

"It's a weevil?" Inej asked, examining it.

"A chemical weevil," said Jesper. "But Wylan still hasn't named it. My vote is for the Wyvil."

"That's terrible," said Wylan.

"It's brilliant." Jesper winked. "Just like you."

Wylan blushed daylily pink.

"I helped as well," added Kuwei, looking sulky.

"He did help," Wylan said.

"We'll make him a plaque," said Kaz. "Tell them how it works."

Wylan cleared his throat. "I got the idea from cane blight—just a little bit of bacteria can ruin a whole crop. Once the weevil is dropped into the silo, it will keep burrowing down, using the refined sugar as fuel until the sugar is nothing but useless mush."

"It reacts to sugar?" asked Jesper.

"Yes, any kind of sugar. Even trace amounts if there's enough moisture present, so keep it away from sweat, blood, saliva."

"Do not lick Wyvil. Does someone want to write that down?"

"Those silos are huge," said Inej. "How much will we need?"

"One vial for each silo," Wylan said.

Inej blinked at the small glass tube. "Truly?"

"Tiny and ferocious," Jesper said. He winked again. "Just like *you*."

Nina burst out laughing, and Inej couldn't help returning Jesper's grin. Her body ached and she would have liked to sleep for two days straight, but she felt some part of herself uncoiling, releasing the terror and anger of the last week.

"The weevil will make the destruction of the sugar look like an accident," said Wylan.

"It will," said Kaz, "until the other merchants learn that Van Eck has been buying up sugar that isn't stored in his silos."

Wylan's eyes widened. *"What?"*

"I used half of the money for our shares. I used the rest to purchase shares on behalf of Van Eck—well, on behalf of a holding company created under Alys' name. Couldn't make it too obvious. The shares were purchased in cash, untraceable. But the certificates authenticating their purchase will be found stamped and sealed at his attorney's office."

"Cornelis Smeet," Matthias said, in surprise. "Deception upon deception. You weren't just trying to figure out where Alys Van Eck was being kept when you broke into his office."

"You don't win by running one game," said Kaz. "Van Eck's reputation will take a hit when the sugar is lost. But when the people who paid him to keep it safe find out he profited from their loss, they'll look more closely at those silos."

"And find the remnants of the weevil," finished Wylan.

"Destruction of property, tampering with the markets," Inej murmured. "It will be the end of him." She thought of Van Eck gesturing to his lackey to take up the mallet. *I don't want it to be a clean break. Shatter the bone.* "Could he go to prison?"

"He'll be charged with violating a contract and attempting to interfere with the market," said Kaz. "There is no greater crime according to Kerch law. The sentences are the same as for murder. He could hang."

"Will he?" Wylan said softly. He used his finger to draw a line across the map of Ketterdam, all the way from Sweet Reef to the Barrel, then on to the Geldstraat, where his father lived. Jan Van Eck had tried to kill Wylan. He'd cast him off like refuse. But Inej wondered if Wylan was ready to doom his father to execution.

"I doubt he'll swing," said Kaz. "My guess is they'll saddle him with a lesser charge. None of the Merchant Council will want to put one of their own on the gallows. As for whether or not he'll actually ever see the inside of a jail cell?" He shrugged. "Depends on how good his lawyer is."

"But he'll be barred from trade," said Wylan, his voice almost dazed. "His holdings will be seized to make good on the lost sugar."

"It will be the end of the Van Eck empire," Kaz said.

"What about Alys?" asked Wylan.

Again Kaz shrugged. "No one is going to believe that girl had anything to do with a financial scheme. Alys will sue for divorce and probably move back in with her parents. She'll cry for a week, sing for two, and then get over it. Maybe she'll marry a prince."

"Or maybe a music teacher," Inej said, remembering Bajan's panic when he heard Alys had been abducted.

"There's just one small problem," said Jesper, "and by *small*, I mean 'huge, glaring, let's scrap this and go get a lager.' The silos. I know we're all about breaching the unbreachable, but how are we supposed to get inside?"

"Kaz can pick the locks," said Wylan.

"No," said Kaz, "I can't."

"I don't think I've ever heard those words leave your lips," said Nina. "Say it again, nice and slow."

Kaz ignored her. "They're quatrefoil locks. Four keys in four locks turned at the same time or they trigger security doors and an alarm. I can pick any lock, but I can't pick four at once."

"Then how do we get in?" Jesper asked.

"The silos also open at the top."

"Those silos are nearly twenty stories high! Is Inej going to go up and down ten of them in one night?"

"Just one," said Kaz.

"And then what?" said Nina, hands back on her hips and green eyes blazing.

Inej remembered the towering silos, the gaps between them.

"And then," said Inej, "I'm going to walk a high wire from one silo to the next."

Nina threw her hands in the air. "And all of it without a net, I suppose?"

"A Ghafa never performs with a net," Inej said indignantly.

"Does a Ghafa frequently perform twenty stories above cobblestones after being held prisoner for a week?"

"There will be a net," said Kaz. "It's in place behind the silo guardhouse already, under a stack of sandbags."

The silence in the tomb was sudden and complete. Inej couldn't believe what she was hearing. "I don't need a net."

Kaz consulted his watch. "Didn't ask. We have six hours to sleep and heal up. I'll nab supplies from the Cirkus Zirkoa. They're camped on the western outskirts of town. Inej, make a list of what you'll need. We hit the silos in twenty-four hours."

"Absolutely not," said Nina. "Inej needs to rest."

"That's right," Jesper agreed. "She looks thin enough to blow away in a stiff breeze."

"I'm fine," said Inej.

Jesper rolled his eyes. "You always say that."

"Isn't that how things are done around here?" asked Wylan. "We all tell Kaz we're fine and then do something stupid?"

"Are we that predictable?" said Inej.

Wylan and Matthias said in unison, "*Yes.*"

"Do you want to beat Van Eck?" Kaz asked.

Nina blew out an exasperated breath. "Of course."

Kaz's eyes scanned the room, moving from face to face. "Do you? Do you want your money? The money we fought, and bled, and nearly drowned for? Or do you want Van Eck to be glad he picked a bunch of nobodies from the Barrel to scam? Because no one else is going to get him for us. No one else is going to care that he cheated us or that we risked our lives for nothing. No one else is going to make this right. So I'm asking, do you want to beat Van Eck?"

"Yes," said Inej. She wanted some kind of justice.

"Soundly," said Nina.

"Around the ears with Wylan's flute," said Jesper.

One by one, they nodded.

"The stakes have changed," said Kaz. "Based on Van Eck's little demonstration today, wanted posters with our faces on them are probably already going up all over Ketterdam, and I suspect he'll be offering a handsome reward. He's trading on his credibility, and the sooner we destroy it, the better. We're going to take his money, his reputation, and his freedom all in one night. But that means we don't stop. Angry as he is, tonight Van Eck is going to eat a fine dinner and fall off to a fitful sleep in his soft merch bed. Those *stadwatch* grunts will rest their weary heads until they get to the next shift, wondering if maybe they'll earn a little overtime. But *we don't stop*. The clock is ticking. We can rest when we're rich. Agreed?"

Another round of nods.

"Nina, there are guards who walk the perimeter of the silos. You'll be the distraction, a distressed Ravkan, new to the city, looking for work in the warehouse district. You need to keep them occupied long enough for the rest of us to get inside and for Inej to scale the first silo. Then—"

"On one condition," said Nina, arms crossed.

"This is not a negotiation."

"Everything is a negotiation with you, Brekker. You probably bartered your way out of the womb. If I'm going to do this, I want us to get the rest of the Grisha out of the city."

"Forget it. I'm not running a charity for refugees."

"Then I'm out."

"Fine. You're out. You'll still get your share of the money for your work on the Ice Court job, but I don't need you on this crew."

"No," said Inej quietly. "But you need me."

Kaz rested his cane across his legs. "It seems everyone is forming alliances."

Inej remembered the way the sun had caught the brown in his eyes only hours before. Now they were the color of coffee gone bitter in the brewing. But she was not going to back down.

"They're called friendships, Kaz."

His gaze shifted to Nina. "I don't like being held hostage."

"And I don't like shoes that pinch at the toes, but we must all suffer. Think of it as a challenge for your monstrous brain."

After a long pause, Kaz said, "How many people are we talking about?"

"There are less than thirty Grisha in the city that I know of, other than the Council of Tides."

"And how would you like to corral them? Hand out pamphlets directing them to a giant raft?"

"There's a tavern near the Ravkan embassy. We use it to leave messages and exchange information. I can get the word out from there. Then we just need a ship. Van Eck can't watch all the harbors."

Inej didn't want to disagree, but it had to be said. "I think he can. Van Eck has the full power of the city government behind him. And you didn't see his reaction when he discovered Kaz had dared to take Alys."

"Please tell me he actually frothed at the mouth," said Jesper.

"It was a close thing."

Kaz limped to the tomb door, staring out into the darkness. "Van Eck won't have made the choice to involve the city lightly. It's a risk, and he wouldn't take that risk if he didn't intend to capitalize on it to the fullest. He'll have every harbor and watchtower on the coast on full alert, with orders to question anyone trying to leave Ketterdam. He'll just claim that he knows Wylan's captors may plan to take him from Kerch."

"Trying to get all of the Grisha out will be extremely dangerous," said

Matthias. "The last thing we need is for a group of them to fall into Van Eck's hands when he may still have a store of *parem*."

Jesper tapped his fingers on the grips of his revolvers. "We need a miracle. And possibly a bottle of whiskey. Helps lubricate the brainpan."

"No," said Kaz slowly. "We need a ship. A ship that couldn't possibly be suspect, that Van Eck and the *stadwatch* would never have cause to stop. We need one of *his* ships."

Nina wriggled to the edge of her chair. "Van Eck's trading company must have plenty of ships heading to Ravka."

Matthias folded his huge arms, considering. "Get the Grisha refugees out on one of Van Eck's own vessels?"

"We'd need a forged manifest and papers of transit," said Inej.

"Why do you think they kicked Specht out of the navy?" Kaz asked. "He was forging leave documents and supply orders."

Wylan pulled on his lip. "But it's not just a question of a few documents. Let's say there are thirty Grisha refugees. A ship's captain is going to want to know why thirty people—"

"Thirty-one," Kuwei said.

"Are you actually following all of this?" said Jesper incredulously.

"A ship to Ravka," said Kuwei. "I understand that very well."

Kaz shrugged. "If we're going to steal a boat, we might as well put you on it."

"Thirty-one it is," said Nina with a smile, though if the muscle twitching in Matthias' jaw was any indication, he wasn't nearly so thrilled.

"Okay," said Wylan, smoothing a crease in the map. "But a ship's captain is going to wonder why there are thirty-one people being added to his manifest."

"Not if the captain thinks he's in on a secret," said Kaz. "Van Eck will write a passionately worded letter calling upon the captain to use the utmost discretion in transporting these valuable political refugees and asking him to keep them hidden from anyone susceptible to Shu bribes— including the *stadwatch*—at all costs. Van Eck will promise the captain a huge reward when he returns, just to make sure *he* doesn't get any ideas about selling out the Grisha. We already have a sample of Van Eck's handwriting. We just need his seal."

"Where does he keep it?" Jesper asked Wylan.

"In his office. At least that's where it used to be."

"We'll have to get in and out without him noticing," said Inej. "And we'll have to move quickly after that. As soon as Van Eck realizes the seal is missing, he'll be able to guess what we're up to."

"We broke into the Ice Court," said Kaz. "I think we can manage a mercher's office."

"Well, we did almost die breaking into the Ice Court," said Inej.

"Several times, if memory serves," noted Jesper.

"Inej and I lifted a DeKappel from Van Eck. We already know the layout of the house. We'll be fine."

Wylan's finger was once more tracing the Geldstraat. "You didn't have to get into my father's safe."

"Van Eck keeps the seal in a safe?" said Jesper with a laugh. "It's almost like he *wants* us to take it. Kaz is better at making friends with combination locks than with people."

"You've never seen a safe like this," Wylan said. "He had it installed after the DeKappel was stolen. It has a seven-digit combination that he resets every day, and the locks are built with false tumblers to confuse safecrackers."

Kaz shrugged. "Then we go around it. I'll take expediency over finesse."

Wylan shook his head. "The safe walls are made of a unique alloy reinforced with Grisha steel."

"An explosion?" suggested Jesper.

Kaz raised a brow. "I suspect Van Eck will notice that."

"A very small explosion?"

Nina snorted. "You just want to blow something up."

"Actually . . ." said Wylan. He cocked his head to one side, as if he were listening to a distant song. "Come morning, there would be no hiding we'd been there, but if we can get the refugees out of the harbor before my father discovers the theft . . . I'm not exactly sure where I can get the materials, but it just might work. . . ."

"*Inej*," Jesper whispered.

She leaned forward, peering at Wylan. "Is that a scheming face?"

"Possibly."

Wylan seemed to snap back to reality. "It is *not*. But . . . but I do think I have an idea."

"We're waiting, merchling," Kaz said.

"The weevil is basically just a much more stable version of auric acid."

"Yes," said Jesper. "Of course. And that is?"

"A corrosive. It gives off a minor amount of heat once it starts to react, but it's incredibly powerful and incredibly volatile. It can cut through Grisha steel and just about anything else other than balsa glass."

"Glass?"

"The glass and the sap from the balsa neutralize the corrosion."

"And where does one come by such a thing?"

"We can find one of the ingredients I need in an ironworks. They use the corrosive to strip oxidation off metals. The other might be tougher to come by. We'd need a quarry with a vein of auris or a similar halide compound."

"The closest quarry is at Olendaal," said Kaz.

"That could work. Once we have both compounds, we'll have to be very careful with the transport," Wylan continued. "Actually, we'll have to be more than careful. After the reaction is completed, auric acid is basically harmless, but while it's active . . . Well, it's a good way to lose your hands."

"So," said Jesper, "*if* we get these ingredients, *and* manage to transport them separately, *and* activate this auric acid, *and* don't lose a limb in the process?"

Wylan tugged at a lock of his hair. "We could burn through the safe door in a matter of minutes."

"Without damaging the contents inside?" asked Nina.

"Hopefully."

"Hopefully," repeated Kaz. "I've worked with worse. We'll need to find out which ships are departing for Ravka tomorrow night and get Specht started on the manifest and papers of transit. Nina, once we've got a vessel chosen, can your little band of refugees make it to the docks on their own or will they need their hands held for that too?"

"I'm not sure how well they know the city," admitted Nina.

Kaz drummed his fingers over the head of his cane. "Wylan and I can tackle the safe. We can send Jesper to escort the Grisha and we can map a route so Matthias can get Kuwei to the docks. But that leaves only Nina to distract the guards and work the net for Inej at the silos. The net needs at least three people on it for it to be worth anything."

Inej stretched, gently rolled her shoulders. It was good to be among these people again. She'd been gone for only a few days, and they were sitting in a damp mausoleum, but it still felt like a homecoming.

"I told you," she said. "I don't work with a net."

12

KAZ

They stayed up planning well past midnight. Kaz was wary of the changes to the plan as well as the prospect of managing Nina's pack of Grisha. But though he gave no indication to the others, there were elements of this new course that appealed to him. It was possible that Van Eck would piece together what the Shu were doing and go after the city's remaining Grisha himself. They were a weapon Kaz didn't want to see in the mercher's arsenal.

But they couldn't let this little rescue slow them down. With so many opponents and the *stadwatch* involved, they couldn't afford it. Given enough time, the Shu would stop worrying about those dry-docked warships and the Council of Tides, and find their way to Black Veil. Kaz wanted Kuwei out of the city and removed from play as soon as possible.

At last, they put their lists and sketches aside. The wreckage of their makeshift meal was cleared from the table to avoid attracting the rats of Black Veil, and the lanterns were doused.

The others would sleep. Kaz could not. He'd meant what he'd said. Van Eck had more money, more allies, and the might of the city behind him. They couldn't just be smarter than Van Eck, they had to be relentless. And Kaz could see what the others couldn't. They'd won the battle today; they'd set out to get Inej back from Van Eck and they had. But the merch was still winning the war.

That Van Eck was willing to risk involving the *stadwatch*, and by extension the Merchant Council, meant he really believed he was invulnerable. Kaz still had the note Van Eck had sent arranging the meeting on Vellgeluk, but it was shoddy proof of the man's schemes. He remembered what Pekka Rollins had said back at the Emerald Palace, when Kaz had claimed that the Merchant Council would never stand for Van Eck's illegal activities. *And who's going to tell them? A canal rat from the worst slum in the Barrel? Don't kid yourself, Brekker.*

At the time, Kaz had barely been able to think beyond the red haze of anger that descended when he was in Rollins' presence. It stripped away the reason that guided him, the patience he relied on. Around Pekka, he lost the shape of who he was—no, he lost the shape of who he'd fought to become. He wasn't Dirtyhands or Kaz Brekker or even the toughest lieutenant in the Dregs. He was just a boy fueled by a white flame of rage, one that threatened to burn the pretense of the hard-won civility he maintained to ash.

But now, leaning on his cane among the graves of Black Veil, he could acknowledge the truth of Pekka's words. You couldn't go to war with an upstanding merch like Van Eck, not if you were a thug with a reputation dirtier than a stable hand's boot sole. To win, Kaz would have to level the field. He would show the world what he already knew: Despite his soft hands and fine suits, Van Eck was a criminal, just as bad as any Barrel thug—worse, because his word was worth nothing.

Kaz didn't hear Inej approach, he just knew when she was there, standing beside the broken columns of a white marble mausoleum. She'd found soap to wash with somewhere, and the scent of the dank rooms of Eil Komedie—that faint hint of hay and greasepaint—was gone. Her black hair shone in the moonlight, already tucked tidily away in a coil at her neck, and her stillness was so complete she might have been mistaken for one of the cemetery's stone guardians.

"Why the net, Kaz?"

Yes, why the net? Why something that would complicate the assault he'd planned on the silos and leave them twice as open to exposure? *I couldn't bear to watch you fall.* "I just went to a lot of trouble to get my spider back. I didn't do it so you could crack your skull open the next day."

"You protect your investments." Her voice sounded almost resigned.

"That's right."

"And you're going off island."

He should be more concerned that she could guess his next move. "Rotty says the old man's getting restless. I need to go smooth his feathers."

Per Haskell was still the leader of the Dregs, and Kaz knew he liked the perks of that position, but not the work that went with it. With Kaz gone for so long, things would be starting to unravel. Besides, when Haskell got antsy, he liked to do something stupid just to remind people he was in charge.

"We should get eyes on Van Eck's house too," said Inej.

"I'll take care of it."

"He'll have strengthened his security." The rest went unspoken. There was no one better equipped to slip past Van Eck's defenses than the Wraith.

He should tell her to rest, tell her he would handle the surveillance on his own. Instead, he nodded and set out for one of the *gondels* hidden in the willows, ignoring the relief he felt when she followed.

After the raucous din of the afternoon, the canals seemed more silent than usual, the water unnaturally still.

"Do you think West Stave will be back to itself tonight?" Inej asked, voice low. She'd learned a canal rat's caution when it came to traveling the waterways of Ketterdam.

"I doubt it. The *stadwatch* will be investigating, and tourists don't come to Ketterdam for the thrill of being blown to bits." A lot of businesses were going to lose money. Come tomorrow morning, Kaz suspected the front steps of the Stadhall would be crowded with the owners of pleasure houses and hotels demanding answers. Could be quite a scene. *Good.* Let the members of the Merchant Council concern themselves with problems other than Jan Van Eck and his missing son. "Van Eck will have changed things up since we lifted the DeKappel."

"And now that he knows Wylan is with us," agreed Inej. "Where are we going to meet the old man?"

"The Knuckle."

They couldn't intercept Haskell at the Slat. Van Eck would have been keeping the Dregs' headquarters under surveillance, and now there were probably *stadwatch* swarming over it too. The thought of *stadwatch* grunts searching his rooms, digging through his few belongings, sent fury prickling over Kaz's skin. The Slat wasn't much, but Kaz had converted it from a leaky squat to a place you could sleep off a bender or lie low from the law without freezing your ass off in the winter or being bled by fleas in the summer. The Slat was his, no matter what Per Haskell thought.

Kaz steered the *gondel* into Zovercanal at the eastern edge of the Barrel. Per Haskell liked to hold court at the Fair Weather Inn on the same night every week, meeting up with his cronies to play cards and gossip. There was no way he'd miss it tonight, not when his favored lieutenant—his *missing* favored lieutenant—had fallen out with a member of the Merchant Council and brought so much trouble to the Dregs, not when he'd be the center of attention.

No windows faced onto the Knuckle, a crooked passage that bent between a tenement and a factory that manufactured cut-rate souvenirs. It was quiet, dimly lit, and so narrow it could barely call itself an alley— the perfect place for a jump. Though it wasn't the safest route from the Slat to the Fair Weather, it was the most direct, and Per Haskell never could resist a shortcut.

Kaz moored the boat near a small footbridge and he and Inej took up their places in the shadows to wait, the need for silence understood. Less than twenty minutes later, a man's silhouette appeared in the lamplight at the mouth of the alley, an absurd feather jutting from the crown of his hat.

Kaz waited until the figure was almost level with him before he stepped forward. "Haskell."

Per Haskell whirled, pulling a pistol from his coat. He moved quickly despite his age, but Kaz had known he would be packing iron and was ready. He gave Haskell's shoulder a quick jab with the tip of his cane, just enough to send a jolt of numbness to his hand.

Haskell grunted and the gun slipped from his grasp. Inej caught it before it could hit the ground and tossed it to Kaz.

"Brekker," Haskell said angrily, trying to wiggle his numb arm. "Where the hell have you been? And what kind of skiv rolls his own boss in an alley?"

"I'm not robbing you. I just didn't want you to shoot anyone before we had a chance to talk." Kaz handed the gun back to Haskell by its grip. The old man snatched it from his palm, grizzled chin jutting out stubbornly.

"Always overstepping," he grumbled, tucking the weapon into a pocket of his nubbly plaid jacket, unable to reach his holster with his incapacitated arm. "You know what trouble you brought down on me today, boy?"

"I do. That's why I'm here."

"There were *stadwatch* crawling all over the Slat and the Crow Club. We had to shut the whole place down, and who knows when we'll be able to start up again. What were you thinking, kidnapping a mercher's son? This was the big job you left town for? The one supposed to make me wealthy beyond my wildest dreams?"

"I didn't kidnap anyone." Not strictly true, but Kaz figured the subtleties would be lost on Per Haskell.

"Then what in Ghezen's name is going on?" Haskell whispered

furiously, spittle flying. "You've got my best spider," he said, gesturing to Inej. "My best shooter, my Heartrender, my biggest bruiser—"

"Muzzen is dead."

"Son of a bitch," Haskell swore. "First Big Bolliger, now Muzzen. You trying to gut my whole gang?"

"No, sir."

"*Sir.* What are you about, boy?"

"Van Eck is playing a fast game, but I'm still a step ahead of him."

"Don't look like it from here."

"Good," said Kaz. "Better no one sees us coming. Muzzen was a loss I didn't anticipate, but give me a few more days and not only will the law be off your back, your coffers will be so heavy you'll be able to fill your bathtub with gold and take a swim in it."

Haskell's eyes narrowed. "How much money are we talking?"

That's the way, Kaz thought, watching greed light Haskell's gaze, the lever at work.

"Four million *kruge.*"

Haskell's eyes widened. A life of drink and hard living in the Barrel had turned the whites yellowy. "You trying to cozy me?"

"I told you this was a big haul."

"Don't matter how high the pile of scrub is if I'm in prison. I don't like the law in my business."

"I don't either, sir." Haskell might mock Kaz's manners, but he knew the old man lapped up every gesture of respect, and Kaz's pride could take it. Once he had his own share of Van Eck's money, he wouldn't have to obey another order or soothe Per Haskell's vanity ever again. "I wouldn't have gotten us into this if I didn't know we'd come out of it clean as choirboys and rich as Saints. All I need is a little more time."

Kaz couldn't help but be reminded of Jesper bargaining with his father, and the thought didn't sit well with him. Per Haskell had never cared for anyone other than himself and the next glass of lager, but he liked to think of himself as the patriarch of a big, criminally inclined family. Kaz could admit he had a fondness for the old man. He'd given Kaz a place to begin and a roof over his head—even if Kaz had been the one to make sure it didn't leak.

The old man hooked his thumbs in the pockets of his waistcoat, making a great show of considering Kaz's offer, but Haskell's greed was more reliable than a faithfully wound clock. Kaz knew he'd already started thinking of ways to spend the *kruge*.

"All right, boy," said Haskell. "I can portion you a little more rope to hang yourself. But I find out you're running game on me and you'll regret it."

Kaz schooled his features to seriousness. Haskell's threats were almost as empty as his boasts.

"Of course, sir."

Haskell snorted. "The deal is the deal," he said. "And the Wraith stays with me."

Kaz felt Inej stiffen by his side. "I need her for the job."

"Use Roeder. He's spry enough."

"Not for this."

Now Haskell bristled, puffing his chest out, the false sapphire of his tie pin glinting in the dim light. "You see what Pekka Rollins is up to? He just opened a new gambling hall right across from the Crow Club." Kaz had seen it. The Kaelish Prince. Another jewel in Rollins' empire, a massive betting palace decked out in garish green and gold as some ridiculous homage to Pekka Rollins' homeland. "He's muscling in on our holdings," said Haskell. "I need a spider, and she's the best."

"It can wait."

"I say it can't. Head on down to the Gemensbank. You'll see my name at the top of her contract, and that means I say where she goes."

"Understood, sir," said Kaz. "And as soon as I find her, I'll let her know."

"She's right—" Haskell broke off, his jaw dropping in disbelief. "She was right here!"

Kaz forced himself not to smile. While Per Haskell had been blustering, Inej had simply melted into the shadows and silently scaled the wall. Haskell searched the length of the alley and peered up at the rooftops, but Inej was long gone.

"You bring her back here," Haskell said furiously, "*right now.*"

Kaz shrugged. "You think I can climb these walls?"

"This is my gang, Brekker. She doesn't belong to you."

"She doesn't belong to anyone," Kaz said, feeling the singe of that angry white flame. "But we'll all be back at the Slat soon enough." Actually, Jesper would be headed out of the city with his father, Nina would be off to Ravka, Inej would be on a ship under her own command, and Kaz would be getting ready to split from Haskell forever. But the old man would have his *kruge* to comfort him.

"Cocky little bastard," growled Haskell.

"Cocky little bastard who's about to make you one of the richest bosses in the Barrel."

"Get out of my way, boy. I'm late for my game."

"Hope the cards are hot." Kaz moved aside. "But you may want these." He held out his hand. Six bullets lay in his gloved palm. "In case of a tussle."

Haskell whisked the pistol from his pocket and flipped open the barrel. It was empty. "You little—" Then Haskell barked a laugh and plucked the bullets from Kaz's hand, shaking his head. "You've got the devil's own blood in you, boy. Go get my money."

"And then some," murmured Kaz as he tipped his hat and limped back down the alley to the *gondel*.

Kaz kept sharp, relaxing only slightly when the boat slid past the boundaries of the Barrel and into the quieter waters that bordered the financial district. Here the streets were nearly empty and the *stadwatch* presence was thinner. As the *gondel* passed beneath Ledbridge, he glimpsed a shadow separating itself from the railing. A moment later, Inej joined him in the narrow boat.

He was tempted to steer them back to Black Veil. He'd barely slept in days, and his leg had never fully recovered from what he'd put it through at the Ice Court. Eventually, his body was going to stop taking orders.

As if she could read his mind, Inej said, "I can handle the surveillance. I'll meet you back on the island."

Like hell. She wasn't going to be rid of him that easily. "What direction do you want to approach Van Eck's house from?"

"Let's start at the Church of Barter. We can get eyes on Van Eck's house from the roof."

Kaz wasn't thrilled to hear it, but he took them up Beurscanal, past the Exchange and the grand facade of the Geldrenner Hotel, where Jesper's father was probably snoring soundly in his suite.

They docked the *gondel* near the church. The glow of candlelight spilled from the doors of the main cathedral, left open and unlocked at all hours, welcoming those who wished to offer prayers to Ghezen.

Inej could have climbed the outer walls with little effort, and Kaz might have managed it, but he wasn't going to test himself on a night when his leg was screaming with every step. He needed access to one of the chapels.

"You don't have to come up," Inej said as they crept along the perimeter and located one of the chapel doors.

Kaz ignored her and swiftly picked the lock. They slipped inside the darkened chamber, then took the stairs up two flights, the chapels stacked one on top of another like a layered cake, each commissioned by a separate merchant family of Kerch. One more lock to pick and they were scaling another damned staircase. This one curled in a tight spiral up to a hatch in the roof.

The Church of Barter was built on the plan of Ghezen's hand, the vast cathedral located in the palm, with five stubby naves radiating along the four fingers and thumb, each fingertip terminating in a stack of chapels.

They'd climbed the chapels at the tip of the pinky and now cut down to the roof of the main cathedral, and then up the length of Ghezen's ring finger, picking their way along a jagged mountain range of slippery gables and narrow stone spines.

"Why do gods always like to be worshipped in high places?" Kaz muttered.

"It's men who seek grandeur," Inej said, springing nimbly along as if her feet knew some secret topography. "The Saints hear prayers wherever they're spoken."

"And answer them according to their moods?"

"What you want and what the world needs are not always in accord, Kaz. Praying and wishing are not the same thing."

But they're equally useless. Kaz bit back the reply. He was too focused on not plummeting to his death to properly engage in an argument.

At the tip of the ring finger, they stopped and took in the view. To the southwest, they could see the high spires of the cathedral, the Exchange, the glittering clock tower of the Geldrenner Hotel, and the long ribbon of the Beurscanal flowing beneath Zentsbridge. But if they looked east, this particular rooftop gave them a direct view of the Geldstraat, the Geldcanal beyond, and Van Eck's stately home.

It was a good vantage point to observe the security Van Eck had put in place around the house and on the canal, but it wouldn't give them all the information they needed.

"We're going to have to get closer," said Kaz.

"I know," said Inej, drawing a length of rope from her tunic and looping it over one of the roof's finials. "It will be faster and safer for me to case Van Eck's house on my own. Give me a half hour."

"You—"

"By the time you make it back to the *gondel*, I'll have all the information we need."

He was going to kill her. "You dragged me up here for nothing."

"Your pride dragged you up here. If Van Eck senses anything amiss tonight, it's all over. This isn't a two-person job and you know it."

"Inej—"

"My future is riding on this too, Kaz. I don't tell you how to pick locks or put together a plan. This is what I'm good at, so let me do my job." She yanked the rope taut. "And just think of all the time you'll have for prayer and quiet contemplation on the way down."

She vanished over the side of the chapel.

Kaz stood there, staring at the place she'd been only seconds before. She'd tricked him. The decent, honest, pious Wraith had outsmarted him. He turned to look back at the long expanse of roof he was going to have to traverse to get back to the boat.

"Curse you and all your Saints," he said to no one at all, then realized he was smiling.

Kaz was in a decidedly less amused frame of mind by the time he sank into the *gondel*. He didn't mind that she'd duped him, he just hated that she was right. He knew perfectly well that he was in no shape to try to slink into Van Eck's house blind tonight. It *wasn't* a two-person job, and it wasn't the way they operated. She was the Wraith, the Barrel's best thief of secrets. Gathering intelligence without being spotted was her specialty, not his. He could also admit that he was grateful to just sit for a moment, stretch out his leg as water lapped gently at the sides of the canal. So why had he insisted that he accompany her? That was dangerous thinking—the kind of thinking that had gotten Inej captured in the first place.

I can best this, Kaz told himself. By midnight tomorrow, Kuwei would be on his way out of Ketterdam. In a matter of days, they would have their reward. Inej would be free to pursue her dream of hunting slavers, and he'd be rid of this constant distraction. He would start a new gang, one built from the youngest, deadliest members of the Dregs. He'd rededicate himself to the promise he'd made to Jordie's memory, the pains-taking task of pulling Pekka Rollins' life apart piece by piece.

And yet, his eyes kept drifting to the walkway beside the canal, his impatience growing. He was better than this. Waiting was the part of the criminal life so many people got wrong. They wanted to act instead of hold fast and gather information. They wanted to know instantly with-out having to learn. Sometimes the trick to getting the best of a situation was just to wait. If you didn't like the weather, you didn't rush into the storm—you waited until it changed. You found a way to keep from get-ting wet.

Brilliant, thought Kaz. *So where the hell is she?*

A few long minutes later, she dropped soundlessly into the *gondel*.

"Tell me," he said as he set them moving down the canal.

"Alys is still in the same room on the second floor. There's a guard posted outside her door."

"The office?"

"Same location, right down the hall. He's had Schuyler locks installed on all of the house's exterior windows." Kaz blew out an annoyed breath. "Is that a problem?" she asked.

"No. A Schuyler lock won't stop any pick worth his stones, but they're time-consuming."

"I couldn't make sense of them, so I had to wait for one of the kitchen staff to open the back door." He'd done a shoddy job of teaching her to pick locks. She could master a Schuyler if she put her mind to it. "They were taking deliveries," Inej continued. "From the little bit I was able to hear, they're preparing for a meeting tomorrow night with the Merchant Council."

"Makes sense," said Kaz. "He'll act the role of the distraught father and get them to add more *stadwatch* to the search."

"Will they oblige?"

"They have no reason to deny him. And they're all getting fair warning to sweep their mistresses or whatever else they don't want discovered in a raid under the rug."

"The Barrel won't go easy."

"No," said Kaz as the *gondel* slid past the shallow sandbar that abutted Black Veil and into the island's mists. "No one wants the merchers poking around in our business. Any notion of what time this little meeting of the Council will take place?"

"The cooks were making noises about setting a full table for dinner. Could make for a good distraction."

"Exactly." This was them at their best, with nothing but the job between them, working together free of complications. He should leave it at that, but he needed to know. "You said Van Eck didn't hurt you. Tell me the truth."

They'd reached the shelter of the willows. Inej kept her eyes on the droop of their white branches. "He didn't."

They climbed out of the *gondel*, made sure it was thoroughly camouflaged, and picked their way up the shore. Kaz followed Inej, waiting, letting her weather change. The moon was starting to set, limning the graves of Black Veil, a miniature skyline etched in silver. Her braid had come uncoiled down her back. He imagined wrapping it around his hand, rubbing his thumb over the pattern of its plaits. And then what? He shoved the thought away.

When they were only a few yards from the stone hull, Inej halted and watched the mists wreathing the branches. "He was going to break my legs," she said. "Smash them with a mallet so they'd never heal."

Thoughts of moonlight and silken hair evaporated in a black bolt of fury. Kaz saw Inej tug on the sleeve of her left forearm, where the Menagerie tattoo had once been. He had the barest inkling of what she'd endured there, but he knew what it was to feel helpless, and Van Eck had managed to make her feel that way again. Kaz was going to have to find a new language of suffering to teach that smug merch son of a bitch.

Jesper and Nina were right. Inej needed rest and a chance to recover after the last few days. He knew how strong she was, but he also knew what captivity meant to her.

"If you're not up for the job—"

"I'm up for the job," she said, her back still to him.

The silence between them was dark water. He could not cross it. He couldn't walk the line between the decency she deserved and the violence this path demanded. If he tried, it might get them both killed. He could only be who he truly was—a boy who had no comfort to offer. So he would give her what he could.

"I'm going to open Van Eck up," he said quietly. "I'm going to give him a wound that can't be sewn shut, that he'll never recover from. The kind that can't be healed."

"The kind you endured?"

"Yes." It was a promise. It was an admission.

She took a shaky breath. The words came like a string of gunshots, rapid-fire, as if she resented the very act of speaking them. "I didn't know if you would come."

Kaz couldn't blame Van Eck for that. Kaz had built that doubt in her with every cold word and small cruelty.

"We're your crew, Inej. We don't leave our own at the mercy of merch scum." It wasn't the answer he wanted to give. It wasn't the answer she wanted.

When she turned to him, her eyes were bright with anger.

"He was going to *break my legs*," she said, her chin held high, the barest quaver in her voice. "Would you have come for me then, Kaz? When I couldn't scale a wall or walk a tightrope? When I wasn't the Wraith anymore?"

Dirtyhands would not. The boy who could get them through this, get their money, keep them alive, would do her the courtesy of putting her out of her misery, then cut his losses and move on.

"I would come for you," he said, and when he saw the wary look she shot him, he said it again. "I would come for you. And if I couldn't walk,

I'd crawl to you, and no matter how broken we were, we'd fight our way out together—knives drawn, pistols blazing. Because that's what we do. We never stop fighting."

The wind rose. The boughs of the willows whispered, a sly, gossiping sound. Kaz held her gaze, saw the moon reflected there, twin scythes of light. She was right to be cautious. Even of him. Especially of him. Cautious was how you survived.

At last she nodded, the smallest dip of her chin. They returned to the tomb in silence. The willows murmured on.

13
NINA

Nina woke well before dawn. As usual, her first conscious thought was of *parem*, and as usual, she had no appetite. The ache for the drug had nearly driven her mad last night. Trying to use her power when the Kherguud soldiers attacked had left her desperate for *parem*, and she'd spent the long hours tossing and turning, digging bloody half-moons into her palms.

She felt wretched this morning, and yet a sense of purpose made it easier to rise from her bed. The need for *parem* had dimmed something in her, and sometimes Nina was afraid that whatever spark had gone out would never return. But today, though her bones hurt and her skin felt dry and her mouth tasted like an oven that needed cleaning, she felt *hopeful*. Inej was back. They had a job. And she was going to do some good for her people. Even if she had to blackmail Kaz Brekker into being a decent person to manage it.

Matthias was already up, seeing to their weapons. Nina stretched and yawned, adding a little extra arch to her back, pleased at the way his gaze darted over her figure before guiltily jumping back to the rifle he was loading. *Gratifying.* She'd practically thrown herself at him the other day. If Matthias didn't want to take advantage of the offer, she could make damn sure he regretted it.

The others were awake and moving around the tomb as well—everyone except Jesper, who was still snoring contentedly, his long legs sticking out from beneath a blanket. Inej was making tea. Kaz was sitting at the table trading sketches back and forth with Wylan as Kuwei looked on, occasionally offering a suggestion. Nina let her eyes study those two Shu faces next to each other. Wylan's manner and posture were utterly different, but when both boys were at rest, it was nearly impossible to tell them apart. *I did that*, Nina thought. She remembered the sway of the ship's lanterns in the little cabin, Wylan's ruddy curls, disappearing beneath her fingertips to be replaced by a sheaf of thick black hair, his wide blue eyes, afraid but stubbornly brave, turning gold and changing shape. It had felt like magic, true magic, the kind in the stories the teachers at the Little Palace had told to try to get them to sleep. And it had all belonged to her.

Inej came to sit beside her with two cups of hot tea in hand.

"How are you this morning?" she asked. "Can you eat?"

"I don't think so." Nina forced herself to take a sip of tea, then said, "Thank you for what you did last night. For standing by me."

"It was the right thing to do. I don't want to see anyone else made a slave."

"Even so."

"You're very welcome, Nina Zenik. You may repay me in the customary way."

"Waffles?"

"Lots of them."

"You need them. Van Eck didn't feed you, did he?"

"I wasn't particularly obliging, but he tried for a while."

"And then?"

"And then he decided to torture me."

Nina's fists clenched. "I'm going to string his innards up like party garlands."

Inej laughed and settled her head on Nina's shoulder. "I appreciate the thought. Truly. But that debt is mine to pay." She paused. "The fear was the worst of it. After the Ice Court, I almost thought I was beyond fear."

Nina rested her chin atop Inej's silky hair. "Zoya used to say that fear is a phoenix. You can watch it burn a thousand times and still it will return." The need for *parem* felt that way too.

Matthias appeared in front of them. "We should go soon. We have little more than an hour before sunrise."

"What exactly are you wearing?" Nina asked, staring at the tufted cap and woolly red vest Matthias had put on over his clothes.

"Kaz procured papers for us in case we're stopped in the Ravkan quarter. We're Sven and Catrine Alfsson. Fjerdan defectors seeking asylum at the Ravkan embassy."

It made sense. If they were stopped, there was no way Matthias could pass himself off as Ravkan, but Nina could easily manage Fjerdan.

"Are we married, Matthias?" she said, batting her lashes.

He consulted the papers and frowned. "I believe we're brother and sister."

Jesper ambled over, rubbing the sleep from his eyes. "Not creepy at all."

Nina scowled. "Why did you have to make us siblings, Brekker?"

Kaz didn't look up from whatever document he was examining. "Because it was easier for Specht to forge the papers that way, Zenik. Same parents' names and birthplace, and he was working to accommodate your noble impulses at short notice."

"We don't look anything alike."

"You're both tall," Inej offered.

"And neither of us have gills," said Nina. "That doesn't mean we look related."

"Then tailor him," Kaz said coldly.

The challenge in Kaz's eyes was clear. So he knew she'd been struggling. Of course he did. Dirtyhands never missed a trick.

"I don't want to be tailored," said Matthias. She had no doubt it was true, but she suspected he was also trying to salve her pride.

"You'll be fine," said Jesper, breaking the tension. "Just keep the soulful glances to a minimum and try not to grope each other in public." She should be so lucky.

"Here," Matthias said, handing her the blonde wig she'd used for the Smeet job and a pile of clothes.

"These better be my size," Nina said grumpily. She was tempted to strip down in the middle of the tomb, but she thought Matthias might keel over from the sheer impropriety of it all. She grabbed a lantern and marched into one of the side catacombs to change. She didn't have a mirror, but she could tell the dress was spectacularly dowdy, and she had no words for the little knitted vest. When she emerged from the passage, Jesper doubled over laughing, Kaz's brows shot up, and even Inej's lips twitched.

"Saints," Nina said sourly. "How bad is it?"

Inej cleared her throat. "You do look a bit . . ."

"Enchanting," said Matthias.

Nina was about to snap that she didn't appreciate the sarcasm when she saw the expression on his face. He looked like someone had just given him a tuba full of puppies.

"You could be a maiden on the first day of *Roennigsdjel*."

"What is *Roennigsdjel*?" asked Kuwei.

"Some festival," replied Nina. "I can't remember. But I'm pretty sure it involves eating a lot of elk. Let's go, you big goon—and I'm supposed to be your sister, stop looking at me like that."

"Like what?"

"Like I'm made of ice cream."

"I don't care for ice cream."

"Matthias," Nina said, "I'm not sure we can continue to spend time together." But she couldn't quite keep the satisfaction from her voice. Apparently she was going to have to stock up on ugly knitwear.

Once they were clear of Black Veil, they followed the canals northwest, slipping in with the boats heading to the morning markets near the Stadhall. The Ravkan embassy was at the edge of the government sector, tucked into a wide bend in the canal that backed on a broad thoroughfare. The thoroughfare had once been a marsh but had been filled in and bricked over by a builder who had intended to use the site for a large hotel and parade ground. He had run out of funds before construction could start. Now it was home to a teeming marketplace of wooden stalls and rolling carts that appeared every morning and vanished every evening when the *stadwatch* patrolled. It was where refugees and visitors, new immigrants and old expatriates came to find familiar faces and customs. The few cafés nearby served *pelmeni* and salted herring, and old men sat at the outdoor tables, sipping *kvas* and reading their Ravkan news sheets, weeks out of date.

When Nina had first been stranded in Ketterdam, she'd thought of seeking sanctuary at the embassy, but she was afraid that she'd be sent back home to where she was supposed to be serving in the Second Army. How could she possibly explain that she couldn't return to Ravka until she'd freed a Fjerdan *drüskelle* she'd helped to imprison on false charges? After that, she'd rarely visited Little Ravka. It was just too painful to walk these streets that were so much like home and so unlike home at the same time.

Still, when she glimpsed the golden Lantsov double eagle flying on its pale blue field, her heart leapt like a horse clearing a jump. The market reminded her of Os Kervo, the bustling town that had served as capital to West Ravka before the unification—the embroidered shawls and gleaming samovars, the scent of fresh lamb being cooked on a spit, the woven wool hats, and battered tin icons glinting in the early morning sun. If she ignored the narrow Kerch buildings with their gabled roofs, she could almost pretend she was home. A dangerous illusion. There was no safety to be had on these streets.

Homesick as she was, as Nina and Matthias passed peddlers and merchants, some small, shameful thing inside her cringed at how old-fashioned everything looked. Even the people, clinging to traditional Ravkan dress, looked like relics of another time, objects salvaged from the pages of a folktale. Had the year she'd spent in Ketterdam done this to her? Somehow changed the way she saw her own people and customs? She didn't want to believe that.

As Nina emerged from her thoughts, she realized that she and Matthias were attracting some very unfriendly glances. No doubt there was quite a bit of prejudice against Fjerdans among Ravkans, but this was something different. Then she glanced up at Matthias and sighed. His expression was troubled, and when he looked troubled, he looked terrifying. The fact that he was built like the tank they'd driven out of the Ice Court didn't help either.

"Matthias," she murmured in Fjerdan, giving his arm what she hoped was a friendly, siblinglike nudge, "must you glower at everything?"

"I'm not glowering."

"We're Fjerdans in the Ravkan sector. We already stand out. Let's not give everyone another reason to think you're about to lay siege to the market. We need to get this task done without drawing unwanted attention. Think of yourself as a spy."

His frown deepened. "Such work is beneath an honest soldier."

"Then pretend to be an actor." He made a disgusted sound. "Have you ever even been to the theater?"

"There are plays every season in Djerholm."

"Let me guess, sober affairs that last several hours and tell epic tales of the heroes of yore."

"They're actually very entertaining. But I've never seen an actor who knows how to properly hold his sword."

Nina snorted a laugh.

"What?" Matthias said, perplexed.

"Nothing. Really. Nothing." She'd educate Matthias on innuendo another time. Or maybe she wouldn't. He was so much more fun when he was completely oblivious.

"What are those?" he asked, gesturing to one of the vendors' blankets. It was laden with tidy rows of what looked like sticks and chips of rock.

"Bones," she said. "Fingers, knuckles, vertebrae, broken bits of wrists. Saints' bones. For protection."

Matthias recoiled. "Ravkans carry around human bones?"

"You talk to trees. It's superstition."

"Are they really meant to come from Saints?"

She shrugged. "They're bones sifted from graveyards and battle-grounds. There are plenty of those in Ravka. If people want to believe they're carrying Sankt Egmond's elbow or Sankta Alina's pinky toe—"

"Who decided Alina Starkov was a Saint anyway?" Matthias said grumpily. "She was a powerful Grisha. They're not the same thing."

"Are you so sure?" Nina said, feeling her temper rise. It was one thing for her to think Ravkan customs seemed backward, quite another to have Matthias questioning them. "I've seen the Ice Court for myself now, Matthias. Is it easier to believe that place was fashioned by the hand of a god or by Grisha with gifts your people didn't understand?"

"That's completely different."

"Alina Starkov was our age when she was martyred. She was just a girl, and she sacrificed herself to save Ravka and destroy the Shadow Fold. There are people in your country who worship her as a Saint too."

Matthias frowned. "It's not—"

"If you say natural, I'll give you giant buck teeth."

"Can you actually do that?"

"I can certainly try." She wasn't being fair. Ravka was home to her; it was still enemy territory to Matthias. He might have found a way to accept her, but asking him to accept an entire nation and its culture was going to take a lot more work. "Maybe I should have come alone. You could go wait by the boat."

He stiffened. "Absolutely not. You have no idea what might be waiting for you. The Shu may have already gotten to your friends."

Nina did not want to think about that. "Then you need to calm down and try to look friendly."

Matthias shook out his arms and relaxed his features.

"Friendly, not sleepy. Just . . . pretend everyone you meet is a kitten you're trying not to scare."

Matthias looked positively affronted. "Animals love me."

"Fine. Pretend they're toddlers. Shy toddlers who will wet themselves if you're not nice."

"Very well, I'll try."

As they approached the next stall, the old woman tending to it looked up at Matthias with suspicious eyes. Nina nodded encouragingly at him.

Matthias smiled broadly and boomed in a singsong voice, "Hello, little friend!"

The woman went from wary to baffled. Nina decided to call it an improvement.

"And how are you today?" Matthias asked.

"Pardon?" the woman said.

"Nothing," Nina said in Ravkan. "He was saying how beautifully the Ravkan women age."

The woman gave a gap-toothed grin and ran her eyes up and down Matthias in an appraising fashion. "Always had a taste for Fjerdans. Ask him if he wants to play Princess and Barbarian," she said with a cackle.

"What did she say?" asked Matthias.

Nina coughed and took his arm, leading him away. "She said you're a very nice fellow, and a credit to the Fjerdan race. Ooh, look, blini! I haven't had proper blini in forever."

"That word she used: *babink*," he said. "You've called me that before. What does it mean?"

Nina directed her attention to a stack of paper-thin buttered pancakes. "It means sweetie pie."

"Nina—"

"Barbarian."

"I was just asking, there's no need to name-call."

"No, *babink* means barbarian." Matthias' gaze snapped back to the old woman, his glower returning to full force. Nina grabbed his arm. It was like trying to hold on to a boulder. "She wasn't insulting you! I swear!"

"Barbarian isn't an insult?" he asked, voice rising.

"No. Well, yes. But not in this context. She wanted to know if you'd like to play Princess and Barbarian."

"It's a game?"

"Not exactly."

"Then what is it?"

Nina couldn't believe she was actually going to attempt to explain this. As they continued up the street, she said, "In Ravka, there's a popu-lar series of stories about, um, a brave Fjerdan warrior—"

"Really?" Matthias asked. "He's the hero?"

"In a manner of speaking. He kidnaps a Ravkan princess—"

"That would never happen."

"In the story it does, and"—she cleared her throat—"they spend a long time getting to know each other. In his cave."

"He lives in a cave?"

"It's a very nice cave. Furs. Jeweled cups. Mead."

"Ah," he said approvingly. "A treasure hoard like Ansgar the Mighty. They become allies, then?"

Nina picked up a pair of embroidered gloves from another stand. "Do you like these? Maybe we could get Kaz to wear something with flowers. Liven up his look."

"How does the story end? Do they fight battles?"

Nina tossed the gloves back on the pile in defeat. "They get to know each other *intimately*."

Matthias' jaw dropped. "In the cave?"

"You see, he's very brooding, very manly," Nina hurried on. "But he falls in love with the Ravkan princess and that allows her to civilize him—"

"To *civilize* him?"

"Yes, but that's not until the third book."

"There are three?"

"Matthias, do you need to sit down?"

"This culture is disgusting. The idea that a Ravkan could civilize a Fjerdan—"

"Calm down, Matthias."

"Perhaps I'll write a story about insatiable Ravkans who like to get drunk and take their clothes off and make unseemly advances toward hapless Fjerdans."

"Now *that* sounds like a party." Matthias shook his head, but she could see a smile tugging at his lips. She decided to push the advantage. "*We* could play," she murmured, quietly enough so that no one around them could hear.

"We most certainly could not."

"At one point he bathes her."

Matthias' steps faltered. "Why would he—"

"She's tied up, so he has to."

"Be silent."

"Already giving orders. That's very barbarian of you. Or we could mix it up. I'll be the barbarian and you can be the princess. But you'll have to do a lot more sighing and trembling and biting your lip."

"How about I bite *your* lip?"

"Now you're getting the hang of it, Helvar."

"You're trying to distract me."

"I am. And it's working. You haven't so much as glared at anyone for almost two blocks. And look, we're here."

"Now what?" Matthias asked, scanning the crowd.

They'd arrived at a somewhat ramshackle-looking tavern. A man stood out front with a wheeled cart, selling the usual icons and small statues of Sankta Alina rendered in the new style—Alina with fist raised, rifle in hand, the crushed bodies of winged volcra beneath her boots. An inscription at the statue's base read *Rebe dva Volkshiya*, Daughter of the People.

"Can I help you?" the man asked in Ravkan.

"Good health to young King Nikolai," Nina replied in Ravkan. "Long may he reign."

"With a light heart," the man replied.

"And a heavy fist," said Nina, completing the code.

The peddler glanced over his shoulder. "Take the second table to your left as you enter. Order if you like. Someone will be with you shortly."

The tavern was cool and dark after the brightness of the plaza, and Nina had to blink to make out the interior. The floor was sprinkled with sawdust and at a few of the small tables, people were gathered in conversation over glasses of *kvas* and dishes of herring.

Nina and Matthias took a seat at the empty table.

The tavern door slammed shut behind them. Immediately, the other customers shoved away from their tables, chairs clattering to the floor, guns pointed at Nina and Matthias. *A trap.*

Without pausing to think, Nina and Matthias leapt to their feet and positioned themselves back to back, ready to fight—Matthias with pistol raised and Nina with hands up.

From the back of the tavern, a hooded girl emerged, her collar drawn up to cover most of her face. "Come quietly," she said, golden eyes flashing in the dim light. "There's no need for a fight."

"Then why all the guns?" Nina asked, stalling for time.

The girl lifted her hand and Nina felt her pulse beginning to drop.

"She's a Heartrender!" Nina shouted.

Matthias yanked something from his pocket. Nina heard a pop and a *whoosh*, and a moment later the air filled with a dark red haze. Had Wylan made a duskbomb for Matthias? It was a *drüskelle* technique for obscuring the sight of Grisha Heartrenders. In the cover of the haze, Nina flexed her fingers, hoping her power would respond. She felt nothing from the bodies surrounding them, no life, no movement.

But from the edges of her consciousness she sensed something else, a different kind of awareness, a pocket of cold in a deep lake, a bracing shock that seemed to wake her cells. It was familiar—she'd felt something similar when she'd brought down the guard the night they'd kidnapped Alys, but this was much stronger. It had shape and texture. She let herself dive into the cold, reaching for that sense of wakefulness blindly, greedily, and arced her arms forward in a movement that was as much instinct as skill.

The tavern windows crashed inward in a hail of glass. Fragments of bone shot through the air, peppering the armed men like shrapnel. *The relics from the vendors' carts*, Nina realized in a flash of understanding. She'd somehow controlled the bones.

"They have reinforcements!" one of the men yelled.

"Open fire!"

Nina braced for the impact of the bullets, but in the next second she felt herself yanked off her feet. One moment she was standing on the floor of the tavern and the next her back was slamming against the roof beams as she gazed down at the sawdust far below. All around her, the men who'd attacked her and Matthias hung aloft, also pinned to the ceiling.

A young woman stood at the doorway to the kitchen, black hair shining nearly blue in the dim light.

"Zoya?" Nina gasped as she stared down, trying to catch her breath.

Zoya stepped into the light, a vision in sapphire silk, her cuffs and hem embroidered in dense whorls of silver. Her heavily lashed eyes widened. "Nina?" Zoya's concentration wavered, and they all dropped a foot through the air before she tossed her hands up and they were once more slammed against the beams.

Zoya stared up at Nina in wonder. "You're alive," she said. Her gaze slid to Matthias, thrashing like the biggest, angriest butterfly ever pinned to a page. "And you've made a new friend."

14

WYLAN

Wylan hadn't been on a browboat of this size since he'd tried to leave the city six months ago, and it was hard not to remember that disaster now, especially when thoughts of his father were so fresh in his mind. But this boat was considerably different from the one he'd tried to take that night. This browboat ran the market line twice a day. Inbound, it would be crowded with vegetables, livestock, whatever farmers were bringing to the market squares scattered around the city. As a child, he'd thought everything came from Ketterdam, but he'd soon learned that, though just about anything could be had in the city, little of it was produced there. The city got its exotics—mangoes; dragon fruit; small, fragrant pineapples—from the Southern Colonies. For more ordinary fare, they relied on the farms that surrounded the city.

Jesper and Wylan caught an outbound boat crammed with immigrants fresh from the Ketterdam harbor and laborers looking for farmwork instead of the manufacturing jobs offered in the city. Unfortunately, they'd boarded far enough south that all the seats were already taken, and Jesper was looking positively sulky about it.

"Why can't we take the Belendt line?" Jesper had complained only hours before. "It goes past Olendaal. The boats on the market line are filthy and there's never any place to sit."

"Because you two will stand out on the Belendt line. Here in Ketterdam, you're nothing to look at—assuming Jesper doesn't wear one of his brighter plaids. But give me one good reason other than farmwork you'd see a Shu and a Zemeni traipsing around the countryside."

Wylan hadn't considered how conspicuous he might be outside the city with his new face. But he was secretly relieved Kaz didn't want them on the Belendt line. It might have been more comfortable, but the memories would have been too much on the day he would finally see where his mother had been laid to rest.

"Jesper," Kaz had said, "keep your weapons hidden and your eyes open. Van Eck has to have people watching all the major transportation hubs, and we don't have time to fake up identification for Wylan. I'll get the corrosive from one of the shipyards on Imperjum. Your first priority is to find the quarry and get the other mineral we need for the auric acid. You go to Saint Hilde if and only if there's time."

Wylan felt his chin lift, that simmering, stubborn feeling overtaking him. "I need to do this. I've never been to my mother's grave. I'm not leaving Kerch without saying goodbye."

"Trust me, you care more than she does."

"How can you say that? Don't you remember your mother and father at all?"

"My mother is Ketterdam. She birthed me in the harbor. And my father is profit. I honor him daily. Be back by nightfall or don't come back at all. Either of you. I need crew, not sentimental nubs." Kaz handed Wylan the travel money. "Make sure *you* buy the tickets. I don't want Jesper wandering off to take a spin at Makker's Wheel."

"This song is getting old," muttered Jesper.

"Then learn a new refrain."

Jesper had just shaken his head, but Wylan could tell Kaz's barbs still stung. Now Wylan looked at Jesper leaning back on the railing, eyes shut, profile turned to the weak spring sun.

"Don't you think we should be more cautious?" Wylan asked, his own face buried in the collar of his coat. They'd barely dodged two *stadwatch* as they'd boarded.

"We're already out of the city. Relax."

Wylan glanced over his shoulder. "I thought they might search the boat."

Jesper opened one eye and said, "And hold up traffic? Van Eck's already making trouble at the harbors. If he jams up the browboats, there'll be a riot."

"Why?"

"Look around. The farms need laborers. The plants need workers. The Kerch will only abide so much inconvenience for a rich man's son, especially when there's money to be made."

Wylan tried to make himself relax and unbuttoned the roughspun coat Kaz had obtained for him. "Where does he get all the clothes and uniforms from anyway? Does he just have a giant closet somewhere?"

"Come here."

Warily, Wylan sidled closer. Jesper reached for his collar and flipped it, giving it a tug so Wylan could twist around and just make out a blue ribbon pinned there.

"This is how actors mark their costumes," Jesper said. "This one belonged to . . . Josep Kikkert. Oh, he's not bad. I saw him in *The Madman Takes a Bride*."

"Costumes?"

Jesper flipped the collar back, and as he did, his fingers brushed against the nape of Wylan's neck. "Yup. Kaz cut a secret entrance into the wardrobe rooms of the Stadlied opera house years ago. That's where he gets a lot of what he needs and where he stashes the rest. Means he can never be caught with a fake *stadwatch* uniform or house livery in a raid."

Wylan supposed it made sense. He watched the sunlight flashing off the water for a while, then focused on the railing and said, "Thanks for coming with me today."

"Kaz wasn't going to let you go by yourself. Besides, I owe you. You came with me to meet my dad at the university, and you stepped in when he started getting inquisitive."

"I don't like lying."

Jesper turned around, balancing his elbows on the railing and gazing out at the grassy banks that sloped down to the canal. "So why did you do it?"

Wylan didn't really know why he'd made up that crazy story about luring Jesper into a bad investment. He hadn't even been totally sure what he was going to say when he opened his mouth. He just couldn't stand to see Jesper—confident, smiling Jesper—with that lost look on his face, or the terrible mix of hope and fear in Colm Fahey's gaze as he waited for an answer from his son. It reminded Wylan too much of the way his own father had looked at him, back when he'd still believed Wylan could be cured or fixed. He didn't want to see the expression in Jesper's father's eyes change from worry to anguish to anger.

Wylan shrugged. "I'm making a habit of rescuing you. For exercise."

Jesper released a guffaw that had Wylan looking frantically over his shoulder again, afraid of drawing attention.

But Jesper's mirth was short-lived. He shifted his position at the rail, scrubbed his hand over the back of his neck, fiddled with the brim of his hat. He was always in motion, like a lanky piece of clockwork that ran on invisible energy. Except clocks were simple. Wylan could only guess at Jesper's workings.

At last Jesper said, "I should have gone to see him today."

Wylan knew he was talking about Colm. "Why didn't you?"

"I have no idea what to say to him."

"Is the truth out of the question?"

"Let's just say I'd rather avoid it."

Wylan looked back at the water. He'd started to think of Jesper as fearless, but maybe being brave didn't mean being unafraid. "You can't run from this forever."

"Watch me."

Another farmhouse slid by, little more than a white shape in the early morning mist, lilies and tulips stippling the fields before it in fractured constellations. Maybe Jesper could keep running. If Kaz kept coming along with miracle scores, maybe Jesper could always stay one step ahead.

"I wish I'd brought flowers for her," Wylan said. "Something."

"We can pick some on the way," said Jesper, and Wylan knew he was seizing the change in subject with both hands. "Do you remember her much?"

Wylan shook his head. "I remember her curls. They were the most beautiful reddish gold."

"Same as yours," said Jesper. "Before."

Wylan felt his cheeks pink for no good reason. Jesper was just stating a fact, after all.

He cleared his throat. "She liked art and music. I think I remember sitting at the piano bench with her. But it might have been a nanny." Wylan lifted his shoulders. "One day she was sick and going to the country so her lungs could recover, and then she was gone."

"What about the funeral?"

"My father told me she'd been buried at the hospital. That was all. We just stopped talking about her. He said it didn't pay to dwell on the past. I don't know. I think he really loved her. They fought all the time, sometimes about me, but I remember them laughing a lot together too."

"I have trouble imagining your father laughing, even smiling. Unless he's rubbing his hands together and cackling over a pile of gold."

"He isn't evil."

"He tried to kill you."

"No, he destroyed our ship. Killing me would have been an added benefit." That wasn't entirely true, of course. Jesper wasn't the only one trying to keep a step ahead of his demons.

"Oh, then you're absolutely right," said Jesper. "Not evil at all. I'm sure he also had good reasons for not letting you grieve for your mother."

Wylan tugged at a thread unraveling from the sleeve of his coat. "It wasn't all his fault. My father seemed sad most of the time. And far away. That was around the same time he realized I wasn't . . . what he'd hoped for."

"How old were you?"

"Eight, maybe? I'd gotten really good at hiding it."

"How?"

A faint smile touched Wylan's lips. "He would read to me or I'd ask one of the nannies to, and I'd memorize whatever they said. I even knew when to pause and turn the pages."

"How much could you remember?"

"A lot. I sort of set the words to music in my head like songs. I still do it sometimes. I'll just claim I can't read someone's writing and get them to read the words aloud, set it all to a melody. I can hold it in my head until I need it."

"Don't suppose you could apply that skill to card counting."

"Probably. But I'm not going to."

"Misspent gifts."

"You're one to talk."

Jesper scowled. "Let's enjoy the scenery."

There wasn't much to look at yet. Wylan realized how tired he felt. He wasn't used to this life of fear, moving from one moment of worry to the next.

He thought about telling Jesper how it had all started. Would it be a relief to have the whole shameful story out in the open? Maybe. But some part of him wanted Jesper and the others to keep believing that he'd left his father's house intending to set up in the Barrel, that he'd chosen this life.

As Wylan got older, Jan Van Eck had made it increasingly clear that there was no place for his son in his household, especially after his marriage to Alys. But he didn't seem to know what to do with Wylan. He took to making pronouncements about his son, each one more dire than the last.

You can't be sent to seminary because you can't read.

I can't apprentice you somewhere because you may reveal yourself to be defective.

You are like food that spoils too easily. I can't even put you on a shelf somewhere to keep without making a stink.

Then, six months ago, Wylan's father had summoned him to his office. "I've secured you a position at the music school in Belendt. A personal secretary has been hired on and will meet you at the school. He will handle any mail or business beyond your capabilities. It is a ridiculous waste of both money and time, but I must accept what is possible where you are concerned."

"For how long?" Wylan had asked.

His father shrugged. "As long as it takes people to forget I had a son. Oh, don't look at me with that wounded expression, Wylan. I am honest, not cruel. This is best for both of us. You'll be spared the impossible task of trying to step into the role of a merchant's son, and I'll be spared the embarrassment of watching you attempt it."

I treat you no more harshly than the world will. That was his father's refrain. Who else would be so frank with him? Who else loved him enough to tell him the truth? Wylan had happy memories of his father reading him stories—dark tales of forests full of witches and rivers that spoke. Jan Van Eck had done his best to care for his son, and if he'd failed, then the defect lay with Wylan. His father might sound cruel, but he wasn't just protecting himself or the Van Eck empire, he was protecting Wylan as well.

And everything he said made perfect sense. Wylan could not be trusted with a fortune because he would be too easily swindled. Wylan could not go to university because he'd be the target of mockery. *This is best for both of us.* His father's ire had been unpleasant, but it was his logic that haunted Wylan—that practical, irrefutable voice that spoke in Wylan's head whenever he thought about attempting something new, or trying to learn to read again.

It had hurt to be sent away, but Wylan had still been hopeful. A life in Belendt sounded magical to him. He didn't know much about it other than that it was the second-oldest city in Kerch and located on the shores of the Droombeld River. But he'd be far away from his father's friends and business associates. Van Eck was a common enough name, and that far from Ketterdam, being a Van Eck wouldn't mean being one of *those* Van Ecks.

His father handed him a sealed envelope and a small stack of *kruge* for travel money. "These are your enrollment papers, and enough money to see you to Belendt. Once you're there, have your secretary see the bursar. An account has been opened in your name. I've also arranged for chaperones to travel with you on the browboat."

Wylan's cheeks had flooded red with humiliation. "I can get to Belendt."

"You've never traveled outside Ketterdam on your own, and this is not the time to start. Miggson and Prior have business to see to for me in Belendt. They'll escort you there and ensure that you're successfully situated. Understood?"

Wylan understood. He was unfit to even board a boat out of the city by himself.

But things would be different in Belendt. He packed a small suitcase with a change of clothes and the few things he would need before his trunks arrived at the school, along with his favorite pieces of sheet music. If he could read letters as well as he read a tablature, he'd have no problems at all. When his father had stopped reading to him, music had given him new stories, ones that unfolded from his fingers, that he could write himself into with every played note. He tucked his flute into his satchel, in case he wanted to practice on the trip.

His goodbye to Alys had been brief and awkward. She was a nice girl, but that was the whole problem—she was only a few years older than Wylan. He wasn't sure how his father could walk down the street beside her without shame. But Alys didn't seem to mind, maybe because around her, his father became the man Wylan remembered from his childhood— kind, generous, patient.

Even now, Wylan could not name the specific moment when he knew his father had given up on him. The change had been slow. Jan Van Eck's patience had worn quietly away like gold plate over cruder metal, and when it was gone, it was as if his father had become someone else entirely, someone with far less luster.

"I wanted to say goodbye and wish you well," Wylan said to Alys. She had been seated in her parlor, her terrier dozing at her feet.

"Are you going away?" she asked, looking up from her sewing and noticing his bag. She was hemming curtains. Kerch women—even the wealthy ones—didn't bother with anything as frivolous as embroidery or needlepoint. Ghezen was better served by tasks that benefited the household.

"I'll be traveling to the music school at Belendt."

"Oh, how wonderful!" Alys had cried. "I miss the country so much. You'll be so glad of the fresh air, and you're sure to make excellent friends." She'd set down her needle and kissed both his cheeks. "Will you come back for the holidays?"

"Perhaps," Wylan said, though he knew he wouldn't. His father wanted him to disappear, so he would disappear.

"We'll make gingerbread then," Alys said. "You will tell me all your adventures, and soon we'll have a new friend to play with." She patted her belly with a happy smile.

It had taken Wylan a moment to understand what she meant, and then he'd just stood there, clutching his suitcase, nodding his head, smiling mechanically as Alys talked about their holiday plans. Alys was pregnant. That was why his father was sending him away. Jan Van Eck was to have another heir, a proper heir. Wylan had become expendable. He would vanish from the city, take up occupation elsewhere. Time would pass and no one would raise a brow when Alys' child was groomed to be the head of the Van Eck empire. *As long as it takes people to forget I had a son.* That hadn't been an idle insult.

Miggson and Prior arrived at eight bells to see Wylan to the boat. No one came to say a last goodbye, and when he'd walked past his father's office, the door was closed. Wylan refused to knock and plead for a scrap of affection like Alys' terrier begging for treats.

His father's men wore the dark suits favored by merchants and said little to Wylan on the walk over to the dock. They purchased tickets for the Belendt line, and once they were aboard the boat, Miggson had buried his head in a newspaper while Prior leaned back in his seat, hat tilted downward, lids not quite closed. Wylan couldn't be sure if the man was sleeping or staring at him like some kind of drowsy-eyed lizard.

The boat was nearly empty at that hour. People dozed in the stuffy cabin or ate whatever dinner they'd packed, ham rolls and insulated flasks of coffee balanced on their laps.

Unable to sleep, Wylan had left the heat of the cabin and walked to the prow of the boat. The winter air was cold and smelled of the slaughter-houses on the outskirts of the city. It turned Wylan's stomach, but soon the lights would fade and they'd be in the open country. He was sorry they weren't traveling by day. He would have liked to see the windmills keeping watch over their fields, the sheep grazing in their pastures. He sighed, shivering in his coat, and adjusted the strap of his satchel. He should try to rest. Maybe he could wake up early and watch the sunrise.

When he turned, Prior and Miggson were standing behind him.

"Sorry," Wylan said. "I—" And then Prior's hands were tight around his throat.

Wylan gasped—or he tried to; the sound that came from him was barely a croak. He clawed at Prior's wrists, but the man's grip was like iron, the pressure relentless. He was big enough that Wylan could feel himself being lifted slightly as Prior pushed him against the railing.

Prior's face was dispassionate, nearly bored, and Wylan understood then that he would never reach the school in Belendt. He'd never been meant to. There was no secretary. No account in his name. No one was expecting his arrival. The supposed enrollment papers in his pocket might say anything at all. Wylan hadn't even bothered to try to read them. He was going to disappear, just as his father had always wanted, and he'd hired these men to do the job. His father who had read him to sleep at night, who'd brought him sweet mallow tea and honeycomb when he'd been sick with lung fever. *As long as it takes people to forget I had a son.* His father was going to erase him from the ledger, a mistaken calculation, a cost that could be expunged. The tally would be made right.

Black spots filled Wylan's vision. He thought he could hear music.

"You there! What's going on?"

The voice seemed to come from a great distance. Prior's grip loosened very slightly. Wylan's toes made contact with the deck of the boat.

"Nothing at all," said Miggson, turning to face the stranger. "We just caught this fellow looking through the other passengers' belongings."

Wylan made a choked sound.

"Shall I . . . shall I fetch the *stadwatch* then? There are two officers in the cabin."

"We've already alerted the captain," said Miggson. "We'll be dropping him at the *stadwatch* post at the next stop."

"Well, I'm glad you fellows were being so vigilant." The man turned to go.

The boat lurched slightly. Wylan wasn't going to wait to see what happened next. He shoved against Prior with all his might—then, before he could lose his nerve, he dove over the side of the boat and into the murky canal.

He swam with every bit of speed he could muster. He was still dizzy and his throat ached badly. To his shock, he heard another splash and knew one of the men had dived in after him. If Wylan showed up somewhere still breathing, Miggson and Prior probably wouldn't get paid.

He changed his stroke, making as little noise as possible, and forced himself to think. Instead of heading straight to the side of the canal the way his freezing body longed to, he dove under a nearby market barge and came up on its other side, swimming along with it, using it as cover. The dead weight of his satchel pulled hard at his shoulders, but he couldn't make himself relinquish it. *My things*, he thought nonsensically, *my flute*. He didn't stop, not even when his breathing grew ragged and his limbs started to turn numb. He forced himself to drive onward, to put as much distance as he could between himself and his father's thugs.

But eventually, his strength started to give out and he realized he was doing more thrashing than swimming. If he didn't get to shore, he would drown. He paddled toward the shadows of a bridge and dragged himself from the canal, then huddled, soaked and shaking in the icy cold. His bruised throat scraped each time he swallowed, and he was terrified that every splash he heard was Prior coming to finish the job.

He needed to make some kind of plan, but it was hard to form whole thoughts. He checked his trouser pockets. He still had the *kruge* his father had given him tucked safely away. Though the cash was wet through, it was perfectly good for spending. But where was Wylan supposed to go? He didn't have enough money to get out of the city, and if his father sent men looking for him, he'd be easily tracked. He needed to get somewhere safe, someplace his father wouldn't think to look. His limbs felt weighted with lead, the cold giving way to fatigue. He was afraid that if he let himself close his eyes, he wouldn't have the will to open them again.

In the end, he'd simply started walking. He wandered north through the city, away from the slaughterhouses, past a quiet residential area where lesser tradesmen lived, then onward, the streets becoming more crooked and more narrow, until the houses seemed to crowd in on him. Despite the late hour, there were lights in every window and shop front. Music spilled out of run-down cafés, and he glimpsed bodies pressed up against each other in the alleys.

"Someone dunk you, lad?" called an old man with a shortage of teeth from a stoop.

"I'll give him a good dunking!" crowed a woman leaning on the stairs.

He was in the Barrel. Wylan had lived his whole life in Ketterdam, but he'd never come here. He'd never been allowed to. He'd never *wanted* to. His father called it a "filthy den of vice and blasphemy" and "the shame of the city." Wylan knew it was a warren of dark streets and hidden passages. A place where locals donned costumes and performed unseemly acts, where foreigners crowded the thoroughfares seeking vile entertainments, where people came and went like tides. The perfect place to disappear.

And it had been—until the day the first of his father's letters had arrived.

With a start, Wylan realized Jesper was pulling at his sleeve. "This is our stop, merchling. Look lively."

Wylan hurried after him. They disembarked at the empty dock at Olendaal and walked up the embankment to a sleepy village road.

Jesper looked around. "This place reminds me of home. Fields as far as the eye can see, quiet broken by nothing but the hum of bees, fresh air." He shuddered. "Disgusting."

As they walked, Jesper helped him gather wildflowers from the side of the road. By the time they'd made it to the main street, he had a respectable little bunch.

"I guess we need to find a way to the quarry?" Jesper said.

Wylan coughed. "No we don't, just a general store."

"But you told Kaz the mineral—"

"It's present in all kinds of paints and enamels. I wanted to make sure I had a reason to go to Olendaal."

"Wylan Van Eck, you lied to *Kaz Brekker*." Jesper clutched a hand to his chest. "And you got away with it! Do you give lessons?"

Wylan felt ridiculously pleased—until he thought about Kaz finding out. Then he felt a little like the first time he'd tried brandy and ended up spewing his dinner all over his own shoes.

They located a general store halfway up the main street, and it took them only a few moments to purchase what they needed. On the way out, a man loading up a wagon exchanged a wave with them. "You boys looking for work?" he asked skeptically. "Neither of you looks up to a full day in the field."

"You'd be surprised," said Jesper. "We signed on to do some work out near Saint Hilde."

Wylan waited, nervous, but the man just nodded. "You doing repairs at the hospital?"

"Yup," Jesper said easily.

"Your friend there don't talk much."

"Shu," said Jesper with a shrug.

The older man gave some kind of grunt in agreement and said, "Hop on in. I'm going out to the quarry. I can take you to the gates. What are the flowers for?"

"He has a sweetheart out near Saint Hilde."

"Some sweetheart."

"I'll say. He has terrible taste in women."

Wylan considered shoving Jesper off the wagon.

The dirt road was bordered on each side by what looked like barley and wheat fields, the flat expanses of land dotted occasionally by barns and windmills. The wagon kept up a fast clip. *A little too fast*, Wylan thought as they jounced over a deep rut. He hissed in a breath.

"Rains," said the farmer. "No one's got around to laying sand yet."

"That's okay," said Jesper with a wince as the wagon hit another bone-rattling divot in the ground. "I don't really need my spleen in one piece."

The farmer laughed. "It's good for you! Jogs the liver!"

Wylan clutched his side, wishing he'd shoved Jesper out of the wagon after all and jumped right down with him. Luckily, only a mile later, the wagon slowed before two stone posts that marked a long gravel drive.

"This is as far as I go," said the farmer. "Not a place I want truck with. Too much suffering. Sometimes when the wind blows right, you can hear 'em, laughing and shrieking."

Jesper and Wylan exchanged a glance.

"You saying it's haunted?" asked Jesper.

"I suppose."

They said their thanks and gratefully slid down to the ground. "When you're done here, head up the road a couple miles," said the driver. "I got two acres still need working. Five *kruge* a day and you can sleep in the barn instead of out in the field."

"Sounds promising," said Jesper with a wave, but as they turned to make their way up the road to the church, he grumbled, "We're walking back. I think I bruised a rib."

When the driver was gone from view, they shrugged out of their coats and caps to reveal the dark suits Kaz had suggested they wear underneath, and tucked them behind a tree stump. "Tell them you were sent by Cornelis Smeet," Kaz had said. "That you want to make sure the grave is being well maintained for Mister Van Eck."

"Why?" Wylan had asked.

"Because if you claim to be Jan Van Eck's son, no one is going to believe you."

The road was lined with poplars, and as they crested the hill, a building came into view: three stories of white stone fronted by low, graceful stairs leading to an arched front door. The drive was neatly laid with gravel and bordered by low yew hedges on either side.

"Doesn't look like a church," said Jesper.

"Maybe it used to be a monastery or a school?" Wylan suggested. He listened to the gravel crunch beneath his shoes. "Jesper, do you remember much about your mother?"

Wylan had seen a lot of different smiles from Jesper, but the one that spread across his face now was new, slow, and as closely held as a winning hand. All he said was, "Yeah. She taught me to shoot."

There were a hundred questions Wylan wanted to ask, but the closer they drew to the church, the less he seemed able to capture a thought and hold it. On the left of the building, he could see an arbor covered with new-blooming wisteria, the sweet scent of the purple blossoms heavy on the spring air. A little past the church's lawn and to the right, he saw a wrought-iron gate and a fence surrounding a graveyard, a tall stone figure at its center—a woman, Wylan guessed, probably Saint Hilde.

"That must be the cemetery," Wylan said, clutching his flowers tighter. *What am I doing here?* There was that question again, and suddenly he didn't know. Kaz had been right. This was stupid, sentimental. What good would seeing a gravestone with his mother's name on it do? He wouldn't even be able to read it. But they'd come all this way.

"Jesper—" he began, but at that moment a woman in gray work clothes rounded the corner pushing a wheelbarrow mounded with earth.

"*Goed morgen*," she called to them. "Can I help you?"

"And a fine morning it is," said Jesper smoothly. "We come to you from the offices of Cornelis Smeet."

She frowned and Wylan added, "On behalf of the esteemed Councilman Jan Van Eck."

Apparently she didn't notice the quaver in his voice, because her brow cleared and she smiled. Her cheeks were round and rosy. "Of course. But I confess to being surprised. Mister Van Eck has been so generous with us, yet we hear from him so rarely. Nothing's wrong, is it?"

"Not at all!" said Wylan.

"Just a new policy," said Jesper. "More work for everyone."

"Isn't that always the way?" The woman smiled again. "And I see you brought flowers?"

Wylan looked down at the bouquet. It seemed smaller and more straggly than he'd thought. "We . . . yes."

She wiped her hands on her shapeless smock and said, "I'll take you to her."

But instead of turning in the direction of the graveyard, she headed back toward the entrance. Jesper shrugged, and they followed. As they made their way up the low stone steps, something cold crawled over Wylan's spine.

"Jesper," he whispered. "There are bars on the windows."

"Antsy monks?" Jesper offered, but he was not smiling.

The front parlor was two stories high, its floor set with clean white tiles painted with delicate blue tulips. It looked like no church Wylan had ever seen. The hush in the room was so deep, it felt almost suffocating. A large desk was placed in the corner, and on it was set a vase of the wisteria Wylan had seen outside. He inhaled deeply. The smell was comforting.

The woman unlocked a large cabinet and sifted through it for a moment, then removed a thick file.

"Here we are: Marya Hendriks. As you can see, everything is in order. You can have a look while we get her cleaned up. Next time you can avoid a delay if you notify us ahead of your visit."

Wylan felt an icy sweat break out over his body. He managed a nod.

The woman removed a heavy key ring from the cabinet and unlocked one of the pale blue doors that led out of the parlor. Wylan heard her turn the key in the lock from the other side. He set the wildflowers down on the desk. Their stems were broken. He'd been clutching them too tightly.

"What is this place?" Wylan said. "What did they mean, *get her cleaned up*?" His heart ticked a frantic beat, a metronome set to the wrong rhythm.

Jesper was flipping through the folder, his eyes skimming the pages.

Wylan leaned over his shoulder and felt a hopeless, choking panic grip him. The words on the page were a meaningless scrawl, a black mess of insect legs. He fought for breath. "Jesper, please," he begged, his voice thin and reedy. *"Read it to me."*

"I'm sorry," Jesper said hurriedly. "I forgot. I . . ." Wylan couldn't make sense of the look on Jesper's face—sadness, confusion. "Wylan . . . I think your mother's alive."

"That's impossible."

"Your father had her committed."

Wylan shook his head. That couldn't be. "She got sick. A lung infection—"

"He states that she's a victim of hysteria, paranoia, and persecution disorder."

"She can't be alive. He—he remarried. What about Alys?"

"I think he had your mother declared insane and used it as grounds for divorce. This isn't a church, Wylan. It's an asylum."

Saint Hilde. His father had been sending them money every year—but not as a charitable donation. *For her upkeep. For their silence.* The room was suddenly spinning.

Jesper pulled him into the chair behind the desk and pressed against Wylan's shoulder blades, urging him forward. "Put your head between your knees, focus on the floor. Breathe."

Wylan forced himself to inhale, exhale, to gaze at those charming blue tulips in their white tile boxes. "Tell me the rest."

"You need to calm down or they're going to know something's wrong."

"Tell me the rest."

Jesper blew out a breath and continued to flip through the file. "Son of a bitch," he said after a minute. "There's a Transfer of Authority in the file. It's a copy."

Wylan kept his eyes on the tiled floor. "What? What is that?"

Jesper read, *"This document, witnessed in the full sight of Ghezen and in keeping with the honest dealings of men, made binding by the courts of Kerch and its Merchant Council, signifies the transfer of all property, estates, and legal holdings from Marya Hendriks to Jan Van Eck, to be managed by him until Marya Hendriks is once again competent to conduct her own affairs."*

" 'The transfer of all property,' " Wylan repeated. *What am I doing here? What am I doing here? What is she doing here?*

The key turned in the lock of the pale blue door and the woman—*a nurse*, Wylan realized—sailed back through, smoothing the apron of her smock.

"We're ready for you," she said. "She's quite docile today. Are you all right?"

"My friend's feeling a bit faint. Too much sun after all those hours in Mister Smeet's office. Could we trouble you for a glass of water?"

"Certainly!" said the nurse. "Oh, you do look a bit done under."

She disappeared behind the door again, following the same routine of unlocking and locking it. *She's making sure the patients don't get out.*

Jesper squatted in front of Wylan and put his hands on his shoulders.

"Wy, listen to me. You have to pull yourself together. Can you do this? We can leave. I can tell her you're not up to it, or I can just go in myself. We can try to come back some—"

Wylan took a deep, shuddering breath through his nose. He couldn't fathom what was happening, couldn't understand the scope of it. *So just do one thing at a time.* It was a technique one of his tutors had taught him to try to keep him from getting overwhelmed by the page. It hadn't worked, particularly not when his father was looming over him, but Wylan had managed to apply it elsewhere. *One thing at a time. Stand up.* He stood up. *You're fine.* "I'm fine," he said. "We are not leaving." It was the one thing he was certain of.

When the nurse returned, he accepted the water glass, thanked her, drank. Then he and Jesper followed her through the pale blue door. He couldn't bring himself to gather the wilting wildflowers scattered on the desk. *One thing at a time.*

They walked past locked doors, some kind of exercise room. From somewhere, he heard moaning. In a wide parlor, two women were playing what looked like a game of *ridderspel*.

My mother is dead. She's dead. But nothing in him believed it. Not anymore.

Finally the nurse led them to a glassed-in porch that had been located on the west side of the building so it would capture all the warmth of the sun's setting rays. One full wall was composed of windows, and through them the green spill of the hospital's lawn was visible, the graveyard in the distance. It was a pretty room, the tiled floor spotless. A canvas with the beginnings of a landscape emerging from it leaned on an easel by the window. A memory returned to Wylan: his mother standing at an easel in the back garden of the house on Geldstraat, the smell of linseed oil, clean brushes in an empty glass, her thoughtful gaze assessing the lines of the boathouse and the canal beyond.

"She paints," Wylan said flatly.

"All the time," the nurse said cheerily. "Quite the artist is our Marya."

A woman sat in a wheeled chair, head dipping as if she was fighting not to doze off, blankets piled up around her narrow shoulders. Her face was lined, her hair a faded amber, shot through with gray. *The color of my hair*, Wylan realized, *if it had been left out in the sun to fade.* He felt a surge of relief. This woman was far too old to be his mother. But then her chin lifted and her eyes opened. They were a clear, pure hazel, unchanged, undiminished.

"You have some visitors, Miss Hendriks."

His mother's lips moved, but Wylan couldn't hear what she said.

She looked at them with sharp eyes. Then her expression wavered, became vague and questioning as the certainty left her face. "Should I . . . should I know you?"

Wylan's throat ached. *Would you know me*, he wondered, *if I still looked like your son?* He managed a shake of his head.

"We met . . . we met long ago," he said. "When I was just a child."

She made a humming noise and looked out at the lawn.

Wylan turned helplessly to Jesper. He was not ready for this. His mother was a body long buried, dust in the ground.

Gently, Jesper led him to the chair in front of Marya. "We have an hour before we have to start the walk back," he said quietly. "Talk to her."

"About what?"

"Remember what you said to Kaz? We don't know what may happen next. This is all we've got." Then he rose and crossed to where the nurse was tidying up the paints. "Tell me, Miss . . . I'm ashamed to say I didn't catch your name."

The nurse smiled, her cheeks round and red as candied apples. "Betje."

"A charming name for a charming girl. Mister Smeet asked that I have a look at all the facilities while we're here. Would you mind giving me a quick tour?"

She hesitated, glancing over at Wylan.

"We'll be fine here," Wylan managed in a voice that sounded too loud and too hearty to his ears. "I'll just run through some routine questions. All part of the new policy."

The nurse twinkled at Jesper. "Well then, I think we might have a quick look around."

Wylan studied his mother, his thoughts a jangle of misplayed chords. They'd cut her hair short. He tried to picture her younger, in the fine black wool gown of a mercher's wife, white lace gathered at her collar, her curls thick and vibrant, arranged by a lady's maid into a nautilus of braids.

"Hello," he managed.

"Did you come for my money? I don't have any money."

"I don't either," Wylan said faintly.

She was not familiar, exactly, but there was something in the way she tilted her head, the way she sat, her spine still straight. As if she was at the piano.

"Do you like music?" he asked.

She nodded. "Yes, but there isn't much here."

He pulled the flute from his shirt. He'd traveled the whole day with it tucked up against his chest like some kind of secret, and it was still warm from his body. He'd planned to play it beside her grave like some kind of idiot. How Kaz would have laughed at him.

The first few notes were wobbly, but then he got control of his breath. He found the melody, a simple song, one of the first he'd learned. For a moment, she looked as if she was trying to remember where she might have heard it. Then she simply closed her eyes and listened.

When he was finished, she said, "Play something cheerful."

So he played a Kaelish reel and then a Kerch sea shanty that was better suited to the tin whistle. He played every song that came into his head, but nothing mournful, nothing sad. She didn't speak, though occasionally, he saw her tap her toe to the music, and her lips would move as if she knew the words.

At last he put the flute down in his lap. "How long have you been here?"

She stayed silent.

He leaned forward, seeking some answer in those vague hazel eyes. "What did they do to you?"

She laid a gentle hand on his cheek. Her palm felt cool and dry. "What did they do to you?" He couldn't tell if it was a challenge or if she was just repeating his words.

Wylan felt the painful press of tears in his throat and fought to swallow them.

The door banged open. "Well now, did we have a good visit?" said the nurse as she entered.

Hastily, Wylan tucked the flute back into his shirt. "Indeed," he said. "Everything seems to be in order."

"You two seem awfully young for this type of work," she said, dimpling at Jesper.

"I might say the same for you," he replied. "But you know how it is, the new clerks get stuck with the most menial tasks."

"Will you be back again soon?"

Jesper winked. "You never do know." He nodded at Wylan. "We have a boat to catch."

"Say goodbye, Miss Hendriks!" urged the nurse.

Marya's lips moved, but this time Wylan was close enough to hear what she muttered. *Van Eck.*

On the way out of the hospital, the nurse kept up a steady stream of chatter with Jesper. Wylan walked behind them. His heart hurt. What had his father done to her? Was she truly mad? Or had he simply bribed the right people to say so? Had he drugged her? Jesper glanced back at Wylan once as the nurse gibbered on, his gray eyes concerned.

They were almost to the pale blue door when the nurse said, "Would you like to see her paintings?"

Wylan jerked to a halt. He nodded.

"I think that would be most interesting," said Jesper.

The woman led them back the way they'd come and then opened the door to what appeared to be a closet.

Wylan felt his knees buckle and had to grab the wall for balance. The nurse didn't notice—she was talking on and on. "The paints are expensive, of course, but they seem to bring her so much pleasure. This is just the latest batch. Every six months or so we have to put them on the rubbish heap. There just isn't space for them."

Wylan wanted to scream. The closet was crammed with paintings—landscapes, different views of the hospital grounds, a lake in sun and shadow, and there, repeated again and again, was the face of a little boy with ruddy curls and bright blue eyes.

He must have made some kind of noise, because the nurse turned to him. "Oh dear," she said to Jesper, "your friend's gone quite pale again. Perhaps a stimulant?"

"No, no," said Jesper, putting his arm around Wylan. "But we really should be going. It's been a most enlightening visit."

Wylan didn't register the walk down the drive bordered by yew hedges or retrieving their coats and caps from behind the tree stump near the main road.

They were halfway back to the dock before he could bring himself to speak. "She knows what he did to her. She knows he had no right to take her money, her life." *Van Eck*, she'd said. She was not Marya Hendriks, she was Marya Van Eck, a wife and mother stripped of her name and her fortune. "Remember when I said he wasn't evil?"

Wylan's legs gave out and he sat down hard, right there in the middle of the road, and he couldn't bring himself to care because the tears were coming and there was no way he could stop them. They gusted through his chest in ragged, ugly sobs. He hated that Jesper was seeing him cry, but there was nothing he could do, not about the tears, not about any of it. He buried his face in his arms, covering his head as if, were he to only will it strongly enough, he could vanish.

He felt Jesper squeeze his arm.

"It's okay," Jesper said.

"No, it's not."

"You're right, it's not. It's rotten, and I'd like to string your father up in a barren field and let the vultures have at him."

Wylan shook his head. "You don't understand. It was me. I caused this. He wanted a new wife. He wanted an heir. A real heir, not a moron who can barely spell his own name." He'd been eight when his mother had been sent away. He didn't have to wonder anymore; that was when his father had given up on him.

"Hey," Jesper said, giving him a shake. "*Hey.* Your father could have made a lot of choices when he found out you couldn't read. Hell, he could have said you were blind or that you had trouble with your vision. Or better yet, he could have just been happy about the fact that he had a genius for a son."

"I'm not a genius."

"You're stupid about a lot of things, Wylan, but you are not stupid. And if I ever hear you call yourself a moron again, I'm going to tell Matthias you tried to kiss Nina. With tongue."

Wylan wiped his nose on his sleeve. "He'll never believe it."

"Then I'll tell Nina you tried to kiss Matthias. With tongue." He sighed. "Look, Wylan. Normal people don't wall their wives up in insane asylums. They don't disinherit their sons because they didn't get the child they wanted. You think my dad wanted a mess like me for a kid? You didn't cause this. This happened because your father is a lunatic dressed up in a quality suit."

Wylan pressed the heels of his hands to his swollen eyes. "That's all true, and none of it makes me feel any better."

Jesper gave his shoulder another little shake. "Well, how about this? Kaz is going to tear your father's damn life apart."

Wylan was about to say that didn't help either, but he hesitated. Kaz Brekker was the most brutal, vengeful creature Wylan had ever encountered—and he'd sworn he was going to destroy Jan Van Eck. The thought felt like cool water cascading over the hot, shameful feeling of helplessness he'd been carrying with him for so long. Nothing could make this right, ever. But Kaz could make his father's life very wrong. And Wylan would be rich. He could take his mother from this place. They could go somewhere warm. He could put her in front of a piano, get her to play, take her somewhere full of bright colors and beautiful sounds. They could go to Novyi Zem. They could go anywhere. Wylan lifted his head and wiped away his tears. "Actually, that helps a lot."

Jesper grinned. "Thought it might. But if we don't get on that boat back to Ketterdam, no righteous comeuppance."

Wylan rose, suddenly eager to return to the city, to help bring Kaz's plan to life. He'd gone to the Ice Court reluctantly. He'd aided Kaz grudgingly. Because through all of it, he'd believed that he deserved his father's contempt, and now he could admit that somewhere, in some buried place, he'd hoped there might still be a way back to his father's good favor. Well, his father could keep that good favor and see what it bought him when Kaz Brekker was finished.

"Come on," he said. "Let's go steal all my dad's money."

"Isn't it your money?"

"Okay, let's go steal it back."

They headed off at a run. "I love a little righteous comeuppance," said Jesper. "Jogs the liver!"

15
MATTHIAS

A crowd had gathered outside the tavern, drawn by the sounds of breaking glass and trouble. Zoya lowered Nina and Matthias none-too-gently to the floor, and they were herded quickly out the back of the tavern, surrounded by a small segment of the armed men. The rest remained in the tavern to offer whatever explanations could be given for the fact that a bunch of bones had just flown through the marketplace and shattered the building's windows. Matthias wasn't even sure he understood what had happened. Had Nina controlled those false Saints' relics? Had it been something else altogether? And why had they been attacked?

Matthias thought they would emerge into an alley, but instead they descended a series of ancient-looking steps into a dank tunnel. *The old canal*, Matthias realized as they climbed aboard a boat that passed sound-lessly through the dark. It had been paved over but not entirely filled in. They were traveling beneath the broad thoroughfare that fronted the embassy.

Only a few moments later, Zoya led them up a narrow metal ladder and into a bare room with a ceiling so low Matthias had to bend double. Nina said something to Zoya in Ravkan and then translated Zoya's reply for Matthias. "It's a half room. When the embassy was built, they created a false floor four feet above the original floor. The way it's set into the foundation, it's almost impossible to know there's another room beneath you."

"It's little more than a crawl space."

"Yes, but Ketterdam's buildings don't have basements, so no one would ever think to search below."

It seemed an extreme precaution in what was supposed to be a neutral city, but perhaps the Ravkans had been forced to take extreme measures to protect their citizens. *Because of people like me.* Matthias had been a hunter, a killer, and proud to do his job well.

A moment later, they came upon a group of people huddled together against what Matthias thought might be the eastern wall if he hadn't gotten completely turned around.

"We're under the embassy garden," said Nina.

He nodded. This would be the safest place to keep a group of people if you didn't want to risk voices rising through the embassy floor. There were about fifteen of them, all ages and colors. They seemed to have little in common beyond their wary expressions, but Matthias knew they must all be Grisha. They hadn't needed Nina's warning to seek sanctuary.

"So few?" Matthias said. Nina had estimated the number of Grisha in the city as closer to thirty.

"Maybe the others got out on their own or are just lying low."

Or perhaps they'd already been captured. If Nina did not wish to speak the possibility, he wouldn't either.

Zoya led them through an archway to an area where Matthias was relieved to be able to stand upright. Given the round shape of the room, he suspected they were beneath some kind of false cistern or maybe a folly in the garden. His relief dissolved when one of Zoya's armed men produced a pair of shackles, and Zoya pointed directly at Matthias.

Immediately, Nina stepped in front of him, and she and Zoya began arguing in furious whispers.

Matthias knew exactly who he was dealing with. Zoya Nazyalensky was one of the most powerful witches in Ravka. She was a legendary Squaller, a soldier who had served first the Darkling, then the Sun Summoner, and who had ascended to power as a member of King Nikolai's Grisha Triumvirate. Now that he'd experienced a taste of her abilities for himself, he wasn't surprised at how quickly she'd risen.

The argument was entirely in Ravkan, and Matthias didn't understand a word of it, but the scorn in Zoya's voice was obvious, as were her jabbing gestures toward Matthias and the shackles. He was ready to growl that if the storm witch wanted him locked up, she could try doing it herself and see what happened, when Nina held up her hands.

"No more," she said in Kerch. "Matthias remains free and we continue this conversation in a language we all understand. He has a right to know what's going on."

Zoya's eyes narrowed. She looked from Matthias to Nina and then, in heavily accented Kerch, she said, "Nina Zenik, you are still a soldier of the Second Army, and I am still your commanding officer. You are directly disobeying orders."

"Then you'll just have to put me in chains too."

"Don't think I'm not considering it."

"Nina!" The cry came from a redheaded girl who had appeared in the echoing room.

"Genya!" Nina whooped. But Matthias would have known this woman without any introduction. Her face was covered in scars, and she wore a red silk eye patch embroidered with a golden sunburst. Genya Safin—the renowned Tailor, Nina's former instructor, and another member of the Triumvirate. As Matthias watched them embrace, he felt sick. He'd expected to meet a group of anonymous Grisha, people who had taken refuge in Ketterdam and then found themselves alone and in danger.

People like Nina—not Ravka's highest-ranking Grisha. All his instincts called on him to fight or to be gone from this place as fast as possible, not to stand there like a suitor meeting his beloved's parents. And yet, these were Nina's friends, her teachers. *They're the enemy*, said a voice in his head, and he wasn't sure if it was Commander Brum's or his own.

Genya stepped back, brushing the blonde strands of Nina's wig from her face to get a better look at her. "Nina, how is this possible? The last time Zoya saw you—"

"You were throwing a tantrum," said Zoya, "stomping away from camp with all the caution of a wayward moose."

To Matthias' surprise, Nina actually winced like a child taking a scolding. He didn't think he'd ever seen her embarrassed before.

"We thought you were dead," Genya said.

"She looks half-dead."

"She looks fine."

"You vanished," Zoya spat. "When we heard there were Fjerdans nearby, we feared the worst."

"The worst happened," Nina said. "And then it happened some more." She took Matthias' hand. "But we're here now."

Zoya glared at their clasped hands and crossed her arms. "I see."

Genya raised an auburn brow. "Well, if *he's* the worst that can happen—"

"What are you doing here?" Zoya demanded. "Are you and your Fjerdan . . . accessory trying to get out of Ketterdam?"

"What if we were? Why did you ambush us?"

"There have been attacks on Grisha all over the city. We didn't know who you were or if you might be colluding with the Shu, only that you used the code on the peddler. We always station soldiers in the tavern now. Anyone looking for Grisha is a potential threat."

Given what Matthias had seen of the new Shu soldiers, they were right to be wary.

"We came to offer our help," Nina said.

"What kind of help? You have no idea what forces are at work here, Nina. The Shu have developed a drug—"

"*Jurda parem.*"

"What do you know about *parem?*"

Nina squeezed Matthias' hand. She took a deep breath. "I've seen it used. I've . . . experienced it myself."

Genya's single amber eye widened. "Oh, Nina, no. You didn't."

"Of course she did," said Zoya. "You've always been like this! You sink into trouble like it's a warm bath. Is this why you look like second-day gruel? How could you take a risk like that, Nina?"

"I do not look like gruel," Nina protested, but she had that same chastened look on her face. Matthias couldn't stand it.

"She did it to save our lives," he said. "She did it knowing she might be dooming herself to misery and even death."

"Reckless," Zoya declared.

"Zoya," said Genya. "We don't know the circumstances—"

"We know that she's been missing nearly a year." She pointed an accusing finger at Nina. "And now she shows up with a Fjerdan in tow, one built like a soldier and who uses *drüskelle* fighting techniques." Zoya reached into her pocket and pulled out a handful of bones. "She attacked our soldiers with these, with *bone shards*, Genya. Have you ever heard of such a thing being possible?"

Genya stared at the bones and then at Nina. "Is this true?"

Nina pressed her lips together. "Possibly?"

"*Possibly,*" said Zoya. "And you're telling me we should just trust her?"

Genya looked less certain but said, "I'm telling you we should listen."

"All right," said Zoya. "I wait with open ears and a ready heart. Entertain me, Nina Zenik."

Matthias knew what it was to face the mentors you had idolized, to feel yourself become a nervous pupil again, yearning to please. He turned to Nina and said in Fjerdan, "Do not let them cow you. You are not the girl you were. You are not just a soldier to command."

"So why do I feel like finding a corner to sob in?"

"This is a round room. There are no corners."

"Matthias—"

"Remember what we've been through. Remember what we came here for."

"I thought we were all speaking Kerch," said Zoya.

Nina gave Matthias' hand another squeeze, threw back her head, and said, "I was taken captive by the *drüskelle*. Matthias helped me escape. Matthias was taken captive by the Kerch. I helped him escape. I was taken captive by Jarl Brum. Matthias helped me escape." Matthias wasn't entirely comfortable with how good they both were at being taken prisoner.

"*Jarl Brum?*" Zoya said in horror.

Nina sighed. "It's been a rough year. I swear I'll explain it all to you, and if you decide I should be put in a sack and dropped in the Sokol River, I will go with a minimum of wailing. But we came here tonight because I saw the Kherguud soldiers' attack on West Stave. I want to help get these Grisha out of the city before the Shu find them."

Zoya had to be several inches shorter than Nina, but she still managed to look down her nose when she said, "And how can you help?"

"We have a ship." That wasn't technically true yet, but Matthias wasn't going to argue.

Zoya waved a dismissive hand. "We have a ship too. It's stuck miles off the coast. The harbor has been blockaded by the Kerch and the Council of Tides. No foreign vessel can come or go without express permission from a member of the Merchant Council."

So Kaz had been right. Van Eck was using every bit of his influence with the government to ensure Kaz didn't get Kuwei out of Ketterdam.

"Sure," said Nina. "But our ship belongs to a member of the Kerch Merchant Council."

Zoya and Genya exchanged a glance.

"All right, Zenik," said Zoya. "Now I'm listening."

Nina filled in some of the details for Zoya and Genya, though Matthias noticed that she did not mention Kuwei and that she steered very clear of any talk of the Ice Court.

When they went upstairs to debate the proposal, they left Nina and Matthias behind, two armed guards posted at the entry to the cistern room.

In Fjerdan, Matthias whispered, "If Ravka's spies are worth their salt, your friends are going to realize we were the ones who broke out Kuwei."

"Don't whisper," Nina replied in Fjerdan, but in a normal tone of voice. "It will just make the guards suspicious. And I'll tell Zoya and Genya everything eventually, but remember how keen we were on killing Kuwei? I'm not sure Zoya would make the same choice to spare him, at least not until he's safely on Ravkan soil. She doesn't need to know who's on that boat until it docks in Os Kervo."

Safely on Ravkan soil. The words sat heavy in Matthias' gut. He was eager to get Nina out of the city, but nothing about the prospect of going to Ravka seemed safe to him.

Nina must have sensed his unease, because she said, "Ravka is the safest place for Kuwei. He needs our protection."

"Just what does Zoya Nazyalensky's protection look like?"

"She's really not that bad." Matthias shot her a skeptical look. "Actually, she's terrible, but she and Genya saw a lot of death in the civil war. I don't believe they want more bloodshed."

Matthias hoped that was true, but even if it was, he wasn't sure it would matter. "Do you remember what you said to me, Nina? You wished King Nikolai would march north and raze everything in his path."

"I was angry—"

"You had a right to your anger. We all do. That's the problem. Brum won't stop. The *drüskelle* won't stop. They consider it their holy mission to destroy your kind." It had been his mission too, and he could still feel the distrust, the pull toward hatred. He cursed himself for it.

"Then we'll find a way to change their minds. All of them." She studied him a moment. "You used a duskbomb today. Did you have Wylan make it?"

"Yes," he admitted.

"Why?"

He'd known she wouldn't like it. "I wasn't sure how the *parem* would affect your power. If I had to keep you from the drug, I needed to be able to fight you without hurting you."

"And you brought it today in case we had trouble?"

"Yes."

"With Grisha."

He nodded, waiting for her admonishment, but all she did was watch him, her face thoughtful. She drew nearer. Matthias cast an uneasy glance at the guards' backs, visible through the doorway. "Ignore them," she said. "Why haven't you kissed me, Matthias?"

"This isn't the time—"

"Is it because of what I am? Is it because you still fear me?"

"*No.*"

She paused, and he could see her struggling with what she wanted to say. "Is it because of the way I behaved on the ship? The way I acted the other night . . . when I tried to get you to give me the rest of the *parem*?"

"How can you think that?"

"You're always calling me shameless. I guess . . . I guess I'm ashamed." She shuddered. "It's like wearing a coat that doesn't fit."

"Nina, I gave you my oath."

"But—"

"Your enemies are my enemies, and I will stand with you against any foe—including this accursed drug."

She shook her head as if he was speaking nonsense. "I don't want you to be with me because of an oath, or because you think you need to protect me, or because you think you owe me some stupid blood debt."

"Nina—" he started, then stopped. "Nina, I am with you because you let me be with you. There is no greater honor than to stand by your side."

"Honor, duty. I get it."

Her temper he could bear, but her disappointment was unacceptable. Matthias knew only the language of war. He did not have the words for this. "Meeting you was a disaster."

She raised a brow. "Thank you."

Djel, he was terrible at this. He stumbled on, trying to make her understand. "But I am grateful every day for that disaster. I needed a cataclysm to shake me from the life I knew. You were an earthquake, a landslide."

"I," she said, planting a hand on her hip, "am a delicate flower."

"You aren't a flower, you're every blossom in the wood blooming at once. You are a tidal wave. You're a stampede. You are overwhelming."

"And what would you prefer?" she said, eyes blazing, the slightest quaver to her voice. "A proper Fjerdan girl who wears high collars and dunks herself in cold water whenever she has the urge to do something exciting?"

"That isn't what I meant!"

She sidled closer to him. Again, his eyes strayed to the guards. Their backs were turned, but Matthias knew they must be listening, no matter what language he and Nina were speaking. "What are you so afraid of?" she challenged. "Don't look at them, Matthias. Look at me."

He looked. It was a struggle *not* to look. He loved seeing her in Fjerdan clothes, the little woolly vest, the full sweep of her skirts. Her green eyes were bright, her cheeks pink, her lips slightly parted. It was too easy to imagine himself kneeling like a penitent before her, letting his hands slide up the white curves of her calves, pushing those skirts higher, past her knees to the warm skin of her thighs. And the worst part was that he knew how good she would feel. Every cell in his body remembered the press of her naked body that first night in the whaling camp. "I . . . There is no one I want more; there is nothing I want more than to be overwhelmed by you."

"But you don't want to kiss me?"

He inhaled slowly, trying to bring order to his thoughts. This was all wrong.

"In Fjerda——" he began.

"We're not in Fjerda."

He needed to make her understand. "In Fjerda," he persisted, "I would have asked your parents for permission to walk out with you."

"I haven't seen my parents since I was a child."

"We would have been chaperoned. I would have dined with your family at least three times before we were ever left alone together."

"We're alone together *now*, Matthias."

"I would have brought you gifts."

Nina tipped her head to one side. "Go on."

"Winter roses if I could afford them, a silver comb for your hair."

"I don't need those things."

"Apple cakes with sweet cream."

"I thought *drüskelle* didn't eat sweets."

"They'd all be for you," he said.

"You have my attention."

"Our first kiss would be in a sunlit wood or under a starry sky after a village dance, not in a tomb or some dank basement with guards at the door."

"Let me get this straight," Nina said. "You haven't kissed me because the setting isn't suitably romantic?"

"This isn't about *romance*. A proper kiss, a proper courtship. There's a way these things should be done."

"For proper thieves?" The corners of her beautiful mouth curled and for a moment he was afraid she would laugh at him, but she simply shook her head and drew even nearer. Her body was the barest breath from his now. The need to close that scrap of distance was maddening.

"The first day you showed up at my house for this proper courtship, I would have cornered you in the pantry," she said. "But please, tell me more about Fjerdan girls."

"They speak quietly. They don't engage in flirtations with every single man they meet."

"I flirt with the women too."

"I think you'd flirt with a date palm if it would pay you any attention."

"If I flirted with a plant, you can bet it would stand up and take notice. Are you jealous?"

"All the time."

"I'm glad. What are you looking at, Matthias?" The low thrum of her voice vibrated straight through him.

He kept his eyes on the ceiling, whispering softly. "Nothing."

"Matthias, are you praying?"

"Possibly."

"For restraint?" she said sweetly.

"You really are a witch."

"I'm not proper, Matthias."

"I am aware of this." Miserably, keenly, hungrily aware.

"And I'm sorry to inform you, but you're not proper either."

His gaze dropped to her now. "I—"

"How many rules have you broken since you met me? How many laws? They won't be the last. Nothing about us will ever be proper," she said. She tilted her face up to his. So close now it was as if they were already touching. "Not the way we met. Not the life we lead. And not the way we kiss."

She went up on tiptoe, and that easily, her mouth was against his. It was barely a kiss—just a quick, startling press of her lips.

Before she could even think of moving away, he had hold of her. He knew he was probably doing everything wrong, but he couldn't bring himself to worry, because she was in his arms, her lips were parting, her hands were twining around his neck, and sweet Djel, her tongue was in his mouth. No wonder Fjerdans were so cautious about courtship. If Matthias could be kissing Nina, feeling her nip at his lip with her clever teeth, feel her body fitted against his own, hear her release that little sigh in the back of her throat, why would he ever bother doing anything else? Why would anyone?

"Matthias," Nina said breathlessly, and then they were kissing again.

She was sweet as the first rain, lush as new meadows. His hands curled along her back, tracing her shape, the line of her spine, the emphatic flare of her hips.

"*Matthias*," she said more insistently, pulling away.

He opened his eyes, certain he'd made some horrible mistake. Nina was biting her lower lip—it was pink and swollen. But she was smiling, and her eyes sparkled. "Did I do something wrong?"

"Not at all, you glorious *babink*, but—"

Zoya cleared her throat. "I'm glad you two found a way to spend the time while you waited."

Her expression was pure disgust, but next to her, Genya looked like she was about to burst with glee.

"Perhaps you should put me down?" suggested Nina.

Reality crashed in on Matthias—the guards' knowing looks, Zoya and Genya in the doorway, and the fact that in the course of kissing Nina Zenik with a year's worth of pent-up desire, he had lifted her clear off her feet.

A tide of embarrassment flooded through him. What Fjerdan did such a thing? Gently, he released his hold on her magnificent thighs and let her slide to the ground.

"*Shameless*," Nina whispered, and he felt his cheeks go red.

Zoya rolled her eyes. "We're making a deal with a pair of love-struck teenagers."

Matthias felt another wave of heat in his face, but Nina just adjusted her wig and said, "So you'll accept our help?"

It took them a short time to work out the logistics of how the night would go. Since it might not be safe for Nina to return to the tavern, once she had information on where and when to board Van Eck's ship, she would get a message to the embassy—probably via Inej, since the Wraith could come and go without being seen. The refugees would remain in hiding as long as possible; then Genya and Zoya would get them to the harbor.

"Be prepared for a fight," Matthias said. "The Shu will be watching this sector of town. They haven't had the temerity to attack the embassy or the marketplace yet, but it's only a matter of time."

"We'll be ready, Fjerdan," said Zoya, and in her gaze he saw the steel of a born commander.

On their way out of the embassy, Nina found the golden-eyed Heartrender who had been part of the ambush at the tavern. She was Shu, with a short crop of black hair, and wore a pair of slender silver axes at her hips. Nina had told him she was the only Corporalnik among the Grisha refugees and diplomats.

"Tamar?" Nina said tentatively. "If the Kherguud come, you mustn't allow yourself to be taken. A Heartrender in Shu possession and under the influence of *parem* could irrevocably tip the scales in their favor. You cannot imagine the power of this drug."

"No one will take me alive," said the girl. She slid a tiny, pale yellow tablet from her pocket, displaying it between her fingers.

"Poison?"

"Genya's own creation. It kills instantly. We all have them." She handed it to Nina. "Take it. Just in case. I have another."

"Nina—" Matthias said.

But Nina didn't hesitate. She slipped the pill into the pocket of her skirt before Matthias could speak another word of protest.

They made their way out of the government sector, steering clear of the market stalls and keeping well away from the tavern, where the *stadwatch* had gathered.

Matthias told himself to be alert, to focus on getting them back to Black Veil safely, but he could not stop thinking about that pale yellow pill. The sight of it had brought the dream back as vivid as ever, the ice of the north, Nina lost and Matthias powerless to save her. It had burned the unchecked joy of her kiss right out of him.

The dream had started on the ship, when Nina was in the worst throes of her struggle with *parem*. She'd been in a rage that night, body quaking, clothes soaked through with sweat.

You're not a good man, she'd shouted. *You're a good soldier, and the sad thing is you don't even know the difference.* She'd been miserable later, weeping, sick with hunger, sick with regret. *I'm sorry*, she'd said. *I didn't mean it. You know I didn't mean it.* And a moment later, *If you would just help me.* Her beautiful eyes were full of tears, and in the faint light from the lanterns, her pale skin had seemed gilded in frost. *Please, Matthias, I'm in so much pain. Help me.* He would have done anything, traded anything to ease her suffering, but he'd sworn he would not give her more *parem*. He'd made a vow that he would not let her become a slave to the drug, and he had to honor it, no matter what it cost him.

I can't, my love, he'd whispered, pressing a cold towel to her brow. *I can't get you more parem. I had them lock the door from the outside.*

In a flash her face changed, her eyes slitted. *Then break the fucking door down, you useless skiv.*

No.

She spat in his face.

Hours later, she'd been quiet, her energy spent, sad but coherent. She'd lain on her side, her eyelids a bruised shade of violet, breath coming in shallow pants, and said, "Talk to me."

"About what?"

"About anything. Tell me about the *isenulf*."

He shouldn't have been surprised she knew of the *isenulf*, the white wolves bred to go into battle with the *drüskelle*. They were bigger than ordinary wolves, and though they were trained to obey their masters, they never lost the wild, indomitable streak that separated them from their distant domesticated cousins.

It had been hard to think about Fjerda, the life he'd left behind for good, but he made himself speak, eager for any way to distract her. "Sometimes there are more wolves than *drüskelle*, sometimes more *drüskelle* than wolves. The wolves decide when to mate, with little influence from the breeder. They're too stubborn for that."

Nina had smiled, then winced in pain. "Keep going," she whispered.

"The same family has been breeding the *isenulf* for generations. They live far north near Stenrink, the Ring of Stones. When a new litter arrives, we travel there by foot and by sledge, and each *drüskelle* chooses a pup. From then on, you are each other's responsibility. You fight beside each other, sleep on the same furs, your rations are your wolf's rations. He is not your pet. He is a warrior like you, a brother."

Nina shivered, and Matthias felt a sick rush of shame. In a battle with Grisha, the *isenulf* could help even the odds for a *drüskelle*, trained to come to his aid and tear out his attacker's throat. Heartrender power seemed to have no effect on animals. A Grisha like Nina would be virtually helpless under *isenulf* attack.

"What if something happens to the wolf?" Nina asked.

"A *drüskelle* can train a new wolf, but it is a terrible loss."

"What happens to the wolf if his *drüskelle* is killed?"

Matthias was silent for a time. He did not want to think about this. Trass had been the creature of his heart.

"They are returned to the wild, but they will never be accepted by any pack." And what was a wolf without a pack? The *isenulf* were not meant to live alone.

When had the other *drüskelle* decided Matthias was dead? Had it been Brum who had taken Trass north to the ice? The idea of his wolf left alone, howling for Matthias to come and take him home, carved a hollow ache in his chest. It felt like something had broken there and left an echo, the lonely snap of a branch too heavy with snow.

As if she had sensed his sorrow, Nina had opened her eyes, the pale green of a bud about to unfurl, a color that brought him back from the ice. "What was his name?"

"Trassel."

The corner of her lips tilted. "Troublemaker."

"No one else wanted him."

"Was he a runt?"

"No," Matthias said. "The opposite."

It had taken more than a week of hard travel to reach the Ring of Stones. Matthias hadn't enjoyed the trip. He'd been twelve years old, new to the *drüskelle*, and every day he'd thought about running away. He didn't mind the training. The hours spent running and sparring helped to keep the longing he felt for his family at bay. He wanted to be an officer. He wanted to fight Grisha. He wanted a chance to bring honor to the memory of his parents and his sister. The *drüskelle* had given him purpose. But the rest of it? The jokes in the mess hall? The endless boasting and mindless chatter? That he had no use for. He had a family. They were buried beneath the black earth, their souls gone to Djel. The *drüskelle* were merely a means to an end.

Brum had warned him that he would never become a true *drüskelle* if he did not learn to see the other boys as his brothers, but Matthias didn't believe that. He was the biggest, the strongest, the fastest. He didn't need to be popular to survive.

He'd ridden in the back of the sled for the entirety of the journey, huddled in his furs, speaking to no one, and when they'd finally arrived at the Ring of Stones, he'd hung back, unsure of himself as the other *drüskelle* bolted into the big barn, yelling and shoving one another, each of them diving for the pile of wriggling white wolf pups with their ice-chip eyes.

The truth was that he wanted a wolf pup desperately, but he knew there might not be enough for all of them. It was up to the breeder which boy was paired with each pup and who went home empty-handed. Many of the boys were already talking to the old woman, attempting to charm her.

"You see? This one likes me."

"Look! Look! I got her to sit!"

Matthias knew he should try to be personable, make some kind of effort, but instead he found himself drawn to the kennels in the back of the barn. In the corner, in a wire cage, he caught a yellow flash—light reflecting off a pair of wary eyes. He drew closer and saw a wolf, a pup no longer, but not yet full grown. He growled as Matthias drew closer to the cage, hackles raised, head lowered, teeth bared. The young wolf had a long scar across his muzzle. It had cut across his right eye and changed part of the iris from blue to mottled brown.

"Don't want no business with that one," said the breeder.

Matthias didn't know when she'd snuck up behind him. "Can he see?"

"He can, but he don't like people."

"Why not?"

"He got out when he was still a pup. Made it across two miles of ice fields. Kid found him and cut him up with a broken bottle. Won't let no one near him since, and he's getting too old to train. Probably have to put him down soon."

"Let me take him."

"He'd just as soon tear you to bits as let you feed him, boy. We'll have a pup for you next time."

As soon as the woman walked away, Matthias opened the cage. And just as fast, the wolf lunged forward and bit him.

Matthias wanted to scream as the wolf's teeth sank into his forearm. He toppled to the ground, the wolf on top of him, the pain beyond anything he'd ever known. But he did not make a sound. He held the wolf's gaze as its teeth sank more deeply into the muscle of his arm, a growl rumbling through the animal's chest.

Matthias suspected that the wolf's jaws were strong enough to break bone, but he did not struggle, did not cry out, did not drop his gaze. *I won't hurt you*, he swore, *even if you hurt me.*

A long moment passed, and then another. Matthias could feel blood soaking through his sleeve. He thought he might lose consciousness.

Then, slowly, the wolf's jaws released. The animal sat back, the white fur of his muzzle coated in Matthias' blood, head tilted to one side. The wolf released a huff of breath.

"Nice to meet you too," said Matthias.

He sat up cautiously, bandaged his arm with the bottom of his shirt, and then he and his wolf, both covered in blood, walked back to where the others were playing in a pile of wolf pups and gray uniforms.

"This one's mine," he said as they all turned to stare, and the old woman shook her head. Then Matthias passed out.

That night, on the ship, Matthias had told Nina about Trassel, his fierce nature, his ragged scar. Eventually, she had dozed and Matthias had let himself shut his eyes. The ice was waiting. The killing wind came with white teeth, the wolves howled in the distance, and Nina cried out, but Matthias could not go to her.

The dream had come every night since. It was hard not to see it as some kind of omen, and when Nina had casually dropped that yellow pill into her pocket, it had been like watching the storm come on: the roar of the wind filling his ears, the cold burrowing into his bones, the certainty that he was going to lose her.

"*Parem* might not work on you anymore," he said now. They'd finally reached the deserted canal where they'd moored the *gondel*.

"What?"

"Your power has changed, hasn't it?"

Nina's footsteps faltered. "Yes."

"Because of the *parem*?"

Now Nina stopped. "Why are you asking me this?"

He didn't want to ask her. He wanted to kiss her again. But he said, "If you were captured, the Shu might not be able to use the drug to enslave you."

"Or it could be just as bad as before."

"That pill, the poison Tamar gave you—"

Nina laid a hand on his arm. "I'm not going to be captured, Matthias."

"But if you were—"

"I don't know what the *parem* did to me. I have to believe the effects will wear off in time."

"And if they don't?"

"They have to," she said, brow furrowed. "I can't live like this. It's like . . . being only half of myself. Although . . ."

"Although?" he urged.

"The craving isn't quite so bad right now," she said as if realizing it herself. "In fact, I've barely thought of *parem* since the fight at the tavern."

"Using this new power helped?"

"Maybe," she said cautiously. "And—" She frowned. Matthias heard a low, curling growl.

"Was that your *stomach*?"

"It was." Nina's face split in a dazzling grin. "Matthias, I'm famished."

Could she truly be healing at last? Or had what she'd done at the tavern returned her appetite to her? He didn't care. He was just glad she was smiling that way. He picked her up and spun her in the air.

"You're going to strain something if you keep doing that," she said with another radiant smile.

"You're light as a feather."

"I do not want to see that bird. Now let's go get me a stack of waffles twice as tall as you. I—"

She broke off, the color draining from her face. "Oh, Saints."

Matthias followed her gaze over his shoulder and found himself looking into his own eyes. A poster had been plastered to the wall, emblazoned with a scarily accurate sketch of his face. Above and beside the illustration, written in several different languages, was a single word: WANTED.

Nina snatched the poster from the wall. "You were supposed to be dead."

"Someone must have asked to see Muzzen's body before it was burned." Maybe the Fjerdans. Maybe just someone at the prison. There were more words printed at the bottom in Kerch that Matthias couldn't read, but he understood his own name and the number well enough. "Fifty thousand *kruge*. They're offering a reward for my capture."

"No," Nina said. She pointed to the text beneath the large number and translated, "*Wanted: Matthias Helvar. Dead or alive.* They've put a price on your head."

16

JESPER

When Nina and Matthias came charging into the tomb, Jesper wanted to leap up from the table and waltz with them both. He'd spent the last hour trying to explain to Kuwei how they would reach the embassy, and he was starting to get the distinct impression the kid was playing dumb—possibly because he was enjoying the ridiculous gestures Jesper was making.

"Could you repeat the last part?" Kuwei said now, leaning in a little too close.

"Nina," Jesper said. "Can you help facilitate this exchange?"

"Thank the Saints," said Inej, leaving off her work at the table with Wylan and Kaz. They were assembling the mass of wires and gear Kaz had stolen from the Cirkus Zirkoa. Wylan had spent the last two hours making modifications to ensure Inej's safety at the silos, attaching magnetized clamps that would grip their metal sides.

"Why do you keep staring at him?" Kuwei said. "I look just like him. You could look at me."

"I'm not staring at him," protested Jesper. "I'm . . . overseeing their work." The sooner Kuwei got on that boat, the better. The tomb was starting to feel crowded.

"Did you manage to contact the refugees?" Inej asked, waving Nina over to the table and clearing a place for her to sit.

"Everything went smoothly," said Nina. "Aside from breaking a few windows and nearly getting shot."

Kaz looked up from the table, his interest secured.

"Big trouble in Little Ravka?" asked Jesper.

"Nothing we couldn't handle," Nina said. "Please tell me there's something to eat."

"You're hungry?" said Inej.

They all goggled at Nina. She curtsied. "Yes, yes, Nina Zenik is hungry. Now will someone feed me before I'm forced to cook one of you?"

"Don't be ridiculous," said Jesper. "You don't know how to cook."

Inej was already digging through what remained of their stockpile of food, placing the meager offerings of salt cod, dried meat, and stale crackers before Nina.

"What happened at the tavern?" asked Kaz.

"The refugees are in hiding at the embassy," said Matthias. "We met—"

"Their leader," said Nina. "They'll be waiting for word from us." She shoved two crackers into her mouth. "These are awful."

"Slow down," said Matthias. "You're going to choke."

"Worth it," Nina said, struggling to swallow.

"For crackers?"

"I'm pretending they're pie. When does the boat leave?"

"We found a shipment of molasses headed for Os Kervo leaving at eleven bells," said Inej. "Specht is working on the documents now."

"Good," said Nina, uncrumpling a piece of paper from her pocket and smoothing it onto the table. A sketch of Matthias looked back at them. "We need to get out of town as soon as possible."

"Damn it," Jesper said. "Kaz and Wylan are still in the lead." He gestured to where they'd pasted up the rest of the wanted posters: Jesper, Kaz, and Inej were all there. Van Eck hadn't yet dared to plaster Kuwei Yul-Bo's face over every surface in Ketterdam, but he'd had to maintain the pretense of searching for his son, so there was also a poster offering a reward for Wylan Van Eck's safe return. It showed his old features, but Jesper didn't think it was much of a likeness. Only Nina was missing. She'd never met Van Eck, and though she had connections to the Dregs, it was possible he didn't know of her involvement.

Matthias examined the posters. "One hundred thousand *kruge*!" He shot a disbelieving glower at Kaz. "You're hardly worth that."

The hint of a smile tugged at Kaz's lips. "As the market wills it."

"Tell me about it," said Jesper. "They're only offering thirty thousand for me."

"Your lives are at stake," said Wylan. "How can you act like this is a competition?"

"We're stuck in a tomb, merchling. You take the action where you find it."

"Maybe we should *all* go to Ravka," said Nina, tapping Inej's wanted poster. "It isn't safe for you to remain here."

"It's not a bad idea," said Kaz.

Inej cast him a swift glance. "You'd go to Ravka?"

"Not a chance. I'll lie low here. I want to see Van Eck's life come apart when the hammer falls."

"But you could come," Nina said to Inej. "Jesper? We could bring Colm too."

Jesper thought of his father, stuck in some lavish suite at the Geldrenner, probably wearing the carpet down to the floorboards with his pacing. Just two days had passed since he'd watched his father's broad back disappear between the graves as Rotty shepherded him off Black Veil, but it felt like far longer. Since then, Jesper had nearly been killed by Grisha hunters and had a price placed on his head. But if they could just get this job done tonight, his father wouldn't have to know any of that.

"No way," said Jesper. "I want Da to get his money as fast as possible and then get back to Novyi Zem. I'm not going to sleep easy until he's safe on the farm. We'll hide out at his hotel until Van Eck has been discredited and the sugar market goes crazy."

"Inej?" said Nina.

They all looked to the Wraith—except Jesper. He watched Kaz, curious to see how he would react to the prospect of Inej leaving town. But Kaz's expression was impassive, as if waiting to hear what time dinner might be served.

Inej shook her head. "When I go to Ravka, it will be on my own ship, piloted by my own crew."

Jesper's brows shot up. "Since when are you a seafarer? And what sane person would want to spend more time on a boat?"

Inej smiled. "I've heard this city drives people mad."

Kaz drew his watch from his waistcoat. "We're coming up on eight bells. Van Eck is gathering the Merchant Council at his house for a meeting tonight."

"Do you think they'll devote more resources to the search for Wylan?" asked Nina.

"Probably. It's not our concern anymore. The noise and people coming and going will provide good cover for Wylan and me to get the seal out of the safe. Nina and Inej will hit Sweet Reef at the same time. The guards patrol the silos' perimeter constantly, and it takes about twelve minutes for them to make it around the fence. They always leave someone to watch the gate, so be smart about the approach." He placed a tiny stoppered bottle on the table. "This is coffee extract. Kuwei, Nina, Jesper, I want you all wearing plenty of it. If those Shu soldiers really can scent Grisha, this might throw them off."

"Coffee?" asked Kuwei, popping the cork and taking a tentative sniff.

"Clever," said Jesper. "We used to pack illegal shipments of *jurda* and spices in coffee grounds to throw off the *stadwatch* dogs. Confuses their noses."

Nina took the bottle and dabbed a generous amount of the extract behind her ears and at her wrists. "Let's hope the Kherguud work the same way."

"Your refugees had better be ready," said Kaz. "How many are there?"

"Fewer than we thought. Fifteen and um . . . some of the people from the embassy too. A total of seventeen."

"Plus you, Matthias, Wylan, and Kuwei. Twenty-one. Specht will forge the letter accordingly."

"I'm not going," said Wylan.

Jesper clasped his fingers together to make them stay still. "No?"

"I'm not letting my father run me out of this city again."

"Why is everyone so determined to stay in this miserable town?" Nina grumbled.

Jesper tipped his chair back, studying Kaz. He'd shown no surprise that Wylan wanted to remain in Ketterdam. "You knew," he said, putting the pieces together. "You knew Wylan's mother was alive."

"Wylan's mother is alive?" said Nina.

"Why do you think I let you two go to Olendaal?" Kaz said.

Wylan blinked. "And you knew I was lying about the quarry."

Jesper felt a spike of rage. It was one thing for Kaz to mess with him, but Wylan wasn't like the rest of them. Despite the bad hand he'd drawn with his father, Wylan hadn't let his circumstances or this city knock the goodness out of him. He still believed people could do right. Jesper pointed a finger at Kaz. "You shouldn't have sent him to Saint Hilde blind like that. It was cruel."

"It was necessary."

Wylan's fists were clenched. "Why?"

"Because you still didn't understand what your father really is."

"You could have told me."

"You were angry. Angry wears off. I needed you righteous."

Wylan crossed his arms. "Well, you've got me."

Kaz folded his hands over his cane. "It's getting late, so everybody put away your *Poor Wylan* hankies and set your minds to the task at hand. Matthias, Jesper, and Kuwei will leave for the embassy at half past nine bells. You approach from the canal. Jesper, you're tall, brown, and conspicuous—"

"All synonyms for delightful."

"And that means you'll have to be twice as careful."

"There's always a price to be paid for greatness."

"Try to take this seriously," said Kaz, voice like a rusty blade. Was that actual concern? Jesper tried not to wonder if it was for him or the job. "Move quickly and get everyone to the docks no sooner than ten. I don't want all of you hanging around attracting attention. We meet at Third Harbor, berth fifteen. The ship is called the *Verrhader*. It sails the route from Kerch to Ravka several times a year." He rose. "Stay smart and stay quiet. None of this works if Van Eck gets wise."

"And stay safe," added Inej. "I want to celebrate with all of you when that boat leaves the harbor."

Jesper wanted that too. He wanted to see them all safe on the other side of this night. He raised his hand. "Will there be champagne?"

Nina finished the last of the crackers, licking her fingers. "*I'll* be there, and I'm effervescent."

After that, there was nothing to do but finish packing up their gear. There would be no grand goodbye.

Jesper shuffled over to the table where Wylan was packing his satchel and pretended to search for something he needed in the pile of maps and documents.

He hesitated, then said, "You could stay with me and Da. If you want. At the hotel. If you need a place to wait everything out."

"Really?"

"Sure," Jesper said with a shrug that didn't feel right on his shoulders.

"Inej and Kaz too. We can't all scatter before the comeuppance is delivered."

"And after that? When your father's loan is paid, will you go back to Novyi Zem?"

"I should."

Wylan waited. Jesper didn't have an answer for him. If he went back to the farm, he'd be away from the temptations of Ketterdam and the Barrel. But he might just find some new kind of trouble to get into. And there would be so much money. Even after the loan was paid, there would still be more than three million *kruge*. He shrugged again. "Kaz is the planner."

"Sure," said Wylan, but Jesper could see the disappointment in his face.

"I suppose you've got your future all figured out?"

"No. I just know I'm going to get my mother out of that place and try to build some kind of life for us." Wylan nodded to the posters on the wall. "Is this really what you want? To be a criminal? To keep bouncing from the next score to the next fight to the next near miss?"

"Honestly?" Jesper knew Wylan probably wasn't going to like what he said next.

"It's time," Kaz said from the doorway.

"Yes, this is what I want," said Jesper. Wylan looped his satchel over his shoulder, and without thinking, Jesper reached out and untwisted the strap. He didn't let go. "But it's not all that I want."

"*Now*," said Kaz.

I'm going to beat him over the head with that cane. Jesper released the strap. "No mourners."

"No funerals," Wylan said quietly. He and Kaz vanished through the door.

Nina and Inej were next. Nina had disappeared into one of the passages to change out of the ridiculous Fjerdan costume and don practical trousers, coat, and tunic—all of Ravkan make and cut. She'd taken

Matthias with her and had emerged rumpled and rosy several long minutes later.

"Staying on task?" Jesper couldn't resist asking.

"I'm teaching Matthias all about fun. He's an excellent student. Diligent in his lessons."

"Nina——" Matthias warned.

"Has problems with attitude. Shows room for improvement."

Inej nudged the bottle of coffee extract toward Jesper. "Try to be cautious tonight, Jes."

"I'm about as good at cautious as Matthias is at fun."

"I'm perfectly good at fun," Matthias growled.

"Perfectly," Jesper agreed.

There was more he wanted to say to all of them, mostly Inej, but not in front of the others. *Maybe not ever*, he conceded. He owed Inej an apology. His carelessness had gotten them ambushed at Fifth Harbor before they left for the Ice Court job, and the mistake had nearly cost the Wraith her life. But how the hell did you apologize for that? *Sorry I almost got you stabbed to death. Who wants waffles?*

Before he could ponder it further, Inej had planted a kiss on his cheek, Nina had aimed a single-fingered gesture at the wall of wanted posters, and Jesper was stuck waiting for half past nine bells, alone in the tomb with a glum-looking Kuwei and a pacing Matthias.

Kuwei began reorganizing the notebooks in his pack.

Jesper sat down at the table. "Do you need all of those?"

"I do," said Kuwei. "Have you been to Ravka?"

Poor kid is scared, thought Jesper. "No, but you'll have Nina and Matthias with you."

Kuwei glanced at Matthias and whispered, "He is very stern."

Jesper had to laugh. "He's not what I'd call a party, but he has a few good qualities."

"I can hear you, Fahey," Matthias grumbled.

"Good. I'd hate to have to shout."

"Aren't you even concerned about the others?" Matthias said.

"Of course. But all of us are out of nursery clothes. The time for worrying is over. Now we get to the fun part," he said, tapping his guns. "The doing."

"Or the dying," Matthias muttered. "You know as well as I do that Nina isn't at her best."

"She doesn't have to be tonight. The whole idea is *not* to get into a fight, alas."

Matthias left off his prowling and took a seat at the table across from Jesper. "What happened at the lake house?"

Jesper smoothed out the corner of one of the maps. "I'm not sure, but I think she choked a guy to death with a cloud of dust."

"I don't understand it," said Matthias. "A cloud of dust? She controlled shards of bone today—she could never have done that before *parem*. She seems to think the change is temporary, a residual effect of the drug, but . . ." He turned to Kuwei. "Could the *parem* alter a Grisha's power? Change it? Destroy it?"

Kuwei fiddled with the latch on his travel pack. "I suppose it's possible. She survived the withdrawal. That is rare, and we know so little about *parem*, about Grisha power."

"Didn't carve enough open to solve that riddle?" The words were out of Jesper's mouth before he thought better of them. He knew they weren't fair. Kuwei and his father were Grisha themselves, and neither had been in any position to keep the Shu from experimenting on others.

"You are angry with me?" said Kuwei.

Jesper smiled. "I'm not an angry type of guy."

"Yes, you are," said Matthias. "Angry and frightened."

Jesper sized up the big Fjerdan. "Beg your pardon?"

"Jesper is very brave," protested Kuwei.

"Thank you for noticing." Jesper stretched out his legs and crossed one ankle over the other. "You have something to say, Matthias?"

"Why aren't you going to Ravka?"

"My father—"

"Your father could go with us tonight. And if you're so concerned about him, why weren't you at his hotel today?"

"I don't see how that's any of your business."

"I know what it is to be ashamed of what you are, of what you've done."

"You really want to start this, witchhunter? I'm not ashamed. I'm careful. Thanks to people like you and your *drüskelle* buddies, the world is a dangerous place for people like me. It always has been, and it doesn't look to be getting any better."

Kuwei reached out and touched Jesper's hand, his face imploring. "Understand. Please. What we did, what my father did . . . We were trying to make things better, to make a way for Grisha to . . ." He made a gesture as if he was pressing something down.

"To suppress their powers?" suggested Matthias.

"Yes. Exactly. To hide more easily. If Grisha don't use their powers, they grow ill. They age, tire easily, lose appetite. It's one way the Shu identify Grisha trying to live in secret."

"I don't use my power," said Jesper. "And yet . . ." He held up his fingers, enumerating his points as he made them. "One: On a dare, I ate a literal trough full of waffles doused in apple syrup and almost went back for seconds. Two: A lack of energy has never been my problem. Three: I've never been sick a day in my life."

"No?" said Matthias. "There are many kinds of sickness."

Jesper touched his hands to his revolvers. Apparently the Fjerdan had a lot on his mind tonight.

Kuwei opened his pack and took out a tin of ordinary *jurda*, the kind sold in every corner shop in Ketterdam. "*Jurda* is a stimulant, good for fighting fatigue. My father thinks . . . thought it was the answer to helping our kind. If he can find the right formula, it will allow Grisha to remain healthy while hiding their powers."

"Didn't quite work out that way, did it?" Jesper said. Maybe he was a *little* angry.

"The tests do not go as planned. Someone in the laboratory is loose in his talk. Our leaders find out and see a different destiny for *parem*." He shook his head and gestured to his pack. "Now I try to remember my father's experiments."

"That's what you're scribbling away at in the notebooks?"

"I also keep a journal."

"Must be fascinating. Day one: sat in tomb. Day two: sat in tomb some more."

Matthias ignored Jesper and said, "Have you had any success?"

Kuwei frowned. "Some. I think. In a laboratory with real scientists, maybe more. I'm not my father. He was a Fabrikator. I am an Inferni. This is not what I'm good at."

"What are you good at?" asked Jesper.

Kuwei cast him a speculative glance, then frowned. "I never had a chance to find out. We live a frightened life in Shu Han. It was never home."

That was certainly something Jesper could understand. He picked up the tin of *jurda* and popped the lid open. It was quality stuff, sweetly scented, the dried blossoms nearly whole and a vibrant orange color.

"You think if you have a lab and a few Grisha Fabrikators around, you might be able to re-create your father's experiments and somehow work your way to an antidote?"

"I hope," said Kuwei.

"How would it work?"

"Would it purge the body of *parem*?" asked Matthias.

"Yes. Draw the *parem* out," said Kuwei. "But even if we succeed, how to administer it?"

"You'd have to get close enough to inject it or make someone swallow it," said Matthias.

"And by the time you were within range, you'd be done for," finished Jesper.

Jesper pinched one of the *jurda* blossoms between his fingers. Eventually, someone would figure out how to create their own version of *jurda parem*, and when they did, one of these blossoms might be worth a very pretty fortune. If he focused on its petals, even a little, he could feel them breaking apart into their smaller components. It wasn't exactly seeing, more like sensing all the different, tiny bits of matter that formed a single whole.

He put the flower back in the tin. When he was a little boy, lying in his father's fields, he'd discovered he could leach the color out of a *jurda* blossom petal by petal. One boring afternoon, he'd bleached a swear word into the western pasture in capital letters. His father had been furious, but he'd been scared too. He'd yelled himself hoarse chastising Jesper, and then Colm had just sat there, staring at him, big hands clasped around a mug of tea to keep them from shaking. At first, Jesper thought it was the swear his father was mad about, but that wasn't it at all.

"Jes," he'd said at last. "You must never do that again. Promise me. Your ma had the same gift. It can bring you only misery."

"Promise," Jesper had said quickly, wanting to make things right, still reeling from seeing his patient, mild-mannered father in such a rage. But all he'd thought was, *Ma didn't seem miserable.*

In fact, his mother had seemed to take joy in everything. She was Zemeni born, her skin a deep, plummy brown, and so tall his father had to tilt his head back to look her in the eye. Before Jesper was old enough to work the fields with his father, he'd been allowed to stay home with her. There was always laundry to be done, food to be made, wood to be chopped, and Jesper loved to help her.

"How's my land?" she'd ask every day when his father returned from the fields, and later Jesper would learn that the farm had been in her name, a wedding gift from his father, who had courted Aditi Hilli for nearly a year before she'd deigned to give him the time of day.

"Blooming," he'd say, kissing her cheek. "Just like you, love."

Jesper's da always promised to play with him and teach him to whittle at night, but invariably Colm would eat his dinner and fall asleep by the fire, boots still on, their soles stained orange with *jurda*. Jesper and his mother would pull them off Da's feet, stifling their giggles, then cover him with a blanket and see to the rest of the evening's chores. They'd clear the table and bring the laundry in off the line, and she'd tuck Jesper into bed. No matter how busy she got, no matter how many animals needed skinning, or baskets needed mending, she seemed to have the same infinite energy as Jesper, and she always had time to tell him a story before bed or hum him a song.

Jesper's mother was the one to teach him to ride a horse, bait a line, clean a fish, pluck a quail, to start a fire with nothing but two sticks, and to brew a proper cup of tea. And she taught him to shoot. First with a child's pellet gun that was little more than a toy, then with pistols and rifle. "Anyone can shoot," she'd told him. "But not everybody can aim." She taught him distance sighting, how to track an animal through the brush, the tricks that light can play on your eyes, how to factor wind shear, and how to shoot running, then seated on a horse. There was nothing she couldn't do.

There were secret lessons too. Sometimes, when they got home late, and she needed to get supper on, she'd boil the water without ever heating the stove, make bread rise just by looking at it. He'd seen her pull stains from clothes with a brush of her fingers, and she made her own gunpowder, extracting the saltpeter from a long-dry lake bed near where they lived. "Why pay for something I can make better myself?" she asked. "But we don't mention this to Da, hmm?" When Jesper asked why, she'd just say, "Because he has enough to worry about, and I don't like it when he worries about me." But Da did worry, especially when one of his mother's Zemeni friends came to the door looking for help or healing.

"You think the slavers can't reach you here?" he'd asked one night, pacing back and forth in their cabin as Jesper huddled in his blankets, pretending to sleep so that he could listen. "If word gets out there's a Grisha living here—"

"That word," Aditi said with a wave of one of her graceful hands, "is not our word. I cannot be anything other than what I am, and if my gifts can help people, then it's my duty to use them."

"And what about our son? Do you owe him nothing? Your first duty is to stay safe so we don't lose you."

But Jesper's mother had taken Colm's face in her hands, so gently, so kindly, with all the love shining from her eyes. "What kind of mother would I be to my son if I hid away my talents? If I let fear be my guide in this life? You knew what I was when you asked that I choose you, Colm. Do not now suggest that I be anything less."

And like that his father's frustration was gone. "I know. I just can't bear the thought of losing you."

She laughed and kissed him. "Then you must keep me close," she said with a wink. And the argument would be over. Until the next one.

As it turned out, Jesper's father was wrong. They didn't lose Aditi to slavers.

Jesper woke one night to hear voices, and when he'd wriggled out from under his blankets, he'd seen his mother putting her coat over her long nightgown, fetching a hat and her boots. He'd been seven then, small for his age, but old enough to know the most interesting conversations happened after his bedtime. A Zemeni man stood at the door in dusty riding clothes, and his father was saying, "It's the middle of the night. Surely this can wait until morning."

"If it were Jes who lay suffering, would you say that?" asked his mother.

"Aditi—"

She'd kissed Colm's cheek, then swept Jesper up in her arms. "Is my little rabbit awake?"

"No," he said.

"Well then, you must be dreaming." She tucked him back in, kissed his cheeks and his forehead. "Go to sleep, little rabbit, and I'll be back tomorrow."

But she didn't return the next day, and when a knock came the following morning, it was not his mother, just the same dusty Zemeni man.

Colm grabbed his son and was out the door in moments. He pushed a hat onto his head, plunked Jesper down in the saddle in front of him, then kicked his horse into a gallop. The dusty man rode an even dustier horse, and they followed him across miles of cultivated land to a white farmhouse at the edge of a *jurda* field. It was far nicer than their little cabin, two stories high with glass in the windows.

The woman waiting at the door was stouter than his mother, but nearly as tall, her hair piled in thick coils of braids. She waved them inside, saying, "She's upstairs."

In the years after, when Jesper had pieced together what had happened over those terrible days, he remembered very few things: the polished wood floors of the farmhouse and how they felt nearly silky beneath his fingers, the stout woman's eyes, red from crying, and the girl—a child several years older than Jesper with braids like her mother's. The girl had drunk from a well that had been dug too near one of the mines. It was supposed to be boarded up, but someone had simply taken away the bucket. The winch was still there, and the old rope. So the girl and her friends had used one of their lunch pails to bring the water up, cold as morning and twice as clear. All three of them had taken ill that night. Two of them had died. But Jesper's mother had saved the girl, the stout woman's daughter.

Aditi had come to the girl's bedside, sniffed the metal lunch pail, then set her hands to the girl's fevered skin. By noon the next day, the fever had broken and the yellowish tinge was gone from the girl's eyes. By early evening, she sat up and told her mother she was hungry. Aditi smiled once at her and collapsed.

"She didn't take enough care when extracting the poison," the dusty man said. "She absorbed too much of it herself. I've seen it happen before with zowa." *Zowa*. It simply meant "blessed." That was the word Jesper's mother used instead of Grisha. *We're zowa*, she would say to Jesper as she made a flower bloom with a flick of her fingers. *You and me.*

Now there was no one to call upon to save her. Jesper did not know how. If she'd been conscious, if she'd been stronger, she might have been able to heal herself. Instead she slipped away into some deep dream, her breath becoming more and more labored.

Jesper slept, his cheek pressed to his mother's palm, sure that any minute she would wake and stroke his cheek and he would hear her voice say, "What are you doing here, little rabbit?" Instead, he woke to the sound of his father weeping.

They'd taken her back to the farm and buried her beneath a cherry tree that was already beginning to flower. To Jesper, it had seemed too pretty for such a sad day, and even now, seeing those pale pink flowers in a shop window or embroidered on a lady's silks always put him in a melancholy mind. They took him back to the smell of fresh-turned earth, the wind whispering through the fields, his father's trembling baritone singing a lonely kind of song, a Kaelish air in words Jesper didn't understand.

When Colm had finished, the last notes drifting up into the cherry tree's branches, Jesper said, "Was Ma a witch?"

Colm laid a freckled hand on his son's shoulder and drew him close. "She was a queen, Jes," he said. "She was our queen."

Jesper had made dinner for them that night, burnt biscuits and watery soup, but his father ate every bite and read to him from his Kaelish book of Saints until the lights burned low and the pain in Jesper's heart eased enough for him to sleep. And that was the way it had been from then on, the two of them, looking after each other, working the fields, bundling and drying jurda in the summers, trying to make the farm pay. Why hadn't it been enough?

But even as Jesper had the thought, he knew it could never be enough. He could never go back to that life. He hadn't been built for it. Maybe if his mother had lived, she would have taught him to channel his restlessness. Maybe she would have shown him how to use his power instead of hiding it. Maybe he'd have gone to Ravka to be a soldier for the crown. Or maybe he would have ended up right here anyway.

He wiped the stain of the *jurda* from his fingertips and placed the lid back on the tin.

"The Zemeni don't just use the blossoms," he said. "I remember my mother soaking *jurda* stalks in goat's milk. She gave it to me when I'd been out in the fields."

"Why?" asked Matthias.

"To counteract the effects of inhaling *jurda* pollen all day. It's too much for a child's system, and no one wanted me more excitable than I already was."

"The stalks?" repeated Kuwei. "Most people just dispose of them."

"The stalks have a balm in them. The Zemeni drain it for ointments. They rub it on babies' gums and nostrils when they're burning *jurda*." Jesper's fingers drummed on the tin, a thought forming in his mind. Could the secret to the antidote for *jurda parem* be the *jurda* plant itself? He wasn't a chemist; he didn't think like Wylan, and he hadn't been trained as a Fabrikator. But he was his mother's son. "What if there's a version of the balm that would counteract the effects of *jurda parem*? There still wouldn't be a way to admin—"

That was when the window shattered. Jesper had his guns drawn in less than a breath, as Matthias shoved Kuwei down and shouldered his rifle. They edged to the wall and Jesper peeked outside through the smashed stained glass. In the shadows of the cemetery he saw lanterns raised, shifting shapes that had to be people—a lot of people.

"Unless the ghosts just got a lot more lively," Jesper said, "it looks like we have company."

PART FOUR

THE UNEXPECTED VISITOR

17

INEJ

At night, the warehouse district felt like it had shed its skin and taken on a new form. The shantytowns at its eastern edges crackled with life, while the streets of the district itself became a no-man's-land, occupied only by guards at their posts and *stadwatch* grunts walking their beats.

Inej and Nina moored their boat in the wide central canal that ran up the center of the district and made their way down the silent quay, keeping close to the warehouses and away from the streetlamps that lined the water's edge. They passed barges loaded with lumber and vast troughs piled high with coal. Every so often, they'd glimpse men working by lantern light, hefting barrels of rum or bales of cotton. Such valued cargo could not be left unattended overnight. When they had almost reached Sweet Reef, they saw two men unloading something from a large wagon parked by the side of the canal, lit by a single blue-tinged lamp.

"Corpselight," whispered Inej, and Nina shuddered. Bonelights, made from the crushed skeletons of deep-sea fishes, glowed green. But the corpselights burned some other fuel, a blue warning that allowed people to identify the flatboats of the bodymen, whose cargo was the dead.

"What are the bodymen doing in the warehouse district?"

"People don't like to see corpses on the streets or canals. The warehouse district is nearly deserted at night, so this is where they bring the bodies. Once the sun goes down, the bodymen collect the dead and bring them here. They work in shifts, neighborhood by neighborhood. They'll be gone by dawn, and so will their cargo." Out to the Reaper's Barge for burning.

"Why don't they just build a real cemetery?" Nina said.

"No room. I know there was some talk of reopening Black Veil a long time ago, but that all stopped when the Queen's Lady Plague struck. People are too afraid of contagion. If your family can afford it, they send you to a cemetery or graveyard outside Ketterdam. And if they can't . . ."

"No mourners," Nina said grimly.

No mourners, no funerals. Another way of saying good luck. But it was something more. A dark wink to the fact that there would be no expensive burials for people like them, no marble markers to remember their names, no wreaths of myrtle and rose.

Inej took the lead as they approached Sweet Reef. The silos themselves were daunting, vast as sentinel gods, monuments to industry emblazoned with the Van Eck red laurel. Soon everyone would know what that emblem stood for—cowardice and deceit. The circular cluster of Van Eck's silos was surrounded by a high metal fence.

"Razor wire," Nina noted.

"It won't be a problem." It had been invented to keep livestock in their pens. It would present no challenge for the Wraith.

They took up a watch beside the sturdy red-brick wall of a warehouse and held their position, confirming that the guards' routine hadn't changed. Just as Kaz had said, the guards took almost twelve minutes exactly to circle the fence that surrounded the silos. When the patrols were on the eastern side of the perimeter, Inej would have roughly six minutes to cross the wire. Once they passed to the west side, it would be too easy for them to spot her on the wire between the silos, but she'd be almost impossible to see on the roof. During those six minutes, Inej would deal with depositing the weevil in the silo hatch and then detach the line. If it took her longer than six minutes, she'd simply have to wait for the guards to come back around. She'd be unable to see them, but Nina had a powerful bonelight in hand. She would signal Inej with a brief flash of green light when she was clear to make the crossing.

"Ten silos," Inej said. "Nine crossings."

"They're a lot taller up close," said Nina. "Are you ready for this?"

Inej couldn't deny they were intimidating. "No matter the height of the mountain, the climbing is the same."

"That's not technically true. You need ropes, picks—"

"Don't be a Matthias."

Nina covered her mouth in horror. "I'm going to eat twice as much cake to make up for it."

Inej nodded wisely. "Sound policy."

The patrol was setting out from the guardhouse again.

"Inej," Nina said haltingly, "you should know, my power hasn't been the same since the *parem*. If we get into a scuffle—"

"No scuffles tonight. We pass through like ghosts." She gave Nina's shoulders a squeeze. "And I know no fiercer warrior, powers or not."

"But—"

"Nina, the guards."

The patrol had disappeared from view. If they didn't act now, they would have to wait for the next cycle, and it would put them behind schedule.

"On it," Nina said, and strode toward the guardhouse.

In the few steps it took her to cross the space from their warehouse lookout to the pool of lamplight bathing the guardhouse, Nina's whole demeanor changed. Inej couldn't quite explain it, but her steps grew more tentative, her shoulders drooped slightly. She almost seemed to shrink. She was no longer a trained Grisha, but a young, nervous immigrant hoping for a shred of kindness.

"Please to excuse?" Nina said in a ridiculously thick Ravkan accent.

The guard held his weapon at the ready but didn't look particularly concerned. "You shouldn't be here at night."

Nina murmured something, looking up at him with big green eyes. Inej had no idea she could look so thoroughly wholesome.

"What was that?" said the guard, stepping closer.

Inej made her move. She lit the long fuse on the low-grade flash bomb Wylan had given them, then loped for the fence, keeping well away from that pool of light, climbing silently. She was almost directly behind the guard and Nina, then above them. She could hear their voices as she slipped easily between the coils of razor wire.

"I come for job, yes?" Nina said. "To make sugar."

"We don't make it here, just store it. You'll want to go to one of the processing plants."

"But I need job. I . . . I . . ."

"Oh, hey now, don't cry. There, there."

Inej restrained a snort and dropped soundlessly to the ground on the other side of the fence. Through it, she could see the sandbags Kaz had mentioned stacked against the back wall of the guardhouse, and the corner of what must be the net he'd planned for her to use.

"Your . . . uh . . . your fella looking for work too?" the guard was asking.

"I have no . . . how you say? *Fella?*"

The gate beside the guardhouse didn't lock from the inside, so Inej pushed it open, leaving it just barely ajar for Nina, and hurried to the shadows at the base of the nearest silo.

She heard Nina say her goodbyes and walk off in the direction opposite their lookout. Then Inej waited. The minutes passed, and just as she became convinced the bomb was defective, a loud *pop* sounded and a bright flash of light crackled from the warehouse they'd used to spy on the guards. The guard emerged again, rifle raised, and took a few paces toward the warehouse.

"Hello?" he shouted.

Nina slipped from the shadows behind him and was inside the gate in a matter of moments. She closed it securely and headed for the second silo, disappearing into the dark. From there, she would be able to signal Inej as the guards made their rounds.

The guard returned to his post, walking backward in case some threat still waited in the warehouses beyond. Finally, he turned and gave the gate a shake to make sure it was locked, then headed inside the guardhouse.

Inej waited for the signal from Nina, then scampered up the rungs welded to the side of the silo. One story, two stories, ten. At the carnival, her uncle would have kept the audience entertained during her ascent. *No trick like this has ever been attempted before, and certainly never by one so young! Above you, behold the terrifying high wire.* A spotlight would come on, lighting the wire so that it looked like the frailest skein of cobweb strung across the tent. *Gentlemen, take your lady's hand in yours. See how slender her fingers are? Now imagine if you will, trying to walk across something so slender, so fragile as that! Who would dare such a thing? Who would dare to defy death itself?*

Then Inej would stand at the top of the pole and, hands on hips, shout, "I will!"

And the crowd would gasp.

But wait, no, this can't be right, her uncle would say, *a little girl?*

At this point, the crowd would always go wild. Women would swoon. Sometimes one of the men would try to stop the show.

There was no crowd tonight, only the wind, the cold metal beneath her fingers, the bright face of the moon.

Inej reached the top of the silo and looked out over the city below. Ketterdam gleamed with golden light, lanterns moving slowly across the canals, candles left burning in windows, shops and taverns still shining bright for the evening's business. She could make out the glittering spangle of the Lid, the colorful lanterns and showy cascade bulbs of the Staves.

In just a few short days, Van Eck's fortunes would be ruined and she would be free of her contract with Per Haskell. *Free.* To live as she wished. To seek forgiveness for her sins. To pursue her purpose. Would she miss this place? This crowded mess of a city she'd come to know so well, that had somehow become her home? She felt certain she would. So tonight, she would perform for her city, for the citizens of Ketterdam, even if they did not know to applaud.

Though it took a bit of muscle, she managed to loosen the wheel of the silo hatch and wrench it open. She reached into her pocket and took out the capped vial of the chemical weevil. Following Wylan's instructions, she gave it a firm shake, then spilled the contents into the silo. A low hiss filled the air, and as she watched, the sugar moved as if something was alive beneath its surface. She shivered. She'd heard of workers dying in silos, getting caught inside when the grain or corn or sugar gave way beneath their feet, being slowly suffocated to death. She closed the hatch and sealed it tight.

Then she reached down to the first rung of the metal ladder and attached the magnetized clamp Wylan had given her. It certainly felt like a solid grip. With the press of a button, two magnetized guide wires sprang free and attached to the silo with a soft *clang*. She removed a crossbow and a heavy coil of wire from her pack, then looped one end of the wire through the clamp, secured it tightly, and attached the guide wires. The other end was fastened to a magnetized clamp loaded into the crossbow. She released the trigger. The first shot went astray, and she had to wind the wire back. The second shot hooked to the wrong rung. But the third shot latched properly in place on the next silo. She twisted the clamp until the tension in the line felt right. They'd used similar gear before, but never on a distance so wide or a climb so high. It didn't matter. The distance, the danger would be transformed upon the wire, and she would be transformed too. On the high wire, she was beholden to no one, a creature without past or present, suspended between earth and sky.

It was time. You could learn the swings, but you had to be born to the wire.

Inej's mother had told her that gifted wire walkers were descended from the People of the Air, that they'd once had wings, and that in the right light, those wings could still be glimpsed on the humans to whom they showed favor. After that, Inej was perpetually twisting this way and that in front of mirrors and checking her shadow, ignoring the laughter of her cousins, to see if perhaps her own wings might be showing.

When her father grew tired of her pestering him every day, he allowed her to begin her education on the low ropes, barefoot, so that she could get a feel for walking forward and backward, keeping her center balanced. She'd been bored senseless, but she'd dutifully gone through the exercises each day, testing her strength, trying the feel of leather shoes that would allow her to grip the stiffer, less friendly wire. If her father got distracted, she would flip into a handstand so that when he turned back to her, she was traversing the rope on her hands. He agreed to raise the rope a few inches, let her try a proper wire, and at each level, Inej mastered one skill after another—cartwheels, flips, keeping a pitcher of water perched on her head. She familiarized herself with the slender, flexible pole that would allow her to keep her balance at greater heights.

One afternoon her uncle and cousins had been setting up a new act. Hanzi was going to push Asha across the wire in a wheelbarrow. The day was hot and they'd decided to take a break for lunch and go for a swim in the river. Alone in the quiet camp, Inej scaled one of the platform rigs they'd erected, making sure her back was to the sun so that she'd have a clear view of the wire.

That high up, the world became a reflection of itself, its shapes stunted, its shadows elongated, familiar in its forms but somehow untrustworthy, and as Inej placed her slippered foot on the wire, she'd felt a sudden moment of doubt. Though this was the same width of wire she'd walked for weeks without fear, it seemed far thinner now, as if in this mirror world, the wire obeyed different rules. *When fear arrives, something is about to happen.*

Inej breathed deeply, tucked her hips beneath her navel, and took her first steps on the air. Beneath her the grass was an undulating sea. She felt her weight shift, listed left, felt the pull of the earth, gravity ready to unite her with her shadow far below.

Her muscles flexed, she bent her knees, the moment passed, and then there was only her and the wire. She was already halfway across when she realized she was being watched. She let her vision expand, but kept her focus. Inej would never forget the look on her father's face as he returned from the river with her uncle and cousins, his head tilted up at her, mouth a startled black O, her mother emerging from the wagon and pressing a hand over her heart. They had stayed silent, afraid to break her concentration—her first audience on the wire, mute with terror that felt to her like adulation.

Once she'd climbed down, her mother had spent the better part of an hour alternating between hugging her and shrieking at her. Her father had been stern, but she hadn't missed the pride in his gaze or the grudging admiration in her cousins' eyes.

When one of them had taken her aside later and said, "How do you walk so fearlessly?" she'd simply shrugged and said, "It's just walking."

But that wasn't true. It was better than walking. When others walked the wire, they fought it—the wind, the height, the distance. When Inej was on the high wire, it became her world. She could feel its tilt and pull. It was a planet and she was its moon. There was a simplicity to it that she never felt on the swings, where she was carried away by momentum. She loved the stillness she could find on the wire, and it was something no one else understood.

She had fallen only once, and she still blamed it on the net. They'd strung it up because Hanzi was adding a unicycle to his act. One moment Inej was walking and the next she was falling. She barely had time to register it before she hit the net—and bounced right out of it onto the ground. Inej felt somewhat startled to discover how very hard the earth was, that it would not soften or bend for her. She broke two ribs and had a lump on her head the size of a fat goose egg.

"It's good that it's so large," her father murmured over it. "That means the blood is not inside her brain."

As soon as Inej's bandages came off, she was back on the wire. She never worked with a net again. She knew it had made her careless. But looking down now, she could admit she wouldn't have minded a little insurance. Far below, the moonlight caught the curves of the cobblestones, making them look like the black seeds of some exotic fruit. But the net stashed behind the guardhouse was useless with only Nina there to hold it, and regardless of what Kaz had originally intended, the new plan hadn't been built around someone in plain sight holding a net. So Inej would walk as she had always done, with nothing to catch her, borne aloft by her invisible wings.

Inej slid the balance pole from its loop on her vest and, with a flick, extended it to its full length. She tested its weight in her hands, flexed her toes in her slippers. They were leather, stolen from the Cirkus Zirkoa at her request. Their smooth soles lacked the firm, tactile grip of her beloved rubber shoes, but the slippers allowed her to release more easily.

At last the signal came from Nina, a brief flash of green light.

Inej stepped out onto the wire. Instantly, the wind snatched at her and she released a long breath, feeling its persistent tug, using the flexible pole to pull her center of gravity lower.

She let her knees bounce once. Thankfully, the wire had almost no give. She walked, feeling the hard press of it beneath the arches of her feet. With each step, it bowed slightly, eager to twist away from her gripping toes.

The air felt warm against her skin. It smelled of sugar and molasses. Her hood was down and she could feel the hairs from her braid escaping to tickle her face. She focused on the wire, feeling the familiar kinship she'd experienced as a child, as if the wire were clinging to her as closely as she clung to it, welcoming her into that mirror world, a secret place occupied by her alone. In moments, she'd reached the rooftop of the second silo.

She stepped onto it, retracting the balance pole and returning it to its sling. She took a sip of water from the flask in her pocket, allowed herself the briefest moment to stretch. Then she opened the hatch and dropped in the weevil. Again she heard that crackling hiss, and her nose filled with the smell of burning sugar. It was stronger this time, a sweet, dense cloud of perfume.

Suddenly, she was back at the Menagerie, a thick hand grasping her wrist, demanding. Inej had gotten good at anticipating when a memory might seize her, bracing for it, but this time she wasn't prepared. It came at her, more insistent than the wind on the wire, sending her mind sprawling. Though he smelled of vanilla, beneath it, she could smell garlic. She felt the slither of silk all around her as if the bed itself were a living thing.

Inej didn't remember all of them. As the nights at the Menagerie had strung together, she had become better at numbing herself, vanishing so completely that she almost didn't care what was done to the body she left behind. She learned that the men who came to the house never looked too closely, never asked too many questions. They wanted an illusion, and they were willing to ignore anything to preserve that illusion. Tears, of course, were forbidden. She had cried the first night. Tante Heleen had used the switch on her, then the cane, then choked her until she'd passed out. The next time, Inej's fear was greater than her sorrow.

She learned to smile, to whisper, to arch her back and make the sounds Tante Heleen's customers required. She still wept, but the tears were never shed. They filled the empty place inside her, a well of sadness where, each night, she sank like a stone. The Menagerie was one of the most expensive pleasure houses in the Barrel, but its customers were no kinder than those who frequented the dollar houses and alley girls. In some ways, Inej came to understand, they were worse. *When a man spends that much coin,* said the Kaelish girl, Caera, *he thinks he's earned the right to do whatever he wants.*

There were young men, old men, handsome men, ugly men. There was the man who cried and struck her when he could not perform. The man who wanted her to pretend it was their wedding night and tell him that she loved him. The man with sharp teeth like a kitten who had bitten at her breasts until she'd bled. Tante Heleen added the price of the blood-speckled sheets and the days of work Inej missed to her indenture. But he hadn't been the worst. The worst had been a Ravkan man who had chosen her in the parlor, the man who smelled of vanilla. Only when they were back in her room amid the purple silks and incense did he say, "I've seen you before, you know."

Inej had laughed, thinking this was part of the game he wished to play, and poured him wine from a golden carafe. "Surely not."

"It was years ago, at one of the carnivals outside Caryeva."

Wine sloshed over the lip of the glass. "You must have me confused with someone else."

"No," he said, eager as a boy. "I'm sure of it. I saw your family perform there. I was on military leave. You couldn't have been more than ten, the barest slip of a girl, walking the high wire without fear. You wore a headdress covered in roses. At one point, you bobbled. You lost your footing and the petals of your crown came loose in a cloud that drifted down, down." He fluttered his fingers through the air as if miming a snowfall. "The crowd gasped—and so did I. I came back the second night, and it happened again, and even though then I knew it was all part of the act, I still felt my heart clench as you pretended to regain your balance."

Inej tried to steady her shaking hands. The rose headdress had been her mother's idea. "You make it look too easy, *meja*, scampering around like a squirrel on a branch. They must believe you are in danger even if you are not."

That had been Inej's worst night at the Menagerie, because when the man who smelled of vanilla had begun to kiss her neck and peel away her silks, she hadn't been able to leave her body behind. Somehow his memory of her had tied her past and present together, pinned her there beneath him. She'd cried, but he hadn't seemed to mind.

Inej could hear the hissing of the sugar as the weevil did its work. She forced herself to focus on the sound, to breathe past the constriction in her throat.

I will have you without armor. Those were the words she'd said to Kaz aboard the *Ferolind*, desperate for some sign that he might open himself to her, that they could be more than two wary creatures united by their distrust of the world. But what might have happened if he'd spoken that night? If he had willingly offered her some part of his heart? What if he had come to her, laid his gloves aside, drawn her to him, kissed her mouth? Would she have pulled him closer? Kissed him back? Could she have been herself in such a moment, or would she have broken apart and vanished, a doll in his arms, a girl who could never quite be whole?

It didn't matter. Kaz hadn't spoken, and perhaps that had been best for them both. They could continue on with their armor intact. She would have her ship and he would have his city.

Inej reached out to close the hatch and took a deep breath of coal-tinged air, coughing the sweetness of the ruined sugar from her lungs. Then she stumbled as she felt a hand grab the back of her neck, shove her forward.

She felt her center of gravity shift as she was sucked into the yawning mouth of the silo.

18

KAZ

Getting into the house wasn't nearly as difficult as it should have been, and it put Kaz on edge. Was he giving Van Eck too much credit? *The man thinks like a merch*, Kaz reminded himself as he tucked his cane beneath his arm and eased down a drainpipe. *He still believes his money keeps him safe.*

The easiest points of entry were the windows on the house's top floor, accessible only from the roof. Wylan wasn't up to the climb or the descent, so Kaz would go first and get him inside via the lower floors.

"Two good legs and he still needs a ladder," Kaz muttered, ignoring the twinge his leg gave in agreement.

He wasn't thrilled to be on another job with Wylan, but Wylan's knowledge of the house and his father's habits would be useful if any surprises cropped up, and he was best equipped to handle the auric acid. Kaz thought of Inej, perched on the roof of the Church of Barter, the city lights glinting below. *This is what I'm good at, so let me do my job*. Fine. He would let them all do their jobs. Nina would hold up her end of the mission, and Inej had seemed confident enough in her ability to walk the wire—with little rest and without the security of a net. *Would she have told you if she was afraid? Is that something you've ever shown sympathy for?*

Kaz shook the thought from his mind. If Inej didn't doubt her abilities, then he shouldn't either. Besides, if they wanted that seal for Nina's darling refugees, he had his own problems to contend with.

Luckily, Van Eck's security system wasn't one of them. Inej's surveillance had indicated that the locks were Schuyler work. They were complicated little bastards, but once you'd cracked one, you'd cracked them all. Kaz had gotten on very friendly terms with a locksmith in Klokstraat who firmly believed Kaz was the son of a wealthy merchant who highly valued his collection of priceless snuffboxes. Consequently, Kaz was always first to know exactly how the rich of Ketterdam were keeping their property secure. Kaz had once heard Hubrecht Mohren, Master Thief of Pijl, extemporizing on the beauty of a quality lock while drunk on brown lager in the Crow Club.

"A lock is like a woman," he'd said blearily. "You have to seduce it into giving up its secrets." He was one of Per Haskell's old cronies, happy to talk about better days and big scams, especially if it meant he didn't have to do much work. And that was exactly the kind of muddled wisdom these old cadgers loved to spout. Sure, a lock was like a woman. It was also like a man and anyone or anything else—if you wanted to understand it, you had to take it apart and see how it worked. If you wanted to master it, you had to learn it so well you could put it back together.

The lock on the window gave way in his hands with a satisfying click. He slid open the sash and climbed inside. The tiny rooms on the top floor of Van Eck's house were devoted to the servants' quarters, but all of the staff were currently occupied below with Van Eck's guests. Some of the richest members of the Kerch Merchant Council were filling their bellies in the first-floor dining room, probably listening to Van Eck's tale of woe about his son's kidnapping and commiserating about the gangs controlling the Barrel. From the smell in the air, Kaz suspected ham was on the menu.

He opened the door and quietly made his way to the staircase, then proceeded cautiously down to the second floor. He knew Van Eck's house from when he and Inej had heisted the DeKappel oil, and he always liked returning to a home or a business he'd had cause to visit before. It wasn't just the familiarity. It was as if by returning, he laid claim to a place. *We know each other's secrets*, the house seemed to say. *Welcome back.*

A guard stood at attention at the end of the carpeted hallway in front of what Kaz knew was Alys' door. Kaz checked his watch. There was a brief pop and a flash of light from the window at the end of the hall. At least Wylan was punctual. The guard went to investigate, and Kaz slipped down the hall in the other direction.

He ducked into Wylan's old room—which was now clearly intended to be the nursery. By the light from the street below, he could see its walls had been decorated with an elaborate seascape mural. The bassinet was shaped like a tiny sailing ship, complete with flags and a captain's wheel. Van Eck was really embracing this new heir thing.

Kaz worked the lock on the nursery window and pushed it open, then secured the rope ladder and waited. He heard a loud thud and winced. Apparently Wylan had made it over the garden wall. Hopefully he hadn't broken the containers of auric acid and burned a hole through himself and the rosebushes. A moment later, Kaz heard panting and Wylan rounded the corner, bustling along like a harried goose. When he was below the window, he tucked his satchel carefully against his body and climbed up the rope ladder, sending it swaying wildly left and right. Kaz helped him through the window, then pulled the ladder in and closed the sash. They'd exit the same way.

Wylan looked around the nursery with wide eyes, then just shook his head. Kaz checked the hall. The guard was back at his post in front of Alys' door.

"Well?" Kaz whispered to Wylan.

"It's a slow-burning fuse," said Wylan. "The timing is imprecise."

The seconds ticked by. Finally, another pop sounded. The guard returned to the window, and Kaz gestured for Wylan to follow him along the hallway. Kaz made quick work of the lock on Van Eck's office door, and they were inside in moments.

When Kaz had broken into the house to steal the DeKappel, he'd been surprised by the office's plush trappings. He'd expected severe mercher restraint, but the woodwork was heavily ornamented with swags of laurel leaves; a chair the size of a throne, upholstered in crimson velvet, loomed over the wide, glossy desk.

"Behind the painting," Wylan whispered, gesturing to a portrait of one of the Van Eck ancestors.

"Which member of your hallowed line is that supposed to be?"

"Martin Van Eck, my great-great-grandfather. He was a ship's captain, the first to land at Eames Chin and navigate the river inland. He brought back a shipload of spices and used the profits to buy a second ship—that's what my father told me, anyway. That was the start of the Van Eck fortune."

"And we'll be the end of it." Kaz shook out a bonelight, and the green glow filled the room. "Quite a resemblance," he said, glancing at the gaunt face, the high brow, and stern blue eyes.

Wylan shrugged. "Except for the red hair, I always took after my father. And his father and all the Van Ecks. Well, until now."

They each took a side of the painting and lifted it from the wall.

"Look at you," Kaz crooned as Van Eck's safe came into view. *Safe* didn't even seem like the right word. It was more like a vault, a steel door set into a wall that had itself been reinforced with more steel. The lock on it was Kerch-made but like nothing Kaz had ever seen before, a series of tumblers that could be reset with a random combination of numbers every day. Impossible to crack in less than an hour. But if you couldn't open a door, you just had to make a new one.

The sound of raised voices filtered up from the floor below. The merchers were finding something to disagree about. Kaz wouldn't have minded a chance to eavesdrop on that conversation. "Let's go," he said. "The clock is ticking."

Wylan removed two jars from his satchel. On their own, they were nothing special, but if Wylan was right, once they were combined, the resulting compound would burn through everything except the balsa glass container.

Wylan took a deep breath and held the jars away from his body. "Stay back," he said, and poured the contents of one jar into the other. Nothing happened.

"Well?" Kaz said.

"Move, please."

Wylan took a balsa glass pipette and drew out a small amount of liquid, letting it trickle down the front of the safe's steel door. Instantly, the metal began to dissolve, giving off a noisy crackle that seemed uncomfortably loud in the small room. A sharp metallic smell filled the air, and both Kaz and Wylan covered their faces with their sleeves.

"Trouble in a bottle," Kaz marveled.

Wylan worked steadily, carefully transferring the auric acid from the jar onto the steel, the hole in the safe door growing steadily larger.

"Pick up the pace," Kaz said, eyeing his watch.

"If I spill a single drop of this, it will burn straight through the floor onto my father's dinner guests."

"Take your time."

The acid consumed the metal in rapid bursts, burning quickly and only gradually tapering off. Hopefully, it wouldn't eat through too much of the wall after they left. He didn't mind the idea of the office collapsing on Van Eck and his guests, but not before the night's business was complete.

After what felt like a lifetime, the hole was big enough to reach through. Kaz shone the bonelight inside and saw a ledger, stacks of *kruge,* and a little velvet bag. Kaz drew the bag from the safe, wincing when his arm made contact with the edge of the hole. The steel was still hot enough to singe.

He shook the contents of the bag into his leather-clad palm: a fat gold ring with an engraving of a red laurel and Van Eck's initials.

He tucked the ring into his pocket, then grabbed a couple of stacks of *kruge* and handed one over to Wylan.

Kaz almost laughed at the expression on Wylan's face. "Does this bother you, merchling?"

"I don't enjoy feeling like a thief."

"After everything he's done?"

"Yes."

"So much for righteous. You do realize we're stealing your money?"

"Jesper said the same thing, but I'm sure my father wrote me out of his will as soon as Alys became pregnant."

"That doesn't mean you're any less entitled to it."

"I don't want it. I just don't want *him* to have it."

"What a luxury to turn your back on luxury." Kaz shoved the *kruge* into his pockets.

"How would I run an empire?" Wylan said, tossing the pipette into the safe to smolder. "I can't read a ledger or a bill of lading. I can't write a purchase order. My father is wrong about a lot of things, but he's right about that. I'd be a laughingstock."

"So pay someone to do that work for you."

"Would you?" asked Wylan, his chin jutting forward. "Trust someone with that knowledge, with a secret that could destroy you?"

Yes, thought Kaz without hesitation. *There's one person I would trust. One person I know would never use my weaknesses against me.*

He thumbed quickly through the ledger and said, "When people see a cripple walking down the street, leaning on his cane, what do they feel?" Wylan looked away. People always did when Kaz talked about his limp, as if he didn't know what he was or how the world saw him. "They feel pity. Now, what do they think when they see me coming?"

Wylan's mouth quirked up at the corner. "They think they'd better cross the street."

Kaz tossed the ledger back in the safe. "You're not weak because you can't read. You're weak because you're afraid of people seeing your weakness. You're letting shame decide who you are. Help me with the painting."

They lifted the portrait back into place over the gaping hole in the safe. Martin Van Eck glared down at them.

"Think on it, Wylan," Kaz said as he straightened the frame. "It's shame that lines my pockets, shame that keeps the Barrel teeming with fools ready to put on a mask just so they can have what they want with no one the wiser for it. We can endure all kinds of pain. It's shame that eats men whole."

"Wise words," said a voice from the corner.

Kaz and Wylan whirled. The lamps flared brightly, flooding the room with light, and a figure emerged from a niche in the opposite wall that hadn't been there a moment before: Pekka Rollins, a smug grin on his ruddy face, bracketed by a cluster of Dime Lions all carrying pistols, saps, and axe handles.

"Kaz Brekker," Rollins mocked. "Philosopher crook."

19

MATTHIAS

"Stay down!" Matthias shouted at Kuwei. The Shu boy flattened himself to the floor. A second rattle of gunfire shook the air, shattering another of the stained-glass portholes.

"Either they're interested in wasting a lot of bullets or those are warning shots," said Jesper. In a low crouch, Matthias edged to the other side of the tomb and peered through a thin crack in the stone.

"We're surrounded," he said. The people standing between Black Veil's graves were a far cry from the *stadwatch* officers he'd expected to see. In the flickering light of lanterns and torches, Matthias glimpsed plaid and paisley, striped vests, and checkered coats. The uniform of the Barrel. They carried equally motley weapons—guns, knives as long as a man's forearm, wooden bats.

"I can't make out their tattoos," said Jesper. "But I'm pretty sure that's Doughty up front."

Doughty. Matthias searched his memory, then remembered the man who had escorted them to Pekka Rollins when Kaz had sought a loan. "Dime Lions."

"A lot of them."

"What do they want?" said Kuwei tremulously.

Matthias could hear people laughing, shouting, and beneath it all, the low, fevered buzz that came when soldiers knew they had the advantage, when they scented the promise of bloodshed in the air.

A cheer arose from the crowd as a Dime Lion sprinted forward and hurled something toward the tomb. It soared through one of the broken windows and hit the floor with a clang. Green gas burst from its sides.

Matthias yanked a horse blanket from the floor and threw it over the canister. He shoved it back through the porthole as another stutter of gunfire split the air. His eyes burned, tears streaming down his cheeks.

Now the buzz was cresting. The Dime Lions surged forward.

Jesper squeezed off a shot and one of the advancing crew fell, his torch extinguished on the damp ground. Again and again Jesper fired, his aim unerring as Dime Lions toppled. Their ranks broke as they scattered for cover.

"Keep lining up, boys," Jesper said grimly.

"Come on out!" bellowed Doughty from behind a grave. "You can't shoot us all."

"I can't hear you," shouted Jesper. "Come closer."

"We smashed your boats. You got no way off this island except us. So come quiet or we'll bring just your heads back to the Barrel."

"Watch out!" said Matthias. Doughty had been distracting them. Another canister crashed through a window, then another. "The catacomb!" Matthias roared, and they raced for the opposite end of the tomb, cramming themselves into the passage and sealing the stone door behind them. Jesper tore off his shirt and shoved it into the gap between the door and the floor.

The dark was almost complete. For a moment, there was only the sound of the three of them coughing and gasping, trying to dislodge the gas from their lungs. Then Jesper shook out a bonelight and their faces were lit by an eerie green glow.

"How the hell did they find us?" he asked.

"It doesn't matter," said Matthias. There was no time to think about how Black Veil had been compromised. All he knew was that if Pekka Rollins had sent his gang after them, Nina might be in danger too. "What are our assets?"

"Wylan left us with a bunch of those violet bombs in case we ran into trouble with the Shu soldiers, and I've got a couple of flash bombs too. Kuwei?"

"I have nothing," he said.

"You have that damn travel pack," said Jesper. "There's nothing useful in there?"

Kuwei clutched the bag to his chest. "My notebooks," he said with a sniff.

"What about the leavings from Wylan's work?" asked Matthias. No one had bothered to clear anything away.

"It's just some of the stuff he used to make the fireworks for Goedmedbridge," said Jesper.

A flurry of shouts came from outside.

"They're going to blow the door to the tomb," said Matthias. It was what he would have done if he'd wanted prisoners instead of casualties, though he felt certain Kuwei was the only one of them the Dime Lions cared about extracting alive.

"There have to be at least thirty toughs out there looking to skin our hides," said Jesper. "There's only one way out of the tomb, and we're on a damn island. We're done for."

"Maybe not," said Matthias, considering the ghostly green glow of the bonelight. Though he did not have Kaz's gift for scheming, he'd been raised in the military. There might be a way out of this.

"Are you crazy? The Dime Lions have to know how badly outnumbered we are."

"True," said Matthias. "But they don't know that two of us are Grisha."

They thought they were hunting a scientist, not an Inferni, and Jesper had long kept his Fabrikator powers a secret.

"Yeah, two Grisha with barely any training," said Jesper.

A loud *boom* sounded, shaking the tomb walls and sending Matthias careening into the others.

"They're coming!" cried Kuwei.

But no footsteps sounded, and there was another series of shouts from outside. "They didn't use a big enough charge," said Matthias. "They want you alive, so they're being cautious. We have one more chance. Kuwei, how much heat can you produce from a flame?"

"I can make a fire burn more intensely, but it's hard to maintain."

Matthias remembered the violet flames licking over the body of the flying Shu soldier, inextinguishable. Wylan had said they burned hotter than ordinary fire.

"Give me one of the bombs," he told Jesper. "I'm going to blow the back of the catacomb."

"Why?"

"To make them think we're blasting our way out the other side," Matthias said, setting the bomb at the farthest end of the stone passage.

"Are you sure you aren't going to blow us up with it?"

"No," admitted Matthias. "But unless you have some brilliant idea—"

"I—"

"Shooting as many people as possible before we die is not an option."

Jesper shrugged. "In that case, go on."

"Kuwei, as soon as the bomb goes off, get to the front door as fast as you can. The gas should have diffused, but I want you to run. I'll be right behind you, lending cover. Do you know the tomb with the big broken mast?"

"To the right?"

"Yes. Head straight for that. Jesper, grab up all those powders that Wylan left and do the same."

"Why?"

Matthias lit the fuse. "You can follow my orders or you can ask your questions of the Dime Lions. Now, get down."

He shoved them both against the wall, shielding their bodies as a thunderous *boom* sounded from the end of the tunnel.

"Run!"

They burst through the catacomb door.

Matthias kept a hand on Kuwei's shoulder, urging him along as they raced through the remnants of the green gas. "Remember, head straight to the broken mast." He kicked open the tomb door and lobbed a flash bomb into the air. It exploded in shards of diamond-white light, and Matthias ran for cover in the trees, blasting at the Dime Lions with his rifle as he dodged through the graves.

The Dime Lions returned fire and Matthias dove beneath a slump of moss-covered stones. He saw Jesper charge through the tomb door, revolvers blazing, cutting toward the broken stone mast. Matthias lobbed the last flash bomb into the air as Jesper rolled to the right, and the roar of gunfire erupted like a storm breaking as the Dime Lions forgot all promise of discipline or offer of reward and let fly with everything they had. They might have been ordered to keep Kuwei alive, but they were Barrel rats, not trained soldiers.

On his belly, Matthias crawled through the dirt of the graveyard. "Everyone unhurt?" he asked as he reached the broken mast of the mausoleum.

"Out of breath but still breathing," said Jesper. Kuwei nodded, though he was shaking badly. "Fantastic plan, by the way. How is being pinned down here better than being pinned down in the tomb?"

"Did you get Wylan's powders?"

"What was left of them," said Jesper. He emptied his pockets, revealing three packets.

Matthias chose one at random. "Can you manipulate those powders?"

Jesper shifted uneasily. "Yes. I guess. I did something similar at the Ice Court. Why?"

Why. Why. In the *drüskelle* he would have been brigged for insubordination.

"Black Veil is supposedly haunted, yes? We're going to make some ghosts." Matthias glanced around the edge of the mausoleum. "They're moving in. I need you to follow my orders and stop asking questions. Both of you."

"No wonder you and Kaz don't get along," Jesper muttered.

In as few words as he could, Matthias explained what he intended now and when they reached the island's shore—assuming his plan worked.

"I've never done this before," said Kuwei.

Jesper winked at him. "That's what makes it exciting."

"Ready?" said Matthias.

He opened the packet. Jesper raised his hands, and with a light *whump* the powder rose in a cloud. It hung suspended in the air as if time had slowed. Jesper focused, sweat beading on his forehead, then shoved his hands forward. The cloud thinned and rolled over the heads of the Dime Lions, then caught in one of their torches in a burst of green.

The men surrounding the torch holder gasped.

"*Kuwei,*" directed Matthias.

The Shu boy lifted his hands and the flame from the green torch crept along the handle, snaking up the arm of its bearer in a sinuous coil of fire. The man screamed, tossing the torch away, falling to the ground and rolling in an attempt to extinguish the flames.

"Keep going," said Matthias, and Kuwei flexed his fingers, but the green flames went out.

"I'm sorry!" said Kuwei.

"Make another," demanded Matthias. There was no time for cosseting.

Kuwei thrust his hands out again and one of the Dime Lions' lanterns exploded, this time in a whorl of yellow flame. Kuwei shrank back as if he hadn't intended to use so much force.

"Don't lose your focus," Matthias urged.

Kuwei curled his wrists and the flames of the lantern rose in a serpentine arc.

"Hey," said Jesper. "Not bad." He opened another packet of powder and tossed its contents into the air, then arced his arms forward, sending it to meet Kuwei's flame. The twisting thread of fire turned a deep, shimmering crimson. "Strontium chloride," the sharpshooter murmured. "My favorite."

Kuwei flexed one of his fists and another stream of fire joined the flames of the lantern, then another, forming a thick-bodied snake that undulated over Black Veil, ready to strike.

"Ghosts!" one of the Dime Lions shouted.

"Don't be daft," replied another.

Matthias watched that red serpent coil and uncoil in trails of flame, feeling the old fear rise in him. He'd grown comfortable with Kuwei, and yet it had been Inferni fire that consumed his family's village in a border skirmish. Somehow, he'd forgotten the power this boy held within him. *It was a war*, he reminded himself. *And this is one too.*

The Dime Lions were distracted, but it wouldn't last long.

"Spread the fire to the trees," Matthias said, and with a little grunt, Kuwei threw his arms wide. The green leaves fought the onslaught of devouring flame, then caught.

"They got a Grisha," shouted Doughty. "Flank them!"

"To the shore!" said Matthias. "Now!" They sprinted past gravestones and broken stone Saints. "Kuwei, get ready. We need everything you have."

They skittered down the bank, tumbling into the shallows. Matthias grabbed the violet bombs and smashed them open on the hulls of the wrecked boats. Slithering violet flame engulfed them. It had an eerie, almost creamy quality. Matthias had navigated to and from Black Veil enough times to know this was the shallowest part of the canal, the long stretch of sandbar where boats were most likely to run aground, but the opposite shore seemed impossibly far away.

"Kuwei," he commanded, praying that the Shu boy was strong enough, hoping that he could manage the plan Matthias had outlined bare moments earlier, "make a path."

Kuwei shoved his hands forward and the flames poured into the water, sending up a massive plume of steam. At first, all Matthias could see was a wall of billowing white. Then the steam parted slightly and he saw fish flopping in the mud, crabs skittering over the exposed bottom of the canal as violet flames licked at the water to either side.

"All the Saints and the donkeys they rode in on," Jesper said on an awed breath. "Kuwei, you did it."

Matthias turned back to the island and opened fire into the trees.

"Hurry!" he shouted, and they ran over a road that had not been there moments before, bolting for the other side of the canal, for the streets and alleys that might lend them cover. *Unnatural*, a voice clamored in his head. *No*, thought Matthias, *miraculous*.

"You do realize you just led your own little Grisha army?" said Jesper as they hauled themselves out of the mud and hurried through the shadowed streets toward Sweet Reef.

He had. An uncomfortable thought. Through Jesper and Kuwei, he had wielded Grisha power. And yet, Matthias did not feel tainted or somehow marked by it. He remembered what Nina had said about the construction of the Ice Court, that it must be the work of Grisha and not the work of Djel. What if both things were true? What if Djel worked through these people? *Unnatural*. The word had come so easily to him, a way to dismiss what he did not understand, to make Nina and her kind less than human. But what if behind the righteousness that drove the *drüskelle*, there was something less clean or justified? What if it wasn't even fear or anger but simply envy? What did it mean to aspire to serve Djel, only to see his power in the gifts of another, to know you could never possess those gifts yourself?

The *drüskelle* gave their oath to Fjerda, but to their god as well. If they could be made to see miracles where once they'd seen abomination, what else might change? *I have been made to protect you.* His duty to his god, his duty to Nina. Maybe they were the same thing. What if Djel's hand had raised the waters the night of the wrathful storm that wrecked the *drüskelle* ship and bound Matthias and Nina together?

Matthias was running through the streets of a foreign city, into dangers he did not know, but for the first time since he'd looked into Nina's eyes and seen his own humanity reflected back at him, the war inside him quieted.

We'll find a way to change their minds, she'd said. *All of them.* He would locate Nina. They would survive this night. They would free themselves of this damp, misbegotten city, and then . . . Well, then they'd change the world.

20

INEJ

Inej twisted, breaking the clawlike grip on the back of her neck. She scrambled to stop her fall. Her legs found purchase on the silo roof and she yanked herself free, pushing away from the hatch. She rocked back on her heels, knives already released from their sheaths, deadly weight in her hands.

Her mind could not quite make sense out of what she was seeing. A girl stood before her on the silo roof, gleaming like a figure carved of ivory and amber. Her tunic and trousers were the color of cream, banded in ivory leather and embroidered in gold. Her auburn hair hung in a thick braid laced with the glint of jewels. She was tall and slender, maybe a year or two older than Inej.

Inej's first thought was of the Kherguud soldiers that Nina and the others had seen in West Stave, but this girl didn't look Shu.

"Hello, Wraith," the girl said.

"Do I know you?"

"I am Dunyasha, the White Blade, trained by the Sages of Ahmrat Jen, the greatest assassin of this age."

"Doesn't ring a bell."

"I'm new to this city," the girl acknowledged, "but I'm told you are a legend on these filthy streets. I confess, I thought you'd be . . . taller."

"What business?" Inej asked, the traditional Kerch greeting at the beginning of any meeting, though it felt absurd to say it twenty stories in the air.

Dunyasha smiled. It seemed practiced, like the smiles Inej had seen girls give customers in the gilded Menagerie parlor. "A crude greeting for a crude city." She flicked her fingers carelessly toward the skyline, acknowledging and dismissing Ketterdam with a single gesture. "Fate brought me here."

"And does fate pay your wages?" Inej asked, sizing her up. She did not think this ivory-and-amber girl had scaled a silo just to make her acquaintance. In a fight, Dunyasha's height would give her a longer reach, but it might impact her balance. Had Van Eck sent her? And if so, had he sent someone after Nina too? She spared the briefest glance below but could see nothing in the deep shadows of the silos. "Who do you work for?"

Knives appeared in Dunyasha's hands, their edges gleaming brightly. "Our work is death," she said, "and it is holy."

An exultant light filled her eyes, the first true spark of life Inej had seen in her, and then she attacked.

Inej was startled by the girl's speed. Dunyasha moved like painted light, as if she were a blade herself, cutting through the darkness, her knives slicing in tandem, left, right. Inej let her body respond, dodging more on instinct than anything else, backing away from her opponent, but avoiding the silo's edge. She feinted left and slipped past Dunyasha, managing the first thrust of her own.

Dunyasha whirled and evaded the attack easily, weightless as sun gilding the surface of a lake. Inej had never seen someone fight this way, as if she were moving to music only she could hear.

"Are you afraid, Wraith?" Inej felt Dunyasha's knife shred through her sleeve. The sting of the blade was like a burning lash. *Not too deep*, she told herself. Unless of course the blade was poisoned. "I think you are. You cannot fear death and be its true emissary."

Was the girl mad? Or just chatty? Inej bobbed backward, moving in a circle around the silo's roof.

"I was born without fear," Dunyasha continued with a happy chuckle. "My parents thought I would drown because I crawled into the sea as a baby, laughing."

"Perhaps they worried you would talk yourself to death."

Her opponent drove forward with new intensity, and Inej wondered if the girl had only been toying with her in that first aggressive flurry, feeling for her strengths and weaknesses before she seized the advantage. They exchanged thrusts, but Dunyasha was fresh. Inej could feel every ache and injury and trial of the last month in her body—the knife wound that had almost killed her, the trip up the incinerator, the days she'd spent bound in captivity.

"I confess to disappointment," Dunyasha said as her feet skipped nimbly over the silo's roof. "I had hoped you might prove a challenge. But what do I find? A smudge of a Suli acrobat who fights like a common street thug."

It was true. Inej had learned her technique from boys like Kaz and Jesper in the alleys and crooked streets of Ketterdam. Dunyasha didn't have just one mode of attack. She bent like a reed when required, stalked forward like a prowling cat, retreated like smoke. She had no single style that Inej could grasp or predict.

She's better than me. The knowledge had the taste of rot, as if Inej had bitten into a tempting fruit and found it foul. It wasn't just the difference in their training. Inej had learned to fight because she had to if she wanted to survive. She'd wept the night she'd made her first kill. This girl was enjoying herself.

But Ketterdam had taught Inej well. If you couldn't beat the odds, you changed the game. Inej waited for her opponent to lunge, then leapt past her onto the wire stretched between the silos, moving recklessly across it. The wind reached out for her, eager now, sensing opportunity. She considered using the balance pole, but she wanted her hands free.

She felt the wire wobble. *Impossible.* But when she looked back over her shoulder, Dunyasha had followed her out onto the high wire. She was grinning, her white skin glowing as if she'd swallowed the moon.

Dunyasha's hand shot out and Inej gasped as something sharp lodged in her calf. She bent backward, taking the wire in her hands, and flipped her stance so that she was facing her opponent. The girl's wrist snapped out again. Inej felt another bright stab of pain, and when she looked down, she saw a spiked metal star protruding from her thigh.

From somewhere below, she heard shouting, the sounds of a fight. *Nina.* Who or what had Jan Van Eck sent after her? But she could not afford distraction, not on the wire, not faced with this creature.

"I hear you whored for the Peacock," Dunyasha said as she flung another spiked star at Inej, and another. Inej avoided both, but took the next in the meat of her right shoulder. She was bleeding badly. "I would have killed myself and everyone beneath that roof before letting myself be used in such a way."

"You're being used now," Inej replied. "Van Eck isn't worthy of your skill."

"If you must know, Pekka Rollins pays my wages," said the girl, and Inej's footsteps faltered. *Rollins.* "He pays for my travel, my lodgings. But I ask no money for the lives I take. They are the jewels I wear. They are my glory in this world and will bring me honor in the next."

Pekka Rollins. Had he somehow found Kaz? The others? What if Nina was lying dead below? Inej had to get free of this girl. She had to help them. Another silver star came whirring at her and she bent left to avoid it, almost lost her balance. She danced backward on the wire, glimpsed another glint of silver. Pain lanced through her arm and she hissed in a breath.

Our work is death and it is holy. What dark god did this mercenary serve?

Inej imagined some vast deity looming above the city, faceless and featureless, skin taut over its swollen limbs, fattened on the blood of its acolytes' victims. She could feel its presence, the chill of its shadow.

A star lodged in Inej's shin, another in her forearm. She glanced over her shoulder. Only ten more feet and she would be at the first silo. Dunyasha might know more about fighting than Inej ever would, but she didn't know Ketterdam. Inej would race to the bottom of the silo, find Nina. They'd lose this monster in the streets and canals Inej knew so well.

Again, she gauged the distance behind her. Just a few more feet. But when she looked back, Dunyasha was no longer on the wire. Inej saw her bend, saw her hand reach for the magnet. *No.*

"Protect me," she whispered to her Saints.

The line went slack. Inej fell, twisting in the air the way she had as a child, searching for her wings.

21

KAZ

Kaz heard a roaring in his ears. As always, he experienced a strange kind of doubling when he looked at Rollins, as if he'd been up too late and had far too much to drink. The man before him was Pekka Rollins, king of the Barrel, gang lord and impresario. But he was also Jakob Hertzoon, the supposedly upstanding merch who had fed Kaz and Jordie on comfort and confidence, then taken their money and left them helpless in a city that put no value on mercy.

Any sign of the respectable Jakob Hertzoon was gone tonight. Rollins wore a green-striped waistcoat snugly buttoned over the beginnings of a gut and trousers with an emerald sheen. Apparently, he'd replaced the watch Kaz had stolen from him, because he took out a new one and glanced at it now.

"This thing never keeps time quite right," Rollins said, giving the watch a shake, his sideburns quivering slightly as he breathed an exasperated sigh, "but I can't resist a fine bit of shine. Don't suppose you kept the one you took off me?" Kaz said nothing. "Well," Rollins continued with a shrug, snapping the watch shut and returning it to his waistcoat pocket. "Right about now, my lieutenants should be rounding up your crew and a certain priceless hostage at Black Veil Island."

Wylan released a distressed sound.

"I've also prepared something special for the Wraith," said Rollins. "An extraordinary asset, that girl. I didn't like the thought of that particular arrow in your quiver, so I found someone even more extraordinary to take care of her."

A sick sensation settled in Kaz's stomach. He thought of Inej rolling her shoulders, the tidy frame of her body brimming with confidence. *I don't work with a net.*

"Did you really think you'd be that hard to find, Brekker? I've been at this game a long time. All I had to do was think what I'd have done when I was younger and more foolish."

The roaring in Kaz's ears grew louder. "You're working for Van Eck." He'd known it was a possibility, but he'd ignored it. He'd thought that if he moved fast enough, they wouldn't have time to form an alliance.

"I'm working *with* Van Eck. After you came to me looking for cash, I had a feeling he might have need of my services. He was hesitant at first, hasn't had the best luck making deals with Barrel boys. But that little stunt you pulled with his wife drove him right into my loving arms. I told Van Eck you'd always be a step ahead of him because he can't help thinking like a businessman."

Kaz nearly flinched. Hadn't he had the very same thought?

"He's a savvy one, no doubt," continued Rollins, "but a man of limited imagination. Whereas you, Brekker, think like a villainous little thug. You're me with a lot more hair and a lot less style. Van Eck thought he had you all tied up on West Stave, felt pretty good about calling in the *stadwatch* too. But I knew you'd be more slippery than that."

"And you knew I'd come here?"

Rollins chuckled. "I knew you couldn't *resist* it. Oh, I didn't know what plan you'd concoct, but I knew whatever scheme you devised would bring you here. You couldn't pass up the chance to humiliate Van Eck, to take back what you think he owes you."

"The deal is the deal."

Rollins shook his head, clucking like a big mother hen. "You take things too personally, Brekker. You should be focused on the job, but you're too busy holding a grudge."

"That's where you're wrong," said Kaz. "I don't hold a grudge. I cradle it. I coddle it. I feed it fine cuts of meat and send it to the best schools. I nurture my grudges, Rollins."

"I'm glad you've kept your sense of humor, lad. Once you've served your term in stir—assuming Van Eck lets you live—I might just let you come work for me. Shame to see a talent like yours go to waste."

"I'd rather be cooked slow on a spit with Van Eck turning the handle."

Rollins' smile was magnanimous. "I imagine that can be arranged too. I'm nothing if not accommodating." *Just keep talking*, Kaz urged silently, his hand slipping inside Wylan's satchel.

"What makes you think Van Eck will honor his agreement with you any more than he did with us?"

"Because I have the sense to get cash up front. And my demands are decidedly more moderate. A few million *kruge* to rid the Barrel of a nuisance I'd like to see gone anyway? Most reasonable." Rollins hooked his thumbs into his waistcoat. "Fact is, Van Eck and I understand each other. I'm expanding, growing my territory, thinking bigger. The Kaelish Prince is the finest establishment East Stave has ever seen, and it's only the beginning. Van Eck and I are builders. We want to create something that outlasts us. You'll grow into it, boy. Now hand over that seal and come quietly, why don't you?"

Kaz pulled the seal from his pocket, held it up, letting it catch the lamplight, drawing Pekka's gaze. He hesitated.

"Come now, Brekker. You're tough, I confess, but I've got you cornered and outnumbered. You can't make the drop from that window, and

Van Eck has *stadwatch* lining the street below. You're done for, toasted, swinging in the wind, so don't do anything foolish."

But if you couldn't open a door, you just had to make a new one. Rollins was easy to get talking; in fact, Kaz doubted he could stop him if he wanted to. Then it was just a question of keeping Rollins' eyes on the shiny golden seal in Kaz's right hand while he opened the jar of auric acid with the left.

"Get ready," he murmured.

"Kaz——" Wylan protested.

Kaz tossed the seal to Rollins and in the same motion splashed the remaining acid onto the floor. The room filled with heat and the carpet hissed as a plume of acrid smoke rose from it.

"Stop them!" Rollins shouted.

"See you on the other side," said Kaz. He grabbed his cane and smashed it into the boards beneath their feet. The floor gave way with a groan.

They crashed through to the first floor in a cloud of plaster and dust, right onto a dinner table that collapsed beneath their weight.

Candlesticks and dishes went rolling. Kaz sprang to his feet, cane in his hand, gravy dripping from his coat, then hauled Wylan up beside him.

He had a brief moment to register the startled expressions of the merchers around the table, their mouths wide with shock, napkins still in their laps. Then Van Eck was screaming, "Seize them!" and Kaz and Wylan were leaping over a fallen ham and sprinting down the black-and-white-tiled hall.

Two liveried guards stepped in front of the glass-paneled doors that opened onto the back garden, lifting their rifles.

Kaz put on a spurt of speed and dropped into a slide. He braced his cane horizontally across his chest and shot between the guards, letting the cane bash into their shins, knocking them from their feet.

Wylan trailed after him, tumbling down the stairs into the garden. Then they were at the boathouse, over the railing, and into the *gondel* Rotty had kept waiting in the canal.

A bullet pinged into the side of the boat as gunfire peppered the water around them. He and Rotty seized their oars.

"Drop heavy," Kaz shouted, and Wylan let loose with every rocket, flash bomb, and bit of demo he'd been able to fit into the boat. The sky above the Van Eck house exploded in an array of light, smoke, and sound as the guards dove for cover.

Kaz put his arms to work, feeling the boat slide into the current as they passed into the glittering traffic of the Geldcanal.

"In and out without him ever knowing?" said Rotty.

"I was half right," growled Kaz.

"We have to warn the others," Wylan gasped. "Rollins said—"

"Pekka Rollins was there?" Rotty asked, and Kaz heard the fear in his voice. A canal rat would take on a thousand thugs and thieves, merchers and mercenaries, but not Pekka Rollins.

Kaz tipped one of his oars, steering the boat starboard and barely missing a browboat full of tourists.

"We have to go back to Black Veil. The others—"

"Shut up, Wylan, I need to think."

Jesper and Matthias were both good in a fight. If anyone had a chance of getting Kuwei off Black Veil, they did. But how had Pekka found them? Someone must have been followed to the island. They'd all taken risks that day, ventured away from Black Veil. Any one of them might have been spotted and pursued. Nina and Matthias? Wylan and Jesper? Kaz himself? Once Pekka had located their hideout, he would have kept them under surveillance every minute, just waiting for them to separate and make themselves vulnerable.

Kaz flexed his shoulders, and Rotty matched his pace, the strokes of their oars driving the boat forward faster through the current. He needed to get them into traffic and as far away from Van Eck's house as possible. He needed to get to Sweet Reef. Rollins' men would have followed Inej and Nina there from Black Veil. Why had he sent them to the silos alone? Nina and her precious refugees. There would be no grand rescue for the

Grisha tonight. All their chances were shot to hell. *I've also prepared something special for the Wraith.* To hell with revenge, to hell with his schemes. If Rollins had done something to Inej, Kaz would paint East Stave with his entrails.

Think. When one plan was blown, you made a new one. When they backed you into a corner, you cut a hole in the roof. But he couldn't fix something he couldn't catch hold of. The plan had gone slippery. He'd failed them. He'd failed her. All because he seemed to have some kind of blind spot where Pekka Rollins was concerned. Jesper could be dead already. Inej could be bleeding on the streets of Sweet Reef.

He turned his oars. "We're going to the warehouse district."

"What about the others?"

"Jesper and Matthias are fighters, and there's no way Pekka's going to risk harming Kuwei. We're going to Sweet Reef."

"You said we'd be safe on Black Veil," Wylan protested. "You said—"

"There is no *safe*," Kaz snarled. "Not in the Barrel. Not anywhere." He threw his strength into rowing. No seal. No ship. Their money spent.

"What do we do now?" Wylan said quietly, his voice barely audible above the sound of the water and the other boats on the canal.

"Pick up a pair of oars and make yourself useful," said Kaz. "Or I'll put your pampered ass in the drink and let your father fish you out."

22

NINA

Nina heard them before she saw them. She was positioned between the second and third silos, where she could watch Inej's progress and keep an eye on the guardhouse.

Inej had climbed the silo like a tiny, nimble spider moving at a pace that made Nina tired just watching her. The angle was steep enough that she could barely see Inej once she'd reached the top, so Nina couldn't tell what progress she was making with the hatch. But Inej didn't start crossing when Nina gave the first signal, so she must have had some delay with the lines or with the weevil. At the second signal, Nina saw her step out over nothing.

From where Nina waited, the high wire was invisible in the dark, and it looked as if Inej was levitating, each step precise, considered. There—the faintest wobble. Now—a small correction. Nina's heart beat a skittering rhythm as she watched. She had the absurd feeling that if she let her own focus waver for even a second, Inej might fall, as if Nina's concentration and faith were helping keep her aloft.

When Inej finally reached the second silo, Nina wanted to cheer, but she settled for a brief, silent dance. Then she waited for the guards to come back into view on the western side of the perimeter. They stopped at the guardhouse for a few minutes and set out again. Nina was about to signal Inej when she heard the sound of rowdy laughter. The guards noticed too, suddenly alert. Nina saw one of them ignite the signal lantern atop the guardhouse to call reinforcements—a precautionary measure in case of trouble. Riots had been known to happen, and with the chaos in West Stave the previous day, Nina wasn't surprised the guards were quick to call for help.

It seemed they might need it. Nina knew a crew of Barrel thugs when she saw one, and this seemed like a nasty lot, all of them large, thickly muscled, and heavily armed. Most of them had guns, a sure sign they were looking for more than a scuffle. The one in the lead wore a checked waistcoat across his broad chest and was swinging a chain in his hands. On his forearm, Nina could see a circular tattoo. She couldn't make out the details from this distance, but she would have bet good money that it was a lion curled into a crown. The Dime Lions. Pekka Rollins' boys. What the hell were they doing here?

Nina glanced up. Inej would be putting the weevil in the second silo. Hopefully she was out of their view. But just what did Pekka's gang want?

The answer came moments later. "Heard there was a Heartrender hiding out in Sweet Reef," said the boy in the checked waistcoat loudly, still swinging that chain.

Oh, Saints, that's bad. Had the Dime Lions followed her and Inej from Black Veil? Were the others in trouble? And what if Pekka Rollins and his gang knew about the Grisha at the embassy? Some of them were violating their indentures by trying to leave the city. They could be blackmailed or worse. Pekka could sell them to the Shu. *You have your own problems right now, Zenik,* said a voice in her head. *Stop worrying about saving the world and save your own ass.* Sometimes her inner voice could be very wise.

One of the silo guards stepped forward—rather bravely, Nina thought, given the Dime Lions' show of force. She couldn't make out their exchange.

A paper with a vibrant red seal changed hands. The guard gave it to his companion to read. After a moment he shrugged. And then, to Nina's horror, the guard stepped forward and unlocked the gate. The lantern on the roof of the guardhouse flashed again. They were calling off the reinforcements.

The red seal. Van Eck's color. These were his silos, and there was no way the guards would risk opening that gate for anyone their employer hadn't sanctioned. The implications made her head spin. Could Jan Van Eck and Pekka Rollins be working together? If so, the Dregs' chances of getting out of the city alive had just turned to crumbs on a cake plate.

"Come on out, sweet Nina. Pekka's got work for you."

Nina saw that the chain the boy was swinging had a heavy manacle at the end. When she'd first come to Ketterdam, Pekka Rollins had offered her employment and his dubious protection. She'd chosen to sign with the Dregs instead. It seemed Pekka was done abiding by contracts or the laws of the gangs. He was going to clap her in chains, maybe sell her to the Shu or offer her up to Van Eck so that he could dose her with *parem*.

Nina was sheltered in the shadows of the second silo, but there was absolutely no way for her to move more than a few paces without exposing herself. She thought of the poison pill in her pocket.

"Don't make us come get you, girl." The boy was gesturing for the other Dime Lions to fan out.

Nina figured she had two advantages: First, the shackle at the end of that chain meant Pekka probably wanted her alive. He wouldn't want to sacrifice a valuable Grisha Heartrender, so they wouldn't shoot. Second, this assembly of geniuses didn't know the *parem* had disrupted her powers. She might be able to buy herself and Inej some time.

Nina shook out her hair, summoned every bit of her courage, and strolled into the open. Instantly, she heard the sound of triggers cocking.

"Easy now," she said, planting a hand on one hip. "I'm not going to be much good to Pekka if you plug me full of holes like the top of a saltshaker."

"Well, hello, Grisha girl. You gonna make this fun for us?"

Depends on your definition. "What's your name, handsome?"

The boy smiled, revealing a gold tooth and a surprisingly charming dimple. "Eamon."

"That's a nice Kaelish name. *Ken ye hom?*"

"Ma was Kaelish. I don't speak that gibber."

"Well, how about you get your friends here to relax and lower those weapons so I can teach you some new words."

"I don't think so. I know the way them Heartrender powers work. Not letting you get hold of my insides."

"Shame," Nina said. "Listen, Eamon, there's no need for trouble tonight. I just want to know Pekka's terms. If I'm going to cross Kaz, I need to know the pain is worth the price—"

"Kaz Brekker's good as dead, darlin'. And Pekka ain't offering no terms. You're coming with us, in chains or out."

Nina raised her arms and saw the men around her stiffen, ready to fire, regardless of Pekka's orders. She turned the movement into a lazy stretch. "Eamon, you do know that before you clap me in those chains I could turn half these gents' internal organs to goo."

"You're not fast enough."

"I'm fast enough to make sure you never"—her eyes gave a meaningful slide below his belt buckle—"raise a flag on West Stave again."

Now Eamon paled. "You can't do that."

Nina cracked her knuckles. "Can't I?"

A soft *clang* sounded from somewhere above them, and they all pointed their guns skyward. *Damn it, Inej, keep quiet.* But when Nina looked up, her thoughts stuttered to a terrified halt. Inej was back on the wire. And she wasn't alone.

For a moment, Nina thought she might be hallucinating as she watched the figure in white follow Inej onto the wire. She looked like a phantom floating in the air above them. Then she hurled something through the air. Nina caught a glint of metal. She didn't see it hit, but she saw Inej's steps falter. Inej righted herself, her posture ruthless, arms extended for balance.

There had to be a way to help her. Nina reached out to the girl in white with her power, searching for her pulse, the fiber of her muscles, something she could control, but again there was that terrible blindness, that nothingness.

"Not gonna help your friend?" Eamon said.

"She can manage for herself," said Nina.

Eamon smirked. "You're not nearly as tough as we heard. Big talk, no action." He turned to his crew. "I buy drinks all night for the first one to grab her."

They didn't rush her. They weren't foolish enough for that. They advanced slowly, guns raised. Nina threw her hands up. They stopped, wary. But when nothing happened, she saw them exchange glances, a few smiles, and now they were coming faster, losing their fear, ready to take their reward.

Nina risked a glance upward. Inej was still somehow keeping her balance. She seemed to be attempting to make her way back to the first silo, but she'd clearly been injured and her walk was unsteady.

The net. But it was no good to Nina alone. If she had a bit of *parem*, just a taste of it, she could force these big idiots to help her. They'd obey her without thinking.

Her mind reached out, grasping for something, anything. She would not just stand here helpless to be taken captive and watch Inej die. But all she felt was a great black void. There were no convenient bone shards, no dust to seize. The world that had once teemed with life, with heartbeats, breath, the rush of blood, had been stripped bare. It was all black desert, starless sky, barren earth.

One of the Dime Lions rushed forward and then they were all lunging at her, grabbing onto her arms, dragging her toward Eamon, whose face split with a grin, his dimple curving in a half moon.

Nina released a howl of pure rage, thrashing like a wild animal.

She was not helpless. She refused to be. *I know no fiercer warrior, powers or not.*

Then she felt it—there, in that black desert, a pocket of cold so deep it burned. There, past the silos, in the wedge of the canal, on the way to the harbor—the sickboat, piled high with bodies. A throb of recognition pulsed through her. She didn't sense heartbeats or blood flow, but she could feel something else, something other. She thought of the bone shards, remembered the comfort she'd felt on Black Veil, surrounded by graves.

Eamon tried to clap one of the shackles onto her wrist.

"Let's put the collar on her too!" another Dime Lion shouted.

She felt a hand in her hair, her head wrenched back to expose her neck. Nina knew what she was thinking was madness, but she was out of sane choices. With all her remaining strength, she kicked hard at Eamon, breaking his grip. She threw her arms out in a wide arc, focusing this strange new awareness, and she felt the bodies on the barge rise. She clenched her fists. *Come to me.*

The Dime Lions seized her wrists. Eamon struck her across the mouth, but she kept her fists clenched, her mind focused. This wasn't the exhilaration she'd felt on *parem*. That had been heat, fire, light. This was a cold flame, one that burned low and blue. She felt the corpses rise, one after another, answering her call. Nina was conscious of hands on her, chains being lashed around her wrists, but the cold was deeper now, a fast-flowing winter river, black rapids jagged with broken ice.

Nina heard screaming, the rattle of gunfire, and then the twist of metal. The hands on her loosened, and the chains hit the cobblestones with an almost musical jangle. Nina drew her arms toward her, plunging further into the cold of the river.

"What the hell," said Eamon, turning toward the guardhouse. *"What the hell."*

The Dime Lions were backing up now, mission forgotten, terror on their faces, and Nina could see exactly why. A line of people were pushing on the fence, rocking it on its posts. Some were old, some young, but all of them were beautiful—cheeks flushed, lips rosy, hair bright with shine and moving in waves around their faces with the gentle sway of something that grew underwater. They were lovely and they were horrible, because while some of them bore no signs of injury, one had brown blood and vomit splashed all over her dress, another bore a puncture wound gone black with decay. Two were naked and one had a deep, wide gash across her stomach, the plump pink skin falling forward in a flap. All of their eyes shone black, the glassy slate of winter water.

Nina felt a wave of nausea overtake her. She felt strange and a little shameful, as if she was looking into a window she had no right to peek through. But she was out of options. And the truth was, she did not want to stop. She flexed her fingers.

The fence crashed forward in a harsh screech of tearing metal. The Dime Lions opened fire, but the corpses kept coming, without interest or fear.

"It's her!" Eamon screamed, stumbling backward, falling, dragging himself onto his knees as his men fled into the night. "They're coming for the Grisha bitch!"

"Bet you're wishing we'd had that talk now," Nina growled. But she didn't care about the Dime Lions.

She looked up. Inej was still on the wire, but the girl in white was on the roof of the second silo and was reaching for the clamp.

The net, she demanded. *Now*. The corpses moved in a blurry burst of speed, rushing forward, then suddenly halting, as if awaiting instruction. She gathered her concentration and willed them to obey, shoving all her strength and life into their bodies. In seconds they had the net in their hands, and they were running, so fast Nina could not track them.

The high wire went slack. Inej fell. Nina screamed.

Inej's body struck the net, bounced high, struck the net again.

Nina ran to her. "Inej!"

Her body lay in the center of the net, pocked by wicked silver stars, blood oozing from the wounds.

Set her down, Nina commanded, and the corpses obeyed, lowering the net to the paving stones. Nina stumbled to Inej's side and went to her knees. "Inej?"

Inej threw her arms around Nina.

"Never, *ever* do that again," Nina sobbed.

"A net?" said a merry voice. "That seems unfair."

Inej stiffened. The girl in white had reached the bottom of the second silo and was striding toward them.

Nina's arms shot out and the corpses stepped in front of her and Inej. "You sure you want this fight, snowflake?"

The girl narrowed her beautiful eyes. "I bested you," she said to Inej. "You know I did."

"You had a good night," Inej replied, but her voice sounded weak as worn thread.

The girl looked at the army of decaying bodies arrayed before her, appeared to assess her odds. She bowed. "We'll meet again, Wraith." She turned in the direction Eamon and the rest of the Dime Lions had fled, vaulted over the remnants of the fence, and was gone.

"Someone likes drama," Nina said. "I mean really, who wears white to a knife fight?"

"Dunyasha, the White Blade of something or other. She really wants to kill me. Possibly everyone."

"Can you walk?"

Inej nodded, though her face looked ashen. "Nina, are these people . . . are they dead?"

"When you put it that way, it sounds creepy."

"But you didn't use—"

"No. No *parem*. I don't know what this is."

"Can Grisha even—"

"I don't know." Now that the fear of the ambush and Inej's fall were abating, she felt a kind of disgust. What had she just done? What had she tampered with?

Nina remembered asking one of her teachers at the Little Palace where Grisha power came from. She'd been little more than a child then, awed by the older Grisha who came and went from the palace grounds on important missions.

Our power connects us to life in ways ordinary people can never understand, her teacher had said. *That's why using our gift makes us stronger instead of depleting us. We are tied to the power of creation itself, the making at the heart of the world. For Corporalki, that bond is woven even more tightly, because we deal in life and the taking of it.*

The teacher had raised his hands, and Nina felt her pulse slow just slightly. The other students had released gasps and looked around at one another, all of them experiencing the same thing. *Do you feel that?* the teacher asked. *All your hearts, beating in shared time, bound to the rhythm of the world?*

It had been the strangest sensation, the feeling of her body dissolving, as if they were not many students wriggling in their classroom chairs, but one creature, with a single heart, a single purpose. It had lasted only moments, but she'd never forgotten that sense of connection, the sudden understanding that her power would mean she was never alone.

But the power she'd used tonight? It was nothing like that. It was a product of *parem*, not the making at the heart of the world. It was a mistake.

There would be time to worry later. "We need to get out of here," Nina said. She helped Inej to her feet, then looked at the bodies surrounding them. "Saints, they smell awful."

"Nina, what if they can hear you?"

"Can you hear me?" she asked. But the corpses did not respond, and when she reached out to them with her power, they didn't feel alive. There was *something* here, though, something that spoke to her in a way the living no longer could. She thought again of the icy river. She could still feel it around her, around everything, but now it moved in slow eddies.

"What are you going to do with them?" asked Inej.

Nina gave a helpless shrug. "Put them back where they were, I suppose?" She raised her hands. *Go*, she told them as clearly as she could, *be at rest*.

They moved again, a sudden flurry that brought a prayer to Inej's lips. Nina watched them fade, dim shapes in the dark.

Inej gave a slight shudder, then plucked a spiked silver star from her shoulder and let it drop to the ground with a loud *plink*. The bleeding seemed to have slowed, but she definitely needed bandages. "Let's go before the *stadwatch* show up," she said.

"Where?" Nina asked as they set out for the canal. "If Pekka Rollins found us—"

Inej's steps slowed as reality set in. "If Black Veil is compromised, Kaz . . . Kaz told me where to go if things went sour. But . . ."

The words hung in the air between them. Pekka Rollins entering the field meant much more than a foiled plan.

What if Black Veil was blown? What if something had happened to Matthias? Would Pekka Rollins spare his life or simply shoot first and claim his bounty?

The Grisha. What if Pekka had followed Jesper and Matthias to the embassy? What if they'd set out for the docks with the refugees and been captured? Again she thought of the yellow pill in her pocket. She thought of Tamar's ferocious golden eyes, Zoya's imperious gaze, Genya's teasing laugh. They had trusted her. If something had happened to them, she would never forgive herself.

As Nina and Inej traced their steps back to the quay where their boat was moored, she spared one glance at the barge where the last of the corpses was lying down, shifting into place. They looked different now, their color returning to the ashy gray and mottled white that she associated with death. But maybe death wasn't just one thing.

"Where do we go?" Nina asked.

At that moment, they saw two figures racing toward them. Inej reached for her knives and Nina raised her arms, prepared to call her strange soldiers once more. She knew it would be easier this time.

Kaz and Wylan appeared in the light from a streetlamp, their clothes rumpled, their hair covered in bits of plaster—and what might have been gravy. Kaz was leaning heavily on his cane, his pace unrelenting, the sharp features of his face set in determined lines.

"We'll fight our way out together," Inej whispered.

Nina glanced from Inej to Kaz and saw they both wore the same expression. Nina knew that look. It came after the shipwreck, when the tide moved against you and the sky had gone dark. It was the first sight of land, the hope of shelter and even salvation that might await you on a distant shore.

23

WYLAN

I'm going to die and there will be no one to help her. No one to even remember Marya Hendriks.

Wylan wanted to be brave, but he was cold and bruised, and worse—he was surrounded by the bravest people he knew and all of them seemed badly shaken.

They made slow progress through the canals, pausing under bridges and in dark wells of shadow to wait as squads of *stadwatch* boots thundered overhead or along the waterways. They were out in force tonight, their boats cruising along slowly, bright lanterns at their prows. Something had changed in the short time since the showdown on Goedmedbridge. The city had come alive, and it was angry.

"The Grisha—" Nina had attempted.

But Kaz had cut her off quickly. "They're either safe at the embassy or beyond our help. They can fend for themselves. We're going to ground."

And then Wylan knew just how much trouble they were in, because Nina hadn't argued. She'd simply put her head in her hands and gone silent.

"They'll be all right," said Inej, placing an arm around her shoulders. "*He'll* be all right." But her movements were tentative, and Wylan could see blood on her clothes.

After that, no one spoke a word. Kaz and Rotty rowed only sporadically, steering them into the quieter, narrower canals, letting them drift silently whenever possible, until they rounded a bend near Schoonstraat and Kaz said, "Stop." He and Rotty dug in their oars, bringing them flush with the side of the canal, tucked behind the bulk of a vendor's boat. Whatever the floating shop sold, its stalls had been locked tight to protect its stock.

Up ahead, they could see *stadwatch* swarming over a bridge, two of their boats obscuring the passage beneath.

"They're setting up blockades," said Kaz.

They ditched the boat there and continued on foot.

Wylan knew they were headed to another safe house, but Kaz had said it himself: *There is no safe.* Where could they possibly hide? Pekka Rollins was working with Wylan's father. Between them they had to own half the city. Wylan would be captured. And then what? No one would believe he was Jan Van Eck's son. Wylan Van Eck might be despised by his father, but he had rights no Shu criminal could hope for. Would he end up in Hellgate? Would his father find a way to see him executed?

As they got farther from the manufacturing district and the Barrel, the patrols dwindled, and Wylan realized the *stadwatch* must be concentrating their efforts on the less respectable parts of town. Still, they moved in fits and starts, passing along alleys Wylan had never known existed, occasionally entering empty storefronts or the lower levels of unoccupied apartments so they could cut through to the next street. It was as if Kaz had a secret map to Ketterdam that showed the city's forgotten spaces.

Would Jesper be waiting when they finally got wherever they were going? Or was he lying wounded and bleeding on the floor of the tomb with no one to come to his aid? Wylan refused to believe it. The worse the odds, the better Jesper was in a fight. He thought of Jesper pleading with Colm. *I know I let you down. Just give me one more chance.* How often had Wylan spoken almost the same words to his father, hoping every time that he could make good on them? Jesper had to survive. They all did.

Wylan remembered the first time he'd seen the sharpshooter. He'd seemed like a creature from another world, dressed in lime green and lemon yellow, his stride long and loping, as if every step was poured from a bottle with a narrow neck.

On Wylan's first night in the Barrel, he'd wandered from street to street, certain he was about to be robbed, teeth chattering from the cold. Finally, when his skin was turning blue and he couldn't feel his fingers, he'd summoned the courage to ask a man smoking his pipe on the front steps of a house, "Do you know where there might be rooms for rent?"

"Sign right there says vacancy," he said, gesturing across the street with his pipe. "What are you, blind?"

"Must have missed it," Wylan said.

The boardinghouse was filthy but blessedly cheap. He'd rented a room for ten *kruge* and had also paid for a hot bath. He knew he needed to save his money, but if he contracted lung fever the first night, he'd have problems beyond being short of cash. He took the little towel into the bathroom at the end of the hall and washed up quickly. Though the water was hot enough, he felt vulnerable crouching naked in a tub with no lock on the door. He dried his clothes as best he could, but they were still damp when he put them back on.

Wylan spent that night lying on a paper-thin mattress, staring at the ceiling and listening to the sounds of the rooming house around him. On the Geldcanal, the nights were so silent you could hear the water lapping against the sides of the boathouse. But here it might as well have been noon. Music flooded in through the dirty window. People were talking, laughing, slamming doors. The couple in the room above him were fighting. The couple in the room below him were definitely doing something else.

Wylan touched his fingers to the bruises at his throat and thought, *I wish I could ring for tea.* That was the moment he really began to panic. How much more pathetic could he be? His father had tried to have him killed. He had almost no money and was lying on a cot that reeked of the chemicals they'd used to try to rid the mattress of lice. He should be making a plan, maybe even plotting revenge, trying to gather his wits and his resources. And what was he doing? Wishing he could ring for tea. He might not have been happy at his father's house, but he'd never had to work for anything. He'd had servants, hot meals, clean clothes. Whatever it took to survive the Barrel, Wylan knew he didn't have it.

As he lay there, he sought some explanation for what had happened. Surely, Miggson and Prior were to blame; his father hadn't known. Or maybe Miggson and Prior had misunderstood his father's orders. It had just been a terrible mistake. Wylan rose and reached into the damp pocket of his coat. His enrollment papers to the music school in Belendt were still there.

As soon as he drew out the thick envelope, he knew his father was guilty. It was soaked through and smelled of canal, but its color was pristine. No ink had bled through from the supposed documents inside. Wylan opened the envelope anyway. The sheaf of folded papers clung together in a wet lump, but he pried each of them apart. They were all blank. His father hadn't even bothered with a convincing ruse. He'd known Wylan wouldn't try to read the papers. And that his gullible son would never think to suspect his father of lying. *Pathetic.*

Wylan had stayed inside for two days, terrified. But on the third morning, he'd been so hungry that the smell of frying potatoes wafting up from the street had driven him from the safety of his room. He bought a paper cone full of them and scarfed them down so greedily he burned his tongue. Then he made himself walk.

He had only enough money to keep his room for another week, less if he planned on eating. He needed to find work, but he had no idea where to begin. He wasn't big enough or strong enough for a job in the warehouses or shipyards. The softer jobs would require him to read. Was it possible one of the gambling dens or even one of the pleasure houses needed a musician to play in their parlors? He still had his flute. He walked up and down East Stave and along the more well-lit side streets. When it started to get dark, he returned to the boardinghouse, thoroughly defeated. The man with the pipe was still on his steps, smoking. As far as Wylan knew, he never left that perch.

"I'm looking for a job," Wylan said to him. "Do you know anyone who might be hiring?"

The man peered at him through a cloud of smoke. "Young dollop of cream like you should be able to make fine coin on West Stave."

"*Honest* work."

The man had laughed until he started hacking, but eventually he'd directed Wylan south to the tanneries.

Wylan was paid a scraping wage for mixing dyes and cleaning the vats. The other workers were mostly women and children, a few scrawny boys like him. They spoke little, too tired and too ill from the chemicals to do more than complete their work and collect their pay. They were given no gloves or masks, and Wylan was fairly sure he'd be dead of poisoning before he ever had to worry about where he should go with the tiny bit of money he was earning.

One afternoon, Wylan heard the dye chief complaining that they were losing gallons of dye to evaporation because the boilers ran too hot. He was cursing over the cost he'd paid to have two of them fixed and how little good it had done.

Wylan hesitated, then suggested adding seawater to the tanks.

"Why the hell would I want to do that?" said the dye chief.

"It will raise the boiling point," said Wylan, wondering why he'd thought it was a good idea to speak at all. "The dyes will have to get hotter to boil so you'll lose less to evaporation. You'll have to tweak the formula because the saline will build up fast, and you'll have to clean the tanks more regularly because the salt can be corrosive."

The dye chief had merely spat a stream of *jurda* onto the floor and ignored him. But the next week, they tried using saltwater in one of the tanks. A few days later, they were using a mixture of seawater in all of them, and the dye chief started coming to Wylan with more questions. How could they keep the red dye from stiffening the hides? How could they shorten processing and drying times? Could Wylan make a resin to keep the dyes from bleeding?

A week after that, Wylan had been standing at the vats with his wooden paddle, woozy from the dyes, eyes watering, wondering if helping the dye chief meant he could request a raise, when a boy approached him. He was tall, lanky, his skin a deep Zemeni brown, and looked ridiculously out of place on the dying floor. Not just because of his lime plaid waistcoat and yellow trousers, but because he seemed to exude pleasure, as if there was no place he'd rather be than a miserable, foul-smelling tannery, as if he'd just walked into a party he couldn't wait to attend. Though he was skinny, his body fit together with a kind of loose-limbed ease. The dye chief didn't usually like strangers on the dying floor, but he didn't say a word to this boy with the revolvers slung across his hips, just tipped his hat respectfully and went scurrying off.

Wylan's first thought was that this boy had the most perfectly shaped lips he'd ever seen. His second was that his father had sent someone new to kill him. He gripped his paddle. Would the boy shoot him in broad daylight? Did people just do that?

But the boy said, "Hear you know your way around a chemistry set."

"What? I . . . yes. A bit," Wylan had managed.

"Just a bit?"

Wylan had the sense that his next answer was very important. "I have a background." He'd taken to science and math and pursued them diligently, hoping they might somehow compensate for his other failings.

The boy handed Wylan a folded piece of paper. "Then come to this address when you get off work tonight. We might have a job for you." He looked around, as if just noticing the vats and the pallid laborers bent over them. "A real job."

Wylan had stared at the paper, the letters a tangle in front of his eyes. "I—I don't know where this is."

The boy gave an exasperated sigh. "You're not from here, are you?" Wylan shook his head. "Fine. I'll come fetch you, because clearly I don't have anything to do with my time but squire new lilies around town. Wylan, right?" Wylan nodded. "Wylan what?"

"Wylan . . . Hendriks."

"You know much about demo, Wylan Hendriks?"

"Demo?"

"The boom, the bang, the flint and fuss."

Wylan didn't know what he meant at all, but he felt admitting that would be a bad mistake. "Sure," he said with as much confidence as he could muster.

The boy cut him a skeptical glance. "We'll see. Be out front at six bells. And no guns unless you want trouble."

"Of course not."

The boy had rolled his gray eyes and muttered, "Kaz has got to be out of his mind."

At six bells, Jesper arrived to escort Wylan to a bait shop in the Barrel. Wylan had been embarrassed by his rumpled clothes, but they were the only ones he owned, and the paralyzing fear that this was just some elaborate trap concocted by his father had provided ample distraction from his worry. In a back room of the bait shop, Wylan met Kaz and Inej. They told him they needed flash bombs and maybe something with a little more kick. Wylan had refused.

That night, he arrived back at the boardinghouse to find the first letter. The only words he recognized were the name of the sender: Jan Van Eck.

He'd lain awake all night, certain that at any moment Prior would smash through the door and clamp his meaty hands around his neck. He'd thought about running, but he barely had enough money to pay his rent, let alone buy a ticket out of the city. And what hope did he have in the country? No one was going to hire him on as farm labor. The next day, he went to see Kaz, and that night, he built his first explosive for the Dregs. He knew what he was doing was illegal, but he'd made more money for a few hours' work than he made in a week at the tannery.

The letters from his father continued to arrive, once, sometimes twice a week. Wylan didn't know what to make of them. Were they threats? Taunts? He stashed them in a stack beneath his mattress, and sometimes at night he thought he could feel the ink bleeding through the pages, up through the mattress and into his heart like dark poison.

But the more time that passed and the more he worked for Kaz, the less scared he felt. He'd make his money, get out of town, and never speak the name Van Eck again. And if his father decided to have him done away with before then, there was nothing Wylan could do about it. His clothes were ragged and threadbare. He was getting so skinny, he had to cut new holes in his belt. But he would sell himself in the pleasure houses of West Stave before he'd ask for his father's mercy.

Wylan hadn't realized it then, but Kaz had known his true identity all along. Dirtyhands kept tabs on anyone who took up residence in the Barrel, and he'd placed Wylan under Dregs protection, certain that one day a rich mercher's son would come in handy.

He had no illusions about why Kaz had looked out for him, but he also knew he never would have survived this long without his help. And Kaz didn't care if he could read. Kaz and the others teased him, but they'd given him a chance to prove himself. They valued the things he could do instead of punishing him for the things he couldn't.

Wylan had believed that Kaz could get revenge for what had been done to his mother. He'd believed that despite his father's wealth and influence, this crew—*his* crew—was a match for Jan Van Eck. But now his father was reaching out to taunt him yet again.

It was well past midnight when they reached the financial district. They'd arrived in one of the wealthiest areas of the city, not far from the Exchange and the Stadhall. His father's presence felt closer here, and Wylan wondered why Kaz had brought them to this part of town. Kaz led them through an alley to the back of a large building, where a door had been propped open, and they entered a stairwell built around a huge iron lift that they shuffled inside. Rotty remained behind, presumably to keep watch over the entrance. The lift's gate clanged shut and they rode it fifteen stories up, to the building's top floor, then emerged into a hallway laid in patterns of lacquered hardwood, its high ceilings painted a pale, foamy lavender.

We're in a hotel, Wylan realized. *That was the servants' entrance and the staff elevator.*

They knocked on a pair of wide white double doors. Colm Fahey answered, wearing a long nightshirt with a coat thrown over it. They were at the Geldrenner.

"The others are inside," he said wearily.

Colm asked them no questions, just pointed toward the bathroom and poured himself a cup of tea as they tracked mud and misery across the purple carpets. When Matthias saw Nina, he leapt from his seat on the huge aubergine sofa and clasped her in his arms.

"We couldn't get through the blockades to Sweet Reef," he said. "I feared the worst."

Then they were all hugging, and Wylan was horrified to find his eyes filling with tears. He blinked them back. The last thing he needed was for Jesper to see him cry again. The sharpshooter was covered in soot and smelled like a forest fire, but he had that wonderful glimmer-eyed look he always seemed to get when he'd been in a fight. All Wylan wanted to do was stand as close as he possibly could to him and know that he was safe.

Until this moment, Wylan hadn't quite understood how much they meant to him. His father would have sneered at these thugs and thieves, a disgraced soldier, a gambler who couldn't keep out of the red. But they were his first friends, his only friends, and Wylan knew that even if he'd had his pick of a thousand companions, these would have been the people he chose.

Only Kaz stood apart, staring silently out the window to the dark streets below.

"Kaz," said Nina. "You may not be glad we're alive, but we're glad you're alive. Come here!"

"Leave him be," murmured Inej softly.

"Saints, Wraith," said Jesper. "You're bleeding."

"Should I call a doctor?" asked Jesper's father.

"No!" they all replied in unison.

"Of course not," said Colm. "Should I ring for coffee?"

"Yes, please," said Nina.

Colm ordered coffee, waffles, and a bottle of brandy, and while they waited, Nina enlisted their help to locate some shears so that she could cut up the hotel towels for bandages. Once a pair had been found, she took Inej into the bathroom to see to her wounds.

When a knock sounded at the door, they all tensed, but it was only their meal. Colm greeted the maid and insisted that he could manage the cart so that she wouldn't see the strange company that had assembled in his rooms. As soon as the door closed, Jesper jumped up to help him wheel in a silver tray laden with food and stacks of dishes of porcelain so fine it was almost transparent. Wylan hadn't eaten off dishes like these since he'd left his father's house. He realized Jesper must be wearing one of Colm's shirts; it was too big in the shoulders and too short in the sleeves.

"What is this place, anyway?" Wylan asked, looking around the vast room decorated almost entirely in purple.

"The Ketterdam Suite, I believe," said Colm, scratching the back of his neck. "It's considerably finer than my room at the university district inn."

Nina and Inej emerged from the bathroom. Nina heaped a plate with food and plunked down beside Matthias on the couch. She folded one of the waffles in half and took a huge bite, wiggling her toes in bliss.

"I'm sorry, Matthias," she said with her mouth full. "I've decided to run off with Jesper's father. He keeps me in the deliciousness to which I have become accustomed."

Inej had removed her tunic and wore only her quilted vest, leaving her brown arms bare. Strips of towel were tied at her shoulder, both of her forearms, her right thigh and her left shin.

"What exactly happened to you?" Jesper asked her as he handed his father a cup of coffee on a delicate saucer.

Inej perched in an armchair next to where Kuwei had settled himself on the floor. "I made a new acquaintance."

Jesper sprawled out on a settee and Wylan took the other chair, a plate of waffles balanced on his knee. There was a perfectly good table and chairs in the suite's dining room, but apparently none of them had an interest in it. Only Colm had taken a seat there, coffee beside him, along with the bottle of brandy. Kaz remained by the window, and Wylan wondered what he saw through the glass that was so compelling.

"So," Jesper said, adding sugar to his coffee. "Other than Inej making a new pal, what the hell happened out there?"

"Let's see," said Nina. "Inej fell twenty stories."

"We put a serious hole in my father's dining room ceiling," Wylan offered.

"Nina can raise the dead," said Inej.

Matthias' cup clattered against his saucer. It looked ridiculous in his huge hand.

"I can't *raise* them. I mean, they get up, but it's not like they come back to life. I don't think. I'm not totally sure."

"Are you serious?" said Jesper.

Inej nodded. "I can't explain it, but I saw it."

Matthias' brow was furrowed. "When we were in the Ravkan quarter, you were able to summon those pieces of bone."

Jesper took a gulp of coffee. "But what about the lake house? Were you controlling that dust?"

"What dust?" asked Inej.

"She didn't just take out a guard. She choked him with a cloud of dust."

"There's a family graveyard next to the Hendriks lake house," said Wylan, remembering the gated plot that abutted the western wall. "What if the dust was . . . well, bones? People's remains?"

Nina set down her plate. "That's almost enough to make me lose my appetite." She picked it up again. "Almost."

"This is why you asked about *parem* changing a Grisha's power," said Kuwei to Matthias.

Nina looked at him. "Can it?"

"I don't know. You took the drug only once. You survived the withdrawal. You are a rarity."

"Lucky me."

"Is it so bad?" Matthias asked.

Nina plucked a few crumbs from her lap, returning them to her plate. "To quote a certain big blond lump of muscle, it's not natural." Her voice had lost its cheery warmth. She just looked sad.

"Maybe it is," said Matthias. "Aren't the Corporalki known as the Order of the Living and the Dead?"

"This isn't how Grisha power is supposed to work."

"Nina," Inej said gently. "*Parem* took you to the brink of death. Maybe you brought something back with you."

"Well, it's a pretty rotten souvenir."

"Or perhaps Djel extinguished one light and lit another," said Matthias.

Nina cast him a sidelong glance. "Did you get hit on the head?"

He reached out and took Nina's hand. Wylan suddenly felt he was intruding on something private. "I am grateful you're alive," he said. "I am grateful you're beside me. I am grateful that you're *eating*."

She rested her head on his shoulder. "You're better than waffles, Matthias Helvar."

A small smile curled the Fjerdan's lips. "Let's not say things we don't mean, my love."

There was a light tapping at the door. Immediately, they all reached for their weapons. Colm sat frozen in his chair.

Kaz gestured for him to stay where he was and moved silently toward the door. He peered through the peephole.

"It's Specht," he said. They all relaxed, and Kaz opened the door.

They watched in silence as Kaz and Specht exchanged harried whispers; then Specht nodded and disappeared back toward the lift.

"Is there access to the clock tower on this floor?" Kaz asked Colm.

"At the end of the hall," said Colm. "I haven't gone up. The stairs are steep."

Without a word, Kaz was gone. They all stared at one another for a moment and then followed, filing past Colm, who watched them go with weary eyes.

As they walked down the hall, Wylan realized that the entire floor was dedicated to the luxury of the Ketterdam Suite. If he was going to die, he supposed it wouldn't be the worst place to spend his last night.

One by one, they climbed a twisting iron staircase to the clock tower and pushed through a trapdoor. The room at the top was large and cold, taken up mostly by the gears of a huge clock. Its four faces looked out over Ketterdam and the gray dawn sky.

To the south, a plume of smoke rose from Black Veil Island. Looking northeast, Wylan could see the Geldcanal, boats from the fire brigade and the *stadwatch* surrounding the area near his father's house. He remembered the shocked look on his father's face when they'd landed in the middle of his dining room table. If Wylan hadn't been so terrified, he might well have burst out laughing. *It's shame that eats men whole.* If only they'd set the rest of the house on fire.

Far in the distance, the harbors were teeming with *stadwatch* boats and wagons. The city was pocked with *stadwatch* purple, as if it had caught a disease.

"Specht says they've closed the harbors and shut down the browboats," said Kaz. "They're sealing the city. No one will be able to get in or out."

"Ketterdam won't stand for that," said Inej. "People will riot."

"They won't blame Van Eck."

Wylan felt a little ill. "They'll blame us."

Jesper shook his head. "Even if they put every *stadwatch* grunt on the street, they don't have the manpower to lock up the city and search for us."

"Don't they?" said Kaz. "Look again."

Jesper walked to the west-facing window where Kaz was standing. "All the Saints and your Aunt Eva," he said on a gust of breath.

"What is it?" asked Wylan as they peered through the glass.

A crowd was moving east from the Barrel across the Zelver district.

"Is it a mob?" asked Inej.

"More like a parade," said Kaz.

"Why aren't the *stadwatch* stopping them?" Wylan asked as the flood of people passed unhindered from bridge to bridge, through each barricade. "Why are they letting them through?"

"Probably because your father told them to," Kaz said.

As the throng drew closer, Wylan heard singing, chanting, drums. It really did sound like a parade. They poured over Zelverbridge, streaming past the hotel as they made their way to the square that fronted the Exchange. Wylan recognized Pekka Rollins' gang leading the march.

Whoever was up front wore a lion skin with a fake golden crown sewn onto its head.

"Razorgulls," Inej said, pointing behind the Dime Lions. "And there are the Liddies."

"Harley's Pointers," Jesper said. "The Black Tips."

"It's all of them," said Kaz.

"What does it mean?" asked Kuwei. "The purple bands?"

Each member of the mob below wore a strip of purple around his upper left arm.

"They've been deputized," said Kaz. "Specht says word is out all over the Barrel. The good news is they want us alive now—even Matthias. The bad news is they've added bounties for the Shu twins we're traveling with, so Kuwei's face—and Wylan's—are gracing the city walls too."

"And your Merchant Council is just sanctioning this?" said Matthias. "What if they start looting or there's a riot?"

"They won't. Rollins knows what he's doing. If the *stadwatch* had tried to lock down the Barrel, the gangs would have turned on them. Now they're on the right side of the law, and Van Eck has two armies. He's pinning us in."

Inej drew a sharp breath.

"What?" asked Wylan, but when he looked down at the square, he understood. The last group in the parade had come into view. An old man wearing a plumed hat was leading them, and they were cawing at the top of their lungs—like crows. The Dregs, Kaz's gang. They had turned on him.

Jesper slammed his fist against the wall. "Those ungrateful skivs."

Kaz said nothing, just watched the crowd flow past the front of the hotel below, the gangs bunched in colorful swarms, calling insults to one another, cheering like it was some kind of holiday. Even after they'd gone by, their chants hung in the air. Maybe they would march all the way to the Stadhall.

"What will happen now?" asked Kuwei.

"We'll be hunted by every *stadwatch* grunt and Barrel thug in the city, until we're found," said Kaz. "There's no way out of Ketterdam now. Certainly not with you in tow."

"Can we just wait?" asked Kuwei. "Here? With Mister Fahey?"

"Wait for what?" Kaz said. "Someone to come to our rescue?"

Jesper rested his head against the glass. "My father. They'll take him in too. He'll be accused of harboring fugitives."

"No," said Kuwei abruptly. "*No.* Give me to Van Eck."

"Absolutely not," said Nina.

The boy cut his hand through the air sharply. "You saved me from the Fjerdans. If we do not act, then I will be captured anyway."

"Then all of this was for nothing?" Wylan asked, surprised at his own anger. "The risks we took? What we accomplished at the Ice Court? Everything Inej and Nina suffered to get us out?"

"But if I give myself up to Van Eck, then the rest of you can go free," insisted Kuwei.

"It doesn't work that way, kid," said Jesper. "Pekka's got his chance to take Kaz out with the rest of the Barrel backing him, and Van Eck sure as hell doesn't want us walking around free, not knowing what we do. This isn't just about you anymore."

Kuwei moaned and slumped down against the wall. He cast a baleful glance at Nina. "You should have killed me at the Ice Court."

Nina shrugged. "But then Kaz would have killed me and Matthias would have killed Kaz and it would have gotten incredibly messy."

"I can't believe we broke out of the Ice Court but we're trapped in our own town," Wylan said. It didn't seem right.

"Yup," said Jesper. "We are well and truly cooked."

Kaz drew a circle on the window with one leather gloved finger. "Not quite," he said. "I can get the *stadwatch* to stand down."

"No," said Inej.

"I'll give myself up."

"But Kuwei—" said Nina.

"The *stadwatch* don't know about Kuwei. They think they're looking for Wylan. So I'll tell them Wylan is dead. I'll tell them I killed him."

"Are you out of your mind?" said Jesper.

"Kaz," said Inej. "They'll send you to the gallows."

"They'll have to give me a trial first."

"You'll rot in prison before that happens," said Matthias. "Van Eck will never give you a chance to speak in a courtroom."

"You really think they've built a cell that can hold me?"

"Van Eck knows just how good you are with locks," Inej said angrily. "You'll die before you ever reach the jailhouse."

"This is ridiculous," said Jesper. "You're not taking the fall for us. No one is. We'll split up. We'll go in pairs, find a way past the blockades, hide out somewhere in the countryside."

"This is my city," said Kaz. "I'm not leaving it with my tail between my legs."

Jesper released a growl of frustration. "If this is your city, what's left of it? You gave up your shares in the Crow Club and Fifth Harbor. You don't have a gang anymore. Even if you did escape, Van Eck and Rollins would set the *stadwatch* and half the Barrel on you again. You can't fight them all."

"Watch me."

"Damn it, Kaz. What are you always telling me? Walk away from a losing hand."

"I'm giving you a way out. Take it."

"Why are you treating us like a bunch of yellow-bellied skivs?"

Kaz turned on him. "You're the one getting ready to bolt, Jesper. You just want me to run with you so you don't have to feel so bad about it. For all your love of a fight, you're always the first to talk about running for cover."

"Because I want to stay *alive*."

"For what?" Kaz said, his eyes glittering. "So you can play another hand at the tables? So you can find another way to disappoint your father and let down your friends? Have you told your father you're the reason he's going to lose his farm? Have you told Inej you're the reason she almost died at the end of Oomen's knife? That we all almost died?"

Jesper's shoulders bunched, but he didn't back down. "I made a mistake. I let my bad get the best of my good, but for Saints' sake, Kaz, how long are you going to make me pay for a little forgiveness?"

"What do you think my forgiveness looks like, Jordie?"

"Who the hell is Jordie?"

For the briefest moment, Kaz's face went slack, a confused, almost frightened look in his dark eyes—there and gone, so fast Wylan wondered if he'd imagined it.

"What do you want from me?" Kaz snarled, his expression just as closed, just as cruel as ever. "My trust? You had it and you shot it to pieces because you couldn't keep your mouth shut."

"*One time.* How many times have I had your back in a fight? How many times have I gotten it right? Doesn't that count for anything?" Jesper threw up his hands. "I can't win with you. No one can."

"That's right. You can't win. You think you're a gambler, but you're just a born loser. Fights. Cards. Boys. Girls. You'll keep playing until you lose, so for once in your life, just walk away."

Jesper swung first. Kaz dodged right and then they were grappling. They slammed into the wall, knocked heads, drew apart in a flurry of punches and grabs.

Wylan turned to Inej, expecting her to object, for Matthias to separate them, for someone to *do something*, but the others just backed up, making room. Only Kuwei showed any kind of distress.

Jesper and Kaz swung around, crashed into the mechanism of the clock, righted themselves. It wasn't a fight, it was a brawl—graceless, a tangle of elbows and fists.

"Ghezen and his works, someone stop them!" Wylan said desperately.

"Jesper hasn't shot him," Nina said.

"Kaz isn't using his cane," said Inej.

"You think they can't kill each other with their bare hands?"

They were both bleeding—Jesper from a cut on his lip and Kaz from somewhere near his brow. Jesper's shirt was halfway over his head and Kaz's sleeve was tearing at the seam.

The trapdoor sprang open and Colm Fahey's head emerged. His ruddy cheeks went even redder.

"Jesper Llewellyn Fahey, that is *enough!*" he roared.

Jesper and Kaz both startled, and then, to Wylan's shock, they stepped away from each other, looking guilty.

"Just what is going on here?" Colm said. "I thought you were friends."

Jesper ran a hand over the back of his neck, looking like he wanted to vanish through the floorboards. "We . . . uh . . . we were having a disagreement."

"I can see that. I have been very patient with all of this, Jesper, but I am at my limit. I want you down here before I count ten or I will tan your hide so you don't sit for two weeks."

Colm's head vanished back down the stairs. The silence stretched.

Then Nina giggled. "You are in *so* much trouble."

Jesper scowled. "Matthias, Nina let Cornelis Smeet grope her bottom."

Nina stopped laughing. "I am going to turn your teeth inside out."

"That is physically impossible."

"I just raised the dead. Do you really want to argue with me?"

Inej cocked her head to one side. "Jesper *Llewellyn* Fahey?"

"Shut up," said Jesper. "It's a family name."

Inej made a solemn bow. "Whatever you say, Llewellyn."

"Kaz?" Jesper said tentatively.

But Kaz was staring into the middle distance. Wylan thought he knew that look.

"Is that——?" asked Wylan.

"Scheming face?" said Jesper.

Matthias nodded. "Definitely."

"I know how to do it," Kaz said slowly. "How to get Kuwei out, get the Grisha out, get our money, beat Van Eck, and give that son of a bitch Pekka Rollins everything he has coming to him."

Nina raised a brow. "Is that all?"

"How?" asked Inej.

"This whole time, we've been playing Van Eck's game. We've been hiding. We're done with that. We're going to stage a little auction. Right out in the open." He turned to face them, and his eyes gleamed flat and black as a shark's. "And since Kuwei is so eager to sacrifice himself, he's going to be the prize."

PART FIVE

KINGS & QUEENS

24

JESPER

At the base of the iron staircase, Jesper tried to straighten his shirt and dabbed the blood from his lip, though at this point he figured it wouldn't matter if he showed up in nothing but his skivvies. His father was no fool, and that ridiculous story Wylan had concocted to cover for Jesper's mistakes had worn faster than a cheap suit. His father had seen their wounds, he'd heard about their botched plans. He knew they weren't students or victims of a swindle. So what now?

Close your eyes and hope the firing squad has good aim, he thought bleakly.

"Jesper."

He whirled. Inej was right behind him. He hadn't heard her approach, but that was no surprise. *Have you told Inej you're the reason she almost died at the end of Oomen's knife?* Well, Jesper figured he'd be doing a lot of apologizing this morning. Best get to it.

"Inej, I'm sorry—"

"I didn't come looking for an apology, Jesper. You have a weak spot. We all have weak spots."

"What's yours?"

"The company I keep," she said with a slight smile.

"You don't even know what I did."

"Then tell me."

Jesper looked down at his shoes. They were miserably scuffed. "I was in deep with Pekka Rollins for a lot of *kruge*. His goons were putting the pressure on, so I . . . I told them I was leaving town, but that I was about to come into a big score. I didn't say anything about the Ice Court, I swear."

"But it was enough for Rollins to put the puzzle together and prepare an ambush." She sighed. "And Kaz has been punishing you for it ever since."

Jesper shrugged. "Maybe I deserve it."

"Do you know the Suli have no words to say 'I'm sorry'?"

"What do you say when you step on someone's foot?"

"I don't step on people's feet."

"You know what I mean."

"We say nothing. We know the slight was not deliberate. We live in tight quarters, traveling together. There's no time to constantly be apologizing for existing. But when someone does wrong, when we make mistakes, we don't say we're sorry. We promise to make amends."

"I will."

"*Mati en sheva yelu.* This action will have no echo. It means we won't repeat the same mistakes, that we won't continue to do harm."

"I'm not going to get you stabbed again."

"I got stabbed because I let my guard down. You betrayed your crew."

"I didn't mean—"

"It would be better if you *had* meant to betray us. Jesper, I don't want an apology, not until you can promise that you won't keep making the same mistake."

Jesper rocked lightly on his heels. "I don't know how to do that."

"There's a wound in you, and the tables, the dice, the cards—they feel like medicine. They soothe you, put you right for a time. But they're poison, Jesper. Every time you play, you take another sip. You have to find some other way to heal that part of yourself." She laid her hand on his chest. "Stop treating your pain like it's something you imagined. If you see the wound is real, then you can heal it."

A wound? He opened his mouth to deny it, but something stopped him. For all his trouble at the tables and away from them, Jesper had always thought of himself as lucky. Happy, easygoing. The kind of guy people wanted around. But what if he'd been bluffing this whole time? *Angry and frightened*—that's what the Fjerdan had called him. What had Matthias and Inej seen in Jesper that he didn't understand?

"I . . . I'll try." It was the most he could offer right now. He took her hand in his, pressed a kiss to her knuckles. "It may take me a while before I can say those words." His lips tilted in a grin. "And not just because I can't speak Suli."

"I know," she said. "But think on it." She glanced toward the sitting room. "Just tell him the truth, Jesper. You'll both be glad to know where you stand."

"Every time I think about doing that, I feel like hurling myself out a window." He hesitated. "Would you tell your parents the truth? Would you tell them everything you've done . . . everything that happened?"

"I don't know," Inej admitted. "But I'd give anything to have the choice."

Jesper found his father in the purple sitting room, a cup of coffee in his big hands. He'd piled the dishes back onto the silver tray.

"You don't have to clean up after us, Da."

"Someone does." He took a sip of his coffee. "Sit down, Jes."

Jesper didn't want to sit. That desperate itch was crackling through his body. All he wanted was to run straight to the Barrel as fast as his legs could carry him and throw himself down in the first gambling parlor he could find. If he hadn't thought he'd be arrested or shot before he got halfway there, he just might have. He sat. Inej had left the unused vials of the chemical weevil on the table. He picked one up, fiddling with the stopper.

His father leaned back, watching him with those stern gray eyes. Jesper could see every line and freckle on his face in the clear morning light.

"There was no swindle, was there? That Shu boy lied for you. They all did."

Jesper clasped his hands to keep them from fidgeting. *You'll both be glad to know where you stand.* Jesper wasn't sure that was true, but he had no more options. "There have been a lot of swindles, but I was usually on the swindling side. A lot of fights—I was usually on the winning side. A lot of card games." He looked down at the white crescents of his fingernails. "I was usually on the losing side."

"The loan I gave you for your studies?"

"I got in deep with the wrong people. I lost at the tables and I kept losing, so I kept borrowing. I thought I could find a way to dig myself out."

"Why didn't you just stop?"

Jesper wanted to laugh. He had pleaded with himself, screamed at himself to stop. "It isn't like that." *There's a wound in you.* "Not for me. I don't know why."

Colm pinched the bridge of his nose. He looked so weary, this man who could work from sunrise to sunset without ever complaining. "I never should have let you leave home."

"Da—"

"I knew the farm wasn't for you. I wanted you to have something better."

"Then why not send me to Ravka?" Jesper said before he could think better of it.

Coffee sloshed from Colm's cup. "Out of the question."

"Why?"

"Why should I send my son to some foreign country to fight and die in their wars?"

A memory came to Jesper, sharp as a mule kick. The dusty man was standing at the door again. He had the girl with him, the girl who had lived because his mother had died. He wanted Jesper to come with them.

"Leoni is zowa. She has the gift too," he'd said. "There are teachers in the west, past the frontier. They could train them."

"Jesper doesn't have it," Colm said.

"But his mother—"

"He doesn't have it. You have no right to come here."

"Are you sure? Has he been tested?"

"You come back on this land and I'll consider it an invitation to put a bullet between your eyes. You go and you take that girl with you. No one here has the gift and no one here wants it."

He'd slammed the door in the dusty man's face.

Jesper remembered his father standing there, taking great heaving breaths.

"What did they want, Da?"

"Nothing."

"Am I zowa?" Jesper had asked. "Am I Grisha?"

"Don't say those words in this house. Not ever."

"But—"

"That's what killed your mother, do you understand? That's what took her from us." His father's voice was fierce, his gray eyes hard as quartz. "I won't let it take you too." Then his shoulders slumped. As if the words were being torn from him, he'd said, "Do you want to go with them? You can go. If that's what you want. I won't be mad."

Jesper had been ten. He'd thought of his father alone on the farm, coming home to an empty house every day, sitting by himself at the table every night, no one to make him burnt biscuits.

"No," he'd said. "I don't want to go with them. I want to stay with you."

Now he rose from his chair, unable to sit still any longer, and paced the length of the room. Jesper felt like he couldn't breathe. He couldn't be here anymore. His heart hurt. His head hurt. Guilt and love and resentment were all tangled up inside him, and every time he tried to unravel the knot in his gut, it just got worse. He was ashamed of the mess he'd made, of the trouble he'd brought to his father's door. But he was mad too. And how could he be angry at his father? The person who loved him most in the world, who had worked to give him everything he had, the person he'd take a bullet for any day of the week?

This action will have no echo. "I'm going to . . . I'll find a way to make amends, Da. I want to be a better person, a better son."

"I didn't raise you to be a gambler, Jesper. I certainly didn't raise you to be a criminal."

Jesper released a bitter huff of laughter. "I love you, Da. I love you with all my lying, thieving, worthless heart, but yes, you did."

"What?" sputtered Colm.

"You taught me to lie."

"To keep you safe."

Jesper shook his head. "I had a gift. You should have let me use it."

Colm banged his fist against the table. "It's not a gift. It's a curse. It would have killed you the same way it killed your mother."

So much for the truth. Jesper strode to the door. If he didn't get shut of this place, he was going to jump right out of his skin. "I'm dying anyway, Da. I'm just doing it slow."

Jesper strode down the hall. He didn't know where to go or what to do with himself. *Go to the Barrel. Stay off the Stave. There's a game to be had somewhere, just be inconspicuous.* Sure, a Zemeni as tall as a modestly ambitious tree and carrying a price on his head wouldn't be noticed at all. He remembered what Kuwei had said about Grisha who didn't use their power being tired and sickly. He wasn't physically sick, that was true enough. But what if Matthias was right and Jesper had a different kind of sickness? What if all that power inside him just liked to bounce around looking for someplace to go?

He passed an open doorway, then doubled back. Wylan was sitting at a white lacquer piano in the corner, listlessly plunking out one solitary note.

"I like that," he said. "Has a great beat—you can dance to it."

Wylan looked up, and Jesper sauntered into the room, hands swinging restlessly at his sides. He circled its perimeter, taking in all the furnishings—purple silk wallpaper flocked in silver fishes, silver chandeliers, a cabinet full of blown-glass ships. "Saints, this place is hideous."

Wylan shrugged and played another note. Jesper leaned on the piano. "Wanna get out of here?"

Wylan looked up at him, his gaze speculative. He nodded.

Jesper stood up a little straighter. "Really?"

Wylan held his gaze. The air in the room seemed to change, as if it had become suddenly combustible.

Wylan rose from the piano bench. He took a step toward Jesper. His eyes were a clear, luminous gold, like sun through honey. Jesper missed the blue, the long lashes, the tangle of curls. But if the merchling had to be wrapped up in a different package, Jesper could admit he liked this one plenty. And did any of that really matter when Wylan was looking at him like that—head tilted to the side, a slight smile playing over his lips? He looked almost . . . *bold*. What had changed? Had he been afraid Jesper wouldn't make it out of the scrape on Black Veil? Was he just feeling lucky to be alive? Jesper wasn't sure he cared. He'd wanted distraction, and here it was.

Wylan's grin broadened. His brow lifted. If that wasn't an invitation . . .

"Well, hell," Jesper muttered. He closed the distance between them and took Wylan's face in his hands. He moved slowly, deliberately, kept the kiss quiet, the barest brush of his lips, giving Wylan the chance to pull away if he wanted to. But he didn't. He drew closer.

Jesper could feel the heat from Wylan's body against his. He slid his hand to the back of Wylan's neck, tilting his head back, asking for more.

He felt greedy for something. He'd wanted to kiss Wylan since he'd first seen him stirring chemicals in that gruesome tannery—ruddy curls damp with the heat, skin so delicate it looked like it would bruise if you breathed on it too hard. He looked like he'd fallen into the wrong story, a prince turned pauper. From then on, Jesper had been stuck somewhere between the desire to taunt the pampered little merchling into another blush and the urge to flirt him into a quiet corner just to see what might happen. But sometime during their hours at the Ice Court, that curiosity had changed. He'd felt the tug of something more, something that came to life in Wylan's unexpected courage, in his wide-eyed, generous way of looking at the world. It made Jesper feel like a kite on a tether, lifted up and then plummeting down, and he liked it.

So where was that feeling now? Disappointment flooded through him.

Is it me? Jesper thought. *Am I out of practice?* He pushed closer, letting the kiss deepen, seeking that rising, falling, reckless sensation, moving Wylan back against the piano. He heard the keys clank against one another—soft, discordant music. *Appropriate*, he thought. And then, *If I can think about metaphors at a time like this, something is definitely wrong.*

He pulled back, dropped his hands, feeling unspeakably awkward. What did you say after a terrible kiss? He'd never had cause to wonder.

That was when he saw Kuwei standing in the doorway, mouth open, eyes wide and shocked.

"What?" Jesper asked. "Do the Shu not kiss before noon?"

"I wouldn't know," Kuwei said sourly.

Not Kuwei.

"Oh, Saints," Jesper groaned. That wasn't Kuwei in the doorway. It was Wylan Van Eck, budding demolitions expert and wayward rich kid. And that meant he'd just kissed . . .

The real Kuwei plunked that same listless note on the piano, grinning shamelessly up at him through thick black lashes.

Jesper turned back to the door. "Wylan——" he began.

"Kaz wants us in the sitting room."

"I——"

But Wylan was already gone. Jesper stared at the empty doorway. How could he have made a mistake like that? Wylan was taller than Kuwei; his face was narrower too. If Jesper hadn't been so riled up and jittery after the fight with Kaz and the argument with his father, he would never have confused them. And now he'd ruined everything.

Jesper jabbed an accusing finger at Kuwei. "You should have said something!"

Kuwei shrugged. "You were very brave on Black Veil. Since we're all probably going to die——"

"Damn it," Jesper cursed, stalking toward the door.

"You're a very good kisser," called Kuwei after him.

Jesper turned. "How good is your Kerch really?"

"Fairly good."

"Okay, then I hope you understand exactly what I mean when I say you are definitely more trouble than you're worth."

Kuwei beamed, looking entirely too pleased with himself. "Kaz seems to think I'm worth a great deal now."

Jesper rolled his eyes skyward. "You fit right in here."

25

MATTHIAS

They assembled once again in the suite's sitting room. At Nina's request, Colm had ordered another stack of waffles and a bowl of strawberries and cream. A mirror covered most of the suite's far wall, and Matthias could not stop his gaze from straying to it. It was like looking into another reality.

Jesper had slipped off his boots and was seated on the carpet, knees tucked up to his chest, casting furtive glances at Wylan, who had settled on the couch and seemed to be deliberately ignoring him. Inej perched on the windowsill, her balance so perfect it made her appear weightless, a bird poised to take flight. Kuwei had wedged himself into the crook of the settee, one of his notebooks open beside him, and Kaz sat in a high-backed purple chair, his bad leg propped on the low table, cane leaning against his thigh. He'd somehow seen to the torn sleeve of his shirt.

Nina was curled up next to Matthias on the couch, her head resting on his shoulder, her feet tucked beneath her, fingers stained with strawberry juice. He felt strange sitting this way. In Fjerda, even a husband and his wife showed little affection in public. They held hands and might dance at a public ball. But he liked it, and though he could not quite relax, he couldn't bear the thought of her moving away from him.

It was Colm's solid presence that transformed the image in the mirror. He made the people in the reflection seem less dangerous, as if they weren't the team that had broken into the Ice Court and bested the Fjerdan military with little more than their wits and nerve, only a bunch of children worn out after a particularly brutal birthday party.

"All right," said Nina, licking strawberry juice from her fingers in a way that thoroughly defeated Matthias' ability to form a rational thought. "When you say an auction, you don't actually mean—"

"Kuwei is going to sell himself."

"Are you mad?"

"I'd probably be happier if I was," said Kaz. He rested one gloved hand on his cane. "Any Kerch citizen and any free citizen who travels to Kerch has the right to sell his own indenture. It isn't just the law, it's trade, and there's nothing more holy in Kerch. Kuwei Yul-Bo has the sacred right— as sanctioned by Ghezen, god of industry and commerce—to submit his life to the will of the market. He can offer his service at auction."

"You want him to sell himself to the highest bidder?" Inej said incredulously.

"To *our* highest bidder. We're going to fix the outcome so Kuwei gets his fondest wish—a life sipping tea from a samovar in Ravka."

"My father will never allow it," said Wylan.

"Van Eck will be powerless to stop it. The auction of an indenture is protected by the highest laws in the city—secular and religious. Once Kuwei declares his contract open, no one can stop the auction until bidding has closed."

Nina was shaking her head. "If we announce an auction, the Shu will know exactly when and where to find him."

"This is not Ravka," said Kaz. "This is Kerch. Trade is sacred, protected by law. The Merchant Council are duty bound to make sure an auction proceeds without interference. The *stadwatch* will be out in force, and the auction statutes demand that the Council of Tides provide their assistance too. The Merchant Council, the *stadwatch*, the Tides—all required to protect Kuwei."

Kuwei set his notebook down. "The Shu may still have *parem* and Fabrikators."

"That's right," said Jesper. "If that's true, they can make all the gold they want. There would be no way to outbid them."

"That's assuming they have Fabrikators in the city already. Van Eck has done us the courtesy of blockading the harbor."

"Even so——"

"Let me worry about the Shu," said Kaz. "I can control the bidding. But we'll need to make contact with the Ravkans again. They'll have to know what we're planning. At least part of it."

"I can get through to the embassy," said Inej, "if Nina will write the message."

"The streets are closed down by barricades," protested Wylan.

"But not the rooftops," Inej replied.

"Inej," said Nina. "Don't you think you should tell them a bit more about your new friend?"

"Yeah," said Jesper. "Who's this new acquaintance who poked a bunch of holes in you?"

Inej glanced through the window. "There's a new player on the field, a mercenary hired by Pekka Rollins."

"You were defeated in single combat?" Matthias asked in surprise. He had seen the Wraith fight. It would be no small thing to best her.

"Mercenary is a little bit of an understatement," said Nina. "She followed Inej onto the high wire and then threw knives at her."

"Not knives, exactly," said Inej.

"Pointy death doilies?"

Inej rose from the sill. She reached into her pocket and let a pile of what looked like small silver suns clatter onto the table.

Kaz leaned forward and picked one up. "Who is she?"

"Her name is Dunyasha," Inej said. "She called herself the White Blade and a variety of other things. She's very good."

"How good?" asked Kaz.

"Better than me."

"I've heard of her," said Matthias. "Her name came up in an intelligence report the *drüskelle* gathered on Ravka."

"Ravka?" Inej said. "She said she was trained in Ahmrat Jen."

"She claims she has Lantsov blood and that she's a contender for the Ravkan throne."

Nina released a hoot of laughter. "You can't be serious."

"We considered backing her claim to undermine Nikolai Lantsov's regime."

"Smart," said Kaz.

"Evil," said Nina.

Matthias cleared his throat. "He's a new king, vulnerable. There are some questions regarding his own lineage. But the report suggested that Dunyasha is erratic, possibly delusional. We determined she was too unpredictable for such a venture."

"Pekka could have had her follow us from Black Veil last night," Inej said.

"Do we know how Pekka found the hideout?" Nina asked.

"One of his people must have spotted one of us," Kaz replied. "That's all it would take."

Matthias wondered if it was better that they couldn't be sure who was responsible. That way no one had to bear the guilt or the blame.

"Dunyasha had the advantage of surprise," said Inej. "If the hotel is still uncompromised, I can get to the embassy and back unseen."

"Good," said Kaz, but the answer didn't come as quickly as Matthias might have expected. *He fears for her*, Matthias thought, *and he does not like it*. For once, he could sympathize with the *demjin*.

"There's another problem," said Nina. "Matthias, cover your ears."

"No."

"Fine. I'll just have to ensure your loyalty later." She whispered in his ear, "There's a very large bathtub off the master bedroom."

"*Nina.*"

"It was just an observation." Nina plucked the remnants of a waffle from the tray and said, "Ravka can't win the auction. We're broke."

"Oh," said Matthias. "I knew that."

"You did not."

"You think Fjerda isn't aware the Ravkan coffers are empty?"

Nina scowled. "You could have at least pretended to be surprised."

"Ravka's financial woes are no secret. Its treasury was depleted from years of mismanagement by the Lantsov kings and fighting on both of its borders. The civil war didn't help, and the new king has borrowed heavily from the Kerch banks. If we go through with the auction, Ravka won't be able to bid competitively."

Kaz shifted his bad leg. "That's why the Kerch Merchant Council is going to bankroll them."

Jesper burst out laughing. "Fantastic. Any chance they want to buy me a solid-gold bowler hat while they're at it?"

"That's unlawful," said Wylan. "The Council are responsible for running the auction. They can't interfere with its outcome."

"Of course not," said Kaz. "And they know it. Kuwei and his father approached the Merchant Council looking for aid, but they were so afraid of compromising their neutrality, they refused to act. Van Eck saw an opportunity, and he's been operating behind their backs ever since." Kaz settled more deeply in his chair. "What has Van Eck been planning all along? He's been buying up *jurda* farms so that when the secret of *jurda parem* is unleashed, he'll control the *jurda* supply. He wins no matter who has Kuwei. So think like him—think like a merch. When Kuwei Yul-Bo, son of Bo Yul-Bayur, announces the auction, the Council will know the secret of *parem* could become public at any time. They'll finally be free to act and they'll be looking for opportunities to secure their fortunes and Kerch's position in the world economy. They can't involve themselves in the auction, but they can guarantee they make a lot of money what-ever the outcome."

"By buying up *jurda*," said Wylan.

"Exactly. We set up a *jurda* consortium, a chance for willing investors to make a fine dime off the world going to hell. We bring the Council an opportunity and let their greed do the rest."

Wylan nodded, his face growing eager. "The money never goes to the consortium. We funnel it to Ravka so they can afford to bid on Kuwei."

"Something like that," said Kaz. "And we take a little percentage. Just like the banks do."

"But who's going to shill?" Jesper said. "Van Eck has seen all our faces except Nina and Specht. Even if one of us somehow got tailored or we brought on another person, the Merchant Council isn't just going to turn over their money to a newcomer with no real credentials."

"How about a *jurda* farmer who's been holed up in the most expen-sive suite in Ketterdam?"

Colm Fahey looked up from his coffee. "Me?"

"No way, Kaz," said Jesper. "Absolutely not."

"He knows *jurda*, he speaks Kerch and Zemeni, and he looks the part."

"He has an honest face," Jesper said bitterly. "You weren't keeping him safe stashing him in this hotel, you were setting him up."

"I was building us an out."

"A hedge of your own?"

"Yes."

"You are not bringing my father into this."

"He's already in it, Jes. You brought him into it when you had him mortgage his farm to pay for your degree in wasting money."

"*No*," repeated Jesper. "Van Eck is going to make the connection between Colm Fahey and Jesper Fahey. He isn't an idiot."

"But there is no Colm Fahey staying at the Geldrenner. Colm Fahey rented rooms at a little university district inn, and according to the harbormaster's manifests, he left town several nights ago. The man staying here is registered under the name Johannus Rietveld."

"Who the hell is that?" asked Nina.

"He's a farmer from a town near Lij. His family's been there for years. He has holdings in Kerch and in Novyi Zem."

"But who is he really?" said Jesper.

"That doesn't matter. Think of him as a figment of the Merchant Council's imagination, a wonderful dream come to life to help them scrape some profit from the disaster of *parem*."

Colm put his cup down. "I'll do it."

"Da, you don't know what you're agreeing to."

"I'm already harboring fugitives. If I'm going to aid, I may as well abet."

"If this goes wrong—"

"What do I have to lose, Jes? My life is you and the farm. This is the only way I can protect both of those things."

Jesper shoved off from the floor, pacing back and forth in front of the windows. "This is insanity," he said, scrubbing his hand over the back of his neck. "They'll never fall for it."

"We don't ask for too much from any of them," said Kaz. "That's the trick. We set a low floor to enter the fund, say, two million *kruge*. And then we let them wait. The Shu are here. The Fjerdans. The Ravkans. The Council will start to panic. If I had to bet, I'd say we'll have five million from each Council member by the time we're through."

"There are thirteen Council members," said Jesper. "That's sixty-five million *kruge*."

"Maybe more."

Matthias frowned. "Even with all the *stadwatch* at the auction and the presence of the Council of Tides, can we really guarantee Kuwei's safety?"

"Unless you have a unicorn for him to ride away on, there is no scenario that *guarantees* Kuwei's safety."

"I wouldn't count on protection from the Council of Tides either," said Nina. "Have they ever even appeared in public?"

"Twenty-five years ago," said Kaz.

"And you think they're going to show up to protect Kuwei now? We can't send him into a public auction alone."

"Kuwei won't be alone. Matthias and I will be with him."

"Everyone there knows your faces. Even if you had some kind of disguise—"

"No disguise. The Merchant Council are considered his representatives. But Kuwei has the right to choose his own protection for the auction. We'll be up there on the stage with him."

"The stage?"

"Auctions are held at the Church of Barter, right in front of the altar. What could be more holy? It's perfect—an enclosed space with multiple points of entry and easy access to a canal."

Nina shook her head. "Kaz, as soon as Matthias steps on that stage, half the Fjerdan delegation will recognize him, and you're the most wanted man in Ketterdam. If you show up at that auction, you'll both be arrested."

"They can't touch us until after the auction."

"And then what?" said Inej.

"There's going to be one hell of a distraction."

"There has to be another way," said Jesper. "What if we tried making a deal with Rollins?"

Wylan pleated the edge of his napkin. "We don't have anything to offer."

"No more deals," said Kaz. "I never should have gone to Rollins in the first place."

Jesper's brows rose. "Are you actually admitting you made a mistake?"

"We needed capital," Kaz said. His eyes slid briefly to Inej. "And I'm not sorry for it, but it wasn't the right move. The trick to beating Rollins is never sit down at the table with him. He's the house. He has the resources to play until your luck runs out."

"All the same," said Jesper. "If we're going up against the Kerch government, the gangs of the Barrel, and the Shu—"

"And the Fjerdans," added Matthias. "And the Zemeni, and the Kaelish, and whoever else shows up when the auction is announced. The embassies are full and we don't know how far the rumors of *parem* have reached."

"We're going to need help," said Nina.

"I know," said Kaz, straightening his sleeves. "That's why I'm going to the Slat."

Jesper stopped moving. Inej shook her head. They all stared.

"What are you talking about?" said Nina. "There's a price on your head. Everyone in the Barrel knows it."

"You saw Per Haskell and the Dregs down there," said Jesper. "You think you can talk the old man into propping you up when the whole city is about to come down on you like a sack of bricks? You know he doesn't have the stones for that."

"I know," said Kaz. "But we need a bigger crew for this job."

"*Demjin*, this is not a risk worth taking," said Matthias, surprised to find he actually meant it.

"When this is all over, when Van Eck has been put in his place, when Rollins goes running, and the money is paid, these will still be my streets. I can't live in a city where I can't hold up my head."

"If you have a head to hold up," said Jesper.

"I've taken knives, bullets, and too many punches to count, all for a little piece of this town," said Kaz. "This is the city I bled for. And if Ketterdam has taught me anything, it's that you can always bleed a little more."

Nina reached for Matthias' hand. "The Grisha are still stuck at the embassy, Kaz. I know you don't give a damn, but we have to get them out of the city. And Jesper's father. All of us. No matter who wins the auction, Van Eck and Pekka Rollins aren't going to just pack up and go home. Neither will the Shu."

Kaz rose, leaning on his crow's head cane. "But I know the one thing this city is more frightened of than the Shu, the Fjerdans, and all the gangs of the Barrel put together. And Nina, you're going to give it to them."

26

KAZ

Kaz sat in that chair for what felt like hours, answering their questions, letting the pieces of the plan shift into place. He saw the scheme's final shape in his mind, the steps it would take to get them there, the infinite ways they might falter or be found out. It was a mad, spiky monster of a plan, and that was what it had to be for them to succeed.

Johannus Rietveld. He'd told a kind of truth. Johannus Rietveld had never existed. Kaz had used Jordie's middle name and their shared family name to create the farmer's identity years ago.

He wasn't certain why he'd purchased the farm where he'd grown up or why he'd continued to make trades and acquire property under the Rietveld name. Was Johannus Rietveld meant to be his Jakob Hertzoon? A respectable identity like the one Pekka Rollins had crafted to better dupe gullible pigeons? Or had it been some way of resurrecting the family he'd lost? Did it even matter? Johannus Rietveld existed on paper and in bank records, and Colm Fahey was perfect to play the role.

When the meeting finally broke apart, the coffee had gone cold and it was nearly noon. Despite the bright light streaming through the windows, they would all try to get a few hours' rest. He could not. *We don't stop.* Kaz's whole body ached with exhaustion. His leg had ceased throbbing and now it just radiated pain.

He knew how damnably stupid he was being, how unlikely it was that he'd return from the Slat. Kaz had spent his life in a series of dodges and feints. Why come at a problem straight on when you could find some other way to approach? There was always an angle, and he was an expert at finding it. Now he was about to go stomping ahead like an ox yoked to a plow. Odds were good he'd end up beaten, bloodied, and dragged through the Barrel straight to Pekka Rollins' front stoop. But they'd landed in a trap, and if he had to chew his paw off to get them out of it, then that was what he would do.

First he had to find Inej. She was in the suite's lavish white-and-gold bathroom, seated at a vanity table, cutting fresh bandages from the towels.

He strode past her and removed his coat, tossing it onto the sink, beside the basin. "I need your help plotting a route to the Slat."

"I'm coming with you."

"You know I have to face them alone," he said. "They'll be looking for any sign of weakness, Wraith." He turned the spigots, and after a few creaking groans, steaming water poured from the tap. Maybe when he was rolling in *kruge* he'd have running hot water installed in the Slat. "But I can't approach at street level."

"You shouldn't approach at all."

He stripped off his gloves and dunked his hands in the water, then splashed it over his face, running his fingers through his hair. "Talk me through the best route or I'll find my own way there."

He would have preferred to walk instead of climb. Hell, he'd have preferred to be driven there in a carriage-and-four. But if he tried to make it through the Barrel on the streets, he'd be captured before he got anywhere near the Slat. Besides, if he had any chance of making this work, he needed the high ground.

He dug in his coat pockets and held up the tourist map of Ketterdam he'd found in the suite's parlor. It didn't have as much detail as he would have liked, but their real maps of the city had been left on Black Veil.

They laid the map beside the basin and bent to the task as Inej drew a line through the rooftops, describing the best places to cross the canals.

At one point she tapped the map. "This way is faster, but it's steeper."

"I'll take the long way," said Kaz. He wanted his mind on the fight ahead and avoiding notice, not on the chance he was going to tumble to his death.

When he was satisfied he could follow the route from memory, he tucked the map away and took another paper from his pocket. It bore the pale green seal of the Gemensbank. He handed it to her.

"What is this?" she asked, her eyes scanning the page. "It's not . . ." She ran her fingertips over the words as if expecting them to vanish. "My contract," she whispered.

"I don't want you beholden to Per Haskell. Or me." Another half-truth. His mind had concocted a hundred schemes to bind her to him, to keep her in this city. But she'd spent enough of her life caged by debts and obligations, and it would be better for them both when she was gone.

"How?" she said. "The money—"

"It's done." He'd liquidated every asset he had, used the last of the savings he'd accrued, every ill-gotten cent.

She pressed the envelope to her chest, above her heart. "I have no words to thank you for this."

"Surely the Suli have a thousand proverbs for such an occasion?"

"Words have not been invented for such an occasion."

"If I end up on the gallows, you can say something nice over the corpse," he said. "Wait until six bells. If I'm not back, try to get everyone out of the city."

"Kaz—"

"There's a discolored brick in the wall behind the Crow Club. Behind it you'll find twenty thousand *kruge*. It's not much, but it should be enough to bribe a few *stadwatch* grunts." He knew their chances would be slim and that it was his fault. "You'd have a better shot on your own—even better if you left now."

Inej narrowed her eyes. "I'm going to pretend you didn't say that. These are my friends. I'm not going anywhere."

"Tell me about Dunyasha," he said.

"She was carrying quality blades." Inej took the shears from the table of the vanity and began cutting fresh strips of cloth from one of the towels. "I think she may be my shadow."

"Pretty solid shadow if she can throw knives."

"The Suli believe that when we do wrong, we give life to our shadows. Every sin makes the shadow stronger, until eventually the shadow is stronger than you."

"If that were true, my shadow would have put Ketterdam in permanent night."

"Maybe," Inej said, turning her dark gaze to his. "Or maybe you're someone else's shadow."

"You mean Pekka."

"What happens if you make it back from the Slat? If the auction goes as planned and we manage this feat?"

"Then you get your ship and your future."

"And you?"

"I wreak all the havoc I can until my luck runs out. I use our haul to build an empire."

"And after that?"

"Who knows? Maybe I'll burn it to the ground."

"Is that what makes you different from Rollins? That you'll leave nothing behind?"

"I am not Pekka Rollins or his shadow. I don't sell girls into brothels. I don't con helpless kids out of their money."

"Look at the floor of the Crow Club, Kaz." Her voice was gentle, patient—why was it making him want to set fire to something? "Think of every racket and card game and theft you've run. Did all those men and women deserve what they got or what they had taken from them?"

"Life isn't ever what we deserve, Inej. If it were—"

"Did your brother get what he deserved?"

"No." But the denial felt hollow.

Why had he called Jesper by Jordie's name? When he looked into the past, he saw his brother through the eyes of the boy he'd been: brave, brilliant, infallible, a knight bested by a dragon dressed like a merch. But how would he see Jordie now? As a mark? Another dumb pigeon looking for a shortcut? He leaned his hands on the edge of the sink. He wasn't angry anymore. He just felt weary. "We were fools."

"You were children. Was there no one to protect you?"

"Was there anyone to protect *you*?"

"My father. My mother. They would have done anything to keep me from being stolen."

"And they would have been mowed down by slavers."

"Then I guess I was lucky I didn't have to see that."

How could she still look at the world that way? "Sold into a brothel at age fourteen and you count yourself lucky."

"They loved me. They love me. I believe that." He saw her draw closer in the mirror. Her black hair was an ink splash against the white tile walls. She paused behind him. "You protected me, Kaz."

"The fact that you're bleeding through your bandages tells me otherwise."

She glanced down. A red blossom of blood had spread on the bandage tied around her shoulder. She tugged awkwardly at the strip of towel. "I need Nina to fix this one."

He didn't mean to say it. He meant to let her go. "I can help you."

Her gaze snapped to his in the mirror, wary as if gauging an opponent.

I can help you. They were the first words she'd spoken to him, standing in the parlor of the Menagerie, draped in purple silk, eyes lined in kohl. She had helped him. And she'd nearly destroyed him. Maybe he should let her finish the job.

Kaz could hear the drip of the faucet, water striking the basin in an uneven rhythm. He wasn't sure what he wanted her to say. *Tell her to get out*, a voice inside him demanded. *Beg her to stay.*

But Inej said nothing. Instead, she gathered the bandages and shears from the vanity and placed them beside the basin. Then she flattened her palms on the counter and effortlessly levered herself up so that she was seated on it.

They were eye to eye now. He took a step closer and then just stood there, unable to move. He could not do this. The distance between them felt like nothing. It felt like miles.

She reached for the shears, graceful as always, a girl underwater, and offered them to him handle first. They were cool in his hand; the metal unpliable and reassuring. He stepped into the space framed by her knees.

"Where do we start?" she asked. The steam from the basin had curled the wisps of hair that framed her face.

Was he going to do this?

He nodded to her right forearm, not trusting himself to speak. His gloves lay on the other side of the basin, black against the gold-veined marble. They looked like dead animals.

He focused on the shears, cold metal in his hands, nothing like skin. He could not do this if his hands were shaking.

I can best this, he told himself. It was no different than drawing a weapon on someone. Violence was easy.

He slid the blade carefully beneath the bandage on her arm. The towel was thicker than gauze would have been, but the shears were sharp. One snip and the bandage fell away, revealing a deep puncture wound. He cast the fabric aside.

He picked up a strip of fresh towel and stood there, steeling himself.

She lifted her arm. Cautiously, he looped the clean piece of cloth around her forearm. His knuckles brushed against her skin and lightning cracked through him, left him paralyzed, rooted to the earth.

His heart should not be making that sound. Maybe he would never get to the Slat. Maybe this would kill him. He willed his hands to move, knotted the bandage once, twice. It was done.

Kaz took a breath. He knew he should replace the bandage at her shoulder next, but he wasn't ready for that, so he nodded to her left arm. The bandage was perfectly clean and secure, but she didn't question him, just offered her forearm.

This time it was a little easier. He moved slowly, methodically, the shears, the bandage, a meditation. But then the task was complete.

They said nothing, caught in an eddy of silence, not touching, her knees on either side of him. Inej's eyes were wide and dark, lost planets, black moons.

The bandage on her shoulder had been looped under her arm twice and tied near the joint. He leaned in slightly, but the angle was awkward. He couldn't simply wedge the scissors beneath the towel. He would have to lift the edge of the fabric.

No. The room was too bright. His chest felt like a clenched fist. *Stop this.*

He pressed two fingers together. He slid them beneath the bandage.

Everything in him recoiled. The water was cold against his legs. His body had gone numb and yet he could still feel the wet give of his brother's rotting flesh beneath his hands. *It's shame that eats men whole.* He was drowning in it. Drowning in the Ketterdam harbor. His eyes blurred.

"It isn't easy for me either." Her voice, low and steady, the voice that had once led him back from hell. "Even now, a boy will smile at me on the street, or Jesper will put his arm around my waist, and I feel like I'm going to vanish." The room tilted. He clung to the tether of her voice. "I live in fear that I'll see one of her—one of *my*—clients on the street. For a long time, I thought I recognized them everywhere. But sometimes I think what they did to me wasn't the worst of it."

Kaz's vision came back into focus. The water receded. He was standing in a hotel bathroom. His fingers were pressed against Inej's shoulder. He could feel the fine muscles beneath her skin. A pulse beat furiously at her throat, in the soft hollow just beneath her jaw. He realized she had closed her eyes. Her lashes were black against her cheeks. As if in response to his shaking, she had gone even more still. He should say something, but his mouth could not make words.

"Tante Heleen wasn't always cruel," Inej continued. "She'd hug you, hold you close, then pinch you so hard, she broke skin. You never knew if a kiss was coming or a slap. One day you were her best girl, and the next day she'd bring you to her office and tell you she was selling you to a group of men she'd met on the street. She'd make you beg her to keep you." Inej released a soft sound that was almost a laugh. "The first time Nina hugged me, I *flinched*." Her eyes opened. She met his gaze. He could hear the drip of the faucet, see the curl of her braid over her shoulder where it had slipped free of its coil. "Go on," she said quietly, as if she was asking him to continue a story.

He wasn't sure he could. But if she could speak those words into the echo of this room, he could damn well try.

Carefully, he raised the shears. He lifted the bandage, creating a gap, feeling regret and release as he broke contact with her skin. He sliced through the bandage. He could feel the warmth of her on his fingers like fever.

The ruined bandage fell away.

He took up another long strip of towel in his right hand. He had to lean in to loop it behind her. He was so close now. His mind took in the shell of her ear, the hair tucked behind it, that rapid pulse fluttering in her throat. Alive, alive, alive.

It isn't easy for me either.

He looped the bandage around again. The barest touches. Unavoidable. Shoulder, clavicle, once her knee. The water rose around him.

He secured the knot. *Step back.* He did not step back. He stood there, hearing his own breath, hers, the rhythm of them alone in this room.

The sickness was there, the need to run, the need for something else too. Kaz thought he knew the language of pain intimately, but this ache was new. It hurt to stand here like this, so close to the circle of her arms. *It isn't easy for me either.* After all she'd endured, he was the weak one. But she would never know what it was like for him to see Nina pull her close, watch Jesper loop his arm through hers, what it was to stand in doorways and against walls and know he could never draw nearer. *But I'm here now*, he thought wildly. He had carried her, fought beside her, spent whole nights next to her, both of them on their bellies, peering through a long glass, watching some warehouse or merch's mansion. This was nothing like that. He was sick and frightened, his body slick with sweat, but he was here. He watched that pulse, the evidence of her heart, matching his own beat for anxious beat. He saw the damp curve of her neck, the gleam of her brown skin. He wanted to . . . He wanted.

Before he even knew what he intended, he lowered his head. She drew in a sharp breath. His lips hovered just above the warm juncture between her shoulder and the column of her neck. He waited. *Tell me to stop. Push me away.*

She exhaled. "Go on," she repeated. Finish the story.

The barest movement and his lips brushed her skin—warm, smooth, beaded with moisture. Desire coursed through him, a thousand images he'd hoarded, barely let himself imagine—the fall of her dark hair freed from its braid, his hand fitted to the lithe curve of her waist, her lips parted, whispering his name.

All of it there and then gone. He was drowning in the harbor. Her limbs were a corpse's limbs. Her eyes were dead and staring. Disgust and longing roiled in his gut.

He lurched backward, and pain shot through his bad leg. His mouth was on fire. The room swayed. He braced himself against the wall, trying to breathe. Inej was on her feet, moving toward him, her face concerned. He held up a hand to stop her.

"Don't."

She stood in the center of the tile floor, framed by white and gold, like a gilded icon. "What happened to you, Kaz? What happened to your brother?"

"It doesn't matter."

"Tell me. Please."

Tell her, said a voice inside him. *Tell her everything.* But he didn't know how or where to begin. And why should he? So she could find a way to absolve him of his crimes? He didn't want her pity. He didn't need to explain himself, he just needed to find a way to let her go.

"You want to know what Pekka did to me?" His voice was a snarl, reverberating off the tiles. "How about I tell you what I did when I found the woman who pretended to be his wife, the girl who pretended to be his daughter? Or how about I tell you what happened to the boy who lured us in that first night with his mechanical toy dogs? That's a good one. His name was Filip. I found him running a monte game on Kelstraat. I tortured him for two days and left him bleeding in an alley, the key to a windup dog shoved down his throat." Kaz saw Inej flinch. He ignored the sting in his heart.

"That's right," he went on. "The clerks at the bank who turned over our information. The fake attorney. The man who gave me free hot chocolate at Hertzoon's fake office. I destroyed them all, one by one, brick by brick. And Rollins will be the last. These things don't wash away with prayer, Wraith. There is no peace waiting for me, no forgiveness, not in this life, not in the next."

Inej shook her head. How could she still look at him with kindness in her eyes? "You don't ask for forgiveness, Kaz. You earn it."

"Is that what you intend to do? By hunting slavers?"

"By hunting slavers. By rooting out the merchers and Barrel bosses who profit off of them. By being something more than just the next Pekka Rollins."

It was impossible. There was nothing more. He could see the truth even if she couldn't. Inej was stronger than he would ever be. She'd kept her faith, her goodness, even when the world tried to take it from her with greedy hands.

His eyes scanned her face as they always had, closely, hungrily, snatching at the details of her like the thief he was—the even set of her dark brows, the rich brown of her eyes, the upward tilt of her lips. He didn't deserve peace and he didn't deserve forgiveness, but if he was going to die today, maybe the one thing he'd earned was the memory of her— brighter than anything he would ever have a right to—to take with him to the other side.

Kaz strode past Inej, took his discarded gloves from the sink, pulled them on. He shrugged into his coat, straightened his tie in the mirror, tucked his cane under his arm. He might as well go to meet his death in style.

When he turned back to her, he was ready. "Whatever happens to me, survive this city. Get your ship, have your vengeance, carve your name into their bones. But survive this mess I've gotten us into."

"Don't do this," Inej said.

"If I don't, it's all over. There's no way out. There's no reward. There's nothing left."

"Nothing," she repeated.

"Look for Dunyasha's tells."

"What?"

"A fighter always has a tell, a sign of an old injury, a dropped shoulder when they're about to throw a punch."

"Do I have a tell?"

"You square your shoulders before you start a move as if you're about to perform, like you're waiting for the audience's attention."

She looked slightly affronted at that. "And what's yours?"

Kaz thought of the moment on Vellgeluk that had nearly cost him everything.

"I'm a cripple. That's my tell. No one's ever smart enough to look for the others."

"Don't go to the Slat, Kaz. Let us find another way."

"Step aside, Wraith."

"Kaz—"

"If you ever cared about me at all, don't follow."

He pushed past her and strode from the room. He couldn't think of what might be, of what there was to lose. And Inej was wrong about one thing. He knew exactly what he intended to leave behind when he was gone.

Damage.

27
INEJ

S he followed him anyway.

If you ever cared about me at all.

Inej actually snorted as she vaulted over a chimney. It was offensive. She'd had numerous chances to be free of Kaz, and she'd never taken them.

So he wasn't fit for a normal life. Was she meant to find a kindhearted husband, have his children, then sharpen her knives after they'd gone to sleep? How would she explain the nightmares she still had from the Menagerie? Or the blood on her hands?

She could feel the press of Kaz's fingers against her skin, feel the bird's-wing brush of his mouth against her neck, see his dilated eyes. Two of the deadliest people the Barrel had to offer and they could barely touch each other without both of them keeling over. But they'd tried. He'd tried. Maybe they could try again. A foolish wish, the sentimental hope of a girl who hadn't had the firsts of her life stolen, who hadn't ever felt Tante Heleen's lash, who wasn't covered in wounds and wanted by the law. Kaz would have laughed at her optimism.

She thought of Dunyasha, her shadow. What dreams did she have? A throne, as Matthias had suggested? Another kill offered up to her god? Inej had no doubt she would meet the ivory-and-amber girl again. She wanted to believe she would emerge victorious when that time came, but she could not argue with Dunyasha's gifts. Maybe she really was a princess, a girl of noble birth trained in the killing arts, destined for greatness like a heroine in a story. Then what did that make Inej? An obstacle in her path? Tribute on the altar of death? *A smudge of a Suli acrobat who fights like a common street thug.* Or perhaps her Saints had brought Dunyasha to these streets. *Who will remember a girl like you, Miss Ghafa?* Maybe this was the way Inej would be called to account for the lives she had taken.

Maybe. But not yet. She still had debts to pay.

Inej hissed as she slid down a drainpipe, feeling the bandage around her thigh pull free. She was going to leave a trail of blood over the skyline.

They were drawing closer to the Slat, but she kept to the shadows and made sure there was a good distance between her and Kaz. He had a way of sensing her presence when no one else could. He paused frequently, unaware he was being observed. His leg was troubling him worse than he'd let on. But she would not interfere at the Slat. She could abide by his wishes in that, at least, because he was right: In the Barrel, strength was the only currency that mattered. If Kaz didn't face this challenge alone, he could lose everything—not just the chance to garner support from the Dregs, but any chance he would ever have to walk the Barrel freely again. She'd often wished to chip away a bit of his arrogance, but she couldn't bear the idea of seeing Kaz stripped of his pride.

He dodged over the rooftops of Groenstraat, following the route they'd laid out together, and soon enough, the back of the Slat came into view—narrow, leaning lopsided against its neighbors, its shingled gables black with soot.

How many times had she approached the Slat from just this angle? To her, it was the way home. She spotted Kaz's window on the top floor.

She'd spent countless hours perched on that sill, feeding the crows that gathered there, listening to him scheme. Below it, slightly to the left, she spotted the sliver of window that belonged to her own tiny bedroom. It struck her that, whether the auction succeeded or failed, this might be the last time she ever returned to the Slat. She might never see Kaz seated at his desk again or hear the thump of his cane coming up the Slat's rickety steps, letting her know from its rhythm whether it had been a bad night or a good one.

She watched him crawl awkwardly down from the lip of the roof and pick the lock on his own window. Once he was out of sight, she continued over the steep pitch of the gable to the other side of the Slat. She couldn't follow the way he'd gone without giving herself away.

On the front of the house, just below the roofline, she found the old metal hook used for hauling up heavy cargo. She grabbed it, ignoring the disgruntled warbling of startled pigeons, and nudged open the window with her foot, wrinkling her nose at the stink of the bird droppings. She slipped inside, moving across the roof beams, and found a place among the shadows. Then she waited, unsure of what to do next. If anyone looked up, they might see her there, perched in the corner like the spider she was, but why would anyone think to?

Below, the entryway buzzed with activity. Apparently the festive mood of that morning's parade had suffused the day. People came in and out the front door, shouting to one another, laughing and singing. A few Dregs sat on the squeaky wooden staircase, passing a bottle of whiskey back and forth. Seeger—one of Per Haskell's favorite bruisers—kept blowing the same three notes on a tin whistle for all he was worth. A group of rowdies burst through the door and tumbled into the entry, cawing and screeching like fools, stomping the floor, banging into one another like a school of hungry sharks. They carried axe handles studded with rusty nails, cudgels, knives, and guns, and some of them had painted crows' wings in black across their wild eyes. Behind them, Inej glimpsed a few Dregs who didn't seem to share the excitement—Anika with her crop of yellow hair, wiry Roeder who Per Haskell had suggested Kaz use as his spider, the bigger bruisers Keeg and Pim. They hung back against the wall, exchanging unhappy looks as the others whooped and postured. *They're Kaz's best hope for support*, she thought. The youngest members of the Dregs, the kids Kaz had brought in and organized, the ones who worked the hardest and took the worst jobs because they were the newest.

But what exactly did Kaz have in mind? Had he entered his office for a reason or simply because it was the easiest point of access from the roof? Did he mean to speak to Per Haskell alone? The entirety of the staircase was exposed to the entryway. Kaz couldn't even start down it without attracting everyone's notice, unless he planned to do it in disguise. And how he would negotiate the stairs on his bad leg without anyone recognizing his gait was beyond her.

A cheer went up from the people gathered below. Per Haskell had emerged from his office, gray head moving through the crowd. He was dressed in high flash for the festivities today—crimson-and-silver-checked vest, houndstooth trousers—out and about as the lord of the Dregs, the gang Kaz had built up from practically nothing. With one hand, he was waving around the plumed hat he favored so much, and in the other, he carried a walking stick. Someone had secured a cartoonish papier-mâché crow atop it. It made her sick. Kaz had been better than a son to Haskell. A devious, ruthless, murdering son, but even so.

"Think we'll land him tonight, old man?" asked Bastian, tapping a nasty-looking cudgel against his leg.

Haskell lifted the walking stick like a scepter. "If anyone's gonna get that reward, it's one of my lads! Isn't that right?"

They cheered.

"Old man."

Inej's head snapped up as Kaz's rock-salt rasp cut through the noise of the crowd, silencing the rowdy chatter. Every eye turned upward.

He stood at the top of the stairs, looking down four flights of rickety wood. She realized he'd stopped to change his coat and it clung to him in perfectly tailored lines. He stood leaning on his cane, hair neatly pushed back from his pale brow, a black glass boy of deadly edges.

The look of surprise on Haskell's face was nearly comical. Then he started to laugh. "Well, I'll be a son of a bitch, Brekker. You have to be the craziest bastard I ever met."

"I'll take that as a compliment."

"Shouldn't have come here—unless it's to turn yourself in like the smart lad I know you to be."

"I'm through making you money."

Per Haskell's face crumpled in rage. "You ignorant little skiv!" he roared. "Waltzing in here like some merch at his manor."

"You was always acting like you're better than us, Brekker," shouted Seeger, still holding the tin whistle, and a few of the other Dregs nodded. Per Haskell clapped his hands in encouragement.

And it was true. Kaz had always kept himself at a remove from everyone. They'd wanted camaraderie, friendship, but he had never agreed to play their game, only his own. Maybe this reckoning was inevitable. Inej knew Kaz hadn't intended to remain Per Haskell's lieutenant forever. Their triumph at the Ice Court should have made him king of the Barrel, but Van Eck had robbed him of that. The Dregs didn't know the extraordinary things he'd achieved in the last few weeks, the prize he'd wrested from the Fjerdans, or the haul that might still be within his grasp. He faced them alone, a boy with few allies, a stranger to most of them, despite his brutal reputation.

"You got no friends here!" shouted Bastian.

Along the wall, Anika and the others bristled. Pim shook his shaggy head and crossed his arms.

Kaz lifted one shoulder in the barest shrug. "I didn't come looking for friends. And I'm not here for the washed-up cadgers and cowards, or the losers who think the Barrel owes them something for managing to stay alive. I came for the killers. The hard ones. The hungry ones. The people like me. This is my gang," Kaz said, starting down the stairs, cane thumping against the boards, "and I'm done taking orders."

"Go get your reward, lads!" Haskell shouted. There was a brief pause, and for a moment, Inej hoped that no one would listen, that they'd simply mutiny against Haskell. Then the floodgates opened. Bastian and Seeger were the first to rush the stairs, eager to get their shot at Dirtyhands.

But Seeger was slow from the whiskey, and by the time they'd reached Kaz on the third flight of stairs, they were out of breath. Kaz's cane whipped out in two slashing arcs, shattering the bones in Seeger's arms. Instead of engaging Bastian, he slipped past him, uncannily fast despite his bad leg. Before Bastian could turn, Kaz jabbed his cane into the soft space between Bastian's thigh and his knee. He crumpled with a strangled cry.

Another of Haskell's lackeys was already rushing to meet him—a bruiser called Teapot for the way he whistled through his nose when he breathed. A blow from Teapot's bat glanced off Kaz's shoulder as he bobbed left. He swung his cane and struck the bruiser directly in the jaw with the full weight of the crow's head. Inej saw what had to be teeth fly from Teapot's mouth.

Kaz still had the high ground, but he was outnumbered, and now they came in waves. Varian and Swann rushed the third-floor landing, Red Felix on their heels, Milo and Gorka hovering close behind.

Inej clamped her lips together as Kaz took a hit to his bad leg, faltered, barely righted himself in time to dodge a blow from Varian's chain. It smashed into the banister inches from Kaz's head, sending splinters of wood flying. Kaz grabbed the chain and used Varian's momentum to send him hurtling over the broken banister. The crowd surged backward as he struck the entry floor.

Swann and Red Felix came at Kaz from both sides. Red Felix grabbed Kaz's coat, yanking him backward. Kaz slipped free like a magician escaping a straitjacket in a show on East Stave.

Swann swung his spiked axe handle wildly, and Kaz slammed the head of his cane into the side of Swann's face. Even from a distance, Inej saw his cheekbone collapse in a bloody crater.

Red Felix pulled a sap from his pocket and batted hard at Kaz's right hand. The blow was sloppy, but Kaz's cane clattered to the floor, rolling down the stairs. Beatle, lean as a ferret and with the face of one too, scampered up the steps and seized it, tossing it to Per Haskell as his cronies gave a cheer. Kaz planted his hands on either side of the banister and jammed his boots into Red Felix's chest, sending him tumbling backward down the stairs.

Kaz's cane was gone. He spread his gloved hands wide. Again Inej thought of a magician. *Nothing up my sleeves.*

Three more Dregs leapt past Red Felix and converged on him—Milo, Gorka, reedy Beatle with his odd little face and oily hair. Inej dared to blink and Milo had Kaz against the wall, raining blows against his ribs and face. Kaz wrenched back his head and butted his forehead into Milo's with a sickening crunch. Milo took a woozy step, and Kaz pressed the advantage.

But there were too many of them, and Kaz was fighting with his fists alone now, blood pouring down one side of his face, lip split, left eye swelling shut. His movements were slowing.

Gorka hooked an arm around Kaz's throat. Kaz drove an elbow into Gorka's stomach and broke free. He lurched forward, and Beatle grabbed his shoulder, slamming his cudgel into Kaz's gut. Kaz doubled over, spitting blood. Gorka struck the side of Kaz's head with a thick loop of chain. Inej saw Kaz's eyes roll up in his head. He swayed. And then he was on the ground. The crowd in the entry roared.

Inej was moving before she thought of it. She couldn't just watch him die, she wouldn't. They had him down now, heavy boots kicking and stomping at his body. Her knives were in her hands. She'd kill them all. She'd pile the bodies to the rafters for the *stadwatch* to find.

But in that moment, through the wide slats in the banister landing, she saw his eyes were open. His gaze found hers. He'd known she was there all along. Of course he had. He always knew how to find her. He gave the barest shake of his bloodied head.

She wanted to scream. *To hell with your pride, with the Dregs, with this whole wretched city.*

Kaz tried to rise. Beatle kicked him back down. They were laughing now. Gorka raised his leg, balancing his big boot above Kaz's skull, playing to the crowd. Inej saw Pim turn away; Anika and Keeg were bellowing for someone to stop them. Gorka brought his foot down— and screamed, a high-pitched, bobbling squeal.

Kaz was holding Gorka's boot, and Gorka's foot was wrenched to the side at an ugly angle. He hopped on one leg, trying to keep his balance, that strange, shrill wail bleating from his mouth in time with his hops. Milo and Beatle kicked Kaz hard in the ribs, but Kaz didn't flinch. With a strength Inej couldn't fathom, Kaz jammed Gorka's leg upward. The big man shrieked as his knee popped free of its socket. He toppled sideways, blubbering, "My leg! My leg!"

"I recommend a cane," Kaz said.

But all Inej could see was the knife in Milo's hands, long and gleaming. It looked like the cleanest thing about him.

"Don't kill him, you podge!" Haskell bellowed, no doubt still thinking of the reward.

But Milo was apparently beyond listening. He raised the knife and plunged it directly at Kaz's chest. At the last second, Kaz rolled. The knife sank into the floorboards with a loud *thunk*. Milo grabbed the knife to pry it free but Kaz was already moving, and Inej saw he had two rusty nails tucked between his fingers like claws—he'd somehow plucked them from one of the axe handles. He shot upward and jabbed the nails into Milo's throat, embedding them in his windpipe. Milo made a faint, choked whistle before he fell.

Kaz used the banister to haul himself to his feet. Beatle held his hands up, as if forgetting he was still in possession of a cudgel and Kaz was unarmed. Kaz grabbed a fistful of Beatle's hair, yanked back his head, and cracked it against the banister, the sound like a gunshot, the recoil sharp enough that Beatle's head bounced off the wood like a rubber ball. He slumped in a ferrety little pile.

Kaz wiped a sleeve across his face, smearing blood over his nose and forehead, and spat. He adjusted his gloves, looked down at Per Haskell from the second-story landing, and smiled. His teeth were red and wet. The crowd was far larger than when the fight had begun. He rolled his shoulders. "Who's next?" he asked, as if he might have an appointment elsewhere. "Who's coming?" Inej didn't know how he could keep his voice so steady. "This is what I do all day long. I fight. When was the last time you saw Per Haskell take a punch? Lead a job? Hell, when was the last time you saw him out of his bed before noon?"

"You think we're going to applaud because you can take a beating?" Per Haskell sneered. "It don't make up for the trouble you've caused. Bringing the law down on the Barrel, kidnapping a mercher's son—"

"I told you I had no part in that," Kaz said.

"Pekka Rollins says otherwise."

"Good to know you take a Dime Lion's word over one of your own."

An uneasy murmur passed through the crowd below like a wind rustling the leaves. Your gang was your family, the bond strong as blood.

"You're crazy enough to cross a merch, Brekker."

"Crazy enough," conceded Kaz. "But not stupid enough."

Now some of the Dregs were muttering to one another, as if they'd never considered Van Eck might have trumped up the charges. Of course they hadn't. Van Eck was quality. Why would an upright mercher make such a charge against some canal rat if it wasn't true? And after all, Kaz had gone to great lengths to prove he was capable of anything.

"You were seen on Goedmedbridge with the mercher's wife," insisted Per Haskell.

"His wife, not his son. His wife who is home safe, beside her thieving husband, knitting booties and talking to her birds. Think for a minute, Haskell. What possible use could I have for a merch's brat?"

"Bribery, ransom—"

"I crossed Van Eck because he crossed me and now he's using the city's
henchmen and Pekka Rollins and all of you to even the score. It's that
simple."

"I didn't ask for this trouble, boy. Didn't ask for it and don't want it."

"You wanted everything else I've brought to your door, Haskell. You'd
still be running the same penny-poor cons and drinking watered-down
whiskey if it wasn't for me. These walls would be falling down around
your head. You've taken every bit of money and luck I've handed you. You
ate up the profits from Fifth Harbor and the Crow Club like it was your due,
let me do your fighting and your dirty work." His gaze tracked slowly over
the Dregs below. "You all benefited. You reaped the rewards. But first
chance you get, you're ready to cozy up to Pekka Rollins for the pleasure
of fitting me for a noose." Another uneasy rustle from the onlookers.
"But I'm not angry."

There had to be twenty Dregs looking up at Kaz, all of them armed,
and yet Inej could have sworn she sensed their relief. Then she understood—
the fight was just the opening act. They knew Kaz was tough. They
didn't need him to prove it. This was about what Kaz needed. To attempt
a coup against Per Haskell, he would have had to seek out the Dregs indi-
vidually, wasting time and risking capture on the streets of the Barrel.
Now he had an audience, and Per Haskell had been happy to welcome one
and all—a bit of entertainment, the dramatic end of Kaz Brekker, the
Humbling of Dirtyhands. But this was no cheap comedy. It was a bloody
rite, and Per Haskell had let the congregation gather, never realizing that
the real performance had yet to begin. Kaz stood upon his pulpit, wounded,
bruised, and ready to preach.

"I'm not angry," Kaz said again. "Not about that. But you know what
makes me mad? What really gets me riled? Seeing a crow taking orders

from a Dime Lion. Watching you parade around after Pekka Rollins like it's something to be proud of. One of the deadliest gangs in the Barrel bending like a bunch of new lilies."

"Rollins has power, boy," said Per Haskell. "Resources. Lecture me when you've been around a few more years. It's my job to protect this gang, and that's what I did. I kept them safe from your recklessness."

"You think you're *safe* because you rolled over for Pekka Rollins? You think he'll be happy to honor this truce? That he won't get hungry for what you've got? Does that sound like Pekka Rollins to you?"

"Hell no," said Anika.

"Who do you want standing in that doorway when the lion gets hungry? A crow? Or a washed-up rooster who squawks and struts, then sides with a Dime Lion and some dirty merch against one of his own?"

From above, Inej could see the people nearest Per Haskell leaning slightly away from him now. A few were taking long looks at him, at the feather in his hat, at the walking sticks in his hands—Kaz's cane that they'd seen wielded with such bloody precision and the fake crow cane Haskell had contrived to mock him.

"In the Barrel, we don't trade in safety," Kaz said, the abraded burn of his voice carrying over the crowd. "There's only strength and weakness. You don't ask for respect. You earn it." *You don't ask for forgiveness. You earn it.* He'd stolen her line. She almost smiled. "I'm not your friend," he said. "I'm not your father. I'm not going to offer you whiskey or clap you on the back and call you son. But I'll keep money in our coffers. I'll keep our enemies scared enough that they'll scurry when they see that tattoo on your arm. So who do you want in that doorway when Pekka Rollins comes to call?"

The silence swelled, a tick feeding on the prospect of violence.

"Well?" Per Haskell blustered, thrusting his chest out. "Answer him. You want your rightful leader or some jumped-up cripple who can't even walk straight?"

"I may not walk straight," said Kaz. "But at least I don't run from a fight."

He started down the steps.

Varian had risen from the floor after his fall. Though he didn't look entirely steady on his feet, he moved toward the stairs, and Inej had to respect his loyalty to Haskell.

Pim pushed off from the wall and blocked Varian's path. "You're through," he said.

"Get Rollins' men," Per Haskell commanded Varian. "Raise the alarm!" But Anika drew a long knife and stepped in front of the entry door.

"You a Dime Lion?" she asked. "Or are you Dregs?"

Slowly, his limp pronounced but his back straight, Kaz made his way down the final flight of stairs, leaning heavily on the banister. When he reached the bottom, the remaining crowd parted.

Haskell's grizzled face was red with fear and indignation. "You'll never last, boy. Takes more than what you got to get past Pekka Rollins."

Kaz snatched his cane from Per Haskell's hand.

"You have two minutes to get out of my house, old man. This city's price is blood," said Kaz, "and I'm happy to pay with yours."

28

JESPER

Jesper had never seen Kaz so bloodied and banged up—broken nose, split lip, one eye swollen shut. He was clutching his side in a way that made Jesper think at least one of his ribs was broken, and when he coughed into a handkerchief, Jesper saw blood on the white fabric before Kaz shoved it back into his pocket. His limp was worse than ever, but he was still standing, and Anika and Pim were with him. Apparently, they'd left a heavily armed skeleton crew at the Slat in case Pekka got word of Kaz's coup and decided to try to make a territory grab.

"All Saints," Jesper said. "So I guess that went well?"

"About as well as expected."

Matthias shook his head in something between admiration and disbelief. "How many lives do you have, *demjin*?"

"One more, I hope."

Kaz had wriggled out of his coat and managed to yank off his shirt, leaning on the sink in the bathroom.

"For Saints' sake, let us help you," said Nina.

Kaz gripped the end of a bandage in his teeth and tore off a piece. "I don't need your help. Keep working with Colm."

"What is *wrong* with him?" Nina grumbled as they went back to the sitting room to drill Colm on his cover story.

"Same thing that's always wrong with him," said Jesper. "He's Kaz Brekker."

A little more than an hour later, Inej had slipped into the room and handed Kaz a note. It was late afternoon and the windows of the suite were ablaze with buttery gold light.

"Are they coming?" asked Nina.

Inej nodded. "I gave your letter to the guard at the door, and it did the trick. They brought me directly to two members of the Triumvirate."

"Who did you meet with?" said Kaz.

"Genya Safin and Zoya Nazyalensky."

Wylan sat forward. "The Tailor? She's at the embassy?"

Kaz raised a brow. "What an interesting fact to forget to mention, Nina."

"It wasn't relevant at the time."

"Of course it's relevant!" Wylan said angrily. Jesper was a little surprised. Wylan hadn't seemed to mind wearing Kuwei's features at first. He'd almost seemed to welcome the distance it gave him from his father. But that had been before they'd gone to Saint Hilde. And before Jesper had kissed Kuwei.

Nina winced slightly. "Wylan, I thought you were coming to Ravka. You would have been able to meet Genya as soon as we were on the boat."

"We all know where Nina's loyalties lie," said Kaz.

"I didn't tell the Triumvirate about Kuwei."

A faint smile touched Kaz's lips. "Like I said." He turned to Inej. "Did you state our terms?"

"Yes, they'll be at the hotel baths in an hour. I told them to make sure no one saw them enter."

"Let's hope they can handle it," said Kaz.

"They can run a country," said Nina. "They can manage a few simple instructions."

"Is it safe for them on the streets?" asked Wylan.

"They're probably the only Grisha safe in Ketterdam," said Kaz. "Even if the Shu are working up the nerve to start hunting again, they aren't going to start with two highly placed Ravkan dignitaries. Nina, does Genya have the skill to restore Wylan's features?"

"I don't know," said Nina. "She's called the First Tailor, and she's certainly the most gifted, but without *parem* . . ." She didn't have to explain. *Parem* was the only reason Nina had been able to manage Wylan's miraculous transformation into Kuwei. Still, Genya Safin was a legend. Anything might still be possible.

"Kaz," Wylan said, twisting the tail of his shirt. "If she's willing to try—"

Kaz nodded. "But you're going to have to be twice as careful until the auction. Your father doesn't want you showing up to skunk the scam he's pulling on the Merchant Council and the *stadwatch*. You'd be smarter waiting—"

"No," said Wylan. "I'm done being someone else."

Kaz shrugged, but Jesper had the feeling he was getting exactly what he wanted. At least in this case, it was what Wylan wanted too.

"Won't there be hotel guests at the baths?" Jesper asked.

"I had them reserve the whole place for Mister Rietveld," said Nina. "He's very self-conscious about disrobing in front of others."

Jesper groaned. "Please don't talk about my father taking his clothes off."

"It's his webbed feet," said Nina. "So embarrassing."

"Nina and Matthias will stay here," said Kaz.

"I should be there," Nina protested.

"Are you Ravkan or a member of this crew?"

"I'm both."

"Exactly. This conversation is going to be tricky enough without you and Matthias there to muddy it up."

Though they went back and forth for a while, eventually Nina agreed to remain behind if Inej went in her stead.

But Inej only shook her head. "I'd prefer not to."

"Why?" Nina asked. "Someone needs to hold Kaz accountable."

"And you think I can?"

"We should at least try."

"I love you, Nina, but the Ravkan government hasn't treated the Suli very well. I'm not interested in exchanging pleasantries with their leaders." Jesper had never really considered that, and it was clear from the stricken expression on Nina's face that she hadn't either. Inej gave her a tight hug. "Come on," she said. "We'll get Colm to order us something decadent."

"That's your answer for everything."

"You're complaining?" Inej asked.

"I'm stating one of the reasons I adore you."

They went to find Colm, arm in arm, but Nina's teeth were worrying her lower lip. She had to be used to Matthias criticizing her country, but Jesper guessed it stung more coming from Inej. He wanted to tell Nina that you could love something and still see its flaws. At least, he hoped that was true, or he was truly cooked.

As they split to prepare for the meeting with the Ravkans, Jesper followed Wylan down the hall.

"Hey."

Wylan kept going.

Jesper jogged past him and cut off his path, walking backward. "Listen, this thing with Kuwei isn't a thing." He tried again. "There is no thing with Kuwei."

"You don't owe me an explanation. I'm the one who interrupted."

"No, you didn't! Kuwei was sitting at the piano. It was an understandable mistake."

Wylan stopped short. "You thought he was me?"

"Yes!" Jesper said. "See? Just a big mis—"

Wylan's gold eyes flashed. "You really can't tell us apart?"

"I . . . I mean, usually I can, but—"

"We're nothing alike," Wylan said indignantly. "He's not even that good at science! Half his notebooks are full of doodles. Mostly of you. And those aren't good either."

"Really? Doodles of me?"

Wylan rolled his eyes. "Forget it. You can kiss whomever you like, Jesper."

"And I do. As regularly as possible."

"So what's the problem?"

"No problem, I just wanted to give you this."

He placed a tiny oval canvas in Wylan's hand. "I took it when we were at Saint Hilde. I thought it might come in handy if Genya's going to try to put you back to your old merchling self."

Wylan stared down at the canvas. "My mother painted this?"

"It was in that room full of her art."

It was small, unframed, suitable only for a miniature: a portrait of Wylan as a child of around eight years. Wylan curled his fingers over the edge of the painting. "It's how she remembers me. She never got to see me grow up." He frowned. "It's so old. I don't know if it will be useful."

"It's still you," said Jesper. "Same curls. Same worried little divot between the brows."

"And you took this just because you thought it might come in handy?"

"I told you, I like your stupid face."

Wylan ducked his head and slipped the portrait into his pocket. "Thank you."

"Sure." Jesper hesitated. "If you're headed down to the baths, I could come with you. If you wanted."

Wylan nodded anxiously. "I'd like that."

Jesper's newly buoyant mood lasted all the way to the lift, but as they joined Kaz and descended to the hotel's third floor, his nerves started to jangle. They might be walking into a trap, and Kaz wasn't exactly in fighting form.

Some part of Jesper hoped that the Ravkans would say no to this mad plan. Then Kaz would be stymied, and even if they all ended up in Hellgate or swinging from the gallows, his father would at least have a chance to escape unharmed. Colm had spent hours with Nina and Kaz trying to learn his role, running through different scenarios, enduring their endless questions and prodding without complaint. Colm wasn't much of an actor, and he lied about as well as Jesper danced ballet. But Nina would be with him. That had to count for something.

The lift opened and they entered another vast purple-and-white hallway, then followed the sound of running water to a room with a large circular pool at its center, surrounded by a colonnade of arches. Through them, Jesper could see more pools and waterfalls, coves and alcoves, every solid surface decorated in glittering indigo tiles. Now *this* Jesper could get used to: pools of steaming water, fountains dancing and burbling like guests at a party, piles of thick towels and sweet-smelling soaps. A place like this belonged in the Barrel, where it could be properly appreciated, not in the middle of the financial district.

They'd been told they would be meeting with only two members of the Triumvirate, but three people stood by the pool. Jesper knew the one-eyed girl in the red-and-blue *kefta* must be Genya Safin, and that meant the shockingly gorgeous girl with the thick fall of ebony hair was Zoya Nazyalensky. They were accompanied by a fox-faced man in his twenties wearing a teal frock coat, brown leather gloves, and an impressive set of Zemeni revolvers slung around his hips. If these people were what Ravka had to offer, maybe Jesper *should* consider a visit.

"We told the Grisha to come alone," said Kaz.

"I'm afraid that wasn't possible," said the man. "Though Zoya is, of course, a force to be reckoned with, Genya's extraordinary gifts are ill-suited to physical confrontation. I, on the other hand, am well suited to all forms of confrontation, though I'm particularly fond of the physical."

Kaz's eyes narrowed. "Sturmhond."

"He knows me!" Sturmhond said delightedly. He nudged Genya with an elbow. "I told you I'm famous."

Zoya blew out an exasperated breath. "Thank you. He's going to be twice as insufferable now."

"Sturmhond has been authorized to negotiate on behalf of the Ravkan throne," said Genya.

"A pirate?" asked Jesper.

"Privateer," Sturmhond corrected. "You can't expect the king to participate in an auction like this himself."

"Why not?"

"Because he might lose. And it looks very bad when kings lose."

Jesper couldn't quite believe he was having a conversation with *the* Sturmhond. The privateer was a legend. He'd broken countless blockades on behalf of the Ravkans, and there were rumors that . . . "Do you really have a flying ship?" blurted Jesper.

"No."

"Oh."

"I have several."

"Take me with you."

Kaz didn't look remotely entertained. "The Ravkan king lets you negotiate for him in matters of state?" he asked skeptically.

"Occasionally," said Sturmhond. "Especially if less than savory personages are involved. You have a reputation, Mister Brekker."

"So do you."

"Fair enough. So let's say we've both earned the right to have our names bandied about in the worst circles. The king won't drag Ravka into one of your schemes blindly. Nina's note claimed that you have Kuwei

Yul-Bo in your possession. I want confirmation of that fact, and I want the details of your plan."

"All right," said Kaz. "Let's talk in the solarium. I'd prefer not to sweat through my suit." When the rest of them made to follow, Kaz halted and glanced over his shoulder. "Just me and the privateer."

Zoya tossed her glorious black mane and said, "We are the Triumvirate. We do not take orders from Kerch street rats with dubious haircuts."

"I can phrase it as a question if it will make your feathers lie flat," Kaz said.

"You insolent—"

"Zoya," said Sturmhond smoothly. "Let's not antagonize our new friends before they've even had a chance to cheat us. Lead on, Mister Brekker."

"Kaz," Wylan said. "Can't you—"

"Negotiate for yourself, merchling. It's time you learned how." He vanished with Sturmhond back into the corridors.

As their footfalls faded, silence descended. Wylan cleared his throat and the sound bounced around the blue-tiled room like a spring colt let loose in a corral. Genya's face was bemused.

Zoya crossed her arms. "Well?"

"Ma'am . . ." Wylan attempted. "Miss Genya—"

Genya smiled, her scars tugging at the corner of her mouth. "Oh, he *is* sweet."

"You always take to the strays," said Zoya sourly.

"You're the boy Nina tailored to look like Kuwei," Genya said. "And you want me to try to undo her work?"

"Yes," Wylan said, that one word imbued with a whole world of hope. "But I don't have anything to bargain with."

Genya rolled her single amber eye. "Why are the Kerch so focused on money?"

"Says the woman with a bankrupt country," murmured Jesper.

"What was that?" snapped Zoya.

"Nothing," said Jesper. "Just saying Kerch is a morally bankrupt country."

Zoya looked him up and down as if she was considering tossing him into a pool and boiling him alive. "If you want to waste your time and talent on these wretches, feel free. Saints know there's room for improvement."

"Zoya—"

"I'm going to go find a dark room with a deep pool and try to wash some of this country off."

"Don't drown," Genya called as Zoya flounced off, then said conspiratorially, "Maybe she'll do it just to be contrary." She gave Wylan an assessing glance. "It would be difficult. If I'd known you before the changes—"

"Here," Wylan said eagerly. "I have a portrait. It's old, but—"

She took the miniature from him.

"And this," Wylan said, offering her the poster his father had created promising a reward for his safe return.

"Hmm," she said. "Let's find better light."

They fumbled their way around the facilities, poking their heads into rooms full of mud baths and milk baths, and one heated chamber made entirely of jade. They finally settled in a chilly white room with a tub of odd-smelling clay against one wall, and windows all along the other.

"Find a chair," said Genya, "and fetch my kit from the main pool area. It's heavy. You'll find it near the towels."

"You brought your kit?" said Wylan.

"The Suli girl suggested it," said Genya, shooing them off to follow her orders.

"Just as imperious as Zoya," Jesper grumbled as he and Wylan obliged.

"But with better hearing!" she called after them.

Jesper fetched the box from near the main pool. It was built like a small cabinet, its double doors fastened with an elaborate gold clasp. When they returned to the clay room, Genya gestured for Wylan to sit near the window, where the light was best. She rested her fingers under his chin and tilted his face this way and that.

Jesper set down her kit. "What are you looking for?" he asked.

"The seams."

"Seams?"

"No matter how fine a Tailor's work, if you look closely, you can see the seams, the place where one thing ends and another begins. I'm looking for signs of the original structure. The portrait does help."

"I don't know why I'm so nervous," said Wylan.

"Because she might mess up and make you look like a weasel with curls?"

Genya lifted a flame-colored brow. "Maybe a vole."

"Not funny," said Wylan. He'd clenched his hands so tightly in his lap his knuckles had become white stars.

"All right," said Genya. "I can try, but I make no promises. Nina's work is near flawless. Luckily, so am I."

Jesper smiled. "You remind me of her."

"I think you mean she reminds you of *me*."

Genya set to unpacking her kit. It was far more elaborate than the one Jesper had seen Nina use. There were capsules of dye, pots of colored powder, and rows of glass cases filled with what looked like clear gels. "They're cells," said Genya. "For a job like this, I need to work with human tissue."

"Not disgusting at all," said Jesper.

"It could be worse," she said. "I once knew a woman who rubbed whale placenta on her face in the hopes of looking younger. To say nothing of what she did with the monkey saliva."

"Human tissue sounds delightful," amended Jesper.

"That's what I thought."

She pushed up her sleeves, and Jesper saw that the scars on her face also traced over her hands and up her arms. He couldn't imagine what manner of weapon had twisted the tissue in that way.

"You're staring," she said without facing him.

Jesper jumped, cheeks heating. "I'm sorry."

"It's all right. People like to look. Well, not always. When I was first attacked, no one would look at me."

Jesper had heard she'd been tortured during the Ravkan Civil War, but that wasn't the kind of thing you made polite conversation about. "Now I don't know where to look," he admitted.

"Anywhere you like. Just be quiet so I don't make a hideous mess of this poor boy." She laughed at Wylan's expression of terror. "I'm kidding. But do stay still. This is slow work, and you'll need to be patient."

She was right. The work was so slow that Jesper wasn't sure anything was happening. Genya would place her fingertips beneath Wylan's eyes or over his lids, then step back and examine what she'd done—which as far as Jesper could see was nothing. Then she'd reach for one of the glass cases or bottles, dab something on her fingertips, touch Wylan's face again, step back. Jesper's attention wandered. He circled the room, dipped his finger in the clay, regretted it, went searching for a towel. But when he looked at Wylan from a little more distance, he could see that something had changed.

"It's working!" he exclaimed.

Genya cast him a cool glance. "Of course it is."

Periodically, the Tailor would stop and stretch and give Wylan a mirror so that he could consult on what looked right or wrong. An hour later, Wylan's irises had gone from gold to blue and the shape of his eyes had changed as well.

"His brow should be narrower," Jesper said, peering over Genya's shoulder. "Just a little bit. And his lashes were longer."

"I didn't know you were paying attention," murmured Wylan.

Jesper grinned. "I was paying attention."

"Oh good, he's blushing," said Genya. "Excellent for the circulation."

"Do you train Fabrikators at the Little Palace?" asked Wylan.

Jesper scowled. Why did he have to go and start that?

"Of course. There's a school on the palace grounds."

"What if a student were older?" said Wylan, still pushing.

"A Grisha can be taught at any age," said Genya. "Alina Starkov didn't discover her power until she was seventeen years old, and she . . . she was one of the most powerful Grisha who ever lived." Genya pushed at Wylan's left nostril. "It's easier when you're younger, but so is everything. Children learn languages more easily. They learn mathematics more easily."

"And they're unafraid," said Wylan quietly. "It's other people who teach them their limits." Wylan's eyes met Jesper's over Genya's shoulder, and as if he was challenging both Jesper and himself, he said, "I can't read." His skin went instantly blotchy, but his voice was steady.

Genya shrugged and said, "That's because no one took the time to teach you. Many of the peasants in Ravka can't read."

"Lots of people took the time to teach me. They tried plenty of strategies too. I've had every opportunity. But it's something I can't do."

Jesper could see the anxiety in his face, what it cost him to speak those words. It made him feel like a coward.

"You seem to be getting along well enough," said Genya. "Aside from your associations with street thugs and sharpshooters."

Wylan lifted his brows, and Jesper knew he was daring him to speak up, but he remained silent. *It's not a gift. It's a curse.* He walked back to the window, suddenly finding himself deeply interested in the streets below. *That's what killed your mother, do you understand?*

Genya alternated between working and having Wylan hold up the mirror to guide her through tweaks and changes. Jesper watched for a while, went upstairs to check on his father, fetched Genya some tea and Wylan a cup of coffee. When he returned to the clay room, he nearly dropped the mugs.

Wylan was sitting in the last of the afternoon light, the real Wylan, the boy he'd first seen in that tannery, the lost prince who had woken in the wrong story.

"Well?" Genya said.

Wylan fiddled nervously with the buttons on his shirt.

"That's him," said Jesper. "That's our fresh-faced runaway merchling."

Genya stretched and said, "Good, because if I have to spend another minute smelling that clay, I may go mad." It was clear she was tired, but her face was glowing, her amber eye sparkled. This was the way Grisha looked when they used their power. "It would be best to revisit the work anew in the morning, but I have to get back to the embassy. And by tomorrow, well . . ." She shrugged.

By tomorrow the auction would be announced and everything would change.

Wylan thanked her and then kept on thanking her until she physically pushed them out the door so that she could go find Zoya.

Jesper and Wylan took the lift back up to the suite in silence. Jesper glanced into the master bedroom and saw his father asleep atop the covers, his chest reverberating with deep snores. A pile of papers was scattered on the bed next to him. Jesper tidied them into a stack—*jurda* prices, listings of farm acreage outside cities in Novyi Zem.

You don't have to clean up after us, Da.

Someone does.

Back in the sitting room, Wylan was lighting the lamps. "Are you hungry?"

"Famished," said Jesper. "But Da's asleep. I'm not sure we're allowed to ring for food." He cocked his head to one side, peering at Wylan. "Did you have her make you better-looking?"

Wylan pinked. "Maybe you forgot how handsome I am." Jesper raised a brow. "Okay, maybe a little." He joined Jesper by the window looking out over the city. Dusk was falling and the streetlamps had bloomed in orderly formation along the edges of the canals. Patrols of *stadwatch* were visible, moving through the streets, and the Staves were alight with color and sound again. How long would they be safe here? Jesper wondered if the Kherguud were tracking Grisha through the city, seeking out the houses of their indentures. The Shu soldiers might be surrounding the embassy even now. Or maybe this hotel. Could they smell a Grisha fifteen stories up?

Periodically, they could see bursts of fireworks over the Staves. Jesper wasn't surprised. He understood the Barrel. It was always hungry for more—money, mayhem, violence, lust. It was a glutton, and Pekka Rollins had offered up Kaz and the rest of the crew as a feast.

"I know what you were doing back there," Jesper said. "You didn't have to tell her you can't read."

Wylan took the miniature of himself from his pocket and propped it on the end table. Young Wylan's serious blue eyes stared back at them.

"Do you know Kaz was the first person I ever told about . . . my condition?"

"Of all the people."

"I know. It felt like I'd choke on the words. I was so afraid he'd sneer at me. Or just laugh. But he didn't do any of that. Telling Kaz, facing my father, freed something in me. And every time I tell someone new, I feel freer."

Jesper watched a browboat vanish beneath Zentsbridge. It was nearly empty. "I'm not ashamed of being Grisha."

Wylan ran his thumb over the edge of the miniature. He wasn't saying anything, but Jesper could tell he wanted to.

"Go ahead," Jesper said. "Whatever you're thinking, just say it."

Wylan looked up at him. His eyes were the clear, unspoiled blue Jesper remembered—a high mountain lake, an endless Zemeni sky. Genya had done her work well. "I just don't get it. I've spent my whole life hiding the things I can't do. Why run from the amazing things you *can* do?"

Jesper gave an irritated shrug. He'd been mad at his father for almost exactly what Wylan was describing, but now he just felt defensive. These were his choices, right or wrong, and they were long since made. "I know who I am, what I'm good at, what I can and can't do. I'm just . . . I'm what I am. A great shooter, a bad gambler. Why can't that be enough?"

"For me? Or for you?"

"Don't get philosophical on me, merchling."

"Jes, I've thought about this—"

"Thought of me? Late at night? What was I wearing?"

"I've thought about your *powers*," Wylan said, cheeks flushing pinker. "Has it ever occurred to you that your Grisha ability might be part of the reason you're such a good shot?"

"Wylan, you're cute, but you're a whole lot of crazy in one little glass."

"Maybe. But I've seen you manipulate metal. I've seen you direct it. What if you don't miss because you're directing your bullets too?"

Jesper shook his head. This was ridiculous. He was a good shot because he'd been raised on the frontier, because he understood guns, because his mother had taught him to steady his hand, clear his mind, and to sense his target as much as see it. His mother. A Fabrikator. A Grisha, even if she never used that word. *No. That's not how it works.* But what if it was?

He shook off the thought, feeling the need to move ignite over his skin. "Why do you have to say things like that? Why can't you just let things be easy?"

"Because they're *not* easy," Wylan said in his simple, earnest way. No one in the Barrel talked like that. "You keep pretending everything is okay. You move on to the next fight or the next party. What are you afraid is going to happen if you stop?"

Jesper shrugged again. He adjusted the buttons on his shirt, touched his thumbs to his revolvers. When he felt like this, mad and scattered, it was as if his hands had a life of their own. His whole body itched. He needed to get out of this room.

Wylan laid his hand on Jesper's shoulder. "Stop."

Jesper didn't know if he wanted to jerk away or pull him closer.

"Just stop," Wylan said. "Breathe."

Wylan's gaze was steady. Jesper couldn't look away from that clearwater blue. He forced himself to be still, inhaled, exhaled.

"Again," Wylan said, and when Jesper opened his mouth to take another breath, Wylan leaned forward and kissed him.

Jesper's mind emptied. He wasn't thinking of what had happened before or what might happen next. There was only the reality of Wylan's mouth, the press of his lips, then the fine bones of his neck, the silky feel of his curls as Jesper cupped his nape and drew him nearer. This was the kiss he'd been waiting for. It was a gunshot. It was prairie fire. It was the spin of Makker's Wheel. Jesper felt the pounding of his heart—or was it Wylan's?—like a stampede in his chest, and the only thought in his head was a happy, startled, *Oh*.

Slowly, inevitably, they broke apart.

"Wylan," Jesper said, looking into the wide blue sky of his eyes, "I really hope we don't die."

29
NINA

Nina was furious to learn that Genya had tailored not only Wylan but Kaz as well, and she hadn't gotten to watch.

He'd let the Tailor set his nose, reduce the swelling on his eye so that he could actually see, and deal with some of the worst damage he'd taken to his body. But that was all he'd permitted.

"Why?" said Nina. "She could have—"

"She didn't know when to stop," said Kaz.

Nina had a sudden suspicion that Genya had offered to heal Kaz's bad leg. "Well, you look like the worst kind of Barrel thug," Nina complained. "You should have at least let her clean up the rest of your bruising."

"I am the worst kind of Barrel thug. And if I don't look like I just trounced ten of the best toughs Per Haskell had to offer, then no one's going to believe I did. Now let's get to work. You can't throw a party if nobody gets the invitation."

Nina was not looking forward to this particular party, but the next morning, the announcement went in all the daily broadsheets, stuck to the columns at the east and west entries of the Exchange, and tacked to the front door of the Stadhall.

They'd kept it simple:

Kuwei Yul-Bo, son of Bo Yul-Bayur, Chief Chemist of Bhez Ju, makes available his service and will offer his indenture as the market and the hand of Ghezen commands. Those wishing to bid are invited to participate in a free and fair auction in compliance with the laws of Kerch, the rule of the Merchant Council, and the supervision of the Council of Tides at the Church of Barter in four days' time. Parties will convene at noon. Sacred is Ghezen and in commerce we see His hand.

The city had already been in an uproar over the curfews, barricades, and blockades. Now gossip raced through the coffeehouses and taverns, changing and taking on new force from the salons of the Geldstraat all the way to the slums of the Barrel. According to Kaz's new Dregs troops, people were eager for any kind of information on the mysterious Kuwei Yul-Bo, and his auction was already being linked to the bizarre attack on West Stave that had nearly leveled two pleasure houses and left reports of flying men in its wake. Inej staked out the Shu Embassy herself and returned with word that messengers had been coming and going all morning and that she'd seen the ambassador himself storm down to the docks to demand the Council of Tides release one of their dry-docked ships.

"He wants to send for a Fabrikator so they can make gold," said Jesper.

"Pity the harbors are locked down," said Kaz.

The doors to the Stadhall were closed to the public, and the Merchant Council was said to be in an emergency meeting to determine whether they would sanction the auction. This was the test: Would they support the laws of the city, or—given what they at least suspected about Kuwei—would they falter and find some way to deny his rights?

At the top of the clock tower, Nina waited with the others, watching the eastern entrance to the Exchange. At noon, a man in mercher black approached the arch with a stack of documents. A horde of people descended on him, tearing the flyers from his hands.

"Poor little Karl Dryden," said Kaz. Apparently, he was the most junior member of the Council, so he'd been stuck with this job.

Moments later, Inej burst through the door of the suite clutching a flyer. Incredible. Nina had been staring straight at the crowd around Dryden and had never glimpsed her.

"They've validated the auction," she said, and handed the paper to Kaz, who passed it around the group.

All the flyer said was: *In accordance with the laws of Kerch, the Merchant Council of Ketterdam agrees to act as representatives to Kuwei Yul-Bo in the legal auction of his indenture. Sacred is Ghezen and in commerce we see His hand.*

Jesper blew out a long breath and looked at his father, dutifully studying commodities reports and the script Nina and Kaz had prepared for him. "My luck they said yes."

Inej laid a hand on his arm. "It's not too late to change course."

"It is," said Jesper. "It was too late a long time ago."

Nina said nothing. She liked Colm. She cared about Jesper. But this auction was the best chance they had of getting Kuwei to Ravka and saving Grisha lives.

"The merchers are perfect marks," said Kaz. "They're rich and they're smart. That makes them easy to dupe."

"Why?" asked Wylan.

"Rich men want to believe they deserve every penny they've got, so they forget what they owe to chance. Smart men are always looking for loopholes. They want an opportunity to game the system."

"So who's the hardest mark to swindle?" asked Nina.

"The toughest mark is an honest one," said Kaz. "Thankfully, they're always in short supply." He tapped the glass of the clock face, gesturing to Karl Dryden, who was still standing by the Exchange, fanning himself with his hat now that the crowd had dispersed. "Dryden inherited his fortune from his father. Since then, he's been too timid an investor to substantially add to his wealth. He's desperate for a chance to prove himself to the other members of the Merchant Council. We're going to give him one."

"What else do we know about him?" asked Nina.

Kaz almost smiled. "We know he's represented by our good friend and dog lover, Cornelis Smeet."

From their earlier surveillance of Cornelis Smeet's office, they knew the attorney had runners taking documents back and forth to clients all day long, gathering necessary signatures and conveying important information. The messengers were too well paid to consider bribing—especially if one of them turned out to be among those few dreaded honest men.

And in a way, they had Van Eck to thank for the ease with which Kaz baited the trap. Dressed in *stadwatch* uniforms, Anika and Pim stopped Smeet's messengers with impunity, demanding to see their identification while their bags were searched. The documents inside were confidential and sealed, but they weren't after the documents. They just needed to plant a few crumbs to entice young Karl Dryden.

"Sometimes," said Kaz, "a proper thief doesn't just take. He leaves something behind."

Working with Specht, Wylan had created a stamp that could be pressed to the back of a sealed envelope. It gave the impression that the envelope had absorbed the ink from another document, as if some thoughtless clerk had left the papers somewhere damp. When the messengers delivered Dryden's files, if he was curious at all, he'd at least glance at the words that seemed to have leached onto his packet of papers. And he'd find something very interesting indeed—a letter from one of Smeet's other clients. The client's name was unreadable, but the letter was clearly an inquiry: Did Smeet have knowledge of a farmer named Johannus Rietveld, the head of a consortium of Kerch and Zemeni *jurda* growers? He was taking meetings at the Geldrenner Hotel with select investors only. Would an introduction be possible?

Prior to the announcement of Kuwei's auction, the information would have been of mild interest. Afterward, it was the kind of tip that could make fortunes.

Even before they'd baited the trap with the false letter, Kaz had Colm taking meals in the Geldrenner's lavish purple dining room with various members of Kerch's trade and banking community. Colm always sat a good distance away from any other customers, ordered extravagantly, and spoke with his guests in hushed tones. The content of the discussions was completely benign—talk of crop reports and interest rates—but no one in the dining room knew that. Everything was done in conspicuous view of the hotel staff, so that when members of the Merchant Council came asking about how Mister Rietveld spent his time, they got the answers that Kaz wanted them to.

Nina was present at all these meetings, playing the role of Mister Rietveld's multilingual assistant, a Grisha Heartrender seeking work after the destruction of the House of the White Rose. Despite dousing herself in coffee extract to mislead the senses of the Kherguud, she felt exposed just sitting out in the open in the dining room. Kaz had members of the Dregs constantly watching the streets around the hotel for signs of the Shu soldiers. No one had forgotten that they were hunting Grisha, and that Nina might present a very appealing target if they found out about the meetings. Acquiring a Heartrender they could dose with *parem* would mean they could radically alter the course of the auction and might be well worth antagonizing the Council of Tides. Still, Nina felt pretty confident that the merchers who learned of Rietveld's presence at the hotel would be keeping quiet. Kaz had educated her well on the power of greed, and these men wanted every bit of profit for themselves.

Nina also appreciated the attention Kaz had paid to Colm's appearance. He was still dressed as a farmer, but Kaz had made a few subtle improvements—a finer coat, polished boots, a silver tie pin set with a small chunk of raw amethyst. These were the signs of prosperity that the merchers would notice and appreciate—nothing too gaudy or loud, nothing that might provoke suspicion. Merchers were like most men; they wanted to believe they were the ones doing the courting.

As for Nina, Genya had offered up a glorious red *kefta* from her collection and they'd pulled out the embroidery, altering it from blue to black. She and Genya were hardly the same size, but they'd managed to let out the seams and sew in a few extra panels. It had felt strange to wear a proper *kefta* after so long. The one Nina had worn at the House of the White Rose had been a costume, cheap finery meant to impress their clientele. This was the real thing, worn by soldiers of the Second Army, made of raw silk dyed in a red only a Fabrikator could create. Did she even have a right to wear such a thing now?

When Matthias had seen her, he'd frozen in the doorway of the suite, his blue eyes shocked. They'd stood there in silence until he'd finally said, "You look very beautiful."

"You mean I look like the enemy."

"Both of those things have always been true." Then he'd simply offered her his arm.

Nina had been nervous about Colm taking the lead role in this charade. He was most definitely an amateur, and during their first few meetings with bankers and consultants, he'd looked nearly as green as his pea soup. But with every passing hour, his confidence had grown, and Nina had begun to feel the stirrings of hope.

And yet, no member of the Merchant Council had come to see Johannus Rietveld. Maybe Dryden had never seen the trace of the fake document or had decided not to act on it. Or maybe Kaz had just overestimated his greed.

Then, only forty-eight hours before the auction, Johannus Rietveld received a note from Karl Dryden announcing that he would call on Mister Rietveld that day and hoped to discuss matters of business that might be profitable to them both. Jesper tried to calm his father's nerves while Kaz dispatched instructions to Anika and Pim. If they wanted to hook Dryden, they'd need to make sure other, bigger fish were interested in the bait. Nina and Colm had gone through their morning meetings in the dining room as usual, and she'd done her best to try to calm him.

At eleven bells, she spotted two men in staid mercher black entering the dining room. They didn't pause to ask the host where to find Johannus Rietveld, but walked directly to his table—a sure sign they'd been watching him and gathering information.

"They're here," she whispered to Colm, then instantly regretted it when he sat up straighter and started to turn in his seat.

She grabbed his hand. "Look at me," she said. "Ask me about the weather."

"Why the weather?" he said, sweat beading on his brow.

"Well, you could ask me about the latest fashion in footwear if you prefer. I'm just trying to get you to act natural." She was attempting to steady her own heart rate—something she used to be able to do without ridiculous attempts at deep breathing—because she'd recognized the man with Dryden. It was Jan Van Eck.

The men approached the table, then removed their hats.

"Mister Rietveld?"

"Yes?" Colm squeaked. Not an auspicious beginning. Nina gave him the gentlest kick she could manage beneath the table. He coughed. "What business, gentlemen?"

During their preparations, Kaz had insisted that Nina learn all the Merchant Council's house colors and symbols, and Nina recognized their tie pins—a golden wheat sheaf bound with a blue enamel ribbon for the Dryden family, and the red laurel for Van Eck. Even without the pin, she would have recognized Jan Van Eck's resemblance to Wylan. She eyed his receding hairline. Poor Wylan might have to invest in a good tonic.

Dryden cleared his throat importantly. "I am Karl Dryden, and this is the esteemed Jan Van Eck."

"Mister Dryden!" Colm said, his surprise a bit overblown. "I received your note. Unfortunately, my day is fully booked."

"I wonder if we might secure just a few minutes of conversation?"

"We have no wish to waste your time, Mister Rietveld," said Van Eck with a surprisingly charming smile. "Or ours."

"Very well," Jesper's father said, projecting reluctance rather convincingly. "Please join us."

"Thank you," Van Eck said with another smile. "We understand you represent a consortium of *jurda* farmers."

Colm looked around as if concerned that someone might overhear. "It's possible I do. How do you come by this information?"

"I'm afraid that's not within my power to disclose."

"He's hiding something," said Nina.

Dryden and Van Eck frowned in unison.

"I learned from the captain of the ship you traveled on," said Van Eck.

"He's lying," said Nina.

"How could you possibly know that?" Dryden asked irritably.

"I am Grisha," Nina said with a dramatic wave. "No secret is beyond my grasp." She might as well enjoy herself.

Dryden's lower lip disappeared as he sucked on it nervously, and Van Eck said grudgingly, "It's possible some sensitive information may have made its way into our hands through Cornelis Smeet's office."

"I see," said Colm, looking very grim indeed.

Nina wanted to applaud. Now the merchers were on the defensive.

"We are interested in the possibility of adding to your list of investors," said Van Eck.

"I don't need more investors."

"How can that be?" asked Dryden. "You've been in the city less than a week."

"The climate has changed somehow. I don't completely understand it, but there's been a run on *jurda*."

Now Van Eck leaned forward, eyes slightly narrowed. "That *is* interesting, Mister Rietveld. How is it that you appeared in Ketterdam at such a fortuitous time? Why choose now to start a *jurda* consortium?"

So much for the defensive. But Kaz had prepared Colm for this.

"If you must know, a few months ago, someone began buying up *jurda* farms surrounding Cofton, but no one could discover his identity. Some of us realized something must be brewing, so we chose not to sell to him, and instead started our own enterprise."

"An unknown buyer?" asked Dryden curiously. Van Eck looked a bit ill.

"Yes," said Nina. "Mister Rietveld and his partners had no success in learning who he might be. But perhaps you gentlemen might have better luck. There's talk that he's Kerch."

Van Eck sank back in his seat. His pale skin had acquired a clammy sheen. The power at the table had shifted once again. The last thing Van Eck wanted was anyone looking into who had been buying up those *jurda* fields. Nina gave Colm another gentle nudge. The less interested they seemed in the Council's money, the more eager the Council members would be to give it up.

"Actually," continued Colm, "if you suss him out, you might be able to go in on his scheme instead. He may still be seeking investors."

"No," said Van Eck a bit too sharply. "After all, you are here now and able to represent our interests. Why waste time and effort in pointless sleuthing? Each man has the right to seek profit where he finds it."

"All the same," said Dryden. "It's possible this investor knew something about the situation with the Shu—"

Van Eck cast Dryden a warning look; he clearly didn't want Council business spread around so casually. The younger merch shut his mouth with a snap.

But then Van Eck pressed his fingers together and said, "It's certainly worth gathering all the information we can. I will take it upon myself to investigate this other buyer."

"Then perhaps we needn't move quite so soon," said Dryden.

Timid indeed, thought Nina. She glimpsed Anika's signal from across the lobby. "Mister Rietveld, your next appointment?" She cast a meaningful glance at the lobby, where Rotty—looking marvelously dapper in mercher black—led a group of men through the entry and past the dining room.

Van Eck and Dryden exchanged a glance at the sight of Jellen Radmakker, one of the wealthiest investors in all of Kerch, walking through the lobby. In fact, as soon as Dryden's note had arrived requesting a meeting, several investors had been invited to a presentation on Zemeni oil futures that had nothing to do with the fictional Johannus Rietveld. Of course, Van Eck and Dryden didn't know that. The important thing was they believed they might lose their opportunity to invest. Nina was almost sorry she wouldn't get a chance to hear Jesper hold forth on the resources market for an hour.

Nina gave Colm another kick under the table.

"Well," he said hurriedly. "I must be on my way, gentlemen. It's been a pleasure—"

"What's the stake price?" asked Dryden.

"I'm afraid at this late date, I couldn't really take on more—"

"What if we came in together?" Van Eck said.

"Together?"

"The Merchant Council believes *jurda* prices may change soon. Until recently, our hands were bound by our roles as public servants. But the upcoming auction has freed us to pursue new investments."

"Is that legal?" Colm asked, his brow furrowing with every appearance of deepest concern.

"Absolutely. We are prohibited from influencing the outcome of the auction, but an investment in your fund is well within the law and could be mutually beneficial to us both."

"I see how the fund may benefit you, but—"

"You've been courting separate investors. What if the Merchant

Council became your lead investors? What if this became our fund exclusively? The Council represents thirteen of the oldest and most established families in Kerch, with thriving businesses and plenty of capital. The farmers in your consortium could have no better partners."

"I . . . I don't know," said Colm. "That's certainly appealing, but I would need serious security if we were to expose ourselves to risk in this way. If the Council were to back out, we'd lose all our investors at once."

Dryden bristled. "No member of the Merchant Council would violate a contract. We'll enter into it with our own seals and have it witnessed by the judge of your choosing."

Nina could almost see the wheels turning in Van Eck's mind. No doubt there *had* been farmers who refused to sell in Novyi Zem. Now he had the chance to control not only the *jurda* fields he'd purchased, but a good chunk of those he'd failed to acquire as well. Nina also wondered if, given the money the search for his son was costing the city, he was feeling pressure to bring the Council a good opportunity.

"Give us forty-eight hours to—" began Van Eck.

Colm's expression was apologetic. "I'm afraid I must finish my business here by tomorrow night. I've already booked passage."

"The harbors are closed," said Van Eck. "You're not going anywhere."

Jesper's father directed a cold gray glare at Van Eck that raised the hair on Nina's arms. "I feel distinctly bullied, Mister Van Eck, and I don't like it."

For a moment Van Eck held his gaze. Then his greed got the better of him.

"Twenty-four hours, then," said Van Eck.

Colm pretended to hesitate. "Twenty-four hours. But I make no promises. I must do what's best for the consortium."

"Of course," Van Eck said as they rose and shook hands. "We only ask that you make no final decision until we've had a chance to make our case for taking over the fund. I think you'll find our offer very generous."

Colm glanced in the direction that Radmakker had gone. "I suppose I can do that. Good day, gentlemen."

As Nina turned to follow him out of the dining room, Van Eck said, "Miss Zenik."

"Yes?"

"I hear you worked out of the House of the White Rose." His lip curled slightly, as if even saying the name of a brothel constituted debauchery.

"I did."

"I'd heard the Heartrender there occasionally works with Kaz Brekker."

"I've done jobs for Brekker before," Nina conceded easily. Best to go on the offense. She took Van Eck's hand in hers, delighted at the way his whole body seemed to recoil. "But please believe me, if I had *any* idea where he's taken your son, I would tell the authorities."

Van Eck stiffened. Clearly he hadn't intended to take the conversation in that direction. "I . . . thank you."

"I can't imagine the anguish you must be going through. How did Brekker even lay hands on the boy?" Nina continued. "I would have thought your security—"

"Wylan wasn't at home."

"No?"

"He was studying music in Belendt."

"And what do his teachers have to say about the abduction?"

"I . . ." Van Eck looked uneasily at Dryden. "They are flummoxed as well."

"Perhaps he fell in with bad company?"

"Perhaps."

"I hope he didn't cross Kaz Brekker," Nina said with a shudder.

"Wylan wouldn't—"

"Of course not," said Nina as she shook out the cuffs of her *kefta* and prepared to exit the dining room. "Only a fool would."

30

KAZ

Nina was tired, Kaz could see it. They all were. Even he'd had no choice but to rest after the fight. His body had stopped listening to him. He'd passed an invisible limit and simply shut down. He didn't remember falling asleep. He didn't dream. One moment he was resting in the suite's smallest bedroom, on his back, running through the particulars of the plan, and the next he was waking in the dark, panicked, unsure of where he was or how he'd gotten there.

When he reached to turn up the lamp, he felt a sharp twinge of pain. It had been excruciating to endure Genya's faint touches when she'd seen to his injuries, but maybe he should have let the Tailor heal him just a little bit more. He still had a long night ahead of him, and the auction scheme was unlike anything he'd attempted.

In his time with the Dregs, Kaz had seen and heard plenty, but his conversation with Sturmhond in the solarium had topped it all.

They had talked through the details of the auction, what they would need from Genya, how Kaz predicted the betting would go and in what increments. Kaz wanted Sturmhond to enter the fray at fifty million and suspected the Shu would counter by raising ten million or more. Kaz needed to know the Ravkans were committed. Once the auction was announced, it would have to proceed. There could be no backward step.

The privateer was wary, pressing for knowledge on how they'd been hired for the Ice Court job, as well as how they'd managed to find and liberate Kuwei. Kaz gave him enough information to convince the privateer that Kuwei was in fact Bo Yul-Bayur's son. But he had no interest in divulging the mechanics of their schemes or the true talents of his crew. For all Kaz knew, Sturmhond might have something he wanted to steal one day.

At last, Sturmhond straightened the lapels of his teal frock coat and said, "Well, Brekker, it's obvious you only deal in half-truths and outright lies, so you're clearly the man for the job."

"There's just one thing," said Kaz, studying the privateer's broken nose and ruddy hair. "Before we join hands and jump off a cliff together, I want to know exactly who I'm running with."

Sturmhond lifted a brow. "We haven't been on a road trip or exchanged clothes, but I think our introductions were civilized enough."

"Who are you really, privateer?"

"Is this an existential question?"

"No proper thief talks the way you do."

"How narrow-minded of you."

"I know the look of a rich man's son, and I don't believe a king would send an ordinary privateer to handle business this sensitive."

"Ordinary," scoffed Sturmhond. "Are you so schooled in politics?"

"I know my way around a deal. Who are you? We get the truth or my crew walks."

"Are you so sure that would be possible, Brekker? I know your plans now. I'm accompanied by two of the world's most legendary Grisha, and I'm not too bad in a fight either."

"And I'm the canal rat who brought Kuwei Yul-Bo out of the Ice Court alive. Let me know how you like your chances." His crew didn't have clothes or titles to rival the Ravkans, but Kaz knew where he'd put his money if he had any left.

Sturmhond clasped his hands behind his back, and Kaz saw the barest shift in his demeanor. His eyes lost their bemused gleam and took on a surprising weight. No ordinary privateer at all.

"Let us say," said Sturmhond, gaze trained on the Ketterdam street below, "hypothetically, of course, that the Ravkan king has intelligence networks that reach deep within Kerch, Fjerda, and the Shu Han, and that he knows exactly how important Kuwei Yul-Bo could be to the future of his country. Let us say that king would trust no one to negotiate such matters but himself, but that he also knows just how dangerous it is to travel under his own name when his country is in turmoil, when he has no heir and the Lantsov succession is in no way secured."

"So hypothetically," Kaz said, "you might be addressed as Your Highness."

"And a variety of more colorful names. Hypothetically." The privateer cast him an assessing glance. "Just how did you know I wasn't who I claimed to be, Mister Brekker?"

Kaz shrugged. "You speak Kerch like a native—a rich native. You don't talk like someone who came up with sailors and street thugs."

The privateer turned slightly, giving Kaz his full attention. His ease was gone, and now he looked like a man who might command armies. "Mister Brekker," he said. "Kaz, if I may? I am in a vulnerable position. I am a king ruling a country with an empty treasury, facing enemies on all sides. There are also forces within my country that might seize any absence as an opportunity to make their own bid for power."

"So you're saying you'd make an excellent hostage."

"I suspect that the ransom for me would be considerably less than the price Kuwei has on his head. Really, it's a bit of a blow to my self-esteem."

"You don't seem to be suffering," said Kaz.

"Sturmhond was a creation of my youth, and his reputation still serves me well. I cannot bid on Kuwei Yul-Bo as the king of Ravka. I hope your plan will play out the way you think it will. But if it doesn't, the loss of such a prize would be seen as a humiliating blunder diplomatically and strategically. I enter that auction as Sturmhond or as no one at all. If that is a problem—"

Kaz settled his hands on his cane. "As long as you don't try to con me, you can enter as the Fairy Queen of Istamere."

"It's certainly nice to have my options open." He looked back out at the city. "Can this possibly work, Mister Brekker? Or am I risking the fate of Ravka and the world's Grisha on the honor and abilities of a fast-talking urchin?"

"More than a bit of both," said Kaz. "You're risking a country. We're risking our lives. Seems a fair trade."

The king of Ravka offered his hand. "The deal is the deal?"

"The deal is the deal." They shook.

"If only treaties could be signed so quickly," he said, his easy privateer's mien sliding back in place like a mask purchased on West Stave. "I'm going to have a drink and a bath. One can take only so much mud and squalor. As the rebel said to the prince, it's bad for the constitution." He flicked an invisible speck of dust from his lapel and sauntered out of the solarium.

Now Kaz smoothed his hair and pulled on his jacket. It was hard to believe a lowly canal rat had struck a deal with a king. He thought of that broken nose that gave the privateer the look of someone who had been through a fair share of fistfights. For all Kaz knew, he had, but he must have been tailored to disguise his features. Hard to lie low when your face was on the money. In the end, royalty or not, Sturmhond was really just a very grand con man, and all that mattered was that he and his people did their part.

Kaz checked his watch—past midnight, later than he would have liked—and went to find Nina. He was surprised to see Jesper waiting in the hall.

"What is it?" Kaz said, his mind instantly trying to calculate all the things that might have gone wrong as he slept.

"Nothing," Jesper said. "Or no more than usual."

"Then what do you want?"

Jesper swallowed and said, "Matthias gave you the remaining *parem*, didn't he?"

"So?"

"If anything happens . . . the Shu will be at the auction, maybe the Kherguud. There's too much riding on this job. I can't let my father down again. I need the *parem*, as a security measure."

Kaz studied him for a long moment. "No."

"Why the hell not?"

A reasonable question. Giving Jesper the *parem* would have been the smart move, the practical move.

"Your father cares more about you than some plot of land."

"But—"

"I'm not going to let you make yourself a martyr, Jes. If one of us goes down, we all go down."

"This is my choice to make."

"And yet I seem to be the one making it." Kaz headed toward the sitting room. He didn't intend to argue with Jesper, especially when he wasn't entirely sure why he was saying no in the first place.

"Who's Jordie?"

Kaz paused. He'd known the question would come, and yet it was still hard to hear his brother's name spoken. "Someone I trusted." He looked over his shoulder and met Jesper's gray eyes. "Someone I didn't want to lose."

Kaz found Nina and Matthias asleep on the couch in the purple sitting room. Why the two biggest people in their crew had chosen the smallest space to sleep on, he had no idea. He gave Nina a nudge with his cane. Without opening her eyes, she tried to bat it away.

"Rise and shine."

"Go 'way," she said, burying her head in Matthias' chest.

"Let's go, Zenik. The dead will wait, but I won't."

At last she roused herself and pulled on her boots. She had discarded her red *kefta* in favor of the coat and trousers she'd worn during the disastrous botch that had been the Sweet Reef job. Matthias watched her every move, but he did not ask to accompany them. He knew his presence would only increase their risk of exposure.

Inej appeared in the doorway, and they headed for the lift in silence. Curfew was in effect on the streets of Ketterdam, but there was no avoiding this. They would have to rely on luck and Inej's ability to scout the path ahead of them for patrolling *stadwatch*.

They left the back of the hotel and headed toward the manufacturing district. Their progress was slow, a circuitous route around the blockades, full of stops and starts as Inej vanished and reappeared, signaling them to wait or rerouting them with a flick of her hand before she was gone once more.

At last they reached the morgue, an unmarked, gray stone structure on the border of the warehouse district, fronted by a garden no one had tended to in some time. Only the bodies of the wealthy were brought here to be prepared for transportation and burial outside the city. It wasn't the miserable human heap of the Reaper's Barge, but Kaz still felt like he was descending into a nightmare. He thought of Inej's voice echoing off the white tiles. *Go on.*

The morgue was deserted, its heavy iron door sealed tight. He picked the lock and looked once over his shoulder at the shifting shadows of the weedy garden. He couldn't see Inej, but he knew she was there. She would keep watch over the entrance as they got this grim business done.

It was chilly inside, lit only by a lantern with the blue-tinted warning flame of corpselight. There was a processing room and beyond it a large, icy stone chamber lined with drawers big enough to hold bodies. The whole place smelled of death.

He thought of the pulse beating beneath Inej's jaw, the warmth of her skin on his lips. He tried to shake the thought free. He did not want that memory tangling with this room full of rot.

Kaz had never been able to dodge the horror of that night in the Ketterdam harbor, the memory of his brother's corpse clutched tight in his arms as he told himself to kick a little harder, to take one more breath, stay afloat, stay alive. He'd found his way to shore, devoted himself to the vengeance he and his brother were owed. But the nightmare refused to fade. Kaz had been sure it would get easier. He would stop having to think twice before he shook a hand or was forced into close quarters. Instead, things got so bad he could barely brush up against someone on the street without finding himself once more in the harbor. He was on the Reaper's Barge and death was all around him. He was kicking through the water, clinging to the slippery bloat of Jordie's flesh, too frightened of drowning to let go.

The situation had gotten dangerous. When Gorka once got too drunk to stand at the Blue Paradise, Kaz and Teapot had to carry him home. Six blocks they hauled him, Gorka's weight shifting back and forth, slumping against Kaz in a sickening press of skin and stink, then flopping onto Teapot, freeing Kaz briefly—though he could still feel the rub of the man's hairy arm against the back of his neck.

Later, Teapot had found Kaz huddled in a lavatory, shaking and covered in sweat. He'd pleaded food poisoning, teeth chattering as he jammed his foot against the door to keep Teapot out. He could not be touched again or he would lose his mind completely.

The next day he'd bought his first pair of gloves—cheap black things that bled dye whenever they got wet. Weakness was lethal in the Barrel. People could smell it on you like blood, and if Kaz was going to bring Pekka Rollins to his knees, he couldn't afford any more nights trembling on a bathroom floor.

Kaz never answered questions about the gloves, never responded to taunts. He just wore them, day in and day out, peeling them off only when he was alone. He told himself it was a temporary measure. But that didn't stop him from remastering every bit of sleight of hand wearing them, learning to shuffle and work a deck even more deftly than he could barehanded. The gloves held back the waters, kept him from drowning when memories of that night threatened to drag him under. When he pulled them on, it felt like he was arming himself, and they were better than a knife or a gun. Until he met Imogen.

He'd been fourteen, not yet Per Haskell's lieutenant but making a name for himself with every fight and swindle. Imogen was new to the Barrel, a year older than he was. She'd run with a crew in Zierfoort, small-time rackets that she claimed had left her bored. Since she'd arrived in Ketterdam, she'd been hanging around the Staves, picking up small jobs, trying to find her way into one of the Barrel gangs. When Kaz had first seen her, she'd been breaking a bottle over the head of a Razorgull who'd gotten too handsy. Then she'd cropped up again when Per Haskell had him running book on the spring prize fights. She had freckles and a gap between her front teeth, and she could hold her own in a brawl.

One night, when they were standing by the empty ring counting up the day's haul, she'd touched her hand to the sleeve of his coat, and when he looked up, she'd smiled slowly, close-lipped, so he couldn't see the gap in her teeth.

Later, lying on his lumpy mattress in the room he shared at the Slat, Kaz had stared up at the leaky ceiling and thought of the way Imogen had smiled at him, the way her trousers sat low on her hips. She had a sidle when she walked, as if she approached everything from a little bit of an angle. He liked it. He liked her.

There was no mystery to bodies in the Barrel. Space was tight and people took their pleasures where they found them. The other boys in the Dregs talked constantly about their conquests. Kaz said nothing. Fortunately, he said nothing about almost everything, so he had consistency working in his favor. But he knew what he was expected to say, the things he was supposed to want. He did want those things, in moments, in flashes—a girl crossing the street in a cobalt dress that slid from her shoulder, a dancer moving like flames in a show on East Stave, Imogen laughing like he'd told the funniest joke in the world when he hadn't said much at all.

He'd flexed his hands in his gloves, listening to his roommates snore. *I can best this*, he told himself. He was stronger than this sickness, stronger than the pull of the water. When he'd needed to learn the workings of a gambling hall, he'd done it. When he'd decided to educate himself on finance, he'd mastered that too. Kaz thought of Imogen's slow, closed-mouth smile and made a decision. He would conquer this weakness the way he'd conquered everything in his path.

He'd started small, with gestures no one would notice. A game of Three Man Bramble dealt with gloves off. A night spent with them tucked under his pillow. Then, when Per Haskell sent him and Teapot to lay a little hurt on a two-bit brawler named Beni who owed him cash, Kaz had waited until they'd had him in the alley, and when Teapot told Kaz to hold Beni's arms, he'd slipped off his gloves, just as a test, something easy.

As soon as he made contact with Beni's wrists, a rush of revulsion overtook him. But he was prepared and endured it, ignoring the icy sweat that broke over him as he hooked Beni's elbows behind his back. Kaz forced himself to brace Beni's body against his while Teapot reeled off the terms of his loan with Per Haskell, punctuating each sentence with a punch to Beni's face or gut.

I'm all right, Kaz told himself. *I'm handling this.* Then the waters rose.

This time the wave was as tall as the spires on the Church of Barter; it seized him and dragged him down, a weight that he could not escape. He had Jordie in his arms, his brother's rotting fish-belly body clutched against him. Kaz shoved him away, gasping for breath.

The next thing he knew, he was leaning against a brick wall. Teapot was yelling at him as Beni fled. The sky was gray above him, and the stink of the alley filled his nostrils, the ash and vegetable smell of garbage, the ripe tang of old urine.

"What the hell was that, Brekker?" screamed Teapot, face mottled with fury, nose whistling in a way that should have been funny. "You just let him go! What if he'd had a knife on him?"

Kaz registered it only dimly. Beni had hardly touched him, but somehow, without the gloves, it was all so much worse. The press of skin, the pliability of another human body so close to his.

"Are you even listening to me, you sorry, skinny little skiv?" Teapot grabbed him by his shirt, his knuckles brushing Kaz's neck, sending another wave of sickness crashing through him. He shook Kaz until his teeth rattled.

Teapot gave Kaz the beat-down he'd had planned for Beni and left him bleeding in the alley. You didn't get to go soft or give in to distraction, not on a job, not when one of your crew was counting on you. Kaz curled his hands into his sleeves, but never threw a punch.

It had taken him nearly an hour to drag himself from that alley, and weeks to rebuild the damage to his reputation. Any slip in the Barrel could lead to a bad fall. He found Beni and made him wish Teapot had been the one to deliver the beating. He put his gloves back on and didn't take them off. He became twice as ruthless, fought twice as hard. He stopped worrying about seeming normal, let people see a glimmer of the madness within him and let them guess at the rest. Someone got too close, he threw a punch. Someone dared to put hands on him, he broke a wrist, two wrists, a jaw. *Dirtyhands*, they called him. Haskell's rabid dog. The rage inside him burned on and he learned to despise people who complained, who begged, who claimed they'd suffered. *Let me teach you what pain looks like*, he would say, and then he'd paint a picture with his fists.

At the ring, the next time Imogen laid her fingers on his sleeve, Kaz held her gaze until that closed-mouth smile slipped. She dropped her hand. She looked away. Kaz went back to counting the money.

Now Kaz rapped his cane against the morgue floor.

"Let's get this over with," he said to Nina, hearing his voice echo too loudly off the cold stone. He wanted out of this place as fast as possible.

They started on opposite sides, scanning the dates on the drawers, searching for a cadaver that would be in the appropriate state of decomposition. Even the thought ratcheted the tension in his chest tighter. It felt like a scream building. But his mind had conceived of this plan, knowing it would bring him to this place.

"Here," Nina said.

Kaz crossed the room to her. They stood before the drawer, neither of them moving to open it. Kaz knew they'd both seen plenty of dead bodies. You couldn't make a life on the streets of the Barrel or as a soldier in the Second Army without encountering death. But this was different. This was decay.

At last, Kaz hooked the crow's head of his cane under the handle and pulled. The drawer was heavier than he'd anticipated, but it slid open smoothly. He stood back.

"We're sure this is a good idea?" said Nina.

"I'm open to better ones," said Kaz.

She blew out a long breath and then pulled the sheet away from the corpse. Kaz thought of a snake molting.

The man was middle-aged, his lips already blackening with decay.

As a little boy, Kaz had held his breath whenever he'd passed a graveyard, certain that if he opened his mouth, something terrible would crawl in. The room tilted. Kaz tried to breathe shallowly, forcing himself back to the present. He spread his fingers inside his gloves, felt the leather tug, grasped the weight of his cane in his palm.

"I wonder how he died," Nina murmured as she peered at the gray folds of the dead man's face.

"Alone," Kaz said, looking at the man's fingertips. Something had been gnawing at them. The rats had gotten to him before his body was found. Or one of his pets. Kaz pulled the sealed glass container he'd lifted from Genya's kit out of his pocket. "Take what you need."

Standing in the clock tower above Colm's suite, Kaz surveyed his crew. The city was still cloaked in darkness, but dawn would come soon and they would go their separate ways: Wylan and Colm to an empty bakery to wait out the start of the auction. Nina to the Barrel with her assignments in hand. Inej to the Church of Barter to take up her position on the roof.

Kaz would descend to the square in front of the Exchange with Matthias and Kuwei and meet the armed *stadwatch* troop that would escort them into the church. Kaz wondered how Van Eck felt about his own officers protecting the bastard of the Barrel.

He felt more himself than he had in days. The ambush at Van Eck's house had shaken him. He hadn't been ready for Pekka Rollins to reenter the field on those terms. He hadn't been prepared for the shame of it, for the memories of Jordie that had returned with such force.

You failed me. His brother's voice, louder than ever in his head. *You let him dupe you all over again.*

Kaz had called Jesper by his brother's name. A bad slip. But maybe he'd wanted to punish them both. Kaz was older now than Jordie had been when he'd succumbed to the Queen's Lady Plague. Now he could look back and see his brother's pride, his hunger for fast success. *You failed* me*, Jordie. You were older. You were supposed to be the smart one.*

He thought of Inej asking, *Was there no one to protect you?* He remembered Jordie seated beside him on a bridge, smiling and alive, the reflection of their feet in the water beneath them, the warmth of a cup of hot chocolate cradled in his mittened hands. *We were supposed to look out for each other.*

They'd been two farm boys, missing their father, lost in this city. That was how Pekka got them. It wasn't just the enticement of money. He'd given them a new home. A fake wife who made them *hutspot*, a fake daughter for Kaz to play with. Pekka Rollins had lured them with a warm fire and the promise of the life they'd lost.

And that was what destroyed you in the end: the longing for something you could never have.

He scanned the faces of the people he had fought beside, bled with. He'd lied to them and been lied to. He'd brought them into hell and dragged them out again.

Kaz settled his hands over his cane, his back to the city. "We all want different things from this day. Freedom, redemption—"

"Cold hard cash?" suggested Jesper.

"Plenty of that. There are lots of people looking to stand in our way. Van Eck. The Merchant Council. Pekka Rollins and his goons, a few different countries, and most of this Saintsforsaken town."

"Is this supposed to be encouraging?" asked Nina.

"They don't know who we are. Not really. They don't know what we've done, what we've managed together." Kaz rapped his cane on the ground. "So let's go show them they picked the wrong damn fight."

31
WYLAN

What am I doing here?

Wylan bent to the basin and splashed cold water on his face. In just a few hours, the auction would begin. They would abandon the hotel suite before dawn. It was imperative that if anyone came looking for Johannus Rietveld after the auction, they would find him long gone.

He took a final glance in the bathroom's gilded mirror. The face gazing back at him was familiar again, but who was he really? A criminal? A runaway? A kid who was passable—maybe more than passable—at demo?

I'm Marya Hendriks' son.

He thought of his mother, alone, abandoned along with her defective child. Had she not been young enough to produce a proper heir? Had his father known even then that he would want to forever rid himself of any evidence that Wylan had existed?

What am I doing here?

But he knew the answer. Only he could see his father punished for what he'd done. Only he could see his mother freed.

Wylan examined himself in the glass. His father's eyes. His mother's curls. It had felt good to be someone else for a while, to forget he was a Van Eck. But he didn't want to hide anymore. Ever since Prior's fingers had closed over his throat, he'd been running. Or maybe it had started long before then, in the afternoons he'd spent sitting in the pantry or curled into a window seat behind a curtain, hoping everyone would forget him, that the nanny would just go home, that his tutor would never arrive.

His father had wanted Wylan to vanish. He'd wanted him to disappear the way he'd made Wylan's mother disappear, and for a long time, Wylan had wanted the exact same thing. That had all started to change when he came to the Barrel, when he got his first job, when he met Jesper and Kaz and Inej, when he'd begun to realize he was worth something.

Jan Van Eck was not going to get his wish. Wylan wasn't going anywhere.

"I'm here for her," he said to the mirror.

The rosy-cheeked boy in the glass did not look impressed.

The sun had just started to rise as Pim led Wylan and Colm out the back of the hotel and through a series of confusing turns to the square that fronted the Exchange. Ordinarily, the bakery on Beurstraat would have been open at this hour, preparing to serve the traders and merchants on their way to the Exchange. But the auction had upended ordinary business and the baker had closed his shop, maybe hoping to secure a seat to watch the proceedings for himself.

They stood at the door on the deserted square for an excruciatingly long moment as Pim fumbled with the lock. Wylan realized he'd gotten used to the dexterity with which Kaz managed breaking and entering. The door opened with a too-loud jingle and then they were inside.

"No mourners," said Pim. He vanished back through the door before Wylan could reply.

The bakery cases were empty, but the smell of bread and sugar lingered. Wylan and Colm settled themselves on the floor with their backs against the shelves, trying to make themselves comfortable. Kaz had left them with strict instructions, and Wylan had no interest in disregarding them. Johannus Rietveld could never be seen in the city again, and Wylan knew exactly what his father would do to him if he found his son roaming the streets of Ketterdam.

They sat in silence for hours. Colm dozed. Wylan hummed to himself, a tune that he'd had in his head for a while. It would need percussion, something with a *rat-a-tat-tat* like gunfire.

He took a cautious peek through the window and saw a few people headed toward the Church of Barter, starlings taking flight in the square, and there, only a few hundred yards away, the entrance to the Exchange. He didn't need to be able to read the words engraved over the arch. He'd heard his father repeat them countless times. *Enjent, Voorhent, Almhent.* Industry, Integrity, Prosperity. Jan Van Eck had managed two out of three well enough.

Wylan didn't realize Colm was awake until he said, "What made you lie for my son that day in the tomb?"

Wylan lowered himself back down to the floor. He chose his words carefully. "I guess I know what it's like to get things wrong."

Colm sighed. "Jesper gets a lot wrong. He's reckless and foolish and apt to joke when it's not warranted, but . . ." Wylan waited. "What I'm trying to say is, he's a lot of trouble, a whole lot. But he's worth it."

"I—"

"And it's my fault he is the way he is. I was trying to protect him, but maybe I saddled him with something worse than all the dangers I saw lurking out there." Even in the weak morning light trickling through the bakery's window, Wylan could see how weary Colm looked. "I made some big mistakes."

Wylan drew a line on the floor with his finger. "You gave him someone to run to. No matter what he did or what went wrong. I think that's bigger than the big mistakes."

"See now? That's why he likes you. I know, I know—it's none of my business, and I have no idea if he'd be good for you. Probably bring you ten kinds of headache. But I think you'd be good for him."

Wylan's face heated. He knew how much Colm loved Jesper, had seen it in every gesture he'd made. It meant something that he thought Wylan was good enough for his son.

A sound came from near the delivery entrance, and they both stilled.

Wylan rose, heart pounding. "Remember," he whispered to Colm. "Stay hidden."

He made his way past the ovens to the back of the bakery. The smells were stronger here, the darkness more complete, but the room was empty. A false alarm.

"It's not—"

The delivery door flew open. Hands grabbed Wylan from behind. His head was yanked back, his mouth forced open as a rag was stuffed inside. A bag was shoved over his head.

"Hey, little merch," said a deep voice he didn't recognize. "Ready to be reunited with your daddy?"

They wrenched his arms back and dragged him through the delivery door of the bakery. Wylan stumbled, barely able to keep his footing, unable to see or get his bearings. He fell, his knees banging painfully against the cobblestones, and he was yanked back up.

"Don't make me carry you, little merch. Not getting paid for that."

"This way," said one of the others, a girl. "Pekka's on the southern side of the cathedral."

"Hold," said a new voice. "Who do you have there?"

His tone was officious. *Stadwatch*, Wylan thought.

"Someone Councilman Van Eck is going to be very happy to see."

"Is he from Kaz Brekker's crew?"

"Just run along like a good grunt and tell him the Dime Lions have a present waiting for him in the armaments chapel."

Wylan heard crowds a little way off. Were they near the church? A moment later he was pulled roughly forward and the sounds changed. They were inside. The air was cooler, the light dimmer. He was dragged up another set of stairs, his shins banging against their edges, and then shoved into a chair, his hands bound behind his back.

He heard footsteps coming up the stairs, the sound of a door opening.

"We got him," said that same deep voice.

"Where?" Wylan's heart stuttered. *Sound it out, Wylan. A child half your age can read this without trying.* He'd thought he was ready for this.

"Brekker had him stashed in a bakery just a few blocks away."

"How did you find him?"

"Pekka's had us searching the area. Figured Brekker might try to pull some stunt at the auction."

"No doubt intending to humiliate me," said Jan Van Eck.

The bag was yanked from Wylan's head and he looked into his father's face.

Van Eck shook his head. "Every time I think you cannot disappoint me further, you prove me wrong."

They were in a small chapel topped by a dome. The oil paintings on the wall featured battle scenes and piles of armaments. The chapel must have been donated by a family of weapons manufacturers.

Over the last few days, Wylan had studied the layout of the Church of Barter, mapping the rooftop niches and alcoves with Inej, sketching the cathedral and long finger naves of Ghezen's hand. He knew exactly where he was—one of the chapels at the end of Ghezen's pinky. The floor was carpeted, the only door led to the stairway, and the only windows opened onto the roof. Even if he wasn't gagged, he doubted anyone but the paintings would be able to hear him cry for help. Two people stood behind Van Eck: a girl in striped trousers, the yellow hair shaved from half of her head, and a stout boy in plaid and suspenders. Both wore the purple armbands indicating they'd been deputized by the *stadwatch*. Both bore the Dime Lion tattoo.

The boy grinned. "You want me to go get Pekka?" he asked Van Eck.

"No need. I want him keeping his eyes on the preparations for the auction. And this is something I'd prefer to handle myself." Van Eck leaned down. "Listen, boy. The Wraith was spotted with a member of the Grisha Triumvirate. I know Brekker is working with the Ravkans. For all your many shortcomings, you still carry my blood. Tell me what he has planned and I'll see you're taken care of. You'll have an allowance. You can live somewhere in comfort. I'm going to remove your gag. If you scream, I'll let Pekka's friends do whatever they like to you, understood?"

Wylan nodded. His father tugged the rag from his mouth.

Wylan ran his tongue over his lips and spat in his father's face.

Van Eck drew a snowy monogrammed handkerchief from his pocket. It was embroidered with the red laurel. "An apt retort from a boy who can barely form words." He wiped the saliva from his face. "Let's try this again. Tell me what Brekker is planning with the Ravkans and I may let you live."

"The way you let my mother live?"

His father's flinch was barely perceptible, a marionette yanked once by its strings, then allowed to return to rest.

Van Eck folded his soiled handkerchief twice, tucked it away. He nodded to the boy and the girl. "Do whatever you have to. The auction starts in less than an hour, and I want answers before then."

"Hold him up," the stout boy said to the girl. She hauled Wylan to his feet, and the boy slipped a pair of brass knuckles from his pocket. "He's not going to be so pretty after this."

"Who is there to care?" Van Eck said with a shrug. "Just make sure you keep him conscious. I want information."

The boy eyed Wylan skeptically. "You sure you want to do it this way, little merch?"

Wylan summoned every bit of bravado he'd learned from Nina, the will he'd learned from Matthias, the focus he'd studied in Kaz, the courage he'd learned from Inej, and the wild, reckless hope he'd learned from Jesper, the belief that no matter the odds, somehow they would win. "I won't talk," he said.

The first punch shattered two of his ribs. The second had him coughing blood.

"Maybe we should snap your fingers so you can't play that infernal flute," Van Eck suggested.

I'm here for her, Wylan reminded himself. *I'm here for her.*

In the end, he was not Nina or Matthias or Kaz or Inej or Jesper. He was just Wylan Van Eck. He told them everything.

32

INEJ

Getting into the Church of Barter was no easy task this morning. Due to its position near the Exchange and the Beurscanal, its roof didn't conjoin any others, and its entrances were already surrounded by guards when Inej arrived. But she was the Wraith; she was made to find the hidden places, the corners and cracks where no one thought to look.

No weapons would be allowed inside the Church of Barter during the auction, so Jesper's rifle was secured to her back. She waited out of sight until she spotted a group of *stadwatch* grunts rolling a cart full of lumber toward the church's huge double doors. Inej assumed they were the makings of some kind of barricade for the stage or the finger naves. She waited until the cart had rolled to a stop, then tucked her hood into her tunic so it would not trail on the ground and slipped beneath the cart. She latched herself onto the axle, her body bare inches above the cobblestones, and let them wheel her directly down the center aisle. Before they reached the altar, she dropped and rolled between the pews, narrowly missing the cart's wheels.

The floor was cold stone under her belly as she crawled the width of the church, then waited at the end of the aisle and darted behind one of the columns of the western arcade. She moved from column to column, then slipped into the nave that would lead her to the thumb chapels. Once more she dropped into a crawl so that she could use the pews in the nave as cover. She didn't know where the guards might be patrolling, and she had no desire to be caught simply wandering the church.

She reached the first chapel, then climbed the stairs to the orange chapel above. Its altar was rendered in gold, but built to resemble crates of oranges and other exotic fruits. It framed a DeKappel oil that showed a family of merchants dressed in black, cradled in Ghezen's hand, hovering over a citrus grove.

She scaled the altar and launched herself up to the chapel's dome, clinging to it so she was hanging nearly upside down. Once she reached the center of the cupola, she wedged her back against the little dome that crowned the larger dome like a hat. Though she doubted she could be heard here, she waited until the sounds of sawing and hammering from the cathedral began, then positioned her foot in front of one of the slender glass windows that gave light to the chapel and kicked. On the second attempt, the glass fractured, spilling outward. Inej covered her hand with her sleeve to clear away the excess shards and edged out onto the top of the dome. She latched a climbing line to the window and rappelled down the dome's side to the roof of the nave, where she left Jesper's rifle. She didn't want it throwing off her balance.

She was atop Ghezen's thumb. The morning mist had started to burn away and she could feel the day would be a hot one. She followed the thumb back to the steeply gabled spires of the main cathedral and began to climb once more.

This was the highest part of the church, but the terrain was familiar, and that made for easier going. Of all the rooftops in Ketterdam, the cathedral was Inej's favorite. She'd had no good reason to learn its contours. There were plenty of other places from which she could have observed the Exchange or the Beurscanal when a job called for it, but she'd always chosen the Church of Barter. Its spires were visible from almost anywhere in Ketterdam, the copper of its rooftop long since turned to green and crisscrossed by spines of metal scrollwork, full of perfect handholds and offering plenty of cover. It was like a strange gray-green fairyland that no one else in the city ever got to see.

The wire walker in her had imagined running a line between its tallest spires. *Who would dare to defy death itself? I will.* The Kerch would probably consider staging acrobatics atop their cathedral blasphemous. Unless of course she charged admission.

She planted the explosives Kaz had described as their "insurance" in the locations she and Wylan had agreed upon while mapping the cathedral. Only in Kaz's mind could chaos count for security. The bombs were meant to be noisy but would do little damage. Still, if something went wrong and a distraction was needed, they would be there.

When she was done, she took up her perch in one of the metalwork pockets that overlooked the apse and the vast nave of the cathedral. Here, her view of the proceedings would be obstructed by nothing but a series of wide slats and the mesh screen between them. There were times she came here just to listen to the music from the organ or to hear voices raised in song. High above the city, chords from the pipe organ echoing through the stone, she felt closer to her Saints.

The acoustics were good enough that she could have listened to every word of the sermons if she'd wanted to, but she chose to ignore those parts of the service. Ghezen was not her god, and she had no desire to be lectured on how she might better serve him. She wasn't fond of Ghezen's altar either—a graceless, flat lump of rock around which the church had been built. Some called it the First Forge, others the Mortar, but today it would be used as an auction block. It made Inej's stomach turn. She was supposedly an indenture, brought to Kerch of her own free will. That was what the documents said. They didn't tell the story of her abduction, her terror in the belly of a slaver ship, the humiliation she'd suffered at Tante Heleen's hands, or the misery of her existence at the

Menagerie. Kerch had been built on trade, but how much of that trade had been the human kind? A minister of Ghezen might stand at that altar and rail against slavery, but how much of this city had been built on taxes from the pleasure houses? How many members of his congregation employed boys and girls who could barely speak Kerch, who scrubbed floors and folded laundry for pennies as they worked to pay off a debt that never seemed to grow smaller?

If Inej got her money, if she got her ship, she might do her part to change all of that. If she survived this day. She imagined all of them—Kaz, Nina, Matthias, Jesper, Wylan, Kuwei, who'd had so little say in the course of his own life—perched side by side on a wire, their balance precarious, their lives tethered together by hope and belief in one another. Pekka would be prowling the church below, and she suspected Dunyasha would be close by. She'd called the ivory-and-amber girl her shadow, but maybe she was a sign as well, a reminder that Inej hadn't been made for this life. And yet, it was hard not to feel that this city was her home, that Dunyasha was the intruder here.

Now Inej watched the guards doing their last sweep of the church's ground floor, searching the corners and chapels. She knew they might send a few brave officers up to the roof to search, but there were plenty of places to hide, and if need be, she could simply slip back into the dome of the thumb chapel to wait them out.

The guards set up their posts, and Inej heard the captain giving orders for where the members of the Merchant Council were to be seated on the stage. She spotted the university medik who had been brought in to verify Kuwei's health and saw a guard wheel a podium into place where the auctioneer would stand. She felt a surge of irritation when she spotted a few Dime Lions walking the aisles with the guards. They puffed out their chests, enjoying their new authority, brandishing the purple *stadwatch* bands on their arms to one another and laughing. The real *stadwatch* didn't look pleased, and Inej could see at least two members of the Merchant Council observing the proceedings with a wary eye. Were they wondering if they'd gotten more than they'd bargained for by allowing a bunch of Barrel thugs to be deputized? Van Eck had started this dance with Rollins, but Inej doubted the king of the Barrel would let him lead for long.

Inej scanned the skyline, all the way to the harbor and the black obelisk towers. Nina had been right about the Council of Tides. It seemed they preferred to stay cloistered in their watchtowers. Though, since their identities were unknown, Inej supposed they could be sitting in the cathedral right now. She looked toward the Barrel, hoping Nina was safe and had not been discovered, that the heavy *stadwatch* presence at the church would mean easier passage on the streets.

By afternoon, the pews started to fill with curious onlookers— tradesmen in roughspun, jollies and bruisers fresh from the Staves and decked out in their best Barrel flash, flocks of black-clad merchers, some accompanied by their wives, their pale faces bobbing above their white lace collars, heads crowned by braids.

The Fjerdan diplomats came next. They wore silver and white and were bracketed by *drüskelle* in black uniforms, all gilded hair and golden skin. Their size alone was daunting. Inej assumed that Matthias must know some of these men and boys. He would have served with them. What would it be like for him to see them again, now that he'd been branded a traitor?

The Zemeni delegation followed, empty gun belts at their hips, forced to divest themselves of their weapons at the doors. They were just as tall as the *drüskelle*, but leaner of build; some bronze like her, others the same deep brown as Jesper, some with heads shorn, others with hair in thick braids and coiled knots. There, tucked between the last two rows of the Zemeni, Inej caught sight of Jesper. For once, he wasn't the tallest person in a crowd, and with the collar of his waxed cotton duster turned up around his jaw and a hat pulled low over his ears, he was nearly unrecognizable. Or so Inej hoped.

When the Ravkans arrived, the buzz in the room rose to a roar. What did the crowd of tradespeople, merchants, and Barrel rowdies make of this grand international showing?

A man in a teal frock coat led the Ravkan delegation, surrounded by a swarm of Ravkan soldiers in pale blue military dress. This had to be the legendary Sturmhond. He was pure confidence, flanked by Zoya Nazyalensky on one side and Genya Safin on the other, his stride easy and relaxed, as if he were taking a turn about one of his ships. Perhaps she should have met with the Ravkans when she'd had the chance. What might she learn in a month with Sturmhond's crew?

The Fjerdans rose, and Inej thought a fight might break out as the *drüskelle* faced down the Ravkan soldiers, but two members of the Merchant Council rushed forward, backed by a troop of *stadwatch*.

"Kerch is neutral territory," one of the merchers reminded them, his voice high and nervous. "We are here on matters of business, not of war."

"Anyone who violates the sanctity of the Church of Barter will not be allowed to bid," insisted the other, black sleeves flapping.

"Why does your weak king send a filthy pirate to do his bidding?" sneered the Fjerdan ambassador, his words echoing across the cathedral.

"Privateer," corrected Sturmhond. "I suppose he thought my good looks would give me the advantage. Not a concern where you're from, I take it?"

"Preening, ridiculous peacock. You stink of Grisha foulness."

Sturmhond sniffed the air. "I'm amazed you can detect anything over the reek of ice and inbreeding."

The ambassador turned purple, and one of his companions hastily drew him away.

Inej rolled her eyes. They were worse than a couple of Barrel bosses facing off on the Staves.

Bristling and grumbling, the Fjerdans and Ravkans took their seats on opposite sides of the aisle, and the Kaelish delegation entered with little fanfare. But seconds later everyone was on their feet again when some-one shouted, "The Shu!"

All eyes turned to the huge doors of the cathedral as the Shu flowed inside, a tide of red banners marked with the horses and keys, their olive uniforms embellished with gold. Their expressions were stony as they marched up the aisle, then stopped as the Shu ambassador argued angrily that his delegation should be seated at the front of the room and that they were giving the Ravkans and Fjerdans precedence by placing them closer to the stage. Were the Kherguud among them? Inej glanced up at the pale spring sky. She did not like the idea of being plucked from her roost by a winged soldier.

Eventually, Van Eck strode down the aisle from wherever he'd been lurking by the stage and snapped, "If you wished to be seated in the front, you should have forgone the drama of a grand entrance and gotten here on time."

The Shu and the Kerch went back and forth a while longer until at last, the Shu settled in their seats. The rest of the crowd was crackling with murmurs and speculative glances. Most of them didn't know what Kuwei was worth or had only heard rumors of the drug known as *jurda parem*, so they were left to wonder why a Shu boy had drawn such bidders to the table. The few merchers who had seated themselves in the front pews with the intention of placing a bid were exchanging shrugs and shaking their heads in bafflement. Clearly, this was no game for casual players.

The church bells began to chime three bells, just behind those from the Geldrenner clock tower. A hush fell. The Merchant Council gathered on the stage. And then Inej saw every head in the room turn. The great double doors of the church opened and Kuwei Yul-Bo entered, flanked by Kaz and Matthias and an armed *stadwatch* escort. Matthias wore simple tradesman's clothes but managed to look like a soldier on parade nevertheless. With his black eye and split lip, Kaz looked even less reputable than usual, despite the sharp lines of his black suit.

The shouting began immediately. It was hard to know who was causing the loudest uproar. The most wanted criminals in the city were striding down the center aisle of the Church of Barter. At the first glimpse of Kaz, the Dime Lions stationed throughout the cathedral started booing. Matthias had instantly been recognized by his *drüskelle* brethren, who were yelling what Inej presumed were insults at him in Fjerdan.

The sanctity of the auction would protect Kaz and Matthias, but only until the final gavel fell. Even so, neither of them seemed remotely concerned. They walked with backs straight and eyes forward, Kuwei safely wedged between them.

Kuwei was faring less well. The Shu were screaming the same word again and again, *sheyao, sheyao,* and whatever it meant, with every shout, Kuwei seemed to curl further in on himself.

The city auctioneer approached the raised dais and took his place at the podium next to the altar. It was Jellen Radmakker, one of the investors they had invited to Jesper's absurd presentation on oil futures. From the investigation she'd done for Kaz, Inej knew that he was scrupulously honest, a devout man with no family except an equally pious sister who spent her days scrubbing the floors of public buildings in service to Ghezen. He was pale, with tufty orange brows and a hunched posture that gave him the look of a giant shrimp.

Inej scanned the undulating spires of the cathedral, the rooftops of the finger naves radiating from Ghezen's palm. Still no patrol on the roof. It was almost insulting. But maybe Pekka Rollins and Jan Van Eck had something else planned for her.

Radmakker brought his gavel down in three furious swings. "There will be order," he bellowed. The clamor in the room dulled to a discontented murmur.

Kuwei, Kaz, and Matthias climbed the stage and took their places by the podium, Kaz and Matthias partially blocking the still shaking Kuwei from view.

Radmakker waited for absolute quiet. Only then did he begin to recite the rules of the auction, followed by the terms of Kuwei's proffered indenture. Inej glanced at Van Eck. What was it like for him to be so close to the prize he'd sought for so long? His expression was smug, eager. *He's already calculating his next move*, Inej realized. As long as Ravka did not have the winning bid—and how could they, with their war chest badly depleted—Van Eck would get his wish: the secret of *jurda parem* unleashed upon the world. The price of *jurda* would rise to unimaginable heights, and between his secret private holdings and his investments in the *jurda* consortium run by Johannus Rietveld, he would be rich beyond all dreaming.

Radmakker waved forward a medik from the university, a man with a shiny bald pate. He took Kuwei's pulse, measured his height, listened to his lungs, examined his tongue and teeth. It was a bizarre spectacle, uncomfortably close to Inej's memory of being prodded and poked by Tante Heleen on the deck of a slaver ship.

The medik finished and closed up his bag.

"Please make your declaration," said Radmakker.

"The boy's health is sound."

Radmakker turned to Kuwei. "Do you freely consent to abide by the rules of this auction and its outcome?"

If Kuwei replied, Inej couldn't hear it.

"Speak up, boy."

Kuwei tried again. "I do."

"Then let us proceed." The medik stepped down and Radmakker lifted his gavel once more. "Kuwei Yul-Bo freely gives his consent to these proceedings and hereby offers his service for a fair price as guided by Ghezen's hand. All bids will be made in *kruge*. Bidders are instructed to keep silence when not making offers. Any interference in this auction, any bid made in less than good faith will be punished to the fullest extent of Kerch law. The bidding will start at one million *kruge*." He paused. "In Ghezen's name, let the auction commence."

And then it was happening, a clamor of numbers Inej could barely track, the bids climbing as Radmakker jabbed his gavel at each bidder, repeating the offers in staccato bursts.

"Five million *kruge*," the Shu ambassador shouted.

"Five million," repeated Radmakker. "Do I have six?"

"Six," the Fjerdans countered.

Radmakker's bark ricocheted off the cathedral walls like gunfire. Sturmhond waited, letting the Fjerdans and Shu bat numbers back and forth, the Zemeni delegate occasionally upping the price in more cautious increments, trying to slow the bidding's momentum. The Kaelish sat quietly in their pews, observing the proceedings. Inej wondered how much they knew, and if they were unwilling or simply unable to bid.

People were standing now, unable to keep to their seats. It was a warm day, but the activity in the cathedral seemed to have driven the temperature higher. Inej could see people fanning themselves, and even the members of the Merchant Council, gathered like a jury of magpies, had begun to dab at their brows.

When the bidding hit forty million *kruge*, Sturmhond finally raised his hand.

"Fifty million *kruge*," he said. The Church of Barter fell silent.

Even Radmakker paused, his cool demeanor shaken, before he repeated, "Fifty million *kruge* from the Ravkan delegation." The members of the Merchant Council were whispering to one another behind their palms, no doubt thrilled at the commission they were going to earn on Kuwei's price.

"Do I hear another offer?" Radmakker asked.

The Shu were conferring. The Fjerdans were doing the same, though they seemed to be arguing more than discussing. The Zemeni appeared to be waiting to see what would happen next.

"Sixty million *kruge*," the Shu declared.

A counter-raise of ten million. Just as Kaz had anticipated.

The Fjerdans offered next, at sixty million two hundred thousand. You could see it cost their pride something to move in such a small increment, but the Zemeni seemed eager to cool down the bidding too. They bid at sixty million five hundred thousand.

The rhythm of the auction changed, climbing at a slower pace, hovering below sixty-two million until at last that milestone was reached, and the Shu seemed to grow impatient.

"Seventy million *kruge*," said the Shu ambassador.

"Eighty million," called Sturmhond.

"Ninety million." The Shu weren't bothering to wait for Radmakker now.

Even from her perch, Inej could see Kuwei's pale, panic-stricken face. The numbers had gone too high, too fast.

"Ninety-one million," Sturmhond said in a belated attempt to slow the pace.

As if he'd grown tired of the game, the Shu ambassador stepped forward and roared, "One hundred and ten million *kruge*."

"One hundred and ten million *kruge* from the Shu delegation," cried Radmakker, his calm obliterated by the sum. "Do I hear another offer?"

The Church of Barter was silent, as if all those assembled had bent their heads in prayer.

Sturmhond gave a jagged-edged laugh and shrugged. "One hundred and twenty million *kruge*."

Inej bit her lip so hard she drew blood.

Boom. The massive double doors blew open. A wave of seawater crashed through into the nave, frothing between the pews, then vanishing in a cloud of mist. The crowd's excited chatter turned to startled cries.

Fifteen figures cloaked in blue filed inside, their robes billowing as if captured by an invisible wind, their faces obscured by mist.

People were calling for their weapons; some were clutching one another and screaming. Inej saw a mercher hunched over, frantically fanning his unconscious wife.

The figures glided up the aisle, their garments moving in slow ripples.

"We are the Council of Tides," said the blue-cloaked figure in the lead, a female voice, low and commanding. The mist shrouded her face completely, shifting beneath her hood in a continuously changing mask. "This auction is a sham."

Shocked murmurs rose from the crowd.

Inej heard Radmakker call for order, and then she was dodging left, moving on instinct as she heard a soft *whoosh*. A tiny, circular blade cut past her, slicing the sleeve of her tunic and pinging off the copper roof.

"That was a warning," said Dunyasha. She perched on the scrollwork of one of the spires thirty feet from Inej, her ivory hood raised around her face, bright as new snow beneath the afternoon sun. "I will look you in the eye when I send you to your death."

Inej reached for her knives. Her shadow demanded an answer.

PART SIX

ACTION & ECHO

33

MATTHIAS

Matthias held his body quiet, taking in the chaos that had erupted over the Church of Barter. He was keenly aware of the Council members seated behind him, a flock of black-suited ravens squawking at one another, each louder than the next—all but Van Eck, who had settled deeply into his chair, his fingers tented before him, a look of supreme satisfaction on his face. Matthias could see the man called Pekka Rollins leaning on a column in the eastern arcade. He suspected that the gang boss had deliberately positioned himself in Kaz's line of vision.

Radmakker demanded order, his voice rising, the tufts of his pale orange hair quivering with every bang of his gavel. It was hard to tell what had riled up the room more—the possibility that the auction was fixed or the appearance of the Council of Tides. Kaz claimed that no one knew the identities of the Tides—and if Dirtyhands and the Wraith could not suss out such a secret, then no one could. Apparently, they had last appeared in public twenty-five years before to protest the proposed destruction of one of the obelisk towers to create a new shipyard. When the vote had not gone in their favor, they'd sent a huge wave to crush the Stadhall. The Council had reversed themselves and a new Stadhall had been erected on the old site, one with fewer windows and a stronger foundation. Matthias wondered if he would ever grow used to such stories of Grisha power.

It's just another weapon. Its nature depends on who wields it. He would have to keep reminding himself. The thoughts of hatred were so old they had become instincts. That was not something he could cure overnight. Like Nina with *parem*, it might well be a lifelong fight. By now, she would be deep into her assignment in the Barrel. Or she might have been discovered and arrested. He sent up a prayer to Djel. *Keep her safe while I cannot.*

His eyes strayed to the Fjerdan delegation gathered in the front pews and the *drüskelle* there. He knew many of them by name, and they certainly knew him. He could feel the sharp edge of their disgust. One boy glared at him from the first row, quivering with fury, eyes like glaciers, hair so blond it was nearly white. What wounds had his commanders exploited to put that look in his eyes? Matthias held his gaze steadily, taking the brunt of his rage. He could not hate this boy. He'd been him. Eventually, the ice-haired boy looked away.

"The auction is sanctioned by law!" shouted the Shu ambassador. "You have no right to stop the proceedings."

The Tidemakers raised their arms. Another wave crashed through the open doors and roared down the aisle, arcing over the heads of the Shu and hovering there.

"Silence," demanded the lead Tidemaker. She waited for another protest, and when none came, the wave curved backward and sloshed harmlessly to the floor. It slithered up the aisle like a silver snake. "We have received word that these proceedings have been compromised."

Matthias' eyes darted to Sturmhond. The privateer had schooled his features into mild surprise, but even from the stage, Matthias could sense his fear and worry. Kuwei was trembling, eyes closed, whispering to himself in Shu. Matthias could not tell what Kaz was thinking. He never could.

"The rules of the auction are clear," said the Tidemaker. "Neither the indenture nor his representatives are permitted to interfere with the auction's outcome. The market must decide."

The members of the Merchant Council were on their feet now, demanding answers, gathering around Radmakker at the front of the stage. Van Eck made a great show of shouting along with the others, but he paused beside Kaz, and Matthias heard him murmur, "Here I thought I would have to be the one to reveal your scheme with the Ravkans, but it seems the Tides will have the honor." His mouth curved in a satisfied smile. "Wylan took quite a beating before he gave you and your friends up," he said, moving toward the podium. "I never knew the boy had so much spine."

"A false fund was created to swindle honest merchants out of their money," continued the Tidemaker. "That money was funneled to one of the bidders."

"Of course!" said Van Eck in mock surprise. "The Ravkans! We all knew they didn't have the funds to bid competitively in such an auction!" Matthias could hear how greatly he was enjoying himself. "We're aware of how much money the Ravkan crown has borrowed from us over the last two years. They can barely make their interest payments. They don't have one hundred and twenty million *kruge* ready to bid in an open auction. Brekker must be working with them."

All the bidders were out of their seats now. The Fjerdans were shouting for justice. The Shu had begun stamping their feet and banging on the backs of the pews. The Ravkans stood in the middle of the maelstrom, surrounded by enemies on every side. Sturmhond, Genya, and Zoya were at the center of it all, chins held high.

"Do something," Matthias growled at Kaz. "This is about to turn ugly."

Kaz's face was as impassive as always. "Do you think so?"

"Damn it, Brekker. You—"

The Tides raised their arms and the church shook with another resonant *boom*. Water sloshed in through the windows of the upper balcony. The crowd quieted, but the silence was hardly complete. It seethed with angry murmurs.

Radmakker banged his gavel, attempting to reassert some authority. "If you have evidence against the Ravkans—"

The Tidemaker spoke from behind her mask of mist. "The Ravkans have nothing to do with this. The money was transferred to the Shu."

Van Eck blinked, then changed tack. "Well then, Brekker struck some kind of deal with the Shu."

Instantly, the Shu were shouting their denials, but the Tidemaker's voice was louder.

"The false fund was created by Johannus Rietveld and Jan Van Eck."

Van Eck's face went white. "No, that's not right."

"Rietveld is a farmer," stammered Karl Dryden. "I met him myself."

The Tidemaker turned on Dryden. "Both you and Jan Van Eck were seen meeting with Rietveld in the lobby of the Geldrenner Hotel."

"Yes, but it was for a fund, a *jurda* consortium, an honest business venture."

"Radmakker," said Van Eck. "You were there. You met with Rietveld."

Radmakker's nostrils flared. "I know nothing of this Mister Rietveld."

"But I saw you. We both saw you at the Geldrenner—"

"I was there for a presentation on Zemeni oil futures. It was most peculiar, but what of it?"

"No," said Van Eck, shaking his head. "If Rietveld is involved, Brekker is behind it. He must have hired Rietveld to swindle the Council."

"Every one of us put money into that fund at your encouragement," said one of the other councilmen. "Are you saying it's all gone?"

"We knew nothing of this!" countered the Shu ambassador.

"This is Brekker's doing," insisted Van Eck. His smug demeanor was gone, but his composure remained intact. "The boy will stop at nothing to humiliate me and the honest men of this city. He kidnapped my wife, my son." He gestured to Kaz. "Did I imagine you standing on Goedmedbridge in West Stave with Alys?"

"Of course not. I retrieved her from the market square just as you asked," Kaz lied with a smoothness even Matthias found convincing. "She said she was blindfolded and never saw the people who took her."

"Nonsense!" said Van Eck dismissively. "Alys!" he shouted up to the western balcony where Alys was seated, hands folded over her high, pregnant belly. "Tell them!"

Alys shook her head, her eyes wide and baffled. She whispered something to her maid, who called down, "Her captors wore masks and she was blindfolded until she reached the square."

Van Eck released a huff of frustration. "Well, my guards certainly saw him with Alys."

"Men in your employ?" said Radmakker skeptically.

"Brekker was the one who set up the meeting at the bridge!" said Van Eck. "He left a note, at the lake house."

"Ah," said Radmakker in relief. "Can you produce it?"

"Yes! But . . . it wasn't signed."

"Then how do you know it was Kaz Brekker who sent the note?"

"He left a tie pin—"

"His tie pin?"

"No, *my* tie pin, but—"

"So you have no proof at all that Kaz Brekker kidnapped your wife." Radmakker's patience was at an end. "Is the business with your missing son as flimsy? The whole city has been searching for him, rewards have been offered. I pray your evidence is stronger on that account."

"My son—"

"I'm right here, Father."

Every eye in the room turned to the archway by the stage. Wylan leaned against the wall. His face was bloodied and he looked barely able to stand.

"Ghezen's hand," complained Van Eck beneath his breath. "Can no one do their jobs?"

"Were you relying on Pekka Rollins' men?" Kaz mused in a low rasp.

"I—"

"And are you sure they *were* Pekka's men? If you're not from the Barrel, you might find it hard to tell lions from crows. One animal is the same as the next."

Matthias couldn't help the surge of satisfaction he felt as he saw realization strike Van Eck. Kaz had known there was no way to get Wylan into the church without Van Eck or the Dime Lions finding out. So he'd staged a kidnapping. Two of the Dregs, Anika and Keeg, with their armbands and fake tattoos, had simply strolled up to the *stadwatch* with their captive and told the men to fetch Van Eck. When Van Eck arrived in the chapel, what did he see? His son held captive by two gang members bearing the insignia of Pekka's Dime Lions. Matthias hadn't thought they'd rough Wylan up quite so badly, though. Maybe he should have pretended to break sooner.

"Help him!" Radmakker shouted to a *stadwatch* officer. "Can't you see the boy is hurt?"

The officer went to Wylan's side and helped him limp to a chair as the medik hurried forward to attend him.

"Wylan Van Eck?" said Radmakker. Wylan nodded. "The boy we've been tearing apart the city searching for?"

"I got free as soon as I could."

"From Brekker?"

"From Rollins."

"Pekka Rollins took you captive?"

"Yes," said Wylan. "Weeks ago."

"Stop your lies," hissed Van Eck. "Tell them what you told me. Tell them about the Ravkans."

Wylan lifted his head wearily. "I'll say whatever you want, Father. Just don't let them hurt me anymore."

A gasp went up from the crowd. The members of the Merchant Council were looking at Van Eck with open disgust.

Matthias had to stifle a snort. "Has Nina been giving him lessons?" he whispered.

"Maybe he's a natural," said Kaz.

"Brekker is the criminal," said Van Eck. "Brekker is behind this! You all saw him at my house the other night. He broke into my office."

"That's true!" said Karl Dryden eagerly.

"Of course we were there," said Kaz. "Van Eck invited us there to broker a deal for Kuwei Yul-Bo's indenture. He told us we'd be meeting with the Merchant Council. Pekka Rollins was waiting to ambush us instead."

"You're saying he violated a good faith negotiation?" said one of the councilmen. "That seems unlikely."

"But we all saw Kuwei Yul-Bo there too," said another, "though we did not know who he was at the time."

"I've seen the poster offering a reward for a Shu boy matching Kuwei's appearance," Kaz said. "Who provided his description?"

"Well . . ." The merchant hesitated, and Matthias could see suspicion warring with his reluctance to believe the charges. He turned to Van Eck, and his voice was almost hopeful when he said, "Surely, you didn't know the Shu boy you described was Kuwei Yul-Bo?"

Now Karl Dryden was shaking his head, less in denial than disbelief. "It was also Van Eck who pushed us to join Rietveld's fund."

"You were just as eager," Van Eck protested.

"I wanted to investigate the secret buyer purchasing *jurda* farms in Novyi Zem. You said—" Dryden broke off, eyes wide, mouth hanging open. "It was you! You were the secret buyer!"

"Finally," muttered Kaz.

"You cannot possibly believe I would seek to swindle my own friends and neighbors," Van Eck pleaded. "I invested my own money in that fund! I had as much to lose as the rest of you."

"Not if you made a deal with the Shu," said Dryden.

Radmakker banged his gavel once more. "Jan Van Eck, at the very least, you have squandered the resources of this city in pursuing unfounded accusations. At the worst, you have abused your position as a councilman, attempted to defraud your friends, and violated the integrity of this auction." He shook his head. "The auction has been compromised. It cannot go on until we have determined whether any member of the Council knowingly channeled funds to one of the bidders."

The Shu ambassador began yelling. Radmakker banged his gavel.

Then everything seemed to happen at once. Three Fjerdan *drüskelle* surged toward the stage and the *stadwatch* rushed to block them. The Shu soldiers pushed forward. The Tidemakers raised their hands, and then, over all of it, like the keening cry of a woman in mourning, the plague siren began to wail.

The church went silent. People paused, their heads up, ears attuned to that sound, a sound they had not heard in more than seven years. Even in Hellgate, prisoners told stories of the Queen's Lady Plague, the last great wave of sickness to strike Ketterdam, the quarantines, the sickboats, the dead piling up in the streets faster than the bodymen could collect and burn them.

"What is that?" asked Kuwei.

The corner of Kaz's mouth curled. "That, Kuwei, is the sound that death makes when she comes calling."

A moment later, the siren could not be heard at all over the screaming as people shoved toward the church's double doors. No one even noticed when the first shot was fired.

34

NINA

The wheel spun, gold and green panels whirring so fast they became a single color. It slowed and stopped and whatever number came up must have been a good one, because the people cheered. The floor of the gambling palace was uncomfortably warm, and Nina's scalp itched beneath her wig. It was an unflattering bell shape, and she'd paired it with a dowdy gown. For once, she didn't want to draw attention.

She had passed unnoticed through her first stop on West Stave, and through her second, then she'd crossed over to East Stave, doing her best to move unseen through the crowds. They were thinner due to the blockades, but people would not be kept from their pleasures. She'd made a visit to a gambling palace just a few blocks south of this one, and now her work was almost done. Kaz had chosen the establishments with care. This would be her fourth and final destination.

As she smiled and whooped with the other players, she opened the glass case in her pocket and focused on the black cells within it. She could feel that deep cold radiating from it, that sense of something more, something other that spoke to the power inside her. She hesitated only briefly, recalling too clearly the chill of the morgue, the stink of death. She remembered standing over the dead man's body and focusing on the discolored skin around his mouth.

As she'd once used her power to heal or rend skin, or even place a flush in someone's cheeks, she had concentrated on those decaying cells and funneled a slender sheath of necrotic flesh into the compressed glass case. She'd tucked the case into a black velvet pouch and now, standing in this raucous crowd, watching the happy colors of the wheel spin, she felt its weight—dangling from her wrist by a silver cord.

She leaned in to place a bet. With one hand, she set her chips on the table. With the other, she opened the glass case.

"Wish me luck!" she said to the wheel broker, allowing the open bag to brush against his hand, sending those dying cells up his fingers, letting them multiply over his healthy skin.

When he reached for the wheel, his fingers were black.

"Your hand!" exclaimed a woman. "There's something on it."

He scrubbed his fingers over his embroidered green coat as if it were simply ink or coal dust. Nina flexed her fingers, and the cells crawled up the broker's sleeve to the collar of his shirt, bursting in a black stain over one side of his neck, curling under his jaw to his bottom lip.

Someone screamed, and the players backed away from him as the broker looked around in confusion. Players at the other tables turned from their cards and dice in irritation. The pit boss and his minions were moving toward them, ready to shut down whatever fight or problem was disrupting game play.

Hidden by the crowd, Nina swept her arm through the air and a cluster of the cells jumped to a woman beside the wheel broker wearing expensive-looking pearls. A black starburst appeared on her cheek, an ugly little spider that rippled down her chin and over the column of her throat.

"Olena!" her heavyset companion shouted. "Your face!"

Now the screams were spreading as Olena clawed at her neck,

stumbling forward, searching out a mirror as the other customers scattered before her.

"She touched the broker! It got her too!"

"What got her?"

"Get out of my way!"

"What's happening here?" the pit boss demanded, clapping a hand on the baffled broker's shoulder.

"Help me!" the broker begged, holding up his hands. "There's something wrong."

The pit boss took in the black stains on the broker's face and hands, backing away quickly, but it was too late. The hand that had touched the broker's shoulder turned an ugly purplish black, and now the pit boss was screaming too.

Nina watched the terror take on its own momentum, careening through the floor of the gambling hall like an angry drunk. Players knocked over their chairs, stumbling toward the doors, grabbing for chips even as they ran for their lives. Tables overturned, spilling cards, and dice clattered to the floor. People raced for the doors, shoving one another out of the way. Nina went with them, letting herself be carried by the crowd as they fled the gambling hall and lurched into the street. It had been the same at every one of her stops, the slow bleed of fear that crested so suddenly to full-blown panic. And now, at last, she heard it: the siren. Its undulating wail descended over the Stave, rising and falling, echoing over the rooftops and cobblestones of Ketterdam.

Tourists turned to one another with questions in their eyes, but the locals—the performers and dealers and shopkeepers and gamblers of the city—were instantly transformed. Kaz had told her they would know the sound, that they would heed it like children called home by a stern parent.

Kerch was an island, isolated from its enemies, protected by the seas and its immense navy. But the two things its capital was most vulnerable to were fire and disease. And just as fire leapt easily between the tightly packed rooftops of the city, so plague passed effortlessly from body to body, through the thick crowds and cramped living spaces. Like gossip, no one knew exactly where it began or how it moved so quickly, only that it did, through breath or touch, carried on the air or through the canals. The rich suffered less, able to stay sequestered in their grand houses or gardens, or flee the city entirely. The infected poor were quarantined in makeshift hospitals on barges outside the harbor. The plague could not be stopped with guns or money. It could not be reasoned with or prayed away.

Only the very young in Ketterdam didn't have a clear memory of the Queen's Lady Plague, of the sickboats moving through the canals piloted by bodymen with their long oars. Those who had survived it had lost a child or a parent or a brother or a sister, a friend or a neighbor. They remembered the quarantines, the terror that came with even the most basic human contact.

The laws addressing plague were simple and ironclad: When the siren sounded, all private citizens were to return to their homes. The officers of the *stadwatch* were to assemble at separate stations around the city—in case of infection, this was a means of attempting to keep it from spreading to the entirety of the force. They were dispatched only to stop looters, and those men were given triple pay for the risk of policing the streets. Commerce halted and only the sickboats, bodymen, and mediks had free rein of the city.

I know the one thing this city is more frightened of than the Shu, the Fjerdans, and all the gangs of the Barrel put together. Kaz had gotten it right. The barricades, the blockades, the checks on people's papers, all of it would be abandoned in the face of the plague. Of course, none of these people were properly sick, thought Nina as she sped back through the harbor. The necrotic flesh would not spread beyond what Nina had grafted onto their bodies. They would have to have it removed, but no one would grow ill or die. At worst, they'd endure a few weeks of quarantine.

Nina kept her head lowered, her hood up. Though she had been the cause of it all, and though she knew the plague was pure fiction, she still found her heart racing, carried into a gallop by the hysteria bubbling up around her. People were crying, shoving and shouting, arguing over space on the browboats. It was chaos. Chaos of her making.

I did this, she thought wonderingly. *I commanded those corpses, those bits of bone, those dying cells.* What did that make her? If any Grisha had ever had such a power, she'd never heard of it. What would the other Grisha think of her? Her fellow Corporalki, the Heartrenders and Healers? *We are tied to the power of creation itself, the making at the heart of the world.* Maybe she should feel ashamed, maybe even frightened. But she hadn't been made for shame.

Perhaps Djel extinguished one light and lit another. Nina didn't care if it was Djel or the Saints or a brigade of fire-breathing kittens; as she hurried east, she realized that, for the first time in ages, she felt strong. Her breath came easy, the ache in her muscles had dimmed. She was ravenous. The craving for *parem* felt distant, like a memory of real hunger.

Nina had grieved for her loss of power, for the connection she'd felt to the living world. She'd resented this shadow gift. It had seemed like a sham, a punishment. But just as surely as life connected everything, so did death. It was that endless, fast-running river. She'd dipped her fingers into its current, held the eddy of its power in her hand. She was the Queen of Mourning, and in its depths, she would never drown.

35

INEJ

Inej saw the snap of Dunyasha's hand and heard a sound like a wingbeat, then felt something bounce off her shoulder. She caught the silver star before it could fall to the roof. Inej had come prepared this time. Jesper had helped her sew some of the padding from one of the hotel suite's mattresses into her tunic and vest. Years on the farm darning shirts and socks had made him surprisingly handy with a needle, and she was not going to play pincushion for the White Blade again.

Inej leapt forward, speeding toward her opponent, sure-footed on this roof she'd spent so very many hours on. She hurled the star back at Dunyasha. The girl dodged it easily.

"My own blades would not betray me so," she chided, as if scolding a small child.

But Inej hadn't needed to hit her, merely distract her. She flicked her hand as if she was throwing another blade, and as Dunyasha followed the movement, Inej rebounded off the metal spine to her right, letting the ricochet carry her past her opponent. She crouched low, knives in hand, and slashed open the mercenary's calf.

Inej was up again in moments, bouncing backward over one of the scrollwork spines of the church, keeping her eyes on Dunyasha. But the girl just laughed.

"Your spirit brings me pleasure, Wraith. I can't remember the last time anyone drew first blood on me."

Dunyasha leapt onto the scrollwork spine, and now they faced each other, both with blades at the ready. The mercenary lunged deeply, slashing out, but this time, Inej did not let herself follow the instincts she had fought so hard to learn on the streets of Ketterdam. Instead, she responded as an acrobat would. When the swing was coming at you, you didn't try to avoid it; you went to meet it.

Inej ducked close into Dunyasha's reach, as if they were partners in a dance, using the motion of her opponent's attack to knock her off balance. Again Inej struck out with her blade, slicing open the girl's other calf.

This time Dunyasha hissed.

Better than a laugh, thought Inej.

The mercenary whirled, a compact movement, spinning on her toes like a dagger on its point. If she felt any pain, she did not show it. Her hands held two curved blades now, moving in sinuous rhythm as she stalked Inej along the metal spine.

Inej knew she could not move into these blades. *So break the rhythm*, she told herself. She let Dunyasha pursue her, giving up ground, skittering backward along the spine until she saw the shadow of a tall finial behind her. She feinted right, encouraging her opponent to lunge forward. Instead of checking the feint and keeping her balance, Inej continued to let herself fall to the right. In the same movement, she sheathed her blades and seized hold of the finial with one hand, swinging her body around to the other side. Now the finial was between them. Dunyasha grunted in frustration as her blades clanged against metal.

Inej leapt from scroll to scroll, racing over the roof to the thickest of the metal spines, following it up the humped back of the cathedral. It was like walking on the fin of some great sea creature.

Dunyasha followed and Inej had to respect that her movements were just as smooth and graceful with two bleeding calves. "Are you going to run all the way back to the caravan, Wraith? You know it's only a matter of time before this ends and justice is done."

"Justice?"

"You are a murderer and a thief. I was chosen to rid this world of people like you. A criminal may pay my wages, but I have never taken an innocent life."

That word sounded a discordant note inside Inej. Was she innocent? She regretted the lives she'd taken, but she would take them again to save her own life, the lives of her friends. She'd stolen. She'd helped Kaz blackmail good men and bad. Could she say the choices she'd made were the only choices put before her?

Dunyasha approached, the flame of her hair bright against the blue sky, her skin nearly the same ivory as the fine clothes she wore. Somewhere far below their feet, the auction continued in the cathedral, its participants unaware of the battle being waged above. Here, the sun shone bright as a freshly minted coin, wind rushed over the spines and spires of the rooftop in a low moan. *Innocence.* Innocence was a luxury, and Inej did not believe her Saints demanded it.

She drew her knives once more. *Sankt Vladimir, Sankta Alina, protect me.*

"They're charming," Dunyasha said, and pulled two long, straight blades from the sheaths at her waist. "I will give my new knife a handle from your shinbone. It will be your honor to serve me in death."

"I will never serve you," said Inej.

Dunyasha lunged.

Inej stayed close, using every opportunity to keep inside the mercenary's guard and deny her the advantage of her longer reach. She was stronger than she'd been when they'd faced each other on the wire, well rested, well fed. But she was still a girl trained on the streets, not in the towers of some Shu monastery.

Inej's first mistake was a slow recoil. She paid for it in a deep slash to her left bicep. It cut through the padding and made it hard to keep a good grip on the blade in her left hand. Her second error was putting too much force into an upward jab. She leaned in too far and felt Dunyasha's knife skim her ribs. A shallow cut that time, but it had been a close thing.

She ignored the pain and focused on her opponent, remembering what Kaz had told her. *Find her tells. Everyone has them.* But Dunyasha's movements seemed unpredictable. She was equally comfortable with her left and right hands, she favored neither foot, and waited until the last moment to strike, giving no early indication of her intent. She was extraordinary.

"Growing weary, Wraith?"

Inej said nothing, conserving her energy. Though Dunyasha's breathing seemed clear and even, Inej could feel herself dragging slightly. It wasn't much, but it was enough to give the mercenary the advantage. Then she saw it—the slightest hitch of Dunyasha's chest, followed by a lunge. A hitch, then another lunge. The tell was in her breathing. She took in a deep breath before an attack.

There. Inej dodged left, struck quickly, a rapid jab of her blade to Dunyasha's side. *There.* Inej attacked again, and blood flowered on Dunyasha's arm.

Inej drew back, waited as the girl advanced. The mercenary liked to hide her direct assaults with other movement, the whirl of her blades, an unnecessary flourish. It made her hard to read, but *there.* The quick burst of breath. Inej sank low and swept her left leg wide, knocking the mercenary off balance. This was her chance. Inej shot to her feet, using her upward momentum and Dunyasha's descent to shove her blade under the leather guard protecting the girl's sternum.

Inej felt blood on her hand as she wrenched the knife free and Dunyasha released a shocked grunt. The girl stared at her now, clutching her chest with one hand. Her eyes narrowed. There was still no fear there, only a hard, bright resentment, as if Inej had ruined an important party.

"The blood you spill is the blood of kings," seethed Dunyasha. "You are not fit for such a gift."

Inej almost felt sorry for her. Dunyasha really believed she was the Lantsov heir, and maybe she was. But wasn't that what every girl dreamed? That she'd wake and find herself a princess? Or blessed with magical powers and a grand destiny? Maybe there were people who lived those lives. Maybe this girl was one of them. *But what about the rest of us?* What about the nobodies and the nothings, the invisible girls? *We learn to hold our heads as if we wear crowns. We learn to wring magic from the ordinary.* That was how you survived when you weren't chosen, when there was no royal blood in your veins. When the world owed you nothing, you demanded something of it anyway.

Inej raised a brow and slowly wiped the blood of kings on her trousers.

Dunyasha snarled and launched herself at Inej, slashing and jabbing with one arm, the other pressed to her wound, trying to stanch the bleeding. She'd obviously been trained to fight with just one hand. *But she's never had to fight with an injury,* Inej realized. *Maybe the monks skipped that lesson.* And now that she was wounded, her tell was even more obvious.

They had neared the tip of the church's main spine. The scrollwork was loose in places here, and Inej adjusted her footing accordingly, dodging Dunyasha's onslaught easily now, bobbing right and left, taking small victories, a cut here, a jab there. It was a war of attrition, and the mercenary was losing blood quickly.

"You're better than I thought," Dunyasha panted, surprising Inej with the admission. Her eyes were dull with pain; the hand at her sternum was slick and red. Still, her posture was erect, her balance steady as they stood mere feet from each other, perched on the high metal spine.

"Thank you," Inej said. The words felt false in her mouth.

"There is no shame in meeting a worthy opponent. It means there is more to learn, a welcome reminder to pursue humility." The girl lowered her head, sheathed her knife. She placed a fist over her heart in salute.

Inej waited, guard up. Could the girl mean it? This wasn't the way you ended a fight in the Barrel, but the mercenary clearly followed her own code. Inej did not want to be forced to kill her, no matter how soulless she seemed.

"I have learned humility," Dunyasha said, head bowed. "And now you will learn that some are meant to serve. And some are meant to rule."

Dunyasha's face snapped up. She unfurled her palm and released a sharp gust of air.

Inej saw a cloud of red dust and recoiled from it, but it was too late. Her eyes were burning. What was it? It didn't matter. She was blind. She heard the sound of a blade being drawn and felt the slash of a knife. She bobbled backward along the spine, fighting to keep her footing.

Tears streamed down her face as she tried to wipe the dust from her eyes. Dunyasha was nothing but a blurry shape in front of her. Inej held her blade straight out, trying to create distance between them, and felt the mercenary's knife cut across her forearm. The blade slid from Inej's fingers and clattered to the rooftop. *Sankta Alina, protect me.*

But perhaps the Saints had chosen Dunyasha as their vessel. Despite Inej's prayers and penance, maybe judgment had come at last.

I am not sorry, she realized. She had chosen to live freely as a killer rather than die quietly as a slave, and she could not regret that. She would go to her Saints with a ready spirit and hope they would receive her.

The next slice cut across her knuckles. Inej took another step backward, but she knew she was running out of room. Dunyasha was going to drive her right over the edge.

"I told you, Wraith. I am fearless. My blood flows with the strength of every queen and conqueror who came before me."

Inej's foot caught the edge of one of the metal scrolls, and then she understood. She didn't have her opponent's training or education or fine white clothes. She would never be as ruthless and she could not wish to be. But she knew this city inside out. It was the source of her suffering and the proving ground for her strength. Like it or not, Ketterdam— brutal, dirty, hopeless Ketterdam—had become her home. And she would defend it. She knew its rooftops the way she knew the squeaky stairs of the Slat, the way she knew the cobblestones and alleys of the Stave. She knew every inch of this city like a map of her heart.

"The girl who knows no fear," Inej panted as the mercenary's shape wobbled before her.

Dunyasha bowed. "Goodbye, Wraith."

"Then learn fear now before you die." Inej stepped aside, balancing on one foot as Dunyasha's boot came down on the loose piece of scrollwork.

If the mercenary had not been bleeding, she might have taken better heed of the terrain. If she had not been so eager, she might have righted herself.

Instead, she slipped, tipped forward. Inej saw Dunyasha through the blur of her tears. She hung for a moment, silhouetted against the sky, toes seeking purchase, arms outstretched with nothing to grasp, a dancer poised to leap, eyes wide and mouth open in surprise. Even now, in this last moment, she looked like a girl from a story, destined for greatness. She was a queen without mercy, a figure carved in ivory and amber.

Dunyasha fell silently, disciplined to the last.

Inej peered cautiously over the side of the roof. Far below, people were screaming. The mercenary's body lay like a white blossom in a spreading field of red.

"May you make more than misery in your next life," Inej murmured.

She needed to move. The siren still hadn't sounded, but Inej knew she was late. Jesper would be waiting. She sprinted across the cathedral's rooftop, back over Ghezen's thumb to the chapel. She grabbed the climbing line and Jesper's rifle from where she'd lodged it between two pieces of scrollwork. As she scaled the dome and ducked her head into the orange chapel, she could only pray she was not too late. But Jesper was nowhere to be found.

Inej craned her neck, searching the empty chapel.

She needed to locate Jesper. Kuwei Yul-Bo had to die tonight.

36
JESPER

The Council of Tides had arrived in all their splendor, and Jesper couldn't help but be reminded of the Komedie Brute. What was this whole thing but a play Kaz had staged with that poor sucker Kuwei as the star?

Jesper thought of Wylan, who might finally see justice for his mother, of his own father waiting in the bakery. He was sorry for the fight they'd had. Though Inej had said they'd both be glad to know where they stood, Jesper wasn't so sure. He loved an all-out brawl, but exchanging harsh words with his father had left a lump in his gut like bad porridge. They'd been *not* talking about things for so long that actually speaking the truth felt like it had broken some kind of spell—not a curse, but good magic, the kind that kept everyone safe, that might preserve a kingdom under glass. Until an idiot like him came along and used that pretty curio for target practice.

As soon as the Tides were moving up the aisle, Jesper stepped away from the Zemeni delegation and headed toward the church's thumb. He kept his movements slow and his back to the guards who lined the walls, pretending he was trying to get a better view of the excitement.

When he reached the arch that marked the entrance to the thumb nave, he directed his steps toward the cathedral's main doors as if to exit.

"Step back, please," said one of the *stadwatch* grunts, keeping polite for the foreign visitor even as he stretched his neck to see what was happening with the Council of Tides. "The doors must be kept clear."

"I am not feeling well," Jesper said, clutching his stomach, laying on a bit of a Zemeni accent. "I pray you let me pass."

"Afraid not, sir." *Sir!* Such civility for anyone who wasn't a Barrel rat.

"You don't understand," Jesper said. "I must relieve myself *urgently*. I had dinner last night at a restaurant . . . Sten's Stockpot?"

The grunt winced. "Why would you go there?"

"It was in one of the guidebooks." In fact, it was one of the worst restaurants in Ketterdam, but also one of the cheapest. Since it was open at all hours and so affordable, Sten's was one of the few things Barrel thugs and *stadwatch* officers had in common. Every other week, somebody reported some nasty trouble with his gut thanks to Sten and his Saintsforsaken stockpot.

The grunt shook his head and signaled to the *stadwatch* guards at the arch. One of them trotted over.

"This poor bastard went to Sten's. If I let him out the front, the captain's bound to see him. Take him out through the chapel?"

"Why the hell would you eat at Sten's?" the other guard asked.

"My boss doesn't pay me well," said Jesper.

"Sounds familiar," the guard replied, and waved him toward the arch.

Sympathy, camaraderie. *I'm going to pretend to be a tourist more often*, Jesper thought. *I can forgo a few nice waistcoats if the grunts go this easy on me.*

As they passed beneath the arch, Jesper noted the spiral staircase built into it. It led to the upper arcade, and from there he'd have a clear view of the stage. They'd promised not to let Kuwei walk into a disaster on his own, and even if the kid was a troublemaker, Jesper wasn't going to let him down.

Discreetly, Jesper consulted his watch as they made their way toward the chapels at the end of the thumb. At four bells, Inej would be waiting atop the orange chapel's dome to lower down his rifle.

"Oh," Jesper groaned, hoping the guard would pick up his pace. "I'm not sure I'm going to make it."

The guard made a small sound of disgust and lengthened his strides. "What did you order, buddy?"

"The special."

"*Never* order the special. They just reheat whatever they had left over from the day before." They arrived at the chapel and the guard said, "I'll let you through this door. There's a coffeehouse across the way."

"Thanks," said Jesper, and looped his arm around the guard's neck, applying pressure until his body went limp. Jesper slipped the leather strips from around his wrists, secured the guard's hands behind his back, and stuffed the kerchief from his neck into the guard's mouth. Then he rolled the body behind the altar. "Sleep well," Jesper said. He felt bad for the guy. Not bad enough to wake him up and untie him, but still.

He heard a boom from the cathedral and glanced down the length of the nave. Because the thumb of the church was built at a slightly higher level than the cathedral, all he could see were the tops of the heads of the audience's back rows, but it sounded like the Tides were making quite a ruckus. Jesper checked his watch once more and headed up the stairs.

A hand seized hold of his collar and hurled him backward.

He hit the floor of the chapel hard, the wind knocked completely out of him. His attacker stood at the base of the stairs, looking down at him with golden eyes.

His clothes were different from when Jesper had seen him exit the House of the White Rose on West Stave. Now the Kherguud soldier wore an olive drab uniform over his vast shoulders. His buttons gleamed and his black hair had been pulled back in a tight tail, revealing a neck as thick as a ham. He looked like what he truly was—a weapon.

"Glad you dressed for the occasion," Jesper gasped, still trying to regain his breath.

The Shu soldier inhaled deeply, nostrils flaring, and smiled.

Jesper scrambled backward. The soldier followed. Jesper cursed himself for not taking the *stadwatch* grunt's gun. The little pistol was no good for distance shooting, but it would have been better than nothing with a giant staring him down.

He leapt to his feet and sprinted back down the nave. If he could make it to the cathedral . . . he might have some explaining to do. But the Shu soldier wouldn't attack him in the middle of the auction. Would he?

Jesper wasn't going to find out. The soldier slammed into him from behind, dragging him to the ground. The cathedral seemed impossibly far away, the clamor from the auction and the Council of Tides a distant echo bouncing off the high stone walls. *Action and echo*, he thought nonsensically as the soldier flipped him over.

Jesper wriggled like a fish, evading the big man's grip, grateful he was built like a heron on a strict diet. He was on his feet again, but the soldier was fast despite his size. He flung Jesper against the wall and Jesper released a yelp of pain, wondering if he'd broken a rib. *It's good for you. Jogs the liver.*

He couldn't think straight with this oaf manhandling him.

Jesper saw the giant's fist draw back, the gleam of metal on his fingers. *They gave him real brass knuckles*, he realized in horror. *They built them into his hand.*

He ducked left just in time. The soldier's fist struck the wall beside his head with a thunderous crack.

"Slippery," said the soldier in heavily accented Kerch. Again he inhaled deeply.

He caught my scent, Jesper thought. *That day on the Stave. He doesn't care that he might be found by the* stadwatch*, he's been hunting and now he's found his quarry.*

The soldier drew his fist back again. He was going to knock Jesper senseless and then . . . what? Bash down the chapel door and carry him along the street like a sack of grain? Hand him off to one of his winged companions?

At least I'll never be able to disappoint anyone again. They would dose him full of *parem*. Maybe he'd live long enough to make the Shu a new batch of Kherguud.

He dodged right. The soldier's fist pounded another crater into the church wall.

The giant's face contorted in rage. He pinned Jesper by the throat and hauled back to strike a final time.

A thousand thoughts jammed into Jesper's head in a single second: His father's crumpled hat. The gleam of his pearl-handled revolvers. Inej standing straight as an arrow. *I don't want an apology.* Wylan seated at the table in the tomb, gnawing on the edge of his thumb. *Any kind of sugar,* he said, and then . . . *keep it away from sweat, blood, saliva.*

The chemical weevil. Inej had dumped the unused vials on the table in the Ketterdam suite. He'd fidgeted with one when he and his father were arguing. Now Jesper's fingers fumbled in his pants pocket, hand closing over the glass vial.

"*Parem!*" Jesper blurted. It was one of the only Shu words he knew.

The soldier paused, fist in midair. He cocked his head to the side.

Always hit where the mark isn't looking.

Jesper made a show of parting his lips and pretended to shove something between them.

The soldier's eyes widened and his grip loosened as he tried to tear Jesper's hand away. The Kherguud made a sound, maybe a grunt, maybe the beginnings of a protest. It didn't much matter. With his other hand, Jesper smashed the glass vial into the soldier's open mouth.

The giant flinched back as glass shards lodged in his lips and spilled over his chin, blood oozing around them. Jesper rubbed his hand furiously against his shirt, hoping he hadn't nicked his own fingers and let in the weevil. But nothing happened. The soldier didn't seem anything but angry. He growled and seized Jesper's shoulders, lifting him off his feet. *Oh, Saints*, thought Jesper, *maybe he's not going to bother taking me to his pals.* He grabbed at the giant's thick arms, trying to break his hold.

The Kherguud gave Jesper a shake. He coughed, big chest shuddering, and shook Jesper again—a weak, stuttering jiggle.

Then Jesper realized—the soldier wasn't shaking him, the soldier was just shaking.

A low hiss emerged from the giant's mouth, the sound of eggs dropped onto a hot skillet. Pink foam bubbled up from his lips, a froth of blood and saliva that dribbled over his chin. Jesper recoiled.

The soldier moaned. His massive hands released Jesper's shoulders and Jesper edged backward, unable to tear his eyes away from the Kherguud as his body began to convulse, chest heaving. The soldier bent double as a stream of pink bile spewed from his lips, spattering the wall.

"Missed me again," said Jesper, trying not to gag.

The giant tipped sideways and toppled to the floor, still as a fallen oak.

For a moment, Jesper just stared at his enormous body. Then sense returned to him. How much time had he lost? He bolted back toward the chapels at the end of the thumb nave.

Before he reached the door, Inej emerged, hurrying toward him. He'd missed the meet. She wouldn't have come after him unless she thought he was in trouble.

"Jesper, where—"

"Gun," he demanded.

Without another word, she unslung it from her shoulder. He snatched it from her, running back toward the cathedral. If he could just make it up to the arcade.

The siren sounded. Too late. He'd never make it in time. He was going to fail them all. *What good is a shooter without his guns?* What good was Jesper if he couldn't make the shot? They'd be trapped in this city. They'd be jailed, probably executed. Kuwei would be sold to the highest bidder. *Parem* would burn a swath through the world and Grisha would be hunted with even more fervor. In Fjerda, the Wandering Isle, Novyi Zem. The zowa would vanish, pressed into military service, devoured by this curse of a drug.

The siren rose and fell. There were shouts inside the cathedral. People were running for the main doors; soon they'd spill over into the thumb, seeking another way out.

Anyone can shoot, but not everybody can aim. His mother's voice. *We're zowa. You and me.*

Impossible. He couldn't even get eyes on Kuwei from here—and *no one* could shoot around a corner.

But Jesper knew the layout of the cathedral well enough. He knew it was a straight shot up the aisle to where the auction block stood. He could see the second button of Kuwei's shirt in his mind's eye.

Impossible.

A bullet had only one trajectory.

But what if that bullet could be guided?

Not everybody can aim.

"Jesper?" said Inej from behind him. He raised his rifle. It was an ordinary firearm, but he'd converted it himself. There was only a single round inside it—nonlethal, a mixture of wax and rubber. If he missed, someone could be hurt badly. But if he didn't shoot, a lot of people would be hurt. *Hell*, Jesper thought, *maybe if I miss Kuwei, I'll take out one of Van Eck's eyes.*

He'd worked with gunsmiths, made his own ammunition. He knew his guns better than he knew the rules of Makker's Wheel. Jesper focused on the bullet, sensed the smallest parts of it. Maybe he was the same. A bullet in a chamber, spending his whole life waiting for the moment when he would have direction.

Anyone can shoot.

"Inej," he said, "if you have a spare prayer, this would be the time for it."

He fired.

It was as if time slowed—he felt the kick of the rifle, the unstoppable momentum of the bullet. With all his will, he focused on its wax casing and *pulled* to the left, the shot still ringing in his ears. He felt the bullet turn, focused on that button, the second button, a little piece of wood, the threads holding it in place.

It's not a gift. It's a curse. But when it came down to it, Jesper's life had been full of blessings. His father. His mother. Inej. Nina. Matthias leading them across the muddy canal. Kaz—even Kaz, with all his cruelties and failings, had given him a home and a family in the Dregs when Ketterdam might have swallowed him whole. And Wylan. Wylan who had understood before Jesper ever had that the power inside him might be a blessing too.

"What did you just do?" asked Inej.

Maybe nothing. Maybe the impossible. Jesper never could resist long odds.

He shrugged. "The same thing I always do. I took a shot."

37

KAZ

Kaz had been standing next to Kuwei when the bullet struck and had been the first to his side. He heard a smattering of gunfire in the cathedral, most likely panicked *stadwatch* officers with hasty trigger fingers. Kaz knelt over Kuwei's body, hiding his left hand from view, and jabbed a syringe into the Shu boy's arm. There was blood everywhere. Jellen Radmakker had fallen to the stage and was bellowing, "I've been shot!" He had not been shot.

Kaz shouted for the medik. The little bald man stood paralyzed beside the stage where he'd been tending to Wylan, his face horror-stricken. Matthias seized the medik's elbow and dragged him over.

People were still pushing to get out of the church. A brawl had erupted between the Ravkan soldiers and the Fjerdans as Sturmhond, Zoya, and Genya bolted for an exit. The members of the Merchant Council had surrounded Van Eck with a clutch of men from the *stadwatch*. He wasn't going anywhere.

A moment later, Kaz saw Inej and Jesper pushing against the tide of people trying to escape down the center aisle. Kaz let his eyes scan Inej once. She was bloody, and her eyes were red and swollen, but she seemed all right.

"Kuwei—" said Inej.

"We can't help him now," said Kaz.

"Wylan!" Jesper said, taking in the cuts and rapidly forming bruises. "Saints, is all that real?"

"Anika and Keeg did a number on him."

"I wanted it to be believable," said Wylan.

"I admire your commitment to the craft," said Kaz. "Jesper, stay with Wylan. They're going to want to question him."

"I'm fine," said Wylan, though his lip was so swollen it sounded more like, "I'b fibe."

Kaz spared a single nod for Matthias as two *stadwatch* guards lifted Kuwei's body onto a stretcher. Instead of fighting the crowds in the cathedral, they headed for the arch that led to Ghezen's little finger and the exit beyond. Matthias trailed them, pulling the medik along. There could be no questions surrounding Kuwei's survival.

Kaz and Inej followed them into the nave, but Inej paused at the archway. Kaz saw her look once over her shoulder, and when he tracked her gaze he saw that Van Eck, surrounded by furious councilmen, was staring right back at her. He remembered the words she'd spoken to Van Eck on Goedmedbridge, *You will see me once more, but only once.* From the nervous bob of Van Eck's throat, he was remembering too. Inej gave the smallest bow.

They raced up the pinky nave and into the chapel. But the door to the street and the canal beyond was locked. Behind them, the door to the chapel banged shut. Pekka Rollins leaned back against it, surrounded by four of his Dime Lion crew.

"Right on time," said Kaz.

"I suppose you predicted this too, you tricksy bastard?"

"I knew you wouldn't let me walk away this time."

"No," Rollins conceded. "When you came to me looking for money,

I should have gutted you and your friends and saved myself a lot of hassle. That was foolish of me." Rollins began to shrug off his jacket. "I can admit I didn't show you the proper respect, lad, but now you've got it. Congratulations. You're worth the time it's going to take me to beat you to death with that stick of yours." Inej drew her knives. "No, no, little girl," Rollins said warningly. "This is between me and this skivstain upstart."

Kaz nodded to Inej. "He's right. We're long overdue for a chat."

Rollins laughed, unbuttoning his cuffs and rolling up his sleeves. "The time for talk is over, lad. You're young, but I've been brawling since long before you were born."

Kaz didn't move; he kept his hands resting on his cane. "I don't need to fight you, Rollins. I'm going to offer you a trade."

"Ah, a fair exchange in the Church of Barter. You cost me a lot of money and earned me a lot of trouble with your scheming. I don't see what you could possibly have to offer that would satisfy me as much as killing you with my bare hands."

"It's about the Kaelish Prince."

"Three stories of paradise, the finest gambling den on East Stave. You plant a bomb there or something?"

"No, I mean the little Kaelish prince." Rollins stilled. "Fond of sweets, red hair like his father. Doesn't take very good care of his toys."

Kaz reached into his coat and drew out a small crocheted lion. It was a faded yellow, its yarn mane tangled—and stained by dark soil. Kaz let it drop to the floor.

Rollins stared at it. "What is that?" he said, his voice little more than a whisper. Then, as if coming back to himself, he shouted, "*What is that?*"

"You know what it is, Rollins. And weren't you the one who told me how much alike you and Van Eck are? Men of industry, building something to leave behind. Both of you so concerned with your legacy. What good is all that if there's no one to leave it to? So I found myself asking, just who is he building for?"

Rollins clenched his fists, the meaty muscles of his forearms flexing, his jowls quivering. "I will kill you, Brekker. I will kill everything you love."

Now Kaz laughed. "The trick is not to love anything, Rollins. You can threaten me all you like. You can gut me where I stand. But there's no way you'll find your son in time to save him. Shall I have him sent to your door with his throat cut and dressed in his best suit?"

"You trifling piece of Barrel trash," Rollins snarled. "What the hell do you want from me?"

Kaz felt his humor slide away, felt that dark door open inside of him.

"I want you to remember."

"Remember what?"

"Seven years ago you ran a con on two boys from the south. Farm boys too stupid to know any better. You took us in, made us trust you, fed us *hutspot* with your fake wife and your fake daughter. You took our trust and then you took our money and then you took everything." He could see Rollins' mind working. "Can't quite recall? There were so many, weren't there? How many swindles that year? How many unlucky pigeons have you conned in the time since?"

"You have no right—" Pekka said angrily, his chest rising and falling in ragged bursts, his eyes drawn again and again to the toy lion.

"Don't worry. Your boy isn't dead. Yet." Kaz watched Pekka's face closely. "Here, I'll help. You used the name Jakob Hertzoon. You made my brother a runner for you. You operated out of a coffeehouse."

"Across from the park," Pekka said quickly. "The one with the cherry trees."

"That's it."

"It was a long time ago, boy."

"You duped us out of everything. We ended up on the streets and then we died. Both of us in our own way. But only one of us was reborn."

"Is that what this has been about all this time? Why you look at me with murder in those shark's eyes of yours?" Pekka shook his head. "You were two pigeons, and I happened to be the one who plucked you. If it hadn't been me, it would have been someone else."

That dark door opened wider. Kaz wanted to walk through it. He would never be whole. Jordie could never be brought back. But Pekka Rollins could learn the helplessness they'd known.

"Well, it's your bad luck that it was you," he bit out. "Yours and your son's."

"I think you're bluffing."

Kaz smiled. "I buried your son," he crooned, savoring the words. "I buried him alive, six feet beneath the earth in a field of rocky soil. I could hear him crying the whole time, begging for his father. *Papa, Papa.* I've never heard a sweeter sound."

"Kaz—" said Inej, her face pale. This she would not forgive him.

Rollins bulled toward him, grabbed him by his lapels, and slammed him against the chapel wall. Kaz let him. Rollins was sweating like a moist plum, his face livid with desperation and terror. Kaz drank it in. He wanted to remember every moment of this.

"Tell me where he is, Brekker." He smashed Kaz's head against the wall again. *"Tell me."*

"It's a simple trade, Rollins. Just speak my brother's name and your son lives."

"Brekker—"

"Tell me my brother's name," Kaz repeated. "How about another hint? You invited us to a house on Zelverstraat. Your *wife* played the piano. Her name was Margit. There was a silver dog and you called your daughter Saskia. She wore a red ribbon in her braid. You see? I remember. I remember all of it. It's easy."

Rollins released him, paced the chapel, ran his hands through his thinning hair.

"Two boys," he said frantically, searching for the memory. He whirled on Kaz, pointing. "I remember. Two boys from Lij. You had a piddling little fortune. Your brother fancied himself a trader, wanted to be a merch and get rich like every other nub who steps off a browboat in the Barrel."

"That's right. Two more fools for you to cozy. Now tell me his name."

"Kaz and . . ." Rollins clasped his hands on top of his head. Back and forth he crossed the chapel, back and forth, breathing heavily, as if he'd run the length of the city. "Kaz and . . ." He turned back to Kaz. "I can make you rich, Brekker."

"I can make myself rich."

"I can give you the Barrel, influence you've never dreamed of. Whatever you want."

"Bring my brother back from the dead."

"He was a fool and you know it! He was like any other mark, thinking he was smarter than the system, looking to make quick coin. You can't fleece an honest man, Brekker. You know that!"

Greed is my lever. Pekka Rollins had taught him that lesson, and he was right. They'd been fools. Maybe one day Kaz could forgive Jordie for not being the perfect brother he held in his heart. Maybe he could even absolve himself for being the kind of gullible, trusting boy who believed someone might simply want to be kind. But for Rollins there would be no reprieve.

"You tell me where he is, Brekker," Rollins roared in his face. "You tell me where my son is!"

"Say my brother's name. Speak it like they do in the magic shows on East Stave—like an incantation. You want your boy? What right does your son have to his precious, coddled life? How is he different from me or my brother?"

"I don't know your brother's name. I don't know! I don't remember! I was making my name. I was making a little scrub. I thought you two would have a rough week and head home to the country."

"No, you didn't. You never gave us another thought."

"Please, Kaz," whispered Inej. "Don't do this. Don't be this."

Rollins groaned. "I am begging you—"

"Are you?"

"You son of a bitch."

Kaz consulted his watch. "All this time talking while your boy is lost in the dark."

Pekka glanced at his men. He rubbed his hands over his face. Then slowly, his movements heavy, as if he had to fight every muscle of his body to do it, Rollins went to his knees.

Kaz saw the Dime Lions shake their heads. Weakness never earned respect in the Barrel, no matter how good the cause.

"I am begging you, Brekker. He's all I have. Let me go to him. Let me save him."

Kaz looked at Pekka Rollins, Jakob Hertzoon, kneeling before him at last, eyes wet with tears, pain carved into the lines of his flushed face. *Brick by brick.*

It was a start.

"Your son is in the southernmost corner of Tarmakker's Field, two miles west of Appelbroek. I've marked the plot with a black flag. If you leave now, you should get to him in plenty of time."

Pekka lurched to his feet and began calling orders. "Send ahead to the boys to have horses waiting. And get me a medik."

"The plague—"

"The one who's on call for the Emerald Palace. You haul him out of the sick ward yourself if you have to." He jabbed a finger into Kaz's chest. "You'll pay for this, Brekker. You'll pay and keep paying. There will be no end to your suffering."

Kaz met Pekka's gaze. "Suffering is like anything else. Live with it long enough, you learn to like the taste."

"Let's go," said Rollins. He fumbled with the locked door. "Where's the damn key?" One of his men came forward with it, but Kaz noticed the distance he kept from his boss. They'd be telling the story of Pekka Rollins on his knees all over the Barrel tonight, and Rollins must know it too. He loved his son enough to wager the whole of his pride and reputation. Kaz supposed that should count for something. Maybe to someone else it would have.

The door to the street burst open, and a moment later they were gone.

Inej sank down into a squat, pressing her palms to her eyes. "Will he get there in time?"

"For what?"

"To . . ." She stared up at him. He was going to miss that look of surprise. "You didn't do it. You didn't bury him."

"I've never even seen the kid."

"But the lion—"

"It was a guess. Pekka's pride in the Dime Lions is plenty predictable. Kid probably has a thousand lions to play with and a giant wooden lion to ride around on."

"How did you even know he had a child?"

"I figured it out that night at Van Eck's house. Rollins wouldn't stop flapping his gums about the legacy he was building. I knew he had a country house, liked to leave the city. I'd just figured he had a mistress stashed somewhere. But what he said that night made me think again."

"And that he had a son, not a daughter? That was a guess too?"

"An educated one. He named his new gambling hall the Kaelish Prince. Had to be a little red-headed boy. And what kid isn't fond of sweets?"

She shook her head. "What will he find in the field?"

"Nothing at all. No doubt his people will report that his son is safe and sound and doing whatever pampered children do when their fathers are away. But hopefully Pekka will spend a few agonized hours digging in the dirt and wandering in circles before that. The important thing is that he won't be around to back up any of Van Eck's claims and that people will hear he fled the city in a rush—with a medik in tow."

Inej gazed up at him and Kaz could see her completing the puzzle. "The outbreak sites."

"The Kaelish Prince. The Emerald Palace. The Sweet Shop. All businesses owned by Pekka Rollins. They'll be shut down and quarantined for weeks. I wouldn't be surprised if the city closes some of his other holdings as a precaution if they think his staff is spreading disease. It should take him at least a year to recover financially, maybe more if the panic lasts long enough. Of course, if the Council thinks he helped set up the false consortium, they may never grant him a license to operate again."

"Fate has plans for us all," Inej said quietly.

"And sometimes fate needs a little assistance."

Inej frowned. "I thought you and Nina chose four outbreak sites on the Staves."

Kaz straightened his cuffs. "I also had her stop at the Menagerie."

She smiled then, her eyes red, her cheeks scattered with some kind of dust. It was a smile he thought he might die to earn again.

Kaz checked the time. "We should go. This isn't over."

He offered her a gloved hand. Inej heaved a long, shuddering breath, then took it, rising like smoke from a flame. But she did not let go. "You showed mercy, Kaz. You were the better man."

There she went again, seeking decency when there was none to be had. "Inej, I could only kill Pekka's son once." He pushed the door open with his cane. "He can imagine his death a thousand times."

38

MATTHIAS

Matthias jogged along beside Kuwei's lifeless body. Two of the *stadwatch* had hefted the boy onto a stretcher, and they were running toward the Beurscanal with him as the plague sirens wailed. The medik struggled to keep up, his university robes flapping.

When they reached the dock, the medik took Kuwei's wrist in his hand. "This is pointless. He has no pulse. The bullet must have pierced his heart."

Just don't pull that shirt back, Matthias willed silently. Jesper had used a wax-and-rubber bullet that had shattered when it struck the bladder lodged behind Kuwei's shirt button, bursting the bladder's casing and spraying blood and bone matter everywhere. The gore had been collected from a butcher shop, but there was no way the medik could know that. To everyone in the church, it appeared that Kuwei Yul-Bo had been shot in the heart and died immediately.

"Damn it," said the medik. "Where is the emergency boat? And where is the dock steward?"

Matthias suspected he could answer those questions easily enough.

The steward had abandoned his post as soon as he'd heard that plague siren, and even from this narrow vantage point they could see the canal was clogged with watercraft, people shouting and jabbing at the sides of one another's boats with their oars as they tried to evacuate the city before the canals were closed and they were trapped in a plague warren.

"Here, sir!" called a man in a fishing boat. "We can take you to the hospital."

The medik looked wary. "Has anyone aboard shown signs of infection?"

The fisherman gestured to the very pregnant woman lying at the back of the boat, sheltered by an awning. "No, sir. It's just the two of us and we're both healthy, but my wife's about to have a baby. We could use someone like you on board in case we don't make it to the hospital in time."

The medik looked a bit green. "I am not . . . I do not treat female problems. Besides, why aren't you having your baby at home?" he asked suspiciously.

He could care less if Kuwei survives, thought Matthias grimly. *He's looking after his own hide.*

"Don't have a home," said the man. "Just the boat."

The medik looked over his shoulder at the panicked people spilling from the doors of the main cathedral. "All right, let's go. Stay here," he said to Matthias.

"I am his chosen protector," said Matthias. "I go where he goes."

"There isn't room for all of you," said the fisherman.

The *stadwatch* officers exchanged furious whispers, then one of them said, "We'll put him on the boat, but then we have to report to our command station. It's protocol."

Kaz had said the officers wouldn't want to be anywhere near a hospital during a plague outbreak, and he was right. Matthias could hardly blame them.

"But we may need protection," protested the medik.

"For a dead guy?" said the *stadwatch* officer.

"For me! I am a medik traveling during plague time!"

The officer shrugged. "It's protocol."

They hefted the stretcher onto the boat and were gone.

"No sense of duty," huffed the medik.

"He don't look too good," the fisherman said, glancing at Kuwei.

"He's done for," said the medik. "But we must still make the gesture. As our uniformed friends would say, 'It's protocol.'"

The pregnant woman let out a terrible moan and Matthias was pleased to see the medik skitter back against the boat's railing, nearly upending a bucket of squid. Hopefully the squeamish coward would keep well away from Nina and her fake belly. It was a struggle for Matthias to keep his eyes from her when all he wanted was to reassure himself that she was safe. But one glance told him she was better than safe. Her face was aglow, her eyes luminous as emeralds. This was what came of her using her power—no matter what form it took. *Unnatural*, said the old, determined voice. *Beautiful*, said the voice that had spoken the night he'd helped Jesper and Kuwei escape Black Veil. It was newer, less certain, but louder than ever before.

Matthias nodded to the fisherman and Rotty winked back at him, giving a brief tug on the beard of his disguise. He poled the boat rapidly down the canal.

As they approached Zentsbridge, Matthias caught sight of the huge bottleboat parked beneath it. It was wide enough that the hulls scraped as Rotty tried to pass. The bottle man and Rotty broke into a heated argument, and Nina let loose another wail, long and loud enough that Matthias wondered if she was trying to compete with the plague siren.

"Perhaps some deep breathing?" the medik suggested from the railing.

Matthias gave Nina the barest warning glance. They could fake a pregnancy. They couldn't fake an actual birth. At least he didn't think they could. He wouldn't put anything past Kaz at this point.

The medik yelled at Matthias to bring him his bag. Matthias pretended to fuss with it for a moment, extracted the stethoscope, and shoved it beneath a pile of netting—just in case the medik wanted to listen to Nina's belly.

Matthias handed over the bag. "What are you looking for?" he asked, using his bulk to block the medik's view of the bottleboat as Kuwei's body was swapped for the corpse they'd stolen from the morgue the night before. As soon as Sturmhond had gotten Genya out of the church, she'd stopped beneath the bridge to tailor the corpse's face and raise its body temperature. It was imperative that it not look like it had been dead for too long.

"A sedative," said the medik.

"Is that safe for a pregnant woman?"

"For me."

The bottle man shouted a few more coarse words at Rotty—Specht was clearly enjoying himself—and then the fishing boat was past Zentsbridge and sailing along, moving faster now that they'd left the most crowded part of the canal. Matthias could not resist a look back and saw shadows moving behind the stacked wine crates on the bottleboat. There was still more work to be done.

"Where are we going?" said the medik abruptly. "I thought we were headed to the university clinic."

"Waterway was closed," Rotty lied.

"Then take us to Ghezendaal hospital and be quick about it."

That was the idea. The university clinic was closer, but Ghezendaal was smaller, less well staffed, and bound to be overwhelmed by the plague panic, a perfect place to bring a body you didn't want looked at too closely.

They glided to a halt at the hospital's dock and the staff assisted Rotty and Nina out of the boat, then helped lift the stretcher out as well. But as soon as they arrived at the hospital's doors, the nurse on duty there looked at the body on the stretcher and said, "Why would you bring a corpse here?"

"It's protocol!" said the medik. "I am trying to do my duty."

"We're locking down for a plague. We don't have beds to give to dead men. Take him around the back to the wagon bay. The bodymen can come for him tonight."

The staff members disappeared around the corner with the stretcher. By tomorrow a stranger's body would be ashes and the real Kuwei would be free to live his life without constantly looking over his shoulder.

"Well, at least help this woman, she's about to—" The medik looked around but Nina and Rotty had vanished.

"They already went inside," said Matthias.

"But—"

The nurse snapped, "Are you going to stand here all day blocking my doorway or come inside and be of help?"

"I . . . am needed elsewhere," the medik said, ignoring the nurse's disbelieving look. "The rudeness of some people," he sputtered, dusting off his robes as they left the hospital. "I am a scholar of the university."

Matthias bowed deeply. "I thank you for your attempts to save my charge."

"Ah, well, yes. Indeed. I was only doing as my oath demands." The medik looked nervously at the houses and businesses that had already started locking their doors and sealing their shutters. "I really must get to . . . the clinic."

"I'm sure all will be most grateful for your care," Matthias said, certain the medik intended to rush home to his rooms and barricade himself against anyone who so much as sniffled.

"Yes, yes," said the medik. "Good day and good health." He hurried off down the narrow street.

Matthias found himself smiling as he jogged in the opposite direction. He would meet the others back at Zentsbridge, where hopefully Kuwei would soon be revived. He would be with Nina again and maybe, maybe they could begin thinking about a future.

"Matthias Helvar!" said a high, querulous voice.

Matthias turned. A boy stood in the middle of the deserted street. The young *drüskelle* with the ice-white hair who had glared at him so fiercely during the auction. He wore a gray uniform, not the black of a full *drüskelle* officer. Had he followed Matthias from the church? What had he seen?

The boy couldn't have been more than fourteen. The hand he held his pistol in was shaking.

"I charge you with treason," he said, voice breaking, "high treason against Fjerda and your *drüskelle* brothers."

Matthias held up his hands. "I am unarmed."

"You are a traitor to your land and your god."

"We haven't met before."

"You killed my friends. In the raid on the Ice Court."

"I killed no *drüskelle*."

"Your companions did. You're a murderer. You humiliated Commander Brum."

"What's your name?" Matthias asked gently. This boy did not want to hurt anyone.

"It doesn't matter."

"Are you new to the order?"

"Six months," he said, lifting his chin.

"I joined when I was even younger than you. I know what it's like there, the thoughts they put in your head. But you don't have to do this."

The boy shook even harder. "I charge you with treason," he repeated.

"I am guilty," said Matthias. "I've done terrible things. And if you wish it, I will walk back to the church with you right now. I will face your friends and commanding officers and we can see what justice may come."

"You're lying. You even let them kill that Shu boy you were supposed to protect. You're a traitor and a coward." Good, he believed Kuwei was dead.

"I will go with you. You have my word. And you have the gun. There's nothing to fear from me."

Matthias took a step forward.

"Stay where you are!"

"Do not be afraid. Fear is how they control you." *We'll find a way to change their minds.* The boy had only been with the order for six months. He could be reached. "There's so much in the world you don't have to be afraid of, if you would only open your eyes."

"I told you to stay where you are."

"You don't want to hurt me. I know. I was like you once."

"I'm nothing like you," said the boy, his blue eyes blazing. Matthias saw the anger there, the rage. He knew it so well. But he was still surprised when he heard the shot.

39
NINA

Nina pulled off her gown and the heavy rubber belly she had strapped over her tunic while Rotty rid himself of his beard and coat. They tied everything in a bundle and Nina tossed it overboard as they climbed into the bottleboat moored beneath Zentsbridge.

"Good riddance," she said as it sank into the water.

"So little maternal sentiment," Kaz said, emerging from behind the wine crates.

"Where's Inej?"

"I'm fine," said Inej from behind him. "But Kuwei—"

"You're bleeding again," Nina observed as she slid behind the high stacks of crates to join them. There was little traffic on the canal now, but it didn't do to take chances. "And what happened to your eyes?"

"I'd tell you to ask the White Blade, but . . ." Inej shrugged.

"I hope she suffered."

"Nina."

"What? We can't both be merciful and serene."

They were in a pocket of shadowy space between the crates of wine and the stone arch of the bridge. The stretcher with Kuwei's body on it lay atop a makeshift table of crates. Genya was injecting something into the Shu boy's arm as Zoya and the man Nina assumed was Sturmhond looked on.

"How is he?" Nina asked.

"If he has a pulse, I can't find it," said Genya. "The poison did its work."

Maybe too well. Genya had said the poison would lower his pulse and breathing to such an extent that it would mimic death. But the act was uncomfortably convincing. Some part of Nina knew the world might be safer if Kuwei died, but she also knew that if someone else unlocked the secret of *parem*, he was Ravka's best chance at an antidote. They'd fought to free him from the Ice Court. They'd schemed and connived and struggled so that he could be safe to pursue his work among the Grisha. Kuwei was hope.

And he was a boy who deserved a chance to live without a target on his back.

"The antidote?" Nina asked, looking at the syringe in Genya's hand.

"This is the second dose she's injected," said Kaz.

They all watched as Genya checked his pulse, his breathing. She shook her head.

"Zoya," said Sturmhond. His voice had the ring of command.

Zoya sighed and pushed up her sleeves. "Unbutton his shirt."

"What are you doing?" Kaz asked as Genya undid Kuwei's remaining buttons. His chest was narrow, his ribs visible, all of it spattered with the pig's blood they'd encased in the wax bladder.

"I'm either going to wake up his heart or cook him from the inside out," said Zoya. "Stand back."

They did their best to obey in the cramped space. "What exactly does she mean by that?" Kaz asked Nina.

"I'm not sure," Nina admitted. Zoya had her hands out and her eyes closed. The air felt suddenly cool and moist.

Inej inhaled deeply. "It smells like a storm."

Zoya opened her eyes and brought her hands together as if in prayer, rubbing her palms against each other briskly.

Nina felt the pressure drop, tasted metal on her tongue. "I think . . . I think she's summoning lightning."

"Is that safe?" asked Inej.

"Not remotely," said Sturmhond.

"Has she at least done it before?" said Kaz.

"For this purpose?" asked Sturmhond. "I've seen her do it twice. It worked splendidly. Once." His voice was oddly familiar, and Nina had the sense they'd met before.

"Ready?" Zoya asked.

Genya shoved a thickly folded piece of fabric between Kuwei's teeth and stepped back. With a shudder, Nina realized it was to keep him from biting his tongue.

"I really hope she gets this right," murmured Nina.

"Not as much as Kuwei does," said Kaz.

"It's tricky," said Sturmhond. "Lightning doesn't like a master. Zoya's putting her own life at risk too."

"She didn't strike me as the type," Kaz said.

"You'd be surprised," Nina and Sturmhond replied in unison. Again, Nina had the eerie sensation that she knew him.

She saw that Rotty had squeezed his eyes shut, unable to watch. Inej's lips were moving in what Nina knew must be a prayer.

A faint blue glow crackled between Zoya's palms. She took a deep breath and slapped them down on Kuwei's chest.

Kuwei's back bowed, his whole body arcing so sharply Nina thought his spine might snap. Then he slammed back down against the stretcher. His eyes didn't open. His chest remained motionless.

Genya checked his pulse. "Nothing."

Zoya scowled and clapped her palms together again, a light sweat breaking out over her perfect brow. "Are we absolutely sure we want him to live?" she huffed. No one answered, but she kept rubbing her hands together, that crackle building once more.

"What is this even supposed to do?" said Inej.

"Shock his heart into returning to its rhythm," said Genya. "And the heat should help denature the poison."

"Or kill him," said Kaz.

"Or kill him," conceded Genya.

"Now," said Zoya, her voice determined. Nina wondered if she was anxious for Kuwei to survive or if she just hated to fail at anything.

Zoya jolted her open palms against Kuwei's chest. His body bent like a green branch caught by an unforgiving wind, and once more collapsed against the stretcher.

Kuwei gasped, eyes flying open. He struggled to sit up, trying to spit out the wad of fabric.

"Thank the Saints," said Nina.

"Thank *me*," said Zoya.

Genya moved to restrain him, and his eyes widened further as panic seized him.

"Shhh," Nina murmured, moving forward. Kuwei knew Genya and Zoya only as members of the Ravkan delegation. They might as well be strangers. "It's all right. You're alive. You're safe."

Inej joined her at his side, removed the fabric from his mouth, smoothed back his hair. "You're safe," she repeated.

"The auction—"

"It's over."

"And the Shu?"

His golden eyes were terrified, and Nina understood just how frightened he had been.

"They saw you die," Nina reassured him. "So did everyone. Representatives from every country saw you get shot in the heart. The medik and hospital staff will testify to your death."

"The body—"

"By tonight, it will be collected by the bodymen," said Kaz. "It's over."

Kuwei flopped back down, threw an arm over his eyes, and burst into tears. Nina patted him gently. "I know what you mean, kid."

Zoya placed her hands on her hips. "Is anyone going to thank me—or Genya, for that matter—for this little miracle?"

"Thank you for nearly killing and then reviving the most valuable hostage in the world so you could use him for your own gain," Kaz said. "Now you need to go. The streets are almost empty, and you need to get to the manufacturing district."

Zoya's beautiful blue eyes slitted. "Show your face in Ravka, Brekker. We'll teach you some manners."

"I'll keep that in mind. When they burn me on the Reaper's Barge, I definitely want to be remembered as *polite*."

"Come with us now, Nina," urged Genya.

Nina shook her head. "The job isn't over, and Kuwei is too weak to make the walk anyway."

Zoya pursed her lips. "Just don't forget where your loyalties lie." She climbed out of the bottleboat, followed by Genya and Sturmhond.

The privateer turned back to the bottleboat and gazed down at Nina. His eyes were an odd color, and his features didn't quite seem to fit together properly. "In case you're tempted not to return, I want you to know you and your Fjerdan are welcome in Ravka. We can't estimate how much *parem* the Shu may still have or how many of those Kherguud soldiers they've made. The Second Army needs your gifts."

Nina hesitated. "I'm not . . . I'm not what I was."

"You're a soldier," said Zoya. "You're Grisha. And we'd be lucky to have you."

Nina's jaw dropped. That almost sounded like praise.

"Ravka is grateful for your service," Sturmhond said as they turned to go. "And so is the crown." He waved once. In the late afternoon light,

with the sun behind him, he looked less like a privateer and more like . . .
But that was just silly.

"I need to get back to the church," said Kaz. "I don't know what the
Council is going to do with Wylan."

"Go," said Nina. "We'll wait here for Matthias."

"Stay alert," Kaz said. "Keep him out of sight until nightfall. Then you
know where to go."

Kaz climbed from the boat and vanished back in the direction of the
Church of Barter.

Nina didn't think it would be safe to offer Kuwei wine, so she offered
him some water and encouraged him to rest.

"I'm afraid to close my eyes," he said.

Nina strained to see over the lip of the canal and down the street.
"What's taking Matthias so long? Do you think that medik gave him
trouble?" But then she saw him striding toward her across the empty
square. He raised his hand in greeting.

She leapt from the boat and ran to him, throwing herself into his
arms.

"*Drüsje*," he said against her hair. "You're all right."

"Of course I'm all right. You're the one who's late."

"I thought I wouldn't be able to find you in the storm."

Nina pulled back. "Did you stop to get drunk on the way here?"

He cupped her cheek with his hand. "No," he said, and then he
kissed her.

"Matthias!"

"Did I do it wrong?"

"No, you did it splendidly. But I'm the one who always kisses *you*
first."

"We should change that," he said, and then he slumped against her.

"Matthias?"

"It's nothing. I needed to see you again."

"Matthias—oh, Saints." The coat he'd been holding fell away and she saw the bullet wound in his stomach. His shirt was soaked with blood. "Help!" she screamed. "Somebody help!" But the streets were empty. The doors barred. The windows shut up. "Inej!" she cried.

He was too heavy. They sank to the cobblestones and Nina cradled his head gently in her lap. Inej was sprinting toward them.

"What happened?" she asked.

"He's been shot. Oh, Saints, Matthias, who did this?" They had so many enemies.

"It doesn't matter," he said. His breath sounded strange and thready. "All I wanted was to see you once more. Tell you—"

"Get Kuwei," Nina said to Inej. "Or Kaz. He has *parem*. You have to get it for me. I can save him. I can fix him." But was that even true? If she used the drug, would her power return to what it had been? She could try. She had to try.

Matthias grabbed her hand with surprising strength. It was wet with his own blood. "No, Nina."

"I can fight it a second time. I can heal you and then I can fight it."

"It's not worth the risk."

"It's worth every risk," she said. "Matthias—"

"I need you to save the others."

"What others?" she asked desperately.

"The other *drüskelle*. Swear to me you'll at least try to help them, to make them see."

"We'll go together, Matthias. We'll be spies. Genya will tailor us and we'll go to Fjerda together. I'll wear all the ugly knitted vests you want."

"Go home to Ravka, Nina. Be free, as you were meant to be. Be a warrior, as you always have been. Just save some mercy for my people. There has to be a Fjerda worth saving. Promise me."

"I promise." The words were more sob than sound.

"I have been made to protect you. Even in death, I will find a way."

He clasped her hand tighter. "Bury me so I can go to Djel. Bury me so I can take root and follow the water north."

"I promise, Matthias. I'll take you home."

"Nina," he said, pressing her hand to his heart. "I am already home."

The light vanished from his eyes. His chest stilled beneath her hands.

Nina screamed, a howl that tore from the black space where her heart had beat only moments before. She searched for his pulse, for the light and force that had been Matthias. *If I had my power. If I'd never taken* parem. *If I had* parem. She felt the river around her, the black waters of grief. She reached into the cold.

Matthias' chest rose, his body shook.

"Come back to me," she whispered. "Come back."

She could do this. She could give him a new life, a life born of that deep water. He was no ordinary man. He was Matthias, her brave Fjerdan.

"*Come back,*" she demanded. He breathed. His eyelids fluttered and opened. His eyes shone black.

"Matthias," she whispered. "Speak my name."

"Nina."

His voice, his beautiful voice. It was the same. She clutched his hand, searching for him in that black gaze. But his eyes had been the ice of the north, palest blue, pure. This was all wrong.

Inej was kneeling beside her. "Let him go, Nina."

"I can't."

Inej placed her arm around Nina's shoulder. "Let him go to his god."

"He should be here with me."

Nina touched his cold cheek. There must be a way to take this back, to make this right. How many impossible things had they accomplished together?

"You will meet him again in the next life," said Inej. "But only if you suffer this now."

They were twin souls, soldiers destined to fight for different sides, to find each other and lose each other too quickly. She would not keep him here. Not like this.

"In the next life then," she whispered. "Go." She watched his eyes close once more. "*Farvell*," she said in Fjerdan. "May Djel watch over you until I can once more."

40
MATTHIAS

Matthias was dreaming again. Dreaming of her. The storm raged around him, drowning out Nina's voice. And yet his heart was easy. Somehow he knew that she would be safe, she would find shelter from the cold. He was on the ice once more, and somewhere he could hear the wolves howling. But this time, he knew they were welcoming him home.

41

WYLAN

Wylan sat between Alys and Jesper in a pew near the front of the church. The Ravkans, Shu, and Fjerdans had gotten themselves into a tangle of a fistfight that had left several soldiers bruised and bleeding and the Fjerdan ambassador with a dislocated shoulder. There was angry talk of trade sanctions and retribution on all sides. But for now, some semblance of order had been restored. Most of the auction goers had long since fled or been ushered out by the *stadwatch*. The Shu had departed, issuing threats of military action for the death of one of their citizens.

The Fjerdans had apparently marched to the doors of the Stadhall to demand that Matthias Helvar be found and arrested, only to be informed that emergency plague measures prohibited public assembly. They were to return to their embassy immediately or risk being forcibly removed from the streets.

People were bruised and concussed, and Wylan had heard that one woman's hand had been crushed when she'd gotten knocked to the floor during the panicked rush to the cathedral door. But few went to the clinics or hospitals for care. No one wanted to risk exposure to the plague that was spreading through the Barrel. Only the Merchant Council and a few of the *stadwatch* remained near the altar, arguing in hushed tones that occasionally rose to something more like shouting.

Wylan, Jesper, Alys, and her maid were bracketed by *stadwatch*, and Wylan hoped Kaz had been right to insist he remain at the church. He wasn't sure if he felt like the officers were there to protect him or keep him under watch. By the way Jesper kept drumming his fingers on his knees, Wylan suspected he was feeling equally nervous. It didn't help that it hurt every time Wylan breathed or that his head felt like a timpani being savaged by an overenthusiastic percussionist.

He was a mess, there had nearly been a riot, and Ketterdam's reputation was in tatters, and yet Wylan had to smile to himself.

"What are you so happy about?" Jesper asked.

Wylan glanced at Alys and whispered, "We did it. And I know Kaz had his own motives, but I'm pretty sure that we just helped prevent a war." If Ravka had won the auction, the Shu or the Fjerdans would have found some excuse to launch an attack on Ravka to get their hands on Kuwei. Now Kuwei would be safe, and even if someone else eventually developed *parem*, the Ravkans might soon be on their way to developing an antidote.

"Probably," said Jesper, his teeth flashing white. "What's one little international incident among friends?"

"I think Keeg may have broken my nose."

"And after Genya made it so nice and straight."

Wylan hesitated. "You can go if you need to. I know you must be worried about your father."

Jesper glanced at the *stadwatch*. "I'm not sure our new pals would just let me walk out of here. Besides, I don't want anyone following me to him."

And Wylan had heard Kaz tell Jesper to stay.

Alys rubbed a hand over her belly. "I'm hungry," she said, glancing over to where the Merchant Council were still arguing. "When do you think we'll get to go home?"

Wylan and Jesper exchanged a glance.

At that moment, a young man raced up the aisle of the cathedral and handed a sheaf of papers to Jellen Radmakker. They bore the pale green seal of the Gemensbank, and Wylan suspected they would show that all of the Merchant Council's money had been funneled from a false *jurda* fund directly into an account intended for the Shu.

"This is madness!" shouted Van Eck. "You can't possibly believe any of it!"

Wylan stood to get a better look, then sucked in a breath at the sharp clap of pain from his ribs. Jesper put a hand out to steady him. But what Wylan saw near the podium drove all thoughts of pain from his mind: A *stadwatch* officer was clapping shackles on his father, who was thrashing like a fish caught on a line.

"It's Brekker's work," said Van Eck. "He set up the fund. Find the farmer. Find Pekka Rollins. They'll tell you."

"Stop making a spectacle of yourself," Radmakker whispered furiously. "For the sake of your family, show some self-control."

"Self-control? When you have me in chains?"

"Be calm, man. You'll be taken to the Stadhall to await charges. Once you've paid your bail—"

"Bail? I am a member of the Merchant Council. My word—"

"Is worth nothing!" snapped Radmakker, as Karl Dryden bristled in a way that reminded Wylan distinctly of Alys' terrier when he spotted a squirrel. "You should be grateful we don't throw you in Hellgate right now. Seventy million *kruge* of the Council's money has vanished. Kerch has been made a laughingstock. Do you have any idea of the damage you caused today?"

Jesper sighed. "We do all the work and he gets all the credit?"

"What is happening?" Alys asked, reaching for Wylan's hand. "Why is Jan in trouble?"

Wylan felt sorry for her. She was sweet and silly and had never done anything more than marry where her family bid her. If Wylan had the right of it, his father would be brought up on charges of fraud and treason. Knowingly entering into a false contract for the purpose of subverting the market wasn't just illegal, it was considered blasphemy, a blight on the works of Ghezen, and the penalties were harsh. If his father was found guilty, he'd be stripped of his right to own property or hold funds. His entire fortune would pass to Alys and his unborn heir. Wylan wasn't sure Alys was ready for that kind of responsibility.

He gave her hand a squeeze. "It's going to be okay," he said. "I promise." And he meant it. They'd find a good attorney or man of business to help Alys with the estate. If Kaz knew all the swindlers in Ketterdam, then he must know who the honest dealers were too—if for no other reason than to avoid them.

"Will they let Jan come home tonight?" Alys asked, her lower lip wobbling.

"I don't know," he admitted.

"But you'll come back to the house, won't you?"

"I—"

"You stay away from her," Van Eck spat as the *stadwatch* dragged him down the steps from the stage. "Alys, don't listen to him. You're going to need to get Smeet to put up the funds for bail. Go to—"

"I don't think Alys will be able to help with that," said Kaz. He was standing in the aisle, leaning on his crow's head cane.

"Brekker, you wretched little thug. Do you really think this is over?" Van Eck straightened, attempting to reclaim some of his lost dignity. "By this time tomorrow, I'll be out on bail and setting my reputation to rights. There's a way to connect you to the Rietveld fund and I will find it. I swear it."

Wylan felt Jesper stiffen beside him. Colm Fahey was the only connection.

"By all means, swear," said Kaz. "Make a solemn vow. I think we all know what your word is worth. But you may find your resources some-what constrained. The custodian of your estate will be in charge of your funds. I'm not sure how much money Wylan plans to devote to your defense, or your bail, for that matter."

Van Eck laughed bitterly. "I wrote him out of my will as soon as Alys conceived. Wylan will never see a penny of my money."

A murmur of surprise went up from the members of the Merchant Council.

"Are you certain?" Kaz said. "I'm sure Wylan told me you two had reconciled. Of course, that was before all this ugly business."

"My will is perfectly clear. There's a copy of it in—" Van Eck stopped midsentence, and Wylan watched a horrified expression spread over his father's face. "The safe," he whispered.

Understanding struck Wylan bare seconds later. Specht had forged a letter in his father's hand for the ship's captain; why not something else? *Sometimes a proper thief doesn't just take. He leaves something behind.* The night they'd broken into his father's office, Kaz hadn't just tried to steal the seal. He'd replaced Van Eck's will with a forgery. Wylan remembered what Kaz had said: *You do realize we're stealing your money?* He'd meant it.

"There's another copy," said Van Eck. "My attorney—"

"Cornelis Smeet?" said Kaz. "Do you know if he breeds those watch-dogs of his? Funny thing, when you train an animal to obey. Sometimes they get too easy to command. Better to keep them a little wild."

You don't win by running one game. How long had Kaz been planning to hand Wylan his father's empire?

"No," said Van Eck, shaking his head. "No." With surprising strength, he shook off his guards. "You can't give this cretin control of my funds," he shouted, gesturing to Wylan with his shackled hands. "Even if I'd wanted him to inherit, he's incompetent to do so. He can't read, can barely string a basic sentence together on the page. He is an idiot, a soft-minded child."

Wylan registered the horror on the Council members' faces. This was the nightmare he'd had countless times as a child—standing in public, his deficiencies exposed.

"Van Eck!" said Radmakker. "How can you say such a thing about your own blood?"

Van Eck laughed wildly. "This at least I can prove! Give him something to read. Go on, Wylan, show them what a great man of business you will make."

Radmakker laid a hand on his shoulder. "You needn't oblige his ravings, son."

But Wylan cocked his head to one side, an idea forming in his mind. "It's all right, Mister Radmakker," he said. "If it will help us end this tragic business, I will oblige my father. In fact, if you have a Transfer of Authority, I can sign it now and begin assembling funds for my father's defense."

There were murmurs from the stage, and then a file was produced with the indenture documents. Wylan's eyes met Jesper's. Did he understand what Wylan intended?

"These were meant for Kuwei Yul-Bo," said Dryden. "But they haven't been completed. There should be a Transfer of Authority."

He offered the file to Wylan, but Jesper took it and thumbed through.

"*He* must read it!" yelled Van Eck. "Not the other boy!"

"I think your first investment should be a muzzle," murmured Jesper.

He handed Wylan a document. It could have been anything. Wylan saw the words, recognized their shapes, couldn't form their meaning. But he could hear the music in his head, that trick of memory he'd used so often as a child—Jesper's voice reading aloud to him in the entry of Saint Hilde. He saw the pale blue door, smelled the wisteria blooming.

Wylan cleared his throat and pretended to examine the page. "*This document, witnessed in the full sight of Ghezen and in keeping with the honest dealings of men, made binding by the courts of Kerch and its Merchant Council, signifies the transfer of all property, estates, and legal holdings from—*" He paused. "I suppose it will say our names here, *Jan Van Eck to Wylan Van Eck, to be managed by him until Jan Van Eck is once again competent to conduct . . . his own affairs.* Do I really need to continue?"

Van Eck was staring openmouthed at Wylan. The members of the Merchant Council were shaking their heads.

"Certainly not, son," Radmakker said. "You've been through enough, I think." The look he turned on Van Eck now was one of pity. "Take him to the Stadhall. We may need to find him a medik too. Something must have addled his mind, put these mad thoughts in his head."

"It's a trick," said Van Eck. "It's another one of Brekker's tricks." He broke away from his guards and rushed at Wylan, but Jesper stepped in front of him, grabbing him by the shoulders and holding him at bay with straight arms. "You'll destroy everything I've built, everything my father and his father built. You—"

Jesper leaned in and said, quietly enough that no one else could hear, "I can read to him."

"He has a very soothing baritone," added Wylan, and then the guards were hauling his father down the aisle.

"You won't get away with this!" Van Eck screamed. "I know your game now, Brekker. My wits are sharper—"

"You can only sharpen a blade so far," Kaz said as he joined them at the front of the church. "In the end, it comes down to the quality of the metal."

Van Eck was howling. "You don't even know if that's really Wylan! He could be wearing another boy's face! You don't understand—"

The rest of the Merchant Council followed, all looking a bit thunderstruck. "He's come unhinged," said Dryden.

"We should have known he wasn't rational when he allied himself with that miscreant Pekka Rollins."

Wylan handed the Transfer of Authority back to Radmakker. "Maybe it's best that we don't handle this now. I find I'm a bit shaken."

"Of course. We'll see to getting the will from Smeet and making sure all is in order. We can send the appropriate papers to your house."

"My house?"

"Won't you be going home to the Geldstraat?"

"I . . ."

"He will indeed," said Jesper.

"I don't understand," said Alys as her maid patted her hand gently. "Jan has been arrested?"

"Alys," said Kaz. "How would you feel about waiting out all this nasty business in the country? Far away from the threat of plague. Maybe at that nice lake house you mentioned."

Alys' face came alight, but then she hesitated. "Is it wholly proper, do you think? For a wife to abandon her husband at such a time?"

"It's your duty, really," said Kaz. "After all, shouldn't your priority be the baby?"

Jesper nodded sagely. "Good country air, lots of fields for . . . gamboling about. I grew up on a farm. It's why I'm so tall."

Alys frowned. "You're a little too tall."

"It was a really big farm."

"And you could continue your music lessons," said Wylan.

Now Alys' eyes were positively sparkling. "With Mister Bajan?" Her cheeks pinked; she bit her lip. "Perhaps it would be best. For the baby."

42

JESPER

In the gathering evening gloom, they walked to Van Eck's house together, Kaz leaning on his cane, Alys leaning on her maid's arm. The streets were eerily empty. Occasionally, they would see *stadwatch* and Jesper's heart would start to race, wondering if their trouble was going to start all over again. But now that Van Eck and Pekka had been so thoroughly discredited, the *stadwatch* had bigger problems to grapple with, and the outbreaks in the Barrel had given the gangs plenty to occupy them. It seemed the city's citizens, both lawful and unlawful, were seeing to themselves, and were content to leave Jesper and his friends in peace.

But none of that mattered to Jesper. He just needed to know his father was safe. He was tempted to go to the bakery, but he couldn't risk being followed.

It put the itch in him, but for now he could resist it. Maybe using his power had helped. Maybe he was just giddy off the fight. It was too soon to try to untangle it. But tonight at least, he could vow not to do something stupid. He would sit in a room fabricating the color out of a carpet, or take target practice, or have Wylan tie him to a chair if he had to. Jesper wanted to know what happened next. He wanted to be a part of it.

No matter the scandal that had touched the Van Eck name today, the lanterns had still been lit in the windows, and the servants happily opened the door to Alys and young Mister Wylan. As they passed through what looked like the dining room but seemed to be missing a table, Jesper glanced up at the huge hole in the ceiling. He could see straight through to the next floor and some very fancy woodwork.

He shook his head. "You really should be more careful with your things."

Wylan tried to smile, but Jesper could see he was all nerves. He moved from room to room warily, occasionally touching a piece of furniture or a spot on the wall briefly. Wylan was still pretty banged up. They'd sent to the university for a medik, but it might be a long while before anyone was able to come.

When they reached the music room, Wylan finally stopped. He ran a hand over the lid of the pianoforte. "This is the only place in this house I was ever happy."

"Hopefully that can change now."

"I feel like an intruder. Like any minute, my father's going to barge through that door and tell me to get out."

"It will help when the papers are signed. Make it feel more permanent." Jesper grinned. "You were pretty amazing back there, by the way."

"I was terrified. I still am." He looked down at the keys and played a gentle chord. Jesper wondered at how he could have mistaken Kuwei for Wylan. Their hands were completely different, the shape of the fingers, the knuckles. "Jes," Wylan said, "did you mean what you told my father? Will you stay with me? Will you help?"

Jesper leaned back on the pianoforte, resting on his elbows. "Let's see. Live in a luxurious merch mansion, get waited on by servants, spend a little extra time with a budding demolitions expert who plays a mean flute? I guess I can manage it." Jesper's eyes traveled from the top of

Wylan's red-gold curls to the tips of his toes and back again. "But I do charge a pretty steep fee."

Wylan flushed a magnificent shade of pink. "Well, hopefully the medik will be here to fix my ribs soon," he said as he headed back into the parlor.

"Yeah?"

"Yes," said Wylan, glancing briefly over his shoulder, his cheeks now red as cherries. "I'd like to make a down payment."

Jesper released a bark of laughter. He couldn't remember the last time he'd felt this good. And no one was even shooting at him.

The cook laid out a cold supper and Alys retired to her rooms. The rest of them sat together on the steps that led down to the back garden, watching the strange sight of the sun setting over the near-empty Geldcanal, waiting. Only the *stadwatch* boats, the fire brigade, and the occasional medik's boat could be seen gliding along the water, leaving wide, uninterrupted ripples in their wakes. No one ate much. They were all on edge as they waited for night to fall. Had the others made it out safely? Had everything gone as planned? There was still so much to do. Kaz kept perfectly still, but Jesper could sense the tension in him, coiled like a rattler.

Jesper felt the hope in him ebbing away, ground down to nothing by his worry for his father. He explored the house, paced the garden, marveled at the destruction wrought on Van Eck's office. Since when did the sun setting take so long? He could tell himself his father was fine as much as he wanted, but he wouldn't believe it until he saw Colm Fahey's craggy face for himself.

At last night fell, and a long hour later the big bottleboat slid up to the dock at Van Eck's elegant boathouse.

"They made it!" Wylan whooped.

Kaz released a slow breath. Jesper grabbed a lantern and the champagne they'd been chilling. They bounded across the garden, tore open the door, and streamed into the boathouse. Their greetings died on their lips.

Inej and Rotty were helping Kuwei from the bottleboat. Though he looked rumpled and shaky, and his shirt hung open to reveal a chest still spattered with pig's blood, he was in one piece. Jesper's father sat in the boat, his shoulders slumped, looking wearier than Jesper had ever seen him, his freckled face creased with sadness. He rose slowly and climbed onto the dock. He clutched Jesper tightly and said, "You're all right. You're all right."

Nina remained in the boat, resting her head on Matthias' chest. He was laid out beside her, his eyes closed, his color ashen.

Jesper cast Inej a questioning look. Her face was tearstained. She gave a single shake of her head.

"How?" Kaz said quietly.

Fresh tears gathered in Inej's eyes. "We still don't know."

Wylan retrieved a blanket from the house and they spread it in the corner of the boathouse, then Jesper and Rotty helped lift Matthias' massive body out of the boat. The process was awkward, undignified. Jesper couldn't help but think the Fjerdan would have hated that.

They laid him down on the blanket. Nina sat beside him, saying nothing, his hand clutched in hers. Inej brought a shawl that she tucked over Nina's arms, then crouched silently next to her, head nestled against her shoulder.

For a while, none of them knew what to do, but eventually Kaz looked at his watch and signaled silently to them. There was still work that required their attention.

They set about converting the bottleboat. By ten bells, it needed to look less like a merchant's canal shop and more like a bodyman's sickboat. They'd remade crafts many times, using the base of a single vessel as the skeleton for a flower barge, a fishing vessel, a floating market stall. Whatever was necessary for the job. This was an easier transformation. Nothing had to be built, only stripped away.

They lugged the flats of bottles into the house and tore up the top part of the deck to eliminate the storage compartments, making the boat wider and flatter. Colm helped, working side by side with Jesper as they'd done back at the farm. Kuwei drifted between the garden and the boathouse, still weak from his ordeal.

Soon Jesper was sweating, trying to focus on the rhythm of the work, but he couldn't shake the sadness in his heart. He'd lost friends. He'd been on jobs when things had gone wrong. Why did this feel so different?

When the last of the work was finished, Wylan, Kaz, Rotty, Jesper, and his father stood in the garden. There was nothing left to do. The barge was ready. Rotty was dressed head to toe in black, and they'd fashioned a bodyman's hood by tearing apart and restitching one of Van Eck's fine black suits. It was time to go, but none of them moved. All around, Jesper could smell spring, sweet and eager, the scent of lilies and hyacinths, early blooming roses.

"We were all supposed to make it," said Wylan softly.

Maybe that was naive, the protest of a rich merchant's son who'd only had a taste of Barrel life. But Jesper realized he'd been thinking the same thing. After all their mad escapes and close calls, he'd started to believe the six of them were somehow charmed, that his guns, Kaz's brains, Nina's wit, Inej's talent, Wylan's ingenuity, and Matthias' strength had made them somehow untouchable. They might suffer. They might take their knocks, but Wylan was right, in the end they were all supposed to stay standing.

"No mourners," said Jesper, surprised by the ache of tears in his throat.

"No funerals," they all replied softly.

"Go on now," said Colm. "Say your goodbyes."

They walked down to the boathouse. But before Wylan entered, he bent and plucked a red tulip from its bed. They all followed suit and silently filed inside. One by one, they knelt by Nina and rested a flower upon Matthias' chest, then stood, surrounding his body, as if now that it was too late, they might protect him.

Kuwei was the last. There were tears in his golden eyes, and Jesper was glad he'd joined their circle. Matthias was the reason Kuwei and

Jesper had survived the ambush on Black Veil; he was one of the reasons Kuwei would have a chance to truly live as a Grisha in Ravka.

Nina turned her face to the water, looking out at the narrow houses that lined the Geldcanal. Jesper saw that the residents had filled their windows with candles, as if these small gestures might somehow push back the dark. "I'm pretending those lights are for him," she said. She plucked a stray red petal from Matthias' chest, sighed, and released his hand, rising slowly. "I know it's time."

Jesper put his arm around her. "He loved you so much, Nina. Loving you made him better."

"Did it make a difference in the end?"

"Of course it did," said Inej. "Matthias and I didn't pray to the same god, but we knew there was something beyond this life. He went easier to the next world knowing he'd done good in this one."

"Will you stay in Ravka?" asked Wylan.

"Only long enough to arrange transport to Fjerda. There are Grisha who can help me preserve his body for the journey. But I can't go home, I can't rest until he does. I'll take him north. To the ice. I'll bury him near the shore." She turned to them then, as if seeing them for the first time. "What about all of you?"

"We'll have to figure out a way to spend our money," said Kaz.

"What money?" said Jesper. "It all got poured into the Shu coffers. Like they needed it."

"Did it?"

Nina's eyes narrowed and Jesper saw a bit of her spirit return. "Stop playing around, Brekker, or I'll send my unholy army of the dead after you."

Kaz shrugged. "I felt the Shu could manage with forty million."

"The thirty million Van Eck owed us—" murmured Jesper.

"Four million *kruge* each. I'm giving Per Haskell's share to Rotty and Specht. It will be laundered through one of the Dregs' businesses before it passes back through the Gemensbank, but the funds should be in separate accounts for you by the end of the month." He paused. "Matthias' share will go to Nina. I know money doesn't matter to—"

"It matters," said Nina. "I'll find a way to make it matter. What will you do with your shares?"

"Find a ship," said Inej. "Put together a crew."

"Help run an empire," said Jesper.

"Try not to run it into the ground," said Wylan.

"And you, Kaz?" Nina asked.

"Build something new," he said with a shrug. "Watch it burn."

Jesper braced himself and said, "Actually, you should put my share in my father's name. I don't think . . . I don't think I'm ready for that kind of money just yet."

Kaz watched him for a long moment. "That's the right move, Jes."

It was a little like forgiveness.

Jesper felt sorrow dragging at his heart. He was flush with funds for the first time in years. His father's farm was safe. But none of it felt right.

"I thought being rich would make everything better," he said.

Wylan glanced back at his father's mansion. "I could have told you it doesn't work that way."

In the distance, bells began to chime. Jesper went to get his father from the garden. Colm stood near the steps of the house, crumpled hat in his hands.

"At least now we can afford to get you a new hat," said Jesper.

"This one's comfortable."

"I'll come home, Da. When the city is open again. After Wylan gets settled."

"He's a good lad." *Too good for me*, thought Jesper. "I hope you really will come home to visit." Colm looked down at his big hands. "You should meet your mother's people. The girl your mother saved all those years ago . . . I've heard she's very powerful."

Jesper didn't know what to say.

"I . . . I'd like that. I'm sorry for all of this. For getting you mixed up in it. For almost losing what you worked so hard to build. I . . . I guess what I mean is, this action will have no echo."

"Pardon?"

"It sounds better in Suli. I'm going to try, Da."

"You're my son, Jesper. I can't protect you. Maybe I shouldn't have tried. But I will be there even when you falter. Every time."

Jesper hugged his father tight. *Remember this feeling*, he told himself. *Remember all you have to lose.* He didn't know if he was strong enough to keep to the promises he'd made tonight, but he could try to be.

They walked back down to the boathouse and joined the others.

Inej placed her hands on Nina's shoulders. "We'll see each other again."

"Of course we will. You've saved my life. I've saved yours."

"I think you're ahead on that count."

"No, I don't mean in the big ways." Nina's eyes took them all in. "I mean the little rescues. Laughing at my jokes. Forgiving me when I was foolish. Never trying to make me feel small. It doesn't matter if it's next month, or next year, or ten years from now, those will be the things I remember when I see you again."

Kaz offered his gloved hand to Nina. "Until then, Zenik."

"Count on it, Brekker." They shook.

Rotty climbed down into the sickboat. "Ready?"

Kuwei turned to Jesper. "You should visit me in Ravka. We could learn to use our powers *together*."

"How about I push you in the canal and we see if you know how to swim?" Wylan said with a very passable imitation of Kaz's glare.

Jesper shrugged. "I've heard he's one of the richest men in Ketterdam. I wouldn't cross him."

Kuwei gave an affronted sniff and lowered himself onto the floor of the sickboat. He folded his arms neatly over his chest.

"No," said Kaz. "No. The bodymen don't bother to arrange them."

Kuwei let his hands flop to his sides. Colm was next, and Jesper instantly wanted to forget the image of his father laid out like a corpse.

They used the blanket to lift Matthias onto the boat, then slid the fabric from beneath him. Nina took the clutch of tulips from his chest and scattered them on the water. She lay down beside him.

Rotty pushed the long wooden pole against the sandy bottom of the canal. The barge drifted away from the dock. In the dark, he looked like any other bodyman ferrying his grim cargo through the canals. Only the sickboats could pass freely through the city and out of the harbor, collecting the dead to take to the Reaper's Barge for burning.

Rotty would bring them up through the manufacturing district, where the Grisha refugees had fled after the auction, after discarding the blue robes they'd worn to pretend to be the Council of Tides. Kaz had known there was no way to transport that many Grisha without attracting notice. So they'd taken the secret passage from the embassy to the tavern, and then paraded down the street in billowing blue robes, faces shrouded in mist, declaring their power instead of attempting to hide it. Jesper supposed there was a lesson there if he wanted to take it. There were only four real Tidemakers among them, but it had been enough. Of course, there had been the chance the real Council of Tides would show up at the auction, but based on their record, Kaz had thought it was worth the risk.

The Grisha and Sturmhond would be waiting to board the boat not far from Sweet Reef. Once they were all aboard, Rotty would pole them out past the harbor and then send up a flare where Sturmhond's ship would come to meet them. It was the only way to get a group of refugee Grisha, a farmer who'd helped con the entire Merchant Council, and the body of a boy who had—until a few hours ago—been the most wanted hostage in the world, out of the city.

"You'll have to be still," Inej murmured.

"Still as the grave," Nina replied.

The barge slid into the canal, and she lifted her hand in farewell, her palm like a white star, bright against the dark. They stood by the water's edge long after it had faded.

At some point, Jesper realized Kaz was gone.

"Not one for goodbyes, is he?" he muttered.

"He doesn't say goodbye," Inej said. She kept her eyes on the lights of the canal. Somewhere in the garden, a night bird began to sing. "He just lets go."

43

KAZ

Kaz propped his bad leg on a low stool and listened as Anika gave her report on the earnings at the Crow Club and the status of tourist traffic on East Stave. In the three weeks since Kuwei's auction and the plague panic, Kaz had taken over Per Haskell's office on the ground floor of the Slat. He still slept on the top floor, but it was easier to do business from Haskell's lair. He didn't miss the extra trips up and down the stairs, and his old office felt empty now. Whenever he sat down to try to get some work done, he'd find his eyes straying to the window ledge.

The city still hadn't returned to normal, but that had created some interesting opportunities. Prices on the Staves had dropped as people prepared for a long plague outbreak, and Kaz was quick to take advantage. He bought the building next to the Crow Club so that they could expand, and he even managed to acquire a small property on the Lid. When the panic was over and tourism resumed, Kaz was looking forward to fleecing a far higher class of pigeon. He'd also bought out Per Haskell's shares in the Crow Club for a reasonable price. He could have had them for nothing, given the trouble in the Barrel, but he didn't want anyone feeling too sorry for the old man.

When Pekka Rollins returned to the city, Kaz would find a way to cut him out of the business. The last thing he wanted was for the proceeds of his hard work to go into Rollins' coffers.

Once Anika finished her recital, Pim gave the details he'd gathered on Van Eck's trial. The mysterious Johannus Rietveld had not been found, but once Van Eck's accounts had been laid bare, it had quickly become clear he'd been using the information he'd learned on the Merchant Council to buy up *jurda* farms. Beyond swindling his friends, tampering with an auction, and kidnapping his own son, there were even suggestions that he'd hired a team to break into a Fjerdan government building and possibly sabotage his own sugar silos. Van Eck was not out on bail. In fact, it didn't look like he'd be out of jail anytime soon. Though his son had provided a small fund for his legal representation, it could be described as moderate at best.

Wylan had chosen to use a portion of his newfound wealth to restore his home. He'd given Jesper a small allowance to speculate in the markets, and he'd brought his mother home as well. People in the Geldstraat were shocked to see Marya Hendriks sitting in the park with her son or being rowed down the canal by one of their servants. Sometimes they could be glimpsed from the water, standing before their easels in the Van Eck garden.

Alys had stayed with them for a time, but eventually she and her terrier had chosen to escape the city and its gossip. She would finish her confinement in the Hendriks lake house, and was said to be making dubious progress in her singing lessons. Kaz was just glad he didn't live next door.

"That's good work," Kaz said when Pim had finished. He hadn't thought Pim had much talent for gathering intelligence.

"Roeder put together the report," Pim said. "Think he's gunning for a place as your new spider."

"I don't need a new spider," said Kaz.

Pim shrugged. "Wraith's been scarce. People talk."

Kaz dismissed Anika and Pim and sat for a long moment in the quiet office. He'd barely slept in the past few weeks. He'd been waiting nearly half his life for this moment to become a reality, and he was afraid that if he let himself sleep, it might all vanish. Pekka Rollins had fled the city and hadn't returned. Word was he'd holed up with his son in a country house surrounded by armed men at all times. Between the quarantines at the Emerald Palace, the Kaelish Prince, and the Sweet Shop, and the fact that he wasn't around to put things to rights, Pekka Rollins' businesses were on the brink of collapse. There was even talk of mutiny within the Dime Lions. Their boss was gone, and the deal he'd made with Van Eck had made them look no better than a rich man's henchmen. They might as well be *stadwatch*.

Brick by brick. Eventually, Rollins would dig himself out of the rubble. Kaz would have to be ready.

A knock sounded at the door. The one problem with being on the ground floor was that people were a lot more likely to bother you.

"Letter came," Anika said, and tossed it on his desk. "Looks like you're keeping fast company, Brekker," she said with a sly smile.

Kaz let his glance at the door do the talking. He wasn't interested in watching Anika bat her yellow lashes.

"Right," she said, and vanished, closing the door behind her.

Kaz held the letter up to the light. The seal was pale blue wax, marked with a golden double eagle. He slit open the envelope, read the letter's contents, and burned both. Then he wrote a note of his own and sealed it in black wax.

Kaz knew Inej had been staying at Wylan's house. Occasionally, he'd find a scrawled note on his desk—some bit of information about Pekka or the doings at the Stadhall—and he'd know she'd been here in his office. He slipped on his coat, took up his hat and cane, and tucked the paper into his pocket. He could have sent a messenger, but he wanted to deliver this note himself.

Kaz strode past Anika and Pim on the way out of the Slat. "I'll be back in an hour," he said, "and I better not still see you podges wasting your time here."

"Hardly anyone at the club," said Pim. "Tourists are too scared of the plague."

"Go to the rooming houses where all the frightened pigeons are waiting out the panic. Show them you're in the pink of health. Make sure they know you just had a fine time playing Three Man Bramble at the Crow Club. If that doesn't work, get your asses to the harbors and drum up some pigeons from the workers on the boats."

"I just came off a shift," protested Pim.

Kaz settled his hat on his head and ran a thumb over the brim. "Didn't ask."

He cut east through the city. He was tempted to take a detour, just to see for himself how things were proceeding on West Stave. Between the Shu attack and the plague outbreak, the pleasure houses were practically deserted. Several streets had been barricaded to enforce the quarantine surrounding the Sweet Shop and the Menagerie. Rumor had it Heleen Van Houden wasn't going to make her rent that month. A pity.

There were no browboats operating, so he had to make the journey up to the financial district on foot. As he wended his way along a small, deserted canal, he saw a thick mist rising off the water. Only a few steps later, it was so dense he could barely see. The mist clung to his coat, wet and heavy, thoroughly out of place on a warm spring day. Kaz paused on the low bridge that spanned the canal, waiting, cane at the ready. A moment later, three hooded figures emerged to his left. Three more appeared to his right, their blue cloaks moving sinuously through the air, though there was no breeze. That much Kaz had gotten right, but their masks weren't made of mist. Instead, the real Council of Tides—or a very convincing set of pretenders—wore something that gave the impression of looking into a starry night sky. Nice effect.

"Kaz Brekker," said the lead Tidemaker. "Where is Kuwei Yul-Bo?"

"Dead and gone. Burnt to ashes on the Reaper's Barge."

"Where is the *real* Kuwei Yul-Bo?"

Kaz shrugged. "A church full of people saw him get shot. A medik pronounced him dead. Beyond that, I can't help you."

"You do not want the Council of Tides as an enemy, young man. None of your shipments will ever leave port again. We will flood Fifth Harbor."

"By all means, do. I don't own shares in Fifth Harbor anymore. You want to stop my shipments, you'll have to stop every boat coming in and out of the harbor. I'm not a merch. I don't charter ships and register trade manifests. I'm a thief and a smuggler. Try to catch hold of me and you'll find you're trying to hold air."

"Do you know how easy it is to drown?" asked the Tidemaker. He lifted a hand. "It can happen anywhere."

Suddenly Kaz felt his lungs filling with water. He coughed, spat seawater, and bent double, gasping.

"Tell us what we want to know," said the Tidemaker.

Kaz drew a stuttering breath. "I don't know where Kuwei Yul-Bo is. You can drown me where I stand and nothing will change that."

"Then maybe we'll find your friends and drown them in their beds."

Kaz coughed and spat again. "And maybe you'll find the obelisk towers under plague quarantine." The Tides shifted uneasily, the mists moving with them. "I made those sirens sound. I created this plague, and I control it."

"A bluff," said the Tidemaker, his sleeve gliding through the mist.

"Try me. I'll spread sickness around every one of your towers. They'll become epicenters of disease. You think the Merchant Council won't lock you all down? Demand you finally register your identities? They'd probably be happy for the excuse."

"They wouldn't dare. This country would sink were it not for us."

"They won't have a choice. The public will clamor for action. They'll burn the towers from the ground up."

"Monstrous boy."

"Ketterdam is made of monsters. I just happen to have the longest teeth."

"The secret of *jurda parem* can never be revealed to the world. No Grisha would ever be safe again. Not here. Not anywhere."

"Then it's lucky for you it died with that poor Shu kid."

"We won't forget this, Kaz Brekker. One day you'll regret your insolence."

"Tell you what," said Kaz. "When that day comes, mark it on your calendars. I can think of a lot of people who'll want to throw a party."

The figures seemed to blur, and when the mists finally thinned, Kaz saw no trace of the Tides.

He shook his head and set off down the canal. That was the wonderful thing about Ketterdam. It never let you get bored. No doubt the Tides would want something from him in the future, and he'd be obliged to give it to them.

But for now, he had unfinished business.

44

INEJ

Inej didn't think she could make it up the stairs to bed. How had she whiled away so many hours at dinner with Jesper and Wylan?

The cook had been all apologies as the meal was served that night. She still couldn't get quality fresh produce from the markets, what with people so afraid to come into the city. They'd done their best to reassure her and had stuffed themselves on cheese and leek pie, then eaten honey-soaked cakes while sitting on the music room floor. Wylan's mother had retired early. She seemed to be coming back to herself in fits and starts, but Inej suspected it would be a long road.

Wylan played the piano and Jesper sang the dirtiest sea shanty Inej had ever heard. She missed Nina painfully. There had been no letters, and she could only hope her friend had made it to Fjerda safely and found some peace on the ice. When Inej finally had her ship, maybe her first trip would be to Ravka. She could journey inland to Os Alta, try to find her family on one of the old routes they'd traveled, see Nina again. Someday.

Inej had chosen to spend her nights at Wylan's house, returning to the Slat just to fetch her few belongings. With her contract paid and her bank account brimming with funds, she wasn't entirely sure where she belonged. She'd been researching sailing vessels with heavy cannon, and using her knowledge of the city's secrets to begin gathering information that she hoped would lead her to the slavers who did business through the ports of Kerch. The skills she'd acquired as the Wraith would serve her well. But tonight, all she wanted to contemplate was sleep.

She dragged herself up the stairs and crawled into her deliciously comfortable bed. Only when she'd reached over to turn down the lamp did she see the note—a sealed letter in Kaz's messy scrawl. *Sunrise. Fifth Harbor.*

Of course he'd managed to get into the locked house, past the servants and the three fools singing at the top of their lungs. It was only fair, she supposed. She'd been coming and going at the Slat, slipping in and out of windows and doorways, leaving bits of information for Kaz when she needed to. She could have simply knocked on his office door, but it was easier this way.

Kaz had changed. The net. Paying her contract. She could still feel the faint touch of his lips on her skin, his bare hands fumbling with the knots of her bandages. Inej had seen the scant glimmer of what he might become if he let himself. She couldn't bear to see him dressed in armor once more, buttoned back into his immaculate suits and cold demeanor. She wouldn't listen to him talk as if the Ice Court and everything that came after had been just another job, another score, another bit of advantage to be gained.

But she wouldn't ignore his note. It was time to put an end to this thing that had never had a chance to begin. She'd tell him what she'd heard about Pekka, offer to share some of her routes and hiding spots with Roeder. It would be over. She turned down the light, and after a long while, she fell asleep with the note clutched in her hand.

It was hard to force herself from bed the next morning. She'd developed bad habits in the last three weeks—sleeping when she wanted to, eating when she liked. Nina would be proud. Being at Wylan's house felt like she'd entered some kind of enchanted world. She'd been to the house before, when she and Kaz had stolen the DeKappel and then again before the Sweet Reef job. But it was one thing to be a thief in a house and quite another to be a guest. Inej found herself embarrassed by the pleasure of being waited on, and yet, Van Eck's staff seemed glad to have them there. Maybe they'd feared Wylan would close up the house and they'd all lose their employment. Or maybe they thought Wylan deserved some kindness.

One of the maids had set out a lapis silk robe and a little pair of fur-lined slippers by the side of the bed. There was hot water in the pitcher by the basin, a glass bowl full of fresh roses. She washed, brushed out her hair, rebraided it, then dressed and quietly let herself out of the house—through the front door, of all things.

She kept her hood up and moved swiftly as she made her way to the harbor. The streets were still largely empty, especially at this hour of the morning, but Inej knew she could not let down her guard. Pekka Rollins was gone. Van Eck was in jail. But contracted to the Dregs or not, as long as Kaz had enemies on these streets, she did too.

He was standing on the quay, looking out at the water. His black coat fit snugly across his shoulders, the salt wind off the sea ruffling the dark waves of his hair.

She knew she did not have to announce herself, so she stood next to him, taking in the view of the boats at the docks. It looked like several vessels had arrived that morning. Maybe the city was regaining its rhythm.

"How are things at the house?" he asked at last.

"Comfortable," she admitted. "It's made me lazy." For the briefest moment, Inej wondered if Kaz might be jealous of that comfort or if it was simply alien to him. Would he ever let himself rest? Sleep in? Linger over a meal? She would never know.

"I hear Wylan is letting Jesper play the markets."

"*Very* cautiously and with extremely limited sums. Wylan's hoping to channel his love of risk into something productive."

"It might work brilliantly or it could end in total disaster, but that's generally the way Jesper likes to work. At least the odds are better than in any gambling hall."

"Wylan only agreed after Jesper promised to start training with a Fabrikator. Assuming they can find one. It might take a trip to Ravka."

Kaz tilted his head, watching a gull arc above them, wings spread wide. "Tell Jesper he's missed. Around the Slat."

Inej raised a brow. "Around the Slat." From Kaz that was as good as a bouquet of flowers and a heartfelt hug—and it would mean the world to Jesper.

Part of her wanted to draw this moment out, to be near him a while longer, listen to the rough burr of his voice, or just stand there in easy silence as they'd done countless times before. He had been so much of her world for so long. Instead she said, "What business, Kaz? You can't be planning a new job so soon."

"Here," he said, handing her a long glass. With a jolt, she realized he wasn't wearing his gloves. She took it from him tentatively.

Inej put the long glass to her eye and peered out at the harbor. "I don't know what I'm looking for."

"Berth twenty-two."

Inej adjusted the lens and scanned along the docks. There, in the very berth from which they'd set out for the Ice Court, was a tidy little warship. She was sleek and perfectly proportioned, cannons out, a flag bearing the three Kerch fishes flying stiffly from the mainmast.

On her side, spelled out in graceful white script, were the words *The Wraith*.

Inej's heart stuttered. It couldn't be. "That's not—"

"She's yours," said Kaz. "I've asked Specht to help you hire on the right crew. If you'd prefer to take on a different first mate, he—"

"Kaz—"

"Wylan gave me a good price. His father's fleet is full of worthy ships, but that one . . . It suited you." He looked down at his boots. "That berth belongs to you too. It will always be there when—if you want to come back."

Inej could not speak. Her heart felt too full, a dry creek bed ill-prepared for such rain. "I don't know what to say."

His bare hand flexed on the crow's head of his cane. The sight was so strange Inej had trouble tearing her eyes from it. "Say you'll return."

"I'm not done with Ketterdam." She hadn't known she meant it until she'd said the words.

Kaz cast her a swift glance. "I thought you wanted to hunt slavers."

"I do. And I want your help." Inej licked her lips, tasted the ocean on them. Her life had been a series of impossible moments, so why not ask for something impossible now? "It's not just the slavers. It's the procurers, the customers, the Barrel bosses, the politicians. It's everyone who turns a blind eye to suffering when there's money to be made."

"*I'm* a Barrel boss."

"You would never sell someone, Kaz. You know better than anyone that you're not just one more boss scraping for the best margin."

"The bosses, the customers, the politicians," he mused. "That could be half the people in Ketterdam—and you want to fight them all."

"Why not?" Inej asked. "On the seas and in the city. One by one."

"Brick by brick," he said. Then he gave a single shake of his head, as if shrugging off the notion. "I wasn't made to be a hero, Wraith. You should have learned that by now. You want me to be the better man, a good man. I—"

"This city doesn't need a good man. It needs you."

"Inej—"

"How many times have you told me you're a monster? So be a monster. Be the thing they all fear when they close their eyes at night. We don't go after all the gangs. We don't shut down the houses that treat fairly with their employees. We go after women like Tante Heleen, men like Pekka Rollins." She paused. "And think about it this way . . . you'll be thinning the competition."

He made a sound that might almost have been a laugh.

One of his hands balanced on his cane. The other rested at his side next to her. She'd need only move the smallest amount and they would be touching. He was that close. He was that far from reach.

Cautiously, she let her knuckles brush against his, a slight weight, a bird's feather. He stiffened, but he didn't pull away.

"I'm not ready to give up on this city, Kaz. I think it's worth saving." *I think you're worth saving.*

Once they'd stood on the deck of a ship and she'd waited just like this. He had not spoken then and he did not speak now. Inej felt him slipping away, dragged under, caught in an undertow that would take him farther and farther from shore. She understood suffering and she knew it was a place she could not follow, not unless she wanted to drown too.

Back on Black Veil, he'd told her they would fight their way out. *Knives drawn, pistols blazing. Because that's what we do.* She would fight for him, but she could not heal him. She would not waste her life trying.

She felt his knuckles slide against hers. Then his hand was in her hand, his palm was pressed against her own. A tremor moved through him. Slowly, he let their fingers entwine.

For a long while, they stood there, hands clasped, looking out at the gray expanse of the sea.

A Ravkan ship flying the Lantsov double eagle had docked only a few berths over from the *Wraith*, probably unloading a cargo of tourists or immigrants seeking work. The world changed. The world went on.

"Kaz," she asked suddenly. "Why crows?"

"The crow and cup? Probably because crows are scavengers. They take the leavings."

"I don't mean the Dregs tattoo. That's as old as the gang. Why did you adopt it? Your cane. The Crow Club. You could have chosen a new symbol, built a new myth."

Kaz's bitter coffee eyes remained trained on the horizon, the rising sun painting him in pale gold light. "Crows remember human faces. They remember the people who feed them, who are kind to them. And the people who wrong them too."

"Really?"

He nodded slowly. "They don't forget. They tell each other who to look after and who to watch out for. Inej," Kaz said, gesturing out to the harbor with the head of his cane, "look."

She raised the long glass and peered back down at the harbor, at the passengers disembarking, but the image was blurry. Reluctantly, she released his hand. It felt like a promise, and she didn't want to let go. She adjusted the lens, and her gaze caught on two figures moving down the gangplank. Their steps were graceful, their posture straight as knife blades. They moved like Suli acrobats.

She drew in a sharp breath. Everything in her focused like the lens of the long glass. Her mind refused the image before her. This could not be real. It was an illusion, a false reflection, a lie made in rainbow-hued glass. She would breathe again and it would shatter.

She reached for Kaz's sleeve. She was going to fall. He had his arm around her, holding her up. Her mind split. Half of her was aware of his bare fingers on her sleeve, his dilated pupils, the brace of his body around hers. The other half was still trying to understand what she was seeing.

His dark brows knitted together. "I wasn't sure. Should I not have——"

She could barely hear him over the clamor in her heart. "How?" she said, her voice raw and strange with unshed tears. "How did you find them?"

"A favor, from Sturmhond. He sent out scouts. As part of our deal. If it was a mistake——"

"No," she said as the tears spilled over at last. "It was not a mistake."

"Of course, if something had gone wrong during the job, they'd be coming to retrieve your corpse."

Inej choked out a laugh. "Just let me have this." She righted herself, her balance returning. Had she really thought the world didn't change? She was a fool. The world was made of miracles, unexpected earthquakes, storms that came from nowhere and might reshape a continent. The boy beside her. The future before her. Anything was possible.

Now Inej was shaking, her hands pressed to her mouth, watching them move up the dock toward the quay. She started forward, then turned back to Kaz. "Come with me," she said. "Come meet them."

Kaz nodded as if steeling himself, flexed his fingers once more.

"Wait," he said. The burn of his voice was rougher than usual. "Is my tie straight?"

Inej laughed, her hood falling back from her hair.

"That's the laugh," he murmured, but she was already setting off down the quay, her feet barely touching the ground.

"Mama!" she called out. "Papa!"

Inej saw them turn, saw her mother grip her father's arm. They were running toward her.

Her heart was a river that carried her to the sea.

45
PEKKA

Pekka sat in the front room of his country house, peering out from behind one of the white lace curtains. Kaelish lace. Imported from Maroch Glen. Pekka had spared no expense when he'd polished up this place. He'd built the house from the ground up, specifying the dimensions of every room, the varnish for the floors, choosing each fixture and furnishing with care. The Emerald Palace was his great pride, the Kaelish Prince the crown jewel of his empire, a testament to luxury and style, decked out in the highest Barrel flash. But this place was his home, his castle. Its every detail spoke respectability, prosperity, permanence.

Pekka felt safe here, safe with his son and the bodyguards he paid so well. Still, he moved away from the window. Best not to take any chances. Plenty of spots for a marksman to hide out there. Maybe he should cut down the beech trees that bordered the lawn.

He struggled to understand where his life had gone. A month ago he'd been a rich man, a man to be reckoned with, a king. And now?

He clutched his son closer and stroked his red hair. The boy was restless in his lap.

"I want to go play!" Alby said, leaping from Pekka's knee, thumb in his mouth, clutching the soft little lion—one of the many he owned. Pekka could barely stand to look at the thing. Kaz Brekker had bluffed him and he'd fallen for it.

But it was worse than that. Brekker had gotten into his head. Pekka couldn't stop thinking of his boy, his perfect boy buried beneath clods of earth, screaming for him, pleading for his father, and Pekka unable to come to his rescue. Sometimes his son was crying from somewhere in the fields but he didn't know where to dig. Sometimes Pekka was the one lying in the grave, paralyzed as the earth was piled on top of him—light at first, a patter of rain, then in heavy clods that filled his mouth and stole the breath from his chest. Above him he could hear people laughing— boys, girls, women, men. They were silhouettes against a blue dusk sky, their faces lost to shadow, but he knew who they were. All the people he'd swindled, duped, killed. All the sorry sobs he'd sacrificed as he made his climb up the ladder. He still couldn't remember the name of Brekker's brother. What had he been called?

Pekka had been Jakob Hertzoon; he'd worn a thousand different faces. But Kaz Brekker had found him. He'd come for his revenge. If one of those fools could find him, why not another, and another? How many would stand in line to throw the next shovelful of dirt?

Making choices, even simple choices, had become difficult. What tie to wear. What to order for dinner. He doubted himself. Pekka had never doubted himself. He'd started life as a no one. A stone breaker from the Wandering Isle, a sturdy boy valued only for his strong back and his youth, for his ability to swing a pick and carry a load of rocks. But he'd cheated his way onto a boat coming to Ketterdam and made his reputation with his fists. He'd been a boxer, a bruiser, the most feared enforcer in the gangs. He'd survived because he was the wiliest, the toughest, because no one could break his will. Now all he wanted to do was sit inside, drink his whiskey, watch the shadows move across the ceiling. Anything else filled him with a terrible fatigue.

And then one morning he woke to a bright, blue-enamel sky. The air was full of birdsong. He could smell the arrival of summer, real heat in the air, fruit ripening in the orchard.

He dressed. He breakfasted. He spent the morning in the fields, working in the early sun and playing with Alby. When the day grew too hot, they sat on the wide porch and drank cool glasses of lemonade. Then Pekka went inside and actually faced the papers and bills that had been piling up on his desk.

Things were in disastrous shape at the Emerald Palace and the Kaelish Prince. They'd been closed by the city as a health precaution, the doors and windows marked with dire black *X*s to indicate an outbreak site. News from Ketterdam indicated that the plague had been a false alarm, some strange fungus or virus that had struck quickly but seemed to be proving harmless. City officials were cautiously optimistic.

Pekka studied the balance sheets. Both gambling halls might be salvageable in time. He'd take a loss for the year, but once things had calmed down, he'd slap a new coat of paint on the buildings, give them new names, and he'd be back in business. He'd probably have to close the Sweet Shop. No man was going to pull his trousers down when the price might be catching the plague, not when there were so many other establishments willing to cater to him. That was unfortunate. But he'd had setbacks before. He had a good source for "indentures" who would work for nothing. He was still Pekka Rollins, king of the Barrel. And if any of those little skivs roaming the streets had forgotten that fact, he'd be happy to serve them a reminder.

By the time Pekka was done sorting through the masses of correspondence and news, night had fallen. He stretched, downed the last of his whiskey, and looked in on Alby sleeping soundly with that cursed little lion tucked beneath his chin. He said good night to the guards posted outside his son's bedroom, then made his way down the hall.

"Turning in, boss?" asked Doughty. He and another huge bruiser watched over Pekka's quarters at night, men Pekka knew he could trust.

"I am, Doughty. And a good night it'll be too."

When he climbed into bed, he knew he would not dream of his son crying or the grave or that dark chorus standing above him, laughing. Tonight he'd dream of the Wandering Isle, of its rolling green fields and the mists that wreathed its mountains. In the morning, he would rise refreshed and restored, ready to see to the real work of reclaiming his throne.

Instead he woke with the weight of a heavy rock on his chest. His first thought was of the grave, the weight of earth pressing down on him. Then he came back to himself. His bedroom was dark, and someone was on top of him. He gasped and tried to shove up from his sheets, but he felt a pair of knees and elbows locked onto him, the stinging press of a blade against his neck.

"I'll kill you," Pekka gasped.

"You already tried." A woman's voice—no, a girl's.

He opened his mouth to bellow for his guards.

She jabbed at his neck with the knife. Pekka hissed as blood trickled into his collar. "Scream and I'll use this blade to pin your throat to the pillow."

"What do you want?"

"Do you like life, Rollins?" When he didn't answer, she jabbed him again. "I asked you a question. Do you like life?"

"How did you get past my guards?"

"You call those guards?"

"You killed them?"

"I didn't bother."

"The only window is barred. It—"

"I am the Wraith, Rollins. Do you think bars can stop me?"

Brekker's little Suli girl. He cursed the money he'd spent on that Ravkan mercenary.

"So Brekker sent you to deliver a message?" he asked.

"I have my own message to deliver."

"Tell me what deal you struck with Brekker. Whatever he's paying you, I can double it."

"Shhhh," the girl said, pressing down with her knees. Pekka felt something in his shoulder pop. "I left pretty Dunyasha's brains dashed all over the Ketterdam cobblestones. I want you to think about what I could do to you."

"Why don't you just kill me now and save your threats?" He would not be cowed by some slip of a girl from the Menagerie.

"Death is a gift you haven't yet earned."

"You—"

She stuffed something in his mouth.

"You can scream now," she crooned. She peeled back the fabric of his nightshirt, and then her knife was digging into his chest. He screamed around the gag, trying to buck her off.

"Careful now," she said. "You wouldn't want me to slip."

Pekka forced himself to still. He realized how long it had been since he'd felt real pain. No one had dared lift a hand against him in years.

"Better."

She sat back slightly as if to review her work. Panting, Pekka peered down but could see nothing. A wave of nausea rolled through him.

"This was the first cut, Rollins. If you ever think about coming back to Ketterdam, we'll meet again so I can make the second."

She replaced his nightshirt with a little pat and was gone. He didn't hear her leave, only felt her weight release from his chest. He tore the rag from his mouth and rolled over, fumbling for the lamp. Light flooded the room—the dresser, the mirror, the washbasin. There was no one there. He stumbled to the window. It was still barred and locked. His chest burned where she'd used her knife on him.

He lurched to his dressing table and yanked back his blood-soaked nightshirt. She'd made a precise slash, directly above his heart. Blood spilled from it in thick, seeping pulses. *This was the first cut.* Bile rose in his throat.

All the Saints and their mothers, he thought. *She's going to cut the heart from my chest.*

Pekka thought of Dunyasha, one of the most gifted assassins in the world, a creature without conscience or mercy—and the Wraith had bested her. Maybe she really wasn't entirely human.

Alby.

He crashed through the door into the hallway, past the guards still posted there. They came to attention, stunned expressions on their faces, but he raced past them, careening down the hall to his son's room. *Please*, he begged silently, *please, please, please.*

He threw the door open. Light from the hall spilled over the bed. Alby was on his side, sleeping soundly, his thumb tucked into his mouth. Pekka slumped against the doorjamb, weak with relief, holding his nightshirt to his bleeding chest. Then he saw the toy his son was clutching in his arms. The lion was gone. In its place was a black-winged crow.

Pekka recoiled as if he'd seen his son asleep with his cheek on a hairy-legged spider.

He shut the door gently and strode back down the hall.

"Get Shay and Gerrigan out of bed," he said.

"What happened?" asked Doughty. "Should I call a medik?"

"Tell them to start packing our bags. And gather up all the cash we have."

"Where are we going?"

"As far away as we can get."

Rollins slammed the bedroom door behind him. He went back to his window and tested the bars again. Still solid. Still locked. In the black shine of the glass he could see his reflection, and he didn't recognize himself. Who was this man with thinning hair and frightened eyes? There'd been a time when he would have faced any threat with chin up and guns blazing. What had changed? Was it just time? *No*, he realized, *it's success.* He'd gotten comfortable and found that he enjoyed it.

Pekka sat before his mirror and began to wipe the blood from his chest. He'd taken pride in making Ketterdam his. He'd laid the traps, set the fires, put his boot to the necks of all those who'd challenged him, and reaped the rewards of his boldness. Most of the opposition had fallen, easy pickings, the occasional challenge almost welcome for the excitement it brought. He'd broken the Barrel to his whim, written the rules of the game to his liking, rewritten them at will.

The problem was that the creatures who had managed to survive the city he'd made were a new kind of misery entirely—Brekker, his Wraith queen, his rotten little court of thugs. A fearless breed, hard-eyed and feral, hungrier for vengeance than for gold.

Do you like life, Rollins?

Yes, he did, very much indeed, and he intended to go on living for a good long time.

Pekka would count his money. He would raise his son. He'd find himself a good woman or two or ten. And maybe, in the quiet hours, he'd raise a glass to the men like him, to his fellow architects of misfortune who had helped raise Brekker and his crew. He'd drink to the whole sorry lot of them, but mostly to the poor fools who didn't know what trouble was coming.

CAST OF CHARACTERS

Adem Bajan [**ad**-em bah-**zhahn**]
Music instructor indentured to Jan Van Eck

Aditi Hilli [uh-**dee**-tee **hee**-lee] (deceased)
Jesper Fahey's mother

Alina Starkov [uh-**lee**-nuh **stahr**-kovf] (deceased)
Grisha Etherealnik (Sun Summoner); former leader of the
Second Army

Alys Van Eck [**al**-is van ek]
Jan Van Eck's second wife

Anika [**an**-i-*kuh*]
Member of the Dregs

Anya [**ahn**-yuh] (deceased)
Grisha Healer indentured to Councilman Hoede

Bastian [**bas**-chuhn]
   Member of the Dregs

Beatle [**bee**-tuhl]
   Member of the Dregs

Betje [**beh**-chyuh]
   Caretaker at Saint Hilde

Big Bolliger [big **bah**-luh-gur]
   Former member of the Dregs; exiled

Bo Yul-Bayur [boh *yool*-bye-**yur**] (deceased)
   Inventor of *jurda parem* who attempted to defect from the Shu Han;
   Kuwei Yul-Bo's father

Colm Fahey [kohm **fay**-hee]
   Jesper Fahey's father

Cornelis Smeet [kor-**nel**-uhs smeet]
   Jan Van Eck's lawyer and property manager

Danil Markov [**da**-nuhl **mahr**-kovf]
   Grisha Inferni indentured at the Anvil

Darkling [**dahr**-kling]
   Grisha Etherealnik and title held by former leaders of the Second
   Army; real name unknown

David Kostyk [**day**-vid **kah**-stik]
Grisha Fabrikator (Durast); member of the
Ravkan Triumvirate

Dirix [**deer**-iks] (deceased)
Member of the Dregs

Doughty [**dow**-tee]
Member of the Dime Lions

Dunyasha Lazareva [duhn-**yah**-shuh *lahts*-uh-**ray**-vuh]
A mercenary; also known as the White Blade of
Ahmrat Jen

Eamon [**ay**-muhn]
Dime Lions lieutenant

Elzinger [**el**-zing-ur]
Member of the Black Tips

Emil Retvenko [eh-**meel** red-**veng**-koh]
Grisha Squaller indentured to Councilman Hoede's estate

Eroll Aerts [**air**-uhl airts]
Member of the Dime Lions

Filip [**fil**-uhp] (deceased)
Member of the Dime Lions

Geels [geelz]
    Black Tips lieutenant

Genya Safin [**jen**-yuh **saf**-in]
    Grisha Tailor; member of the Ravkan Triumvirate

Gerrigan [**gair**-uh-*ghin*]
    Member of the Dime Lions

Gorka [**gor**-kuh]
    Member of the Dregs

Hanna Smeet [**ha**-nuh smeet]
    Daughter of Cornelis Smeet

Heleen Van Houden [huh-**leen** van **hou**-tuhn]
    Owner and chief procurer of the Menagerie (the House
    of Exotics); also known as the Peacock

Hoede [hohd] (deceased)
    Member of the Kerch Merchant Council

Inej Ghafa [in-**ezh** guh-**fah**]
    Member of the Dregs; spider and secret-gatherer; also known as
    the Wraith

Jan Van Eck [yahn van ek]
    Shipping magnate and prominent merchant; member of the Kerch
    Merchant Council; Wylan Van Eck's father

Jarl Brum [yarl broom]
   Commander of the Fjerdan *drüskelle*

Jellen Radmakker [**yel**-uhn **rahd**-mah-kur]
   Prominent merchant

Jesper Fahey [**jes**-pur **fay**-hee]
   Member of the Dregs; sharpshooter

Jordan Rietveld [**jor**-duhn **reet**-veld] (deceased)
   Kaz Brekker's older brother

Karl Dryden [karl **drye**-duhn]
   Most junior member of the Kerch Merchant Council

Kaz Brekker [kaz **brek**-ur]
   Dregs lieutenant; also known as Dirtyhands

Keeg [keeg]
   Member of the Dregs

Kuwei Yul-Bo [koo-**way yool**-*boh*]
   Grisha Inferni and Shu defector; son of Bo Yul-Bayur

Marya Hendriks [**mahr**-ee-*yuh* **hen**-driks] (deceased)
   Jan Van Eck's first wife; Wylan Van Eck's mother

Matthias Helvar [muh-**tye**-uhs **hel**-vahr]
   Disgraced Fjerdan *drüskelle*

Miggson [**mig**-suhn]
   An employee of Jan Van Eck

Milo [**mye**-loh]
   Member of the Dregs

Muzzen [**muh**-zuhn]
   Member of the Dregs

Naten Boreg [**nay**-tuhn **bor**-eg]
   Member of the Kerch Merchant Council

Nikolai Lantsov [**ni**-koh-lye **lan**-tsovf]
   King of Ravka

Nina Zenik [**nee**-nuh **zen**-uhk]
   Member of the Dregs; Grisha Heartrender

Onkle Felix [**uhng**-kuhl **fee**-liks]
   Chief procurer of the House of the White Rose

Oomen [**oo**-muhn] (deceased)
   Member of the Black Tips

Pekka Rollins [**pek**-uh **rah**-luhnz]
   Dime Lions general

Per Haskell [pair **has**-kuhl]
   Dregs general

Pim [pim]
Member of the Dregs

Prior [**prye**-ur]
An employee of Jan Van Eck

Raske [rask]
Freelance demolitions expert

Red Felix [red **fee**-liks]
Member of the Dregs

Roeder [**roh**-dur]
Member of the Dregs

Rotty [**rah**-tee]
Member of the Dregs

Seeger [**see**-gur]
Member of the Dregs

Shay [shay]
Member of the Dime Lions

Specht [spekt]
Member of the Dregs; forger and former naval officer

Sturmhond [**sturm**-*hahnd*]
Privateer and emissary of the Ravkan government

Swann [swahn]
   Member of the Dregs

Tamar Kir-Bataar [**tay**-mahr *keer*-buh-**tahr**]
   Grisha Heartrender; captain of King Nikolai's personal guard

Varian [**vair**-ee-yuhn]
   Member of the Dregs

Wylan Van Eck [**wye**-luhn van ek]
   Son of Jan Van Eck

Zoya Nazyalensky [**zoi**-yuh *nahz*-yuh-**len**-skee]
   Grisha Squaller; member of the Ravkan Triumvirate

ACKNOWLEDGMENTS

Joanna Volpe a.k.a. the Wolf a.k.a. the funniest, toughest, smartest, most patient agent around—thank you for being my dear friend and ferocious advocate. And to everyone at Team New Leaf—especially Jackie, Jaida, Mike, Kathleen, Mia, Chris, Hilary, Danielle, and Pouya "All Star" Shahbazian—thank you for being an agency, a family, and an army. I love you guys.

Holly Black and Sarah Rees Brennan helped me find the heart of this story when all I could see were its bones. Robin Wasserman, Sarah Mesle, Daniel José Older, and the brilliant Morgan Fahey provided invaluable editorial feedback. Rachael, Robyn, and Flash spent many hours in my living room and garden keeping me company. Amie Kaufman and Marie Lu are hilarious, beautiful warrior angels who put up with a lot of ridiculous e-mails from me. Rainbow Rowell is a Gryffindor, but I guess we're cool. Anne Grasser managed my schedule and my kooky requests with ease and patience. Nina Douglas championed my books in the UK and kept me laughing on the road. Noa Wheeler, thank you for staying in Ketterdam a little while longer and seeing me (and our misfit crew) through this adventure.

As always, I owe a blood debt to Kayte Ghaffar, my right-hand man, my genius on call, who has lent so much time and creativity to me and these books.

Many thanks to my Macmillan family: Jon, Laura, Jean, Lauren, Angus, Liz, Holly, Caitlin, Kallam, Kathryn, Lucy, Katie, April, Mariel, KB, Eileen, Tom, Melinda, Rich (who somehow managed to outdo himself on this cover), every single person in sales who got this book onto shelves, every single person in marketing who got people to pick it up. And a very special thank-you to the incredible team of publicists who have toured with me and taken care of me and listened to me blather in airports—Morgan, Brittany, Mary, Allison, and especially the Marvelous Molly Brouillette, who worked such magic with this series.

Thank you to Steven Klein for his help in thinking about sleight of hand and grand illusions; Angela DePace for helping me finesse the chemical weevil and auric acid; and Josh Minuto, who put the storm in brainstorm when it was time to bring Kuwei back from the dead.

Lulu, thank you for putting off holidays, suffering my moods, and keeping me in peonies. Christine, Sam, Emily, and Ryan, I am so glad we're family. Corn pie for all!

To all of the readers, librarians, bloggers, BookTubers, Instagrammers, booklr denizens, fic writers, artists, and makers of edits and playlists: Thank you for bringing the Grisha world to life beyond the pages of these books. I am truly grateful.

And finally, if you'd like to help stop human trafficking and forced labor in our world, you don't need a schooner and heavy cannon. GAATW.org offers online resources and information on reputable organizations that would welcome your support.

ENTER THE
GRISHAVERSE

THE SHADOW AND BONE TRILOGY

THE SIX OF CROWS DUOLOGY

ALSO AVAILABLE AS GLORIOUS
HARDBACK COLLECTOR'S EDITIONS

© Christina Guerra

LEIGH BARDUGO

is a No. 1 *New York Times*–bestselling author of fantasy novels and the creator of the Grishaverse, which spans the Shadow and Bone Trilogy, the Six of Crows Duology, *The Language of Thorns*, and the King of Scars Duology. Her short stories can be found in multiple anthologies, including *The Best American Science Fiction and Fantasy*. Her other works include *Wonder Woman: Warbringer* and *Ninth House*. Leigh was born in Jerusalem, grew up in Southern California, and graduated from Yale University. These days, she lives and writes in Los Angeles.

leighbardugo.com